Gypsy Spirit

& Other Stories of Childhood, Nature,
Life Choices, Loss, and Love

Ute Carson

Plain View Press   http://plainviewpress.net
1101 W. 34th Street, STE 404, Austin, TX 78705

ISBN: 978-1-63210-076-4
ebook ISBN: 978-1-63210-077-1
Library of Congress Control Number: 2020935342

Cover Art and design by Jeffrey Powers
Photographs by Ute and Cecile Carson
Illustrations Kaius Carson Powers

For our girls
Caitlin, Claudia, Cecile

Contents

Childhood

The House of Childhood

We return to the place
where we first heard voices,
smelled the air and tasted nourishment,
where hands caressed or frightened us,
where comfort was our cocoon
or neglect made us shiver.
The tears of harm are cold,
the tears of joy warm as a lagoon.
We carry the house of childhood within us,
and spying through its translucent walls,
we keep life at a distance—or embrace it.

The Fall

It was May and the sweet fragrance of apple blossoms wafted through the open window. I had propped my elbows on the windowsill in my upstairs bedroom and was gazing at a myriad of pinkish petals illuminating the night like candles. Then I inhaled deeply with my eyes closed.

Mr. Franz's six sturdy apple trees bordered my mother's bountiful flower garden. A white picket fence divided our two properties, and a rusty iron gate hung loosely on its hinges. Low branches tapped it on windy days with an eerie persistence. The trees, all slightly different heights, stretched toward a changing sky. From my perch I could spy out over their tops. There was no official name for the golden sunbaked apples. We called them Paradise Apples. 

The apple trees were planted in a semicircle and nothing was used as fertilizer but horse manure. The apples were the best I've ever eaten, firm and juicy. Although wide grease bands encircled the tree trunks to deter insects, the apple skins were pockmarked where worms had burrowed tunnels through them. But we didn't mind. My mother and father, and my sister Inge and I grew healthy and strong on more than an apple a day.

Apples were part of our daily diet. At breakfast my mother sliced them onto our oatmeal. I took an apple to school in my backpack. Setting off to afternoon sports I ran under the low tree branches, grabbed an apple and sank my teeth into it without slowing down. Apples were often a staple at dinner. One dish of boiled apples and potatoes was called "Himmel und Erde" (heaven and earth). My mother prepared it with a roast seasoned with curry and thyme. My favorite apple dish was a dessert of cored baked apples filled with honey and almonds, and sprinkled with cinnamon.

We made use of apples in many ways. We grated them for upset stomachs, pureed them into applesauce, and canned them. We ate whole apples, core and all. My parents explained to us that "the nutrients are just under the protective envelope—the apple's skin—and in its heart." The only time we pared apples was for a Sunday torte. I remember sitting across from my mother at the kitchen table and watching her quick fingers peel the skin off an apple in one long unbroken ringlet. She worked by feel without ever looking down. Afterwards my sister and I gathered the peelings in a bucket and took them to the pond where ducks splashed toward the water's edge through the slimy algae and gobbled up the apple curls which we dangled over their eager beaks.

Mr. and Mrs. Franz were generous neighbors and at harvest time we were all invited over to pick. My father helped Mr. Franz carry a heavy wooden ladder from tree trunk to tree trunk, its bottom raking the ground through rustling leaves. Then Father placed one foot on the lowest rung to steady the ladder as we took turns climbing up and filling our baskets set on the rung next to our feet. We hooked our bare toes around the slats. Sweat glistened in our armpits and along our hairlines. Our waxy-brown calf muscles hardened as we balanced on tiptoe and reached. Once in a while an apple escaped our grasp and tumbled to the ground. Everyone laughed, "That's how Newton discovered gravity!" I rested after filling several baskets and sat munching on a particularly crisp apple. Inge, who was finicky about eating, scolded me, "Don't crunch."

The apple trees were part of my life. We took our time growing up. We had picnics under those trees with blankets spread on the grass for extra softness. We laughed and talked under the thick dome of their leaves, and my little cousin Ralf used one of the lower branches to steady himself as he learned to walk.

May induced daydreaming to the accompaniment of buzzing bees, busily gathering pollen. I remember being entangled by spider webs suspended between branches, feeling their fine transparent threads against my face.

One warm July evening Mr. Franz had his two grandsons Eric and Wolfgang over. They giggled with the delight of small children, rolling apples back and forth on the lawn between their outspread legs.

With the arrival of October, light came through the branches at a slant and a rough wind ripped loose the blood-red leaves, then scattered them aflutter like a thousand flames. The bees returned, now drawn by the smell of overripe, decomposing fruit. The odor of damp air seeped into my clothes as I shook the branches, and the last stragglers nestled among large serrated leaves fell to the ground.

With the first touch of frost and a nip in the air, my mother and Mrs. Franz circled through the trees in search of the strays and gathered them into their faded red, blue or checkered aprons which they held up by the corners. Apples left on a branch after all the others had been picked tasted especially sweet. They made up for the immature ones in June that had set our teeth on edge.

December lulled me into hibernation, spinning its sleepy time web. The snow came down slowly like confetti, layering the branches with white velvet. And as the trees stored warmth and sap, and the wind blew the remaining crumbled leaves in big swirls, I moved indoors to activities around the old tiled stove and the nearby kitchen table.

But I remember best the summer nights. They would often find me resting my back against a tree trunk and hoping that my boyfriend Ernest would soon join me. I had fallen for Ernest with uninhibited feeling but was not yet sure what do with this new sensation. Sitting under my favorite apple tree I took its pulse. Once I was caught there in a warm drizzle. The bark was singing, and the roots gurgled like underground rivulets. Waves of birds circled the crown, flies droned, and grasshoppers jumped to the rhythm of my heartbeat. Lightning bugs blinked off and on as it got darker. I looked skyward through the dense foliage where throbbing stars were beginning to glisten like insect eyes. I pressed my body into the tree hollow and lifted my face into the spray, letting the soft drops lick my skin with their ticklish tongues. The firmament was silver with moonlight.

I felt as if bees buzzed in my body until I heard Ernest's footsteps bouncing over the cushy grass in my direction. As soon as he stood in front of me all nervous anticipation stopped, and we both were timidly quiet. Ernest gently let himself down next to me. We remained silent. Then the tenseness lifted, and we became animated. We started to trade stories without pausing, as though we would lose the connection between us if we stopped to breathe. The night air pressed against our eager young bodies, and we were camouflaged by softly descending darkness. Ernest kissed me, and I shivered with a fresh awareness like a quivering green leaf. The apple tree branches gave us gentle cover, sheltering our secret.

Our blissful life changed with the onset of World War II. My father and many other men were drafted and we who were left behind retreated into our close family circles and into ourselves. When Ernest was inducted into a youth group, our snuggling together under the apple tree abruptly ended.

Mr. Franz was too old to be drafted. He continued to prune the trees and harvest the apples, which he no longer freely shared with us but sold instead. On a bitter cold January day we heard hacking sounds and saw the first of our beloved trees fall to his axe. In the coming years two more trees shared the same fate. After the felling of the first tree, Mother and I sneaked out before dawn and collected the few logs, branches and wood chips left on the ground. Mr. Franz had stored the rest of the tree safely in his shed before nightfall.

The atmosphere of the war years was gloomy and drab and filled with anxieties. We knitted through long evenings, and my mother taught my sister and me to darn socks and patch torn sweater elbows and legging knees.

One morning Mr. Franz discovered two soldiers in their worn-out, olive-drab uniforms asleep side by side under one of the remaining apple trees. Later I overheard him tell Mother that they had pleaded with him, "Please help us with anything you can spare," and he had handed them some apples. "They went away," he grumbled, "like godless beggars."

There was great joy and relief when my father returned home. The war was over but the postwar chaos and its deprivations were only beginning. The destruction all around us was chilling. We continued to struggle for survival. My father was forced to find odd jobs, mostly manual labor. He no longer had a position as a lecturer in mathematics, because most universities had only partially reopened their doors. He seemed forlorn.

We had sold everything we could spare. We even tearfully parted with Riva, our faithful breeding dog, a golden retriever. A hunter bought her for a bushel of corn, two sacks of potatoes, several bags of coal and a dozen eggs, which kept us going for only a few weeks. But we got by. Somehow my parents found a way to clothe and feed us and even kept the old tiled oven glowing.

Mr. Franz had not totally forgotten us. In August 1946 he delivered a basket of Paradise Apples to our doorstep in exchange for a knitted sweater, which my mother had managed to piece together from leftover yarn. Our delight knew no bounds, but Mother curbed our appetites. She indulged us with one apple each. The rest were reserved for cooking—except for the healthiest, roundest specimens which were set aside for Christmas. We placed them on a newspaper on a shelf next to the canned cabbage and blackberry marmalade in our cool, damp cellar. There they might shrivel a bit but still be a treat for the holidays.

Whenever I was sent to fetch a tin of rations or bring up some coal, I stopped at the display of apples. I fingered them, running my hand over their wrinkly surfaces, then bringing my nose into smelling range, I inhaled the familiar sweet fragrance. Once I lifted the rosiest apple off the shelf only to put it back quickly as if I had been stung.

The Advent season in most German households is a time for baking and making presents. One frosty evening when our stomachs growled like hungry hounds, my mother decided to donate her Paradise Apple while we were busy wrapping and gluing tiny golden angels onto gifts, readying them for delivery to family members and friends. She quartered the reddish ball, then we each dipped our portion into warm honey. We let the taste linger on our tongues before finally swallowing. Later in bed, Inge and I speculated about what might happen at Christmas. We were convinced that Father would share his apple with our mother. He was a very generous man.

I never liked the cellar. Except for a slit of a window at ground level, the cave-like room was dim and musty-smelling. Even on a bright, sunny day little light filtered in. At dusk we switched on the single light bulb that dangled on a wire from the cellar ceiling. The steps down to the cavern were worn and rickety. The cellar floor was made of concrete and was slightly slippery from the permanent moisture. Only the sight of our three remaining Paradise Apples lit up my mood every time I was called upon to go down to the cellar and bring something up.

Two weeks before Christmas, unusually cold winter days arrived. At the gold-green haze of twilight my father returned from the woods with firewood and splintered it for kindling. Earlier that morning my mother had come home from the black market with meager exchanges of flour and shriveled potatoes. Once a master at the stove, her cooking had become uninspired under the burden of the dwindling food supply. This didn't stop us from lying to her at every meal, "It's so good, Mutti." That night, as a small fire crackled in our tiled oven and a pungent odor of sap and cooking oils circulated through the warm kitchen, she told me to fetch a jar of red cabbage. She was making potato dumplings again. Gingerly, I made my way down the cellar steps and pulled the light cord.

That's when I saw him. As soon as the light blinded us both, he spun away from me, his back rounded into a shield, withdrawing his neck into his frayed jacket like a turtle. I froze in my tracks, dumbfounded. I had only seconds to make a choice. I could have withdrawn inconspicuously, silently retracing my steps back up the stairs. I could have ignored his transgression, saved him the embarrassment. But I had seen the bite, a rosy, dripping wound.

Defiantly, I took a stand and waited until my father decided to face me, hand extended, the  forbidden fruit glistening in his cupped palm. Suddenly I stepped forward, a feathery panic in my chest and took the cherished Paradise Apple from him and plunged my teeth into the soft flesh. At that moment innocence changed places with the knowledge of sin. I stood glued to the damp cellar floor. Sharing my father's guilt tasted deliciously sweet. I can't remember how long we stood there in deep shame, our heads bowed toward each other like top-heavy tree crowns, the quiet broken only by the taps of a tattered twig against the glass of the cellar window, which on that night let no light into the darkness, not even the faintest glimmer of a star.

Hope Diamond

"It fits." She pounded the left heel of her travel-weary brown shoes. In its hollow my grandmother had just buried a diamond-in-the-rough. A few days before, sitting on the steps of their ramshackle cottage near the diamond fields of the Namib Desert where my grandfather was an overseer, she had spotted an object in the sand. The African sun had reflected off its glittering surface.

British freighters, anchored in the bay off Lüderitz, were ready to transport German settlers back home following the English takeover of South West Africa in 1919. The diamond mine workers had already been evacuated.

Back in her native Germany my grandmother stored the shoes among other valuables in her closet. "You never know when we might need them," she told my mother.

A war later, fleeing invading Russian troops, my grandmother trekked westward wearing her trusty worn African shoes.

In the icy winter of 1946 I contracted diphtheria. Although I lived in a cocoon of familial love, infected children were forcibly quarantined in a provisional hospital by the American authorities. "Have a heart," my distraught mother pleaded," we have never been apart." She was summarily ushered out.

I was delirious and barely aware of what was going on. I vaguely recall crying "Mutti" during nights of feverish demon-dreams as children around me died in droves. Once I threw my arms around a nurse, thinking she was my mother. Medicines were scarce and penicillin was available only on the black market. There was little hope for me.

My grandmother made contact with a street-smart volunteer in the hospital's storage room where CARE packages containing powdered milk and instant soup arrived from abroad.

Then that night she pried off the heel of her left shoe, lifted the diamond out and spit-polished it with her handkerchief. "Your time has come," she whispered to it and then cloaked herself in a shabby gray coat. Under cover of darkness she descended into the underworld of our city where smugglers eagerly exchanged the new wonder drug for the precious stone. "Just in time," sighed the doctor at the children's ward. I soon recovered.

I was left with fear of separation, a damaged heart valve, and an amazing story. My grandmother had to recount her adventure again and again. It was the ending that I envisioned with vivid imagination.

"After being led through tunnels to a dimly lit shed, a bespectacled man examined the diamond under a magnifying glass and exclaimed: It's real! He then reached up to a shelf behind him and pulled down a box with black lettering: PENICILLIN. He dismissed me abruptly, urging me to go quickly before we were found out." My grandmother assured me that she had not been frightened until that moment. "But then I realized," she confessed, "that I might be followed and robbed." She hurried away, clutching the box of tablets to her chest, then stuffing them into her undergarments. "But where?" I asked with childish curiosity. "Close to my heart," she murmured.

Letting Go

In the wintery spring of 1945, World War II had ended but not the chaos and misery of its survivors. My mother received notice that her husband had been killed. She sought solace in the arms of the messenger, got pregnant, and remarried. The couple moved south looking for work. I was five years-old and left in the care of my maternal grandmother in the bombed-out city of Kassel.

These were the happiest times of my war-torn childhood. I never wanted to leave my grandmother's side. Days were spent gathering twigs and branches for our wood-burning stove, source of warmth and light. We filled baskets with the white flower heads of chamomile, then dried them for brewing tea. We collected sugar beets in the fields, cooked and stirred them into syrup, a delicious treat over our watery oatmeal. But the evenings were the best. Warmed and protected by my grandmother's ample body, we snuggled as she spun stories of imaginary places and events.

Months later my mother called for me. My grandmother prepared me with allusions to a happy family life, and eventually I did thrive in my new environment. We arranged a meeting place where my stepfather waited in a horse-drawn wagon. The exchange was brief. I suddenly felt cramps in my stomach and barely had time to sling my arms around my beloved grandmother's neck before being hoisted onto the wagon seat.

That was the last time I saw my grandmother. She waved and then her hand covered her mouth to stifle a sob. She had to stay behind, war-weary and lonely, while I was ushered toward a fresh beginning. I still see her getting smaller and smaller, sinking into the shadow of the bright morning light.

Bedrock

As I sit drinking coffee this morning, the hot dark liquid energizing me, the sun washing over my skin, gloriously alive and well lived-in, I watch my grandchildren laugh and play among the flowers with reckless abandon. I think back to a tiny girl, my four year-old self, forced from my home, unaware that such a carefree destination might someday be mine. I recall being hoisted aboard a train crammed with wounded and dying soldiers from the front and exclaiming, "It stinks here," and my grandmother hastily hushing me by placing a hand over my mouth as she would do on many occasions during our frightful exodus.

I had an idyllic early childhood. I was born into a cocoon of familial love, desired by my young parents, adored by my paternal grandparents and spoiled by my maternal grandmother. We lived on a wide-roaming estate in Silesia complete with all the amenities of an aristocratic household. Troubles seemed far removed until World War II trampled our comforts and dreams.

Although the worries of my elders for my father and uncles serving on the Russian front cast a shadow over my peaceful existence, I was isolated from the terrible losses my family suffered and spared the worst.

Everything changed once the German army was defeated and Soviet troops moved westward, burning and plundering. We escaped from our castle at the last minute in a horse-drawn wagon. The neighboring villages were up in flames. February 1945 was bitter cold and I was bundled up in furs.

Then good fortune played its hand. Stranded on an icy railway platform in Hirschberg, the nearest town, a train passed through, stopping only long enough for an announcement to be broadcast over the loudspeaker asking for doctors and other medical personnel. My mother, a trained nurse, her identification card held high, was approached by an officer. Moments later, she, my grandmother and I were lifted onto the train which moved very slowly out of the station.

From the interior of the transport I heard moaning. It took my eyes awhile to adjust to the dimness in the long corridor. There were bunks three high on either side of the aisle. I was startled by the many white turbans and bloody wrappings around dangling arms and legs. The air was very stuffy and foul-smelling. Almost immediately, my mother was whisked away and from then on was on nonstop duty while my grandmother and I were shunted into something resembling a lawn chair. I seldom saw my mother except when she flitted by, stopping momentarily to wet my face with kisses. Once she ran through the corridor, halted at a bed, lit a cigarette, and gently placed it between the lips of a soldier, only to be reprimanded by an orderly rushing up behind her and scolding, "No smoking. Fire hazard!" When I asked, "What are we doing in this dark place?" grandmother whispered, "Hush!" and repeated her hand-over-mouth gesture every time I complained, "I'm hungry" or "Let's go back home."

We were served watery milk soup in tin cups which were so different from my white bowls at home with painted flowers trailing along the rims. When it became clear that no other food was forthcoming, I greedily slurped down my soup. I slept on my grandmother's lap, startled awake whenever one of the men cried out. The latrine, located outside the corridor next to the buffers between train cars, was a stink hole. My grandmother held me above it, while burying her nose in her crocheted shawl.

After a day and a night on the rumbling train I started to recognize some of the occupants. When I walked from bed to bed, some of the men would try to grab my arm or long braids. One soldier smiled when I pointed to his bloody bandage and wanted to know, "Are you hurt?" Puzzled by the silent ones, I asked my grandmother, "Why don't they answer me?" "They are sleeping," she replied, which made sense. The blinds were all drawn.

During the second night we were shaken from sleep by an ear-piercing cry, "Mutti! Help me!" In the bunk across from our chair a man had started to thrash, tearing at his sheets and throwing them off. A nurse hurried to his side and pushed a needle into his arm and he quieted down. From then on he lay very still. Death was still unknown to me and I would have fallen back into my slumbers were it not for what happened next. The locomotive let out a loud hoot and the train slowed to a crawl. Several men moved from bed to bed wrapping motionless bodies in soiled bedsheets and knotting the ends together.

As I watched from my safe perch on my grandmother's lap, several blinds sprang up and windows were pushed down. Snowflakes whistled in on steely gusts of wind. Two men grabbed the ends of each sheet, lifted it high and then "... one…two… three…" and the bundle was heaved through the window. They repeated this frightful spectacle all along the corridor. Then the windows were closed again and darkness descended in the carriage, illuminated only by the dim yellow light from dangling bulbs. Anxiously I asked grandmother, "What are they doing?" "They are taking the soldiers to a place to sleep." "Where though?" "In the soft snow."

Now that the bunk across from our chair was empty my grandmother was invited to take it. She collapsed from exhaustion onto the stripped mattress and tried to pull me in next to her. I screamed and kicked free of her grasp. I could not be coaxed into that terrifying bed. Instead I crouched on the floor with my back against a low iron railing, hanging on to my grandmother's hand for dear life.

That night grandmother had a premonition of impending danger. When the train stopped to take on coal, the three of us got off and made our way westward by whatever movable means turned up. We later learned that the train was destroyed in an air attack as it sped toward a tunnel for protection.

By nightfall we reached a well-kept farmhouse and were kindly offered shelter. After a soothing bath, mouse-like bits of scrambled eggs and a few scraps of chicken were served. It was a real feast. My mother even complained of a stomachache after eating solid food for the first time in days. Snuggling under clean, downy bedding and about to doze off, I spotted a stuffed black cat on the shelf above my bed. Suddenly wide awake, I reached for the toy, elated at my discovery. The old farmwoman watched my excitement and told me that I could sleep with the black kitten. "It's yours," she pronounced. Drowsily, I clutched the little creature in my arms. Of course it was mine. It was my toy kitten from home!

The next morning I woke up to familiar kitchen aromas and soon sat with my mother and grandmother, drinking fresh milk from the farm's cow. But then I wondered, where was the kitten? I jumped up and ran back to my bed. It was gone! With bated breath I returned to the kitchen and asked, "Where is my kitten?" Furtive looks flitted between my mother and the farmwoman. "The kitten has left," the woman explained. "It belonged to my son." "But you promised me," I screamed. "Just for the night," the woman replied resolutely. I pushed over my mug of milk and ran to my mother, burying my face in her breasts. "It's MY kitten," I howled and was inconsolable, despite assurances that we would find another kitten later on. I felt betrayed and refused to shake hands with our hosts when we left.

Shortly before the war ended we reached western Germany safely and began to weather its aftermath. A few months later I contracted diphtheria. The Allies quarantined all children with infectious diseases. On a snowy night, I was forcibly disentangled from my mother's gentle arms and taken to a former schoolhouse which had been converted into a makeshift children's hospital. I had a very high fever. Delirious, I remember cold wraps being applied to my hot body. I shivered and then perspired profusely.

It was the large room I recall best. Rows of beds lined the walls and a blackboard from former days hung in plain view. The hospitalized children's names were written on the blackboard and then erased when they died. Many of them died. I owe my survival to the fact that my grandmother sold her valuable diamond on the black market for precious penicillin, a commodity most difficult to obtain in those post-war days. Thanks to the medication, I lived through the critical phase of diphtheria as well as other childhood diseases making the round of the ward—scarlet fever, measles, typhus, and mumps.

By now I knew that if someone pulled a bed sheet over your head you were dead and would soon be rolled out. Parents were not allowed in the big room except to pick up a child who was recovering or, as was more often the case, their child's body. I watched fathers with their hats drawn deep over their foreheads and mothers sinking next to a bed and weeping, only to be gently led out alongside a covered bed on wheels. Later the same bed would be rolled back in, made up for another ailing child.

Although there were no visitation days, parents were permitted to bring presents. Food items were always in short supply. Notes and toys were also highly valued. Because I could not read, a nurse read to me. Grandmother wrote daily. Her encouragements always ended with the same message, "Every sunrise you are in my thoughts and before I fall asleep I think of you again." My mother knitted booties which I happily distributed among my fellow ailing compatriots. She also crocheted slipcovers for the hot water bottles.

The greatest relief from my unrelenting homesickness came on days when it was my turn to sit on one of the broad windowsills spanned above the clanking, steaming radiators. There I crouched next to other children who were able to leave their beds. My mother and grandmother faithfully took turns walking back and forth along the frosty sidewalk and waving. They continued their vigil into the greening season. My stay seemed endless.

Franz was a straw-blond farm boy. His parents brought him fresh produce, sometimes milk and eggs. His bed was wheeled next to mine with just enough space for the nurses and doctors to squeeze through. He cried so hard when his father left that his nose seemed permanently crusted. I was an old-timer by then and offered him my bedtime stories. He had never been told stories or read to. He eagerly grasped the opportunity, and I was in my element. I made up stories about his pigs at home and imagined so many wonderful details that he found himself on a magic carpet, flying over a blooming meadow, watching newborn calves and lambs. After hearing a story about a baby lamb bleating for its mother, he had his mother bring him his toy lamb from home. I can still see his face light up as he showed off the lamb's fluffy pink ears and movable tail. The coat was made from real lamb's wool and was so soft to the touch.

I never knew what Franz suffered from except that his skin was blotched. Bluish spots like big freckles covered his face, neck, arms and even the backs of his hands. Once he had to wear gloves so he wouldn't scratch. During those tormenting days I had to redouble my storytelling efforts to keep his spirits up. When he was not miserable with itching he was fun. He made me laugh. He made funny noises by pumping his palms behind the nurses' backs and doing a grimacing imitation of a doctor's stern voice, "All these cases are severe!" He gravely shook his head, pointing at us "poor little mites."

Franz became my best friend. I worried when he couldn't keep his food down and then fell asleep during our story hour. One night I reached across the short space between us. When I found his hand, smaller than mine, it felt clammy and hung limp in my grasp. But Franz didn't withdraw his hand and from then on let me hold it whenever I reached for it. He once whispered, "Would you like to sleep with my lamb tonight?" As much as I longed to, I declined, sensing his need for comfort.

One night when the moon shone pearly over our beds I slipped out and crept over to Franz, something that was strictly forbidden by the staff. I placed my ear on his chest as I had seen the doctors do and heard no breathing. Tentatively, I touched his cheek, then his forehead, sweaty and cold. Instinctively I reached for the lamb which had slipped out of his arm and lay beside him on the sheet. I took it and fled back to my own bed, and hid it under the blanket. I rolled onto my stomach and tucked the lamb where I believed my heart was, now thumping loudly and very fast. Then I tuned out all the noises in the room, pulled my pillow over my ears and cried as if there was no end to my grief. Next morning, tugging my sheets as tightly around me as I possibly could, I watched as Franz's bed was rolled out.

Weeks later I was released. The doctor who signed the form mumbled, "Like an old woman. Been here too long."

I was jubilant to be reunited with my family and right away I made new friends. But nobody knew how I secretly consoled myself. To this day I have no idea where my idea for an animal cemetery originated. It started with a dead bird which I placed in a cigar box stuffed with cotton I had snitched from my mother's meager toiletries. I found a clearing amidst a knoll of dense trees and shrubbery where nobody could spot me. I used the shovel from my sandbox to dig the first grave and later took a spoon from our kitchen drawer for the tiny creatures. I was always on the lookout for dead animals. I even collected dead bugs. Many of my deceased friends I wrapped in handkerchiefs or rags resembling the shrouds I remembered from the train.

The largest animal was a squirrel which I discovered frozen on the garden path. I was unable to spoon out its grave. Using my fingers like claws I finally loosened the hard ground. I decorated the graves with flowers in the warm season and with branches and Christmas decorations in winter. The bushes around my hidden garden were a wonderful barrier from the world beyond. There I felt secure.

Because I had missed the beginning of first grade, my mother taught me how to read. Armed with books from home and the library I would trot to my beloved hiding place, squat on a mossy stone which I had lugged there and read to my dead friends. I also sang to them, especially at Christmas when the snow decked the graves with white lacy blankets resembling doilies.

As I grew up, I spent less and less time at my cemetery but I retained a fondness for it and cast quick glances its way whenever I walked by.

Looking back I wonder how I lived through those early separations and deaths and still became a trusting person. It may be that I was fortunate to be endowed with strong survival instincts. But beyond that there is no doubt in my mind what I owe my devoted mother and grandmother who never wavered in their steadfast love and unceasing efforts to see me through. They were my bedrock.

Fear Not

It is nap time. Through the slats of our blinds sunrays caper across the tousled brown hair of two year-old Lucas. He is wrapped in a green crocheted blanket and both of us are stretched out on my wide bed facing each other. I squint through my half-shut eyes watching him as his eyes slowly close. "Hand, Omi," he murmurs. I take his little one into my palm and hold it until I feel his fingers relaxing, his body twitching, and him sinking into restful slumber. A current of warmth and security has just passed from me to him. I am transported back seventy years to a time when my grandmother's aged hand held mine.

The end of World War II was near in the late spring of 1945 but the bombardment continued. I would turn five in July. Although I had heard a lot about war I had not experienced it. Just after Christmas I was shaken from my family cocoon in Silesia by Red Army tanks approaching our manor house. My grandmother and mother had been watching their movements from a rooftop cupola as neighboring villages went up in flames. I was fascinated by the sight. It reminded me of a bonfire I had seen in a nearby field last spring. A few days later, under darkness of night we were rushed through snow-laden forests in a covered horse-drawn wagon to the Hirschberg train station. Bundled up in fur coats and with bread from home, we survived the night on the icy platform surrounded by hundreds of people, many starving or freezing to death. When an occasional transport moved slowly through the station people tried to jump onto the freight cars, only to lose their grip and fall back onto the frozen pavement.

Good fortune was with us when a train carrying wounded soldiers westward from the front stopped briefly and a call went out for medical personnel. My mother, a nurse, was hoisted up with my grandmother and me in tow. In the foul smelling interior I encountered fear emanating from the soldiers' bloodstained bodies. The men seemed like scary characters in a storybook to me. But the fairytales I knew ended well. I believed that the moaning men would get better and that the people who had collapsed at the train station would get up and go on. Besides, my grandmother was with me.

We arrived in the west near Kassel and found shelter on the estate of family friends. The cellar doubled as an air raid shelter when a warning was sounded. It was spacious, had dangling lightbulbs, and was a place for us children to play. Only when the rumbling hum of a bomber was heard did the adults join us. Once a bomb destroyed an adjacent building and the walls of the basement began to shake as cement dust drizzled onto our heads. When we children were barred from a certain room in the main house, I learned about sorrow. One adult after another, clutching handkerchiefs, would enter and depart, their eyes wet and red, shutting the door behind them. An older girl whispered, "In there they read the letter that someone has died."

I was in the care of my grandmother when my mother, pregnant with my sister, was called to join her husband in a town farther south where he had found work. My grandmother soon left the crowded estate and found refuge in an attic room on a nearby farm. There I experienced the most joyful days of my childhood, gathering firewood and twigs for our small wrought iron stove, scooping dried elderberries from frozen branches and rejoicing in the green tips of nettles poking through the melting snow which we gathered for a nourishing soup. We were even fortunate to find some wrinkled potatoes stored in a crate in a barn loft. At night I snuggled on a straw mattress under piles of fur coats savoring the comfort of my grandmother's body. She was a fantastic storyteller. The lives of the animals in the fields, the chirping birds and the numerous squirrels unearthing nuts, came alive in her telling.

Then the time came for me to be reunited with my parents and meet my new sister. My grandmother and I shouldered our backpacks with provisions and started our trek south. Because few trains were running, we had to rely mostly on helpful farmers to give us a ride in their carts. We also walked a lot. Kindly strangers took us in the first two nights. On the third day we were given a lift on a tractor hauling a load of manure. At the edge of a village the farmer pointed the way to a community shelter about half an hour away. It was getting dark as we spotted a grass-covered mound which resembled an icehouse. Foreseeing that there would be no toilets or water in the shelter, my grandmother urged me to relieve myself behind a bush and insisted that we take several sips from our water bottle. As we entered the bowel of this well-constructed bunker, it felt like the depth of winter. The steps were slippery and even though we heard a chorus of voices we could barely make out shapes. As our eyes adjusted to the dimness we saw how crowded the interior was. From one end to the other people were squeezed together. A small potbellied pipe stove stood in the middle of the room which gave out little light and even less warmth. The fumes made my grandmother cough. Otherwise there was only candlelight, and the ceiling was marked with circles and swirls from the candle smoke. Like my crayon drawings, I thought. My grandmother spied an empty corner where we unrolled our brown horse blanket. Though we were dressed in several layers of clothing, we didn't shed a single item but bedded down using a lighter blanket as cover. We curled up close, our breath mingling in the frigid air. Suddenly I began to shiver. A black shovel and a huge spiky rake leaning against the adjacent wall loomed like stick figures and a spider web swung back and forth like a net about to entrap me. It was so spooky. There were monsters here! We needed to flee right away! I reached out and murmured haltingly, "Hand, Omi, hand." Holding on tight, I drifted off to sleep and did not wake from restful slumber until my grandmother roused me the next morning for the last stretch of our journey.

The Owl

The past pulled me with mounting force the older I got.

My grandmother, Omi Maria, appeared. She had taught me to trust myself and connect with others. She had given me the backbone to move on and the love that kept me grounded. Now she was showing me how to age gracefully.

Omi Maria was the wise mare, I the young colt trotting in her footsteps.

I thumbed through the yellowed pages of her photo album with pictures blurred like old dreams. I spooled back time and she was a child again with her violin under her chin. Then she was a mother, her arms spread like leafy branches over her children, my mother and two uncles. Now she was a grandmother, leaning her full breasts on the wooden rail of a balcony. This one was my favorite. Her body fruit round, ripe. She smiled. Later the smile was gone but her hair was still charcoal black. It remained black into her eighties. Her eyes were hazel, alert, her skin sun-shy white. She always shielded her face with large straw hats. Sometimes she tied a bandanna around her forehead, a forehead with secretive, wrinkled lines.

Her pictures guarded against forgetfulness. With them I conquered time. I could make her young again or middle-aged. I found her in Silesia, Namibia, then back in Silesia and finally West Germany. But I always perceived her as old. She was a grandmother. I had loved her, and did still.

I remembered at three, maybe even two years old, hearing the humming of tea kettles. Omi Maria brewed teas from catnip, linden blossoms, and fennel. She laced her teas with lemon or currant juice, honey or rum. She had a tea for every ailment.

For Omi Maria, tea, then evening lulled the world.

"Why," I asked as a little girl, "do we go on walks just before dark?"

"Because at dusk we see things we miss in the light of day."

We set out on one of our strolls and our surroundings grew into shadows until the countryside blurred. We walked the fold of a valley between pale, sloping mountains. The sandy road passed a high-steepled church, the last building on the village edge, and then broken down barns, a pasture enclosed by a peeling white fence. Our destination was the ruins of a monastery, formerly part of our family estate in better times. There we sat on a low stone wall and looked up at the hollow windows, the blackened remains of arches above. The moon sent pearls of light down to us. Soon the enfolding darkness stirred Omi Maria's stories.

She talked of things that no longer existed. She recalled bone-chilling nights from her youth here, waking up mornings under sheets stiff from the cold, the castle's servants stoking wood in the fireplaces in the long corridors. She told of English nannies and French tutors, of her body constrained by tightly laced corsets, of feeling free only when riding horses, side-saddle of course. Did I get my love of horses from her?

Omi Maria dazzled me with pictures of fancy balls in rustling gowns and elegant, formal dinners, a life of perished things and vanished voices, of ceremonies, of luxuriant leisure.

"We wore our gowns only once, and then donated them to the theater in Breslau," she told me.

During our nightly walks a silky, soft-plumaged owl often flew over our heads. If we were quiet enough we could distinguish the beat of its wings from the rustling of the trees. Its strange lamenting cry cut through the greyness as it swooped down on a scurrying mouse or a motionless lizard.

Some nights we'd spy the owl, eyes shut, perched on a branch, immobile as a statue. It was a mystical, seemingly prehistoric creature. Omi called its keen sense of hearing and sharp eyesight "the owl's wisdom." I imitated its sound, "Kiwitt." I said it faster and faster, "Kiwitt, kiwitt. Komm mit, komm mit." I asked Omi if those were the words of death. I had heard people in the village call the owl "a death-bird." "Whoever hears a screeching owl must die," the people whispered. It gave them the shakes. "Superstition is often based on seeing or hearing something uncanny," Omi Maria explained. "Owls are gentle creatures. They do not bring death. They simply accompany us."

It was 1945 when we fled from the Russians, leaving the Rapunzel tower of our Silesian castle. Our family found shelter in West Germany, and for some months I was entrusted to Omi Maria's care. We roomed upstairs in an old farm house filled with other refugees. Our few possessions were crammed within four stout walls together with a bed, a table, two chairs, an assortment of dishes and a pot-bellied, iron stove for cooking and for warmth. But most of the warmth emanated from my Omi Maria.

Under a thick feather blanket, her body shielded me with the softness of age. A fledgling, I snuggled in the hollows of her arms, my feet tucked between her thighs. I slept a deep, safe sleep that continued long after Omi Maria slipped out of bed. Upon waking, I heard her bustling about. I saw her in those cold morning hours, crossing in front of the windowpanes iced like glazed glass, starting a peat fire, pouring gooey syrup over watery oatmeal. Late into the night before, we had boiled sugar beets down to molasses. She had given me a wooden ladle to help with the stirring. This was our dinner and also our breakfast, with teas—even then we drank tea—brewed from peppermint leaves we had gathered along the banks of a brook.

There was no running water. Omi pumped water from a well and carried it up to our room by the bucket full. We stuffed rags around the ill-fitting door to keep out the draft. Power lines were down from the Allied bombings, but we had candles. I was happy in this nest. But I had seen enough of war and the struggle for survival to be full of questions.

"Why are people crying? Why is everyone so sad?"

Did these early impressions make me anxious about life? What was in store? Mostly tears and sorrow?

After leaving Silesia, the world changed, but Omi Maria and I still had our long, unhurried evenings. I begged for her stories and she told them over and over, again and again. Night after night her stories lulled me, fantastic falling stars. Often I couldn't tell where her stories left off and my dreams began.

✦

Once again I leafed through the photo album. There was a picture around a Christmas tree with candles weighty on its limbs, bending them toward the ground. It showed a new family getting started. My grandfather, Peter, craned his long neck down toward Omi Maria. Her hair was pulled into a nest on top of her head, her dress collar was turned up. My mother, maybe a year old in this photograph, stood between them, holding her father's hand. The light had turned her hair into spun gold. Peter had blond hair like that. My mother also had Peter's cornflower blue eyes.

There were numerous pictures of sand dunes. Omi Maria had written in her loopy handwriting "Namib Desert" under one. Another photo showed a cactus in the midst of endless whiteness, bearing one tiny yellow blossom.

Stuck between the pages was a faded newspaper clipping. I unfolded it and smoothed it out with the palm of my hand. The edges crumbled. Then I read the headlines:

"Crown Prince Ferdinand assassinated by Serb nationalists. June 28, 1914."

In the back of the album I discovered Omi Maria's notes from South West Africa. I needed to hear her stories again, to glean strength from her memories to wrap into my own. Through sheets now as thin as rice paper I glimpsed what her life there must have been like.

+

Maria's foot rocked the bamboo chair. Specks of light penetrated the canopy of palm trees shading the terrace. No breeze ruffled the branches. The farm "Hoffnung" was a green oasis. Shafts of sun spread a glaze over the sand in the distance.

Maria had changed into sun-resistant clothes fit for the tropics. Her host, a middle-aged gentleman handed her a fruit drink, crystal drops on the rim of the glass.

"You need plenty of salt in this dry heat. I take it you had a good journey? Our "Deutschland" must be a fine ship. Her maiden voyage, too."

"It was a splendid crossing. I was the only woman in first class. I dined every night at the captain's table. My only regret is that my mother was inconsolable at my departure. She thinks me foolish for spending my 21st birthday money on this trip."

Her host reached into his pocket.

"Happy birthday, Maria. This precious stone was harvested in our mining fields. It's not for export but your luggage is unlikely to be searched as you continue your round-the-world voyage."

Maria held a diamond in the rough. It was May 1914.

A month later at breakfast, Maria sensed her host staring at her. As she looked back at him she noticed his eyebrows were pulled up like ruffled umbrellas.

"Germany has gone to war. I received a wire only this morning," he said.

Maria folded her napkin very slowly into a perfect square.

"War? Over the troubles in the Balkans? I'd better pack."

"The "Deutschland" was requisitioned by the military. She sailed last night. By now, we have lost communication with Germany."

Overnight Maria had become a prisoner of circumstance. Though she couldn't yet grasp the consequences, she involuntarily pressed the folded napkin over her mouth to suppress a scream.

Peter and Maria met that fateful day. Upon hearing the news of the outbreak of World War I, Peter, who owned a neighboring ranch, paid a visit and saw Maria framed by a window, playing her violin, her black hair fanning down over her shoulders.

South African colonial forces soon conquered the South West territory and imprisoned the German settlers. There Peter was interned at Aus, a lightly guarded camp about a hundred miles south of Lüderitz. Each day the prisoners were taken out to clear the sand off the tracks of the narrow gauge rail line that ran from Lüderitz to Keetmanshoop. Peter would sneak out at night and join Maria halfway between the camp and the farm.

No lights, only stars on the horizon. The Southern Cross blessed their brief reunions. Peter's firm hands reached around Maria's waist carefully as if gently trying to tame a lion cub.

"I have come to love Africa," Maria murmured. "I would never have thought it possible. The vastness, the loneliness, the heat. It's hypnotic."

"I know what you mean. The African sun did it to me. The sun is the spirit of this place, of its limitless expanses. It is as if this country knows no introspection or regret. We follow the light. One day I'll take you up north to the Etosha Pan. When I camped there after my arrival, I woke up one morning to shuffling sounds. I peeked out of my tent to discover that I was surrounded by a herd of elephants. They had walked up on us as silently as cats on their big, cushioned feet. Here you still feel the presence of the wild. Humans have not completely triumphed. I want to show you that Africa."

In September 1916, a bountiful African spring. Peter was freed from Aus. Peter and Maria recorded their marriage in the registry of the German Lutheran Church at Gibbeon, a sturdy brick building with a blue neon cross on the roof. They promised themselves to each other under the inscription over the altar: "Ehre Sei Gott In Der Höhe."

Maria had not forgotten how to dress well. She still lived out of her steamer trunk, but she had learned to mend. For this festive day she chose an orange dress, with pinned white orange blossoms around its collar. It was a dress she had shown off at the captain's table two years before. Two silver combs tamed the lush hair that crowned Maria's head.

The cross of an Order of Maltese nurses adorned the hospital portal in Keetmanshoop.

The flag was hoisted half-mast. It would have been drawn to the top if a boy had been born. But Maria and Peter had a girl, Gerda, my mother.

Peter leaned against the doorpost of the room. Maria, propped against a feather pillow, tied back her flowing hair. She raised her eyebrows to a perfect arch. A blond baby sprawled on a cushion stitched in old German script.

"Beautiful, simply beautiful." Peter couldn't let go of the sight.

Keetmanshoop was only a way station. They moved to Swakopmund, a romantic harbor and resort where the high surf breaks on the rocky shore.

"A jewel," Maria marveled. "I don't want to leave. Not again."

But they had no choice. In 1919 a freighter anchored off the coast of Swakopmund. Maria, pregnant again, was expelled by the British victors, along with Peter and Gerda.

Five years before, the lighthouse's fog horn had welcomed Maria. Now its blinking light signaled a farewell.

In the bowel of the vessel Maria navigated around suitcases, squeezed past bodies, looking for a berth. The dampness and foul smell of illness worked into her stomach. She rushed back up on deck and vomited over the railing, letting the spray of the sea wet her hair. Water lapped against the flanks of the freighter. Seagulls flew along with the wind, then rested on the foam of the swells and drifted back toward shore.

Maria swayed with the ship and feared for Gerda's safety. The child had followed her onto the deck. She took off her scarf and tied it around Gerda's waist.

Peter was isolated in the men's quarters. Maria and Gerda never changed their clothes on the month-long journey. Sometimes underwear and socks were washed in puddles of rainwater on deck. Maria kept her shoes on at all times. A fellow passenger remarked,

"In your condition, you should take your shoes off and put your feet up."

Maria's legs were swollen like boa constrictors.

Peter, Maria and Gerda lumbered off the boat like cattle. A loyal servant from the pre-war days met the family at disembarkation in the port of Amsterdam.

"Baroness, I hardly recognize you. But you still turn up your collar, I see."

Wrapped in heavy horse blankets and bundled into the carriage, they bumped toward Silesia and home. Maria let Peter lift her legs onto the seat. He pulled her shoes off with difficulty.

"Twist the heel. It will come off," Maria said.

In the hollow of the shoe Maria had hidden her diamond.

A war later this jewel would be sold on the black market in exchange for penicillin to save my life.

Settled on Maria's estate, Peter busied himself with farm duties. He became known for his skill with animals and his outstanding horsemanship. But he was restless. Africa beckoned him. In 1927 he returned, never again to set foot in Europe. Long before his departure, he and Maria had become estranged. She fled to her violin and to poetry, he was bound to an earthy life. They went their separate ways.

During the years between the wars, Maria devoted her life to her three children and to Wolf. I knew nothing of Wolf until one day I pulled a thin leather-bound volume of poetry from the shelf. Many of the poems were hymns of love, and the collection was dedicated to my Omi Maria. I thought I knew my grandmother well, and was surprised that there must have been other important people in her life besides me. Then I remembered a funny incident Omi Maria had told me about when she and a man named Wolf were on a trip to Austria. "We had the name and address of a hotel but couldn't find it. Every person we'd ask, Excuse us, could you tell us the way to Paradise? would burst into laughter."

Only after discovering the love poems did I make the connection.

Maria was only mildly interested in politics. She disliked Hitler more for his crudeness than for his plans for the country, about which she knew next to nothing. But her mind was alert to disquieting changes occurring in Germany.

She had joined a small resistance group of landed aristocrats and opened her castle to the meetings. She was arrested when the Gestapo came looking for guest books which were common then. Fortunately, few visitors had signed.

She was taken to headquarters and led into a sparely furnished room, dark and silent as an underground cave. The lock snapped shut behind her. The furniture, draped with scraps of plastic looked on loan. The officer behind the desk glanced up as Maria's footsteps squeaked over the planks of the wooden floor. With her sweeping gate, she crossed in view of him.

Maria held her head high, especially high, and stated her name with refinement and certainty,

"Maria Baroness von Lüttwitz."

Of course the officer knew her name.

He never took his eyes off Maria. They were bright searchlights more glaring than the polished buttons on his uniform.

"Tell me who your guests were on May 2nd."

"May 2nd?" Maria named a few.

"Only those?"

Maria nodded.

"Friends?"

"Yes, friends."

The officer shuffled through a list. He continued to glower at her with his naked eyes, hard little seeds about to burst behind his wire-rimmed glasses.

"A baroness? Must be nice to live in a castle while a war is going on."

Maria's nostrils quivered once. She held her back straight and kept quiet.

"Count Silverstein. Do you know him?" He asked with a guttural rasp in his voice.

"A neighbor," Maria answered.

A gray stillness settled between them. The officer intensified his stare. Now his eyes were torches. But no names were discernible in Maria's calm composure.

He read from his list.

"Your two sons are fighting for the fatherland."

"And my son-in-law died for it in France."

The officer rubbed his temple in a circular motion. Again his finger traced down the list.

"You may go." Even he recognized a born aristocrat.

Maria's eyes adjusted slowly to the sunlight as she stepped outside. What did she see? A desert fox? Iridescent onyx eyes, horizontal whiskers, taut sinews under russet fur, the tail a flag? Maria blinked twice. Or a hawk with dusty feathers clawing the top of a telegraph pole? It smoothed its ruffled plumage. Its eyes lost focus. Then a tabby, dodging shadows, dashed under a bush. Was she hallucinating or did she hear the owl screech?

Omi Maria lost both of her sons in that war. She had called them her sunshine. I knew them only from pictures, forever young in their pressed uniforms, grins on their faces, certain of their lives.

Uncle Hubertus and Uncle Heio were both casualties of the campaign in Russia. Nobody knew exactly where Uncle Hubertus died. He was listed as missing in action. But Maria received some things from Uncle Heio's commander, a silver cigarette case, a snapshot of his girlfriend, an iron cross on a green velvet ribbon, a note:

Stalingrad—New Year's Eve.

Dear Mother,

We are surrounded by enemy fire and God only knows who will make it out of this inferno alive. We are without rations. My feet bleed from the cold. All my remaining strength in this hellhole comes from memories of you and my happy childhood.

Your loving son, Heio

Every New Year's Eve after the Battle of Stalingrad Omi Maria secluded herself from us and mourned in solitude.

I never knew until after her death. It was then I took one of her dresses off a hanger, a black one with fur on the cuffs and around the collar. I stroked the fur as I had done as a child. When I turned it over, I found a pocket sewn shut. I cut it open. Uncle Heio's last note was tucked inside.

+

I held a picture taken during my last visit with Omi Maria. I had carried the photo in my wallet and it got folded in the middle, bisecting the image. By then she appeared to be all air but the essential features of her face were prominent, accentuating the fine lines around her nose and mouth. I had a vision of an owl unfurling its feathers, readying itself for the long night watch.

I pressed my cheek to the picture.

Ron and I were on our way to Scotland, he to research Robert Owen's socialist reform movement, I to train horses. We stopped before we left to see Omi Maria as she lay dying. She had been moved to my mother's house.

I was young still and could not accept her dying. As she began to slip away I tried to anchor her to this earth. I had planned that she would visit us in Scotland and see our home there. She had never ventured to America.

Gently, firmly, she taught me as she always had.

"Child, growing old has been difficult but dying is much harder."

I made oatmeal and fed her. She swallowed only a little from the tip of the spoon.

"Tea? I can get you any kind you want."

She sipped a few drops while I propped her up.

I tended to things I knew mattered. I clipped her fingernails, her toenails.

"I'd love to have my hair washed," she said one day.

I carried her to the tub. She was all lightness. Her hands were riddled with liver spots, loose skin hung over hollow bones. It pained me to see her belly all bloated. She squeezed my hand ever so gently. After I shampooed her hair I combed the wet ebony strains with her silver African comb.

It consoled me to perform these small acts of love and gratitude. All through my growing-up years, Omi Maria had been the lead mare I galloped after, trying to be strong and independent as she was.

Ron and I could delay no longer. The day before our departure Omi Maria asked to be taken to her apartment.

"I'll be alright for one night," she tried to assure us.

My mother and I fretted.

When I climbed the stairs to her apartment that next morning, my childhood climbed with me. I smelled catnip tea before I opened the door. The table was set for an old-time breakfast for two.

I could hardly eat. My tiny, shrunken Omi Maria huddled under her comforter, her skin so sheer her soul began to shine through. But I could not rob her of her triumph by starting to cry. I talked of Scotland, told her how she would enjoy seeing a new country. I handed her a cup of steaming tea. She spilled it, her hands so unsteady.

In the car loaded for the train station, Ron honked from downstairs.

In Omi Maria's fragile embrace lay strength.

"This is the end, my child. Maybe we get old and ugly to ease the pain of parting."

I saw her tears. I was three years old again and wanted to suck my thumb.

A month had passed since we settled in Scotland. Tired after a day of training horses, I was napping and woke with a start. Why was I in pain? Then I realized, Omi Maria had just died.

My mother later confirmed the hour of her death.

"She died at 6 pm," she told me, "in her own bed at home, with open windows, as she had requested and a wise owl watching over her."

For Omi Maria, evening lulled the world.

I got on with my life but never stopped missing my dear grandmother when great aches came over me in dreams or when no one was watching.

In Search of My Father

I sit cross-legged on a sheepskin rug in front of a glowing fire. A days-long snow storm affects the reflective mood of my present search. A finely bound leather photo album rests on my lap, its pages well thumbed through, its pictures yellowed. But I can make out what my mother, Gerda, has written in her loopy hand under a photo taken the morning after my parents' wedding. "That's how it began." She has underlined BEGAN. My parents had snapped pictures of each other in their sun-flooded hotel room in Brünn where my father had been stationed. Their unmade bed in plain view. My mother is fixing a bra strap and smiling coyly, unaware of the many hardships she would soon have to endure. My father, Gert, is grinning from ear to ear, his head confidently tossed back and holding a white undershirt in front of his privates. I was conceived during that brief golden October honeymoon and was born the following July. My father was killed two weeks before my arrival, shortly after Germany's invasion of France in 1940. My mother survived into old age.

Where does one look for one's dead father? I delved into stories of family and friends, studied this treasured family album, read my father's diary that miraculously survived, and tried to get my mother to share her memories.

The earliest account comes from my grandmother, Aenne. "The umbilical cord was so tough the midwife had difficulty severing it," she told me and "thus I believe our close bond was formed." Gert also seems to have imbibed Grandmother Aenne's passion for classical literature with his mother's milk. She recited ballads from memory to him throughout his childhood. All his short life my father was enamored with Schiller. Had he lived, he planned to study the works of the great 18th century German writers at a university.

I pressed my grandmother for stories and she cobbled together a complex picture of her first-born. "As a child your father had a temper and when he became impatient toys would fly through the air like missiles. But he also had a caring side. After overhearing an adult conversation about his beloved aunt who had fallen on hard times, he secreted part of his weekly allowance onto her nightstand." As my grandmother recalled these memories, tears welled up in her eyes. "My heart is heavy when I talk about your father. The terrible waste of his young life. He was endowed with so many talents. What he could have given to the youth of today!"

From his lawyer father, Karl, Gert learned the art of debating. During a hike along the Baltic coast one summer with a high school friend, he wrote in his diary, "Franz and I argued incessantly about politics. I said as crude as Hitler is, he's bound to fail. Franz is not so sure." Although their political opinions were often naïve they both lamented the Versailles Treaty and hoped for a revival of German national pride. And they had joined the youth movement with its credo of a return to nature. A strange mixture slumbered in my father's admiration for the classics and his nostalgia for the German romantics. Joseph Eichendorff's yearning, dreamy poems were among his favorites.

My father's love for his parents is evident in his diary entries. "My parents' care for me and my siblings is unwavering. They are devoted to making our growing up years happy ones." There was laughter, games and sports. Grandfather Karl was an avid chess player who engaged all his children in the game. Until the outbreak of World War II, the home was a lively haven for family, friends and strangers. Franz recalled, "The door to Gert's house was always open to us." He went on, "Gert had a magic about him. He led the high school debate team with ease and confidence, and without a hint of arrogance."

My father seemed to have known the Baltic coast like his own room at home. He had listened to the sea's boisterous roars and calm murmurs, inhaled the seaweed-scented air, felt the warm sun rippling over his muscles. He had climbed up and down the sand dunes and waded through the many inlets and rivulets around little islands, abloom in spring, butterflies everywhere. The pages in his diary are sparsely filled but they tell about his connection with nature. "The waves wash gently against the beach and the ocean looks like rippled fabric reflecting a blue sky. I inhale the scent of the ocean unspoiled by humans." On a visit to my birthplace on the Baltic coast forty years later, I caught a whiff of the acidic odor from the iodine in the water and felt that I was breathing in my father's world.

My father records two special discoveries from his sojourns with Franz, a jewel and a dead bird. All her life my mother would cling to the rare aquamarine colored shard of amber in the shape of a large teardrop which my father had found and given to her as an engagement present. When you held this fossilized jewel up in natural sunlight the transparent color would turn deep blue and display the outline of a petrified leaf at its center. A mysterious glow enveloped the stone. "History is embedded in amber," my father wrote. "And our personal life is enshrined in this gift from the Baltic Sea."

The second discovery he described this way: "I saw several of my favorite birds, seagulls looping over the dunes in a love dance, wings meeting over their backs. They squawked loudly. Then I stumbled in the sand upon a fallen comrade, grey with black markings on head and wings. When I picked up the lifeless body I noticed a red spot on its beak. It was the sign of a mother bird. I took it home to be preserved by the taxidermist in town." When I was a toddler the stuffed seagull hung over my crib, its bony claws clutching a leafless branch that was festooned to the wall. Sometimes my grandparents would dangle a piece of chocolate from the bird's beak. I remember reaching up to its breast to stroke the so-soft down.

Like his beloved seagulls, my father lived in both kingdoms, the air and the sea. He was skilled at sailing the family sailboat. He built his own glider, and received his glider pilot license when he was eighteen. "Now I can swim *and* fly," he proudly recorded in his diary.

The last entry in his diary is written a few weeks before he was drafted and just before my parents' short engagement. It is about my mother whom he had first met at a party for nurses graduating from the Potsdam hospital on the outskirts of Berlin. "I've got her…I think she's mine!" Numerous exclamation marks run across the page!

My parents were married in a hurry before my father's departure. He was whisked off to France where he spent a few days luxuriating in Paris. By then he knew of the pregnancy and bought my mother an emerald ring with splinters of diamonds surrounding the precious stone. He mailed the ring from Paris along with an enthusiastic note, "This is for our daughter. I know it will be a girl. Should I be wrong (which I doubt) I will make up for the ring and build a glider with our son." He guessed right, and I am here as proof.

My father's regiment was dispatched to the battlefront near Verdun. Shortly thereafter, France surrendered. He was giddy upon hearing the news and confided to Franz his hope that he might be able to return to the Baltic coast in time for my impending birth. But fate was capricious. Maybe my father had a premonition. He had scribbled a sentence on the back of an envelope addressed to my mother which Franz later found in his shirt pocket. It read, "Don't cry if our days turn dark. Know that they have been. That memory will sustain us."

It was Franz who brought the news of my father's death. "We were bivouacked in an abandoned farmhouse. After hearing of France's surrender, we let our guard down and decided to celebrate. Our entire platoon was in a festive mood. There was food stocked in the kitchen of the old farmhouse but not as much liquor in the cupboards as we had hoped. So Gert and I decided to venture down the lane to a house that looked unoccupied. Maybe some lovely French wine would be waiting for us there. As we traipsed through tall weeds and grass not mowed for many moons we laughed at everything and nothing, so great was our relief that the capitulation had been so swift in coming. Everything was eerily quiet when we entered the house. As we had expected, there was no one in sight. Happening upon the cellar steps, we thought that's where the wine would be. Gert descended first, I stumbled after him on the rickety wooden staircase. It was pitch dark. Suddenly I heard a shot. A soldier scrambled out of hiding and up the steps in my direction. I shot him point blank with my revolver. Gert was sprawled at the foot of the stairs, bleeding profusely. As his breathing ebbed, he said calmly and clearly, 'I was so very happy.' He died in my arms."

On a warm summer afternoon last year I walked down the dusty French country road where my father's grave is barely visible among the high grasses of the meadow. An apple orchard borders his resting place and the wooden cross, hastily erected by Franz, is weather-worn and worm-eaten and tips sideways but still marks the spot, a place so far away from his beloved homeland.

What would my relationship with my father have been like had he lived? Would he have helped me through my many teenage troubles? How would he have seen me? What had I and my children and grandchildren inherited from him?

I have my mother's robin-egg blue eyes and straight straw-blond hair. My father's eyes were hazelnut brown, his hair was wavy and dark, his skin olive-tanned. Mine is sun-bleached white. My mother and I look Nordic, my father central European. He was of average height but as he confided in his diary, "I wish that I was tall like my mother." His father was rather short. In the few pictures I have of my father he stands a head above my mother. His posture is confident, his hands strong with nimble looking fingers, gesticulate easily. His eyes seem to twinkle. He must have been a bit vain because he posed in his uniform for an oil portrait. "It looks fetching," he wrote about his military attire.

My mother was by nature warm and lighthearted. Her lifelong struggle with depression was surely prompted by the loss, in quick succession, of her young husband, her two brothers and her Pomeranian homeland. Until her death, my mother always placed a rose near my father's framed picture on his birthday. But she had difficulty talking about him. When I asked questions, she said little more than that he had a great zest for life, before dissolving into prolonged weeping. I couldn't fully imagine my mother's sorrow until I had a baby of my own. How could joy and sadness exist side by side?

Because my mother was in mourning I was two weeks overdue and my birth had to be induced. Maybe I sensed that the world might not be a welcoming place. But following my birth I became my mother's sole comfort. "You are the most precious thing I have left from your father."

Now, with our grandchildren frolicking around us, I feel their hair, gaze at the color of their eyes, and I glimpse my father in their posture, their gestures. I smile when they trample on their building blocks. I watch them fondly as they pick flowers for me, and am amused when they quarrel over some triviality. But mostly I hear them echoing my father's note to Franz on that long-ago summer hike, "The air is for adventure, the sea for dreaming." And I say to my children and grandchildren, "It's time we returned to the Baltic coast. Who wants to go?"

Your Two or Three Year Old

The tempestuous twos are not ushered in with the recurrence of an official birth date. We knew that for Cecile they had arrived when we found her studying her face in a mirror. Looking up, she greeted me, "That's Cecile, Mommy." Thus identifying herself as Cecile, she started down that race course of development from toddler to little girl. She would make many thrilling discoveries during the stretch of that year. Anxieties would overwhelm her at times. Hurdles would frustrate her. But she would achieve independence in many areas, insisting repeatedly with great assurance, "I'll do it."

Life for a two year-old is excitement and mystery. To understand what is going on around her a child has to order her world. An assortment of toys, songs, as well as being read to, are means to that end. An explosion of words occurs between two and three. Speech begins with more rhyme than reason. A verse is memorized with greater ease than a story. "Pat-a-cake, pat-a-cake, baker's man, bake a cake as fast as you can" is popular not just for its play value but for its singsong quality as well. Music becomes an invitation to twirl and spin.

Parents are thrilled when their child puts a complete sentence together for the first time. Events, too, are told in sequence. A breakfast conversation with Cecile might go like this: "Now we all eat. Daddy goes to his office. Caitlin and Claudia go to school. Kitty goes to the bathroom in her box, and Cecile and Mommy go to the big bed and Mommy tells Cecile 'The Frog and the Princess'."

But it's not with words alone that children try to make sense of their existence. Games that are played over and over again, building blocks tumble down and are restacked with enormous perseverance, and puzzles put together with great patience. Simple acts are repeated and gestures are on an even footing with words. Repetition is the name of the game.

Cecile wants to do things herself, from brushing her teeth to giving herself a bath. Lots of extra time has to be allowed for dressing in the morning. It's frustrating when the foot ends up in the wrong pant leg again and again and the zipper has to be turned repeatedly from back to front. There are outbursts of anger when the sock won't let itself be pulled over the heel. Cecile rips the sock off, attacking it by biting it until loose brown threads dangle between her teeth like fangs. But frustrations are overcome by the joy over an accomplished task. "I look so, so pretty," Cecile tells me while stroking her sweater. She has finally managed to get both her arms and her head through the appropriate openings.

The tactile sense is refined. No longer are the lips the primary explorers, the hands now take the lead in touching. Physical sensations are felt in a new way. A cool wind caresses, water splashes with delight over the body of a child and she wonders as she rubs grains of sand inside her palms. She wants to smell every flower in the garden and goes back to the tree to stroke its rough bark.

There is a see-saw movement between clinging and breaking away. The more exploring goes on, the more fixed will be a child's attitude toward the daily routine and the adult world. All rituals like taking a morning stroll, reading, or lullabies before bedtime must be followed meticulously. Any digression is met with annoyance. "Don't put my teddy on that chair." Cecile grabs him away from me. "He sleeps on my pillow." How could I forget? I disturbed her sense of order. To conquer the unknown (often frightening) new territory, the known (mastered) world must appear stable and unalterable. The child might be drawn to a loud noise but only by holding on securely to a pant leg.

The need for mother is at its height for a two-year-old. The child asks for constant reassurance. Even a temporary absence can be experienced with anxiety. The child demands love and security during the time when her will to break away is strongest. Her attempts at venturing out require constant strengthening. My husband suggests that he might give Cecile her bath. "No," protests Cecile, "Mommy has to bathe me." "Why?" my husband tries to find out. Cecile already has an answer which bends reality to fit the needs of her situation. "You are so exhausted, Daddy, you must go to bed. Mommy has to bathe me."

We rejoice in all the modes of affection Cecile gives us at this age. We hug, we snuggle, we hold hands while walking. Cecile sits on our lap when looking at a picture book. But I am more than annoyed when my lovable little girl throws a tantrum and refuses to leave the grocery store without the cans that have kitty pictures on them. Usually compromises or limited choices help Cecile through such a crisis. We settle on five sheets of toilet paper when she really would like to unroll it all, or we can decide to take the baby doll with us to the dinner table when Cecile can't otherwise be persuaded to leave her toys. "No" won't get very far during this stubborn stage of development. A substitute is more readily agreed to. "Let's not color the wall," I tell Cecile who has lifted a purple crayon out of the coloring box and is headed for the yellow wall of her room. "I want to," is her immediate, defiant reply. Only after I show her the new coloring book I have bought her, with flowers and her favorite cat on one of the pages, can she be persuaded to use her artistic talents in a different area. The parents become magicians at diversions.

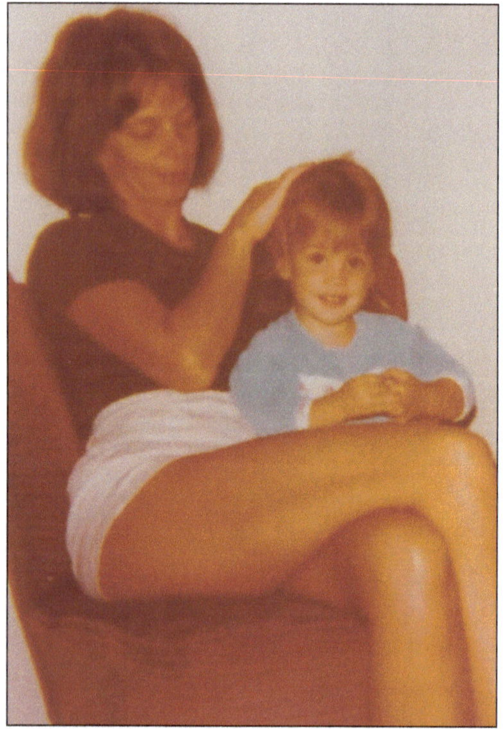

What began in the cradle as an attempt to imitate the expressions of faces or the swinging of a mobile, continues now by imitating tasks or following older siblings and other members of the household around. If her sisters practice cartwheels on the lawn, Cecile tries to do them too and calls, "Watch me." If her dad reads the newspaper, Cecile gets a book and reads it aloud (upside down) next to him. Armed with a watering can she follows our neighbor to "give the flowers a drink."

"The thunder is knocking at my window," Cecile informs me after I rush to her bedside in response to her crying. Another time she calls us because the "duck is going to bite me." There are ducks in the fabric of her curtain. She tells us, "They come out and get in my bed." Since reality and fantasy are not yet separated in her mind, it doesn't help to tell her the ducks are not real and can't leave the material. Instead we let her pet the duck in the curtain and by imitating our voice she tells them, "Go to sleep, duckies, right now." Reassured, Cecile asks that teddy be tucked in tightly next to her.

In the child's imagination objects are alive and toys are animated. Cecile carries on long conversations with her stuffed animals after she has put them to bed. She tells them episodes from the day's activities and scolds them in words overheard in adult conversations. At this age fantasy is a tool by which a child tries to make sense of various realities.

From my desk chair I watch Cecile on the beach. She runs after a seagull, calling it, "Come here, little bird, please come to Cecile." She turns back to the sand and starts digging for the disappearing coquinas. "Why are they playing hide-and-seek?" She laughs when a wave rolls in and fills her dugout hole. Now she stretches out on the ground, digging again and awaiting the return of the next wave to wash over her and her burrow, enchanted by the feel of water and the movement in the sand. The image that suggests itself to me about this age is, "I am the center of the universe."

Watching Cecile draw in the sand, run against the wind, sit in the bathtub trying to soak her shoulder, or hearing her call out, "Look, my belly button is a snail," I realize that she is no longer a toddler but a little girl. She is still quite a distance from doing without our help but I am struck by a certain completion of her self-awareness. Soon Cecile will not only celebrate her third birthday, she will be ready for more people. A good time for nursery school, I am reminded. She is ready to include others beyond the familiar figures. She needs playmates and encounters with selected strangers.

This phase is especially challenging to parents. Don't ever take rebukes personally. I had played joyfully an entire afternoon with Cecile but when my husband returned home from work she rushed into his arms and pushed me away saying, "You go away, now!" She did not love me any less, but the object of her affection centered momentarily on someone else. Difficult not to get your feelings hurt!

We know that each child goes through similar passages between two and three. Each child needs to order the world. She will have her ups-and-downs on the emotional seesaw. She will experience loss, and fear separation, as well as the desire to let go, to become more independent. She will follow some leaders such as parents and siblings, and imitate their behavior. She will feel frustration and anger. But there are the glorious times of achievement when the child is indeed the center of the universe. Beyond the general behavior characteristics, what makes a child your child, our Cecile our two-year-old, is the curious and marvelous fact that each child colors, builds, messes up, and invents the shapes, forms, and shadings of that period in his or her own unique way.

An Emergency Room Experience

I was neither calm nor collected as we rushed our five year-old daughter to the hospital emergency room. She had broken her arm falling from a swing in our backyard. She was in pain and terrified. As I cradled Claudia in my arms, I sang to her. My husband drove us to the hospital. Images of graver accidents flashed through my mind. I heard the sirens of ambulances zooming by with red lights flashing and I began to envision the place to which those racing, squealing vehicles would deliver their sick or injured victims. Although it was some relief to realize that ours was not a life-threatening event, still I was apprehensive.

Once we arrived at the ER, the waiting began. Answering questions about medical history and insurance is surely necessary but is frustrating when you are also simultaneously trying to calm your upset child. We bided our time while our paperwork was reviewed.

Then an aide walked us to a room off the main receiving area, situated Claudia on a cot, took her temperature and paged a pediatric resident. After a long wait, the resident came in and, seeing the disjointed and swollen arm, ordered X-rays. A student nurse arrived and insisted that it was hospital policy that our daughter be placed in a wheelchair for transport to the X-ray station. The rule was waived by the resident when he realized how much calmer Claudia was when carried by her father. The X-ray station was extremely busy. Time dragged. Finally, it was our turn but then one X-ray had to be repeated because Claudia had moved her arm. After that we had a breather. The resident told us he would be back as soon as the films had been read.

A member of an ambulance team provided some distraction when he winked at our daughter and made her smile as he passed by. He later returned to talk with her about her fall and showed her his beeper. She asked him why he was wearing green pants and shirt. He explained and warned her not to play Tarzan on a swing again. They parted as friends.

Preparing a child for an unpleasant procedure requires both frankness and a reassuring manner. Our daughter responded well to comments like, "What a brave girl you are," and "You are doing real well," whereas she flinched and clung to me when she was told to "hold still" by a nurse who came to give her an injection. Hearing Claudia cry, another nurse who happened by our room returned with an inflated sterile glove on which she had drawn a funny face. It worked. Our daughter reached for the glove, laughing. The pediatric resident helped too. He made the waiting bearable by keeping us informed. Comments like, "The films are not back yet," or "Your room is not ready," let us know we had not been forgotten.

What was the orthopedic resident like? He walked into the small room after having seen the films of the broken arm. He looked like Omar Sharif in "Dr. Zhivago." I was immediately skeptical. I hoped that his good looks wouldn't stand in the way of his doctoring. I soon found out that my skepticism was unwarranted. He introduced himself by his first and last names and we shook hands. This bespoke a self-assuredness, a sense that he could comfortably handle the forthcoming medical procedure and that he was at ease with this injured child and her parents. We felt included.

Contrasting behavior may help to drive home the point. A senior staff physician was asked to review the X-rays and check our daughter's finger movements. He did manage to smile at our groggy daughter, but we never heard his name nor were we included in the conversation between him and his entourage. He simply talked past us and generally ignored us, whereas the pediatric resident had explained every aspect of what we should expect. Being included had bolstered our trust and mitigated the feeling of being condescended to.

The orthopedic resident agreed to have us stay during the setting of the arm. Parents can be helpful or a hindrance in such situations. They may add their own anxieties to already tense circumstances, and they have generally a tendency to meddle since they are best qualified to judge their child's behavior. A problem arises only when the child's reactions interfere with a necessary medical procedure. For example, when we returned to have the cast removed, Claudia cried harder and louder than she had immediately following the accident. I knew she cried not because of present discomfort, but because of a painful memory. Although I understood her fear of the repetition of an unpleasant experience, I nevertheless had to be firm with her so that the cast could come off.

Parents can serve several important functions. They can provide security for their child in strange and frightening surroundings, serving as a buffer between the familiar and the unknown. And they can provide an important outlet for the child's aggression which arises from fear. Our daughter was brave with nearly all the strangers in the hospital. Her frustration at not being able to escape the unpleasantness was acted out in hostility toward me, first by pinching me and whispering, "I want to go home... get me away from here," and later by biting my arm. If parents can be included in their child's care, and doctors are not put off by displays of temporary aggression as well as affection between parents and child, a much less anxiety-laden atmosphere will likely result.

Ultimately, it was neither my humming lullabies nor my husband carrying her around but a sedative that allowed Claudia to relax so that the fractured bones could be set. But the fact that the orthopedic resident was willing to wait while we soothed her, rather than immediately increasing the sedative dosage, had a salutary effect on the student who was assisting. He, too, relaxed and ceased his earlier efforts to try to get our daughter to "settle down." When all was over and done, he gave her a big smile.

What made an unpleasant experience bearable was the praiseworthy ability of the two residents to consider the feelings of their patient and her parents while simultaneously skillfully performing their medical tasks. They showed us human kindness. What is more, they taught by example those who worked with them, thereby setting the tone for complex set of human interactions.

Birth As an Art

When I became pregnant for the first time, I had no idea which manner of delivery would be right for me. I did not think myself a likely candidate for natural childbirth. I am squeamish about pain, and the experiences of two friends were not encouraging.

There was Lisa, a good friend from my college years. I visited her in the hospital the day after she had delivered a healthy nine-pound son. "This will be my first and last child," she insisted after I asked how it went. I assumed she meant she would not want another nine-pounder but was immediately told otherwise. "No," she answered, "I would not go through such an ordeal again—ever!"

Then there was Annie. She lived on a small communal farm in Vermont and attended classes at the college where my husband taught. I saw her during her pregnancy and heard about her preparation for childbirth. She decided to have the child on the farm with the other members of the commune assisting. She had her baby and was up the next day preparing a feast, without a thought to the risk she had taken with herself and her child. Annie's rhetoric about pregnancy and birth being little more than everyday events in a woman's life seemed too immature to deserve earnest consideration. But neither was I willing to accept Lisa's description of childbirth as a dreadful experience. For the time being my attitude was, "Let's wait and see."

My physician took a similar approach. Two factors made him skeptical of my candidacy for non-medicated childbirth. I was twenty-nine by the time I delivered, and several complications had occurred during my pregnancy. "But," he said, "we are willing to go along with your wish to give natural childbirth a try. We can always step in if we deem it necessary." That's the way we left it. Meanwhile, I continued to read about all the possible turns a delivery can take. I also never neglected to practice my breathing exercises on our daily walks on the beach. My husband became an expert at detecting false sounds in either deep chest breathing or the panting reserved for the final stages of labor.

My first delivery was a triumph over uncertainty. It also had its comic moments, as well as touches of naïveté. My husband and I were living in a city on the Gulf Coast of Florida. The municipal hospital there had an unalterable rule: No fathers in the delivery room! Not even a reasoned petition from enthusiastic couples like us could change that. My own doctor added his veto to the proposal. Recently the image of the father running out of the delivery room to phone the good news to his relatives had even crept into television ads. Watching those commercials, the doctor's kind but unapologetic words come back to me, "We have enough to do with the mothers and the newborns. What if we also had to cope with fathers unaccustomed to such an experience?" Natural childbirth was tolerated in that setting but never practiced, and gas was administered as a matter of course since, as one nurse explained, "Nobody refuses when it's offered."

I happened to have a doctor's appointment the day before I delivered. I was dilated four centimeters but no one was able to predict the onset of labor. As was my custom, I walked home thinking nothing about the extra stops I had to make to do my breathing. All I felt were some irregular cramps. I went ahead with my normal activities, leaning on the kitchen table whenever I felt uncomfortable. When, that evening, I ordered a second ice cream sundae, my husband didn't blink an eye. He became suspicious only after I insisted he return the movie tickets we had just bought, "I don't believe I can sit in one spot very long anymore," I exclaimed.

Back at our apartment we tried various distractions. A warm sitz-bath felt good for awhile. Fearing that Lisa's childbirth experience might be closer to reality than Annie's, I didn't dare admit that it was becoming difficult to enjoy the comforting water and to relax with my breathing. My husband had placed himself in front of the bathtub and was reading aloud from John Holt's book *How Children Learn.* "Are you listening... that's an interesting point... ." He tried in vain to draw my attention away from myself. I was not taking in a single sentence. Slowly I stepped out of the tub, steadied by my husband. What felt like a mini-explosion made me pass out for a few seconds. Warm fluid gushed down my legs and onto the bathroom floor, soaking the book's pages. My membranes had ruptured with a bang. Now we knew! My husband phoned, and our doctor's reply was, "Bring her over right away." The memories are blurred from then on. In the car I faintly heard my husband's coaching, "Blow out... don't hold your breath... don't panic... go on... you're doing just fine." During this crucial period, when I wasn't in full command of the situation, he was my helpmate and intermediary. After encouraging me in moments of near-panic during our drive, he became my liaison with the hospital staff.

Placed in a wheelchair at the emergency entrance and rushed upstairs, I thought if things get much worse I won't be able to stand it. But they didn't. After the receiving nurse discovered how far the birth had progressed, I was taken straight to the delivery room. Having arrived at my destination, calm set in. A nurse said, "You're in good hands now. The doctor will be here in a minute. Try not to push yet. We will give you some gas to get you through the contractions." I managed a composed reply, "No thank you. I don't need anything. I am just fine."

Nothing was done until my doctor arrived. He repeated the offer of gas. After I declined again, he instructed a nurse, "Let's get to work. I used to do home deliveries this way when I started out as a young man in practice. We didn't have much choice in those days." And, to me, "We won't get around an episiotomy, Ute. Sorry, but we don't want you to tear." I was touched that he told me this and consequently suppressed the urge to correct his mispronunciation of my foreign name, a feat I would not have managed under normal circumstances. When he held up the bloody bundle that was our daughter I burst into tears. There was joy as well as relief after the physical and mental tension of the previous few hours. I was wheeled into the recovery room while our daughter was "cleaned up." When they brought her out to greet my husband, I whispered in her ear, "Tonight to us a girl is born and her name shall be Caitlin." It was two weeks before Christmas. The floor had been decorated with greens by the staff.

Now a convert to natural childbirth, I had to resist becoming a zealous advocate. I faced the birth of our second daughter two years later in an elated mood. It was an easy and joyful event, as close to my friend Annie's experience as I would come. The doctor who had delivered Caitlin also helped bring Claudia into the world. He had had no change of heart about my husband being in the delivery room but because I had proven to him what I could do, the atmosphere was relaxed, even jovial. He did not even offer me "gas." From beginning to end I was confident.

When we left our house most of the world was still asleep. We looked up at a full moon and wondered aloud whether there was something to the belief that more babies are born during full moon than at any other time. We did not stop at the emergency entrance but parked the car and walked the short distance together. It was 7 a.m., the night shift was just leaving, the morning shift arriving. Leaning on my husband's arm, halting every three minutes to do my breathing, we caught inquisitive glances. More than one person asked if we needed assistance.

The second time around my husband was also more relaxed. At one point I had to remind him why we had come. During the elevator ride to the maternity floor he started to engage the attendant in a conversation about natural childbirth which continued while I changed into my hospital gown and which might have gone on and on had I not interrupted. My membranes began to leak just then and the fluid slowly trickled out. I exclaimed, "I'm ready!"

Between contractions, I talked with our doctor about his new house. He in turn left my hands unrestrained, something he had not been willing to do previously. "When you are in pain you might touch the sterile sheets by mistake," he had warned. Claudia was born within fifteen minutes of my arrival in the delivery room. Having pushed her out halfway I couldn't wait to ask, "What is it?" "We're still not there," my doctor answered. "We are just rotating the shoulders out." The nurse was in greater sympathy with my curiosity. "With that much black hair it must be another girl." Claudia's first cry sent chills of joy down my spine. We were the happy parents of another beautiful daughter. Later, the doctor held up the placenta so that I could see the marvelous, complex organ which had sustained our little girl during her gestation.

Our third daughter, Cecile, was born five years later. Hers was a spontaneous birth in a supportive, cooperative setting which I was able to share with the man I love. I would not have chosen a teaching hospital had it not been for the fact that there my husband was allowed into the delivery room. The drabness of its corridors and rooms seemed out of tune with my desire that even my surroundings should resound with joy at the birth of our baby. No colorful curtains or brightly painted walls were to be seen. But because all else was "in place," the unattractiveness of the setting lost significance.

My doctor allowed me great leeway. No IVs, no enema, no prep. I was not flat on my back but on a reclining table, free to move except that my legs were in stirrups. My husband was on one side, a nurse at the other, and a young woman resident stood behind my doctor. She had been there upon our arrival. While waiting for the doctor I had to "blow away" my contractions at a time when the urge to press down was already quite strong. All I saw during the entire procedure were the resident's eyes. In those eyes I could see support as well as understanding, encouragement and approval.

I announced each oncoming contraction to those present. I felt a great need to let them know that I was in control and only temporarily incapacitated. The doctor had placed himself on a stool directly in front of me. Contraction followed contraction in rapid succession. I had learned to meet each one with my breathing but at last it became strenuous to blow them away. "I have a great urge to bear down," I announced. "Can I push now?" "By all means, go ahead," was his reply. As the pressure grew I pushed, and then relaxed. "Thank goodness for these respites," I heard myself panting. "You're doing great. Keep pushing." A contraction was coming, slowly rising. I breathed evenly. The pressure continued to mount. I started panting fast, faster as it reached its crest. Sensations raced from toes to fingertips. I shook my hand as if it burned. Then the pressure ebbed, the undulations receded. I blew out and rested until, when the inexorable flow returned, I prepared to meet it and go with it again.

My husband supported my head in his cupped hands. The young resident massaged my calf to alleviate a muscle spasm. I felt my palms turn clammy. "We'll get it with the next contraction," my doctor coached, "One more push." Flop! At its peak the pressure abated, the gushing blood felt like warm, soothing water, my legs started trembling. "Look at that pretty baby girl! Congratulations!" A squirming, wrinkled bundle was placed on my abdomen. The umbilical cord was cut. The process of wanting to retain what had been part of me for nine months, while needing to let a new person be born, had ended. My husband and I embraced. "Nearly nine pounds, I thought she was big," said the nurse who was weighing her in. "Here, Papa, take her." My husband held her until I was wheeled into the recovery room. I nursed her right away.

The two older girls were able to participate throughout the pregnancy in the development of the baby. Each child had her own concerns. Claudia asked questions such as, "How can the baby see in your tummy?" and "Where does it go to the bathroom?" Caitlin was interested in where and how the baby would come out. They watched me expand, felt the fetal movements and took part in the daily exercises. The high point came when they were allowed to accompany me to one of my regular checkups. They watched the doctor measure my abdomen and they listened through the stethoscope to the baby's heartbeat. All these preparations were crowned by the arrival of their baby sister.

Why should a woman face the anxieties and endure the discomforts of birth when a little pain-relieving medication can make her drowsy or let her sleep throughout? For the sake of the child we may object to sedation. But there are other, more subtle reasons. "I had two children without medication," my neighbor once told me. "With the third one they put me out. I woke up and it was over. All of a sudden there was my child. I felt strange toward it. And then I touched my stomach. The change was too quick. There you are, fat and in pain, and out you go. I got terribly moody afterward." Although post-partum blues are a fairly common occurrence, the joy of having accomplished a life-giving task, of having literally brought a child into the world, mitigates against depression.

"But why," I am often asked, "Do you have to endure it all the way? Why not accept a local anesthetic? You are awake and aware during the birth but your senses are numbed. Why not ask for relief, especially when the baby pushes its way out?" The fact is that the transition period, when the cervix dilates, is the most uncomfortable. Helpful interventions seem to be offered at the wrong time. As a friend put it, "Toward the end, birth is just hard work." My answer in favor of natural childbirth, especially in the final stages, is that you rob yourself of the satisfaction that comes from completing a task.

Dick Read, the founding father of modern natural childbirth, wrote that birth can become an occasion for self-discovery in a woman. Indeed, there were surprises in store for me. I was able to tolerate more discomfort than I had expected. And I displayed some negative behavior during my deliveries. I realized that my fear of losing control, or others taking complete charge of me, tempted me to manipulate the people around me. I used small talk to that end. My subtle message between contractions, when I was panting hard, was, "Don't think for a moment that I'm not in command of myself and the situation."

A young friend of mine is expecting her first child in a couple of months. I know that natural childbirth is not for everybody. Circumstances intervene. Nature makes mistakes. This natural process can be interrupted by complications. But those are exceptions. I have not told my friend that she should opt for natural childbirth. But I have told her it may be worth a try.

A Fluke of Circumstance

A mild August thunderstorm quivered in the air. It was 1976 and I was pregnant. To divert my attention from the inner rumbling, I decided to walk through "Jungle Gardens," lush tropical grounds adjacent to our house. It was a sweltering afternoon as I meandered over pebbly paths under shady palm trees with leaves like elephant ears. I stopped often to practice shallow breathing and deep breathing. Leaning on a railing overlooking a swamp where an alligator family lazed in the mud, I recalled that baby alligators "talk" to their mothers while still in the shell. They have an egg tooth on the tip of their snout which helps them break the shell. The mother assists in the hatching as soon as the baby peeps, then pecks. My due-date was still two weeks away, but my third child was already pecking. She started to descend on my dilating cervix with powerful urgency.

Another moon had passed from old to new. All my girls were born on the first Saturday of the month during a full moon. They all have that lunar connection. On this particular night the sky was athrob with stars, and my fertility goddess was decked out in full majestic splendor, her golden beams like outstretched arms ready to catch a new earthling.

Within twenty minutes of our arrival at the hospital Cecile bolted headlong into life with one cry, faint but audible enough to make my fingers and toes tingle. After the umbilical cord was cut, I nestled her in my arms as happiness pulsed through every cell in my body. My other girls too had bonded with me at first touch but soon after they had attached themselves, they were whisked from me to the nursery. Cecile and I were never separated. We had as close to a home birth experience as a hospital setting can provide.

Right after my easy delivery Cecile was checked over, then handed back to me. And soon we were stretched out on a narrow cot, Cecile curled against my tender breasts like a kitten against its mother's soft belly. It was a perfect fit. Because I had received no medication I was on a natural high, my senses taut as a newly strung bow. Birth had invigorated me.

The recovery room was freezing and cloaked in semi-darkness. I shivered and pulled the thin blanket up over my shoulders. The fertility goddess had been very generous that Saturday night. The recovery room was as busy as an airport terminal. The beds were crammed so close to each other that I could have reached for the hand of a new mother on either side. But I seemed to be the only one who was awake and no one shared my exuberance. Sleep-dazed women moaned or snored under the foggy influence of anesthesia. A woman next to me, her eyes gaping in a state of delirium, murmured unintelligibly. Dense, clinging odors had left traces of clotted blood and disinfectant in the stale air. I stuck my nose under the blanket and inhaled my newborn's alluring fragrance, mixed with the odor of tarry poop. A sense of tranquility pervaded my entire body.

Several times I tried to doze off but could not shake my wide-awake watchfulness. In the half-light of the room my eyes scanned Cecile. The little wisps of her blond hair were damp, her skin creamy from birth. Her fawn eyes opened only once, then closed as I pushed her small mouth toward my left nipple. She suckled like a hungry fish, then, exhausted from the effort, relaxed into a nourishing sleep. I felt my heart in every breath as we began to breathe in unison. The warmth of our two bodies were as one. I imagined the morning sky turning cherry red.

My doctor breezed into the room. As soon as he made out my presence next to the wall, he apologized, "Sorry. No rooms as yet. We'll find one soon. This has been a helluva night." He clearly could not linger. In an effort to be accommodating, he offered "Is there anything we can do for you?" "Yes," I exclaimed, "breakfast." His puzzled expression told me that he had forgotten my speedy delivery and only belatedly recognized my alertness. "Breakfast!" he announced to his nurse who, I am sure, wanted to object that this was not the place for food. Shortly, I got breakfast. The food, white toast and leathery eggs, was not to my liking and the coffee was covered with a bluish sheen. But I was ravenous and devoured it all.

The waiting seemed interminable. To occupy my mind I embarked on an unlikely rumination. Ethologist Konrad Lorenz wrote extensively about early imprinting, rapid learning, and the importance of love objects during the first days of life. He observed that goslings follow the first face they glimpse, fowl or human. We humans bond in various ways with our children throughout their formative years. So what difference does the early environment make? What impact do lights, sounds, smells and physical contact have on a child? My other girls were nursed from the start but also spent time away in the nursery. Every time I visited Caitlin, our oldest, at the baby station she was surrounded by a cacophony of crying infants. Our second, Claudia, whose liver was slow to function, was confined in the hospital for several extra days while I struggled to keep her on a regular nursing schedule. In 1940 my own mother supplied me with plenty of good breast milk but in those days German babies were expected to sleep through the night from day one. Unlike many people my age I do not suffer from insomnia. Was my brain perhaps programmed from inception to sleep through the night? How do bottle-fed babies perceive their environment when rubber is the initial supplier of nourishment? How do tiny humans negotiate a balance between comfort, warmth, security, and harsh reality? Are babies forced from the outset to shuttle between these two perceptual worlds? How do a newborn's surroundings and early emotional experience interact? Animals keep their young at their side until they are weaned to independence. Did Cecile imbibe her confidence about life pressed to my heart while we breathed in unison?

All the while, I continued to wait for a room. To pass the time I now started to hum, very softly, with my lips close to Cecile's ears so as not to disturb the sleeping women. "Kindlein mein, schlaf doch ein, weil die Sternlein kommen, und der Mond kommt auch schon, wieder angeschwommen." I knew that by now the moon had sent all the stars to bed and had itself swum out of view. For all I knew it had already been replaced by the mercilessly blazing Florida sun. But it was still night and cool in the recovery room. As I hummed, I stroked Cecile, then gently tapped my right middle fingers in rhythm with the soothing lullaby. Cecile stirred as if listening, attuned to the harmony of my drumming, her soft lips making smacking sounds as she spontaneously sucked colostrum from my still empty breasts. Music would course through Cecile's life like blood through her body. She hummed before uttering her first words. Was a melody seed planted in the nocturnal recovery room of that hospital?

Lost in thought, I was startled when a nurse came toward me and whispered, "Your husband is in the hallway to pick you up. We need all the beds for the difficult cases. Dr. Smallwood signed your discharge papers before he left for lunch."

I remained in my green delivery gown and kept Cecile tucked into its blousy front. She never made a peep until we were home and snugly tucked in our own big bed in a room painted in joyful daylight colors. All the while my husband, and Caitlin and Claudia, and my mother were ooh-ing and aah-ing over the little bundle. We remained curled up intermittently like two peas in a pod for most of the next few days.

We kept an appointment with our pediatrician later in the week. He was incredulous. "How did you sneak out of the hospital the day she was born?" "We didn't," I replied. "There were no beds available, so by fluke of circumstance Cecile and I were sent home."

Landings

My ordinarily cautious husband was speeding. Pat, the other grandmother, had phoned half an hour ago, "Get on the road, the kids are headed to the hospital." We lived only three hours south of Dallas but this time the drive seemed interminable. "Faster, faster," I urged. "If a policeman should stop us he will surely understand. We are awaiting our first grandchild!" Under the blush of a spectacular sunrise, bluebonnets and Indian paintbrush glowed along the highway. We hurried on. I felt as if I was accepting my first literary award, elated, anxious, not quite believing that it was happening.

At the hospital I left my husband to park the car and hurried past other arriving relatives. I barged directly into the room where our daughter Caitlin lay propped up among multiple pillows. "Mom," she huffed, "join the others in the waiting room. Chris and I can manage." Of course this was theirs to handle. I tucked away the rebuff and wandered slowly toward a chattering crowd of aunts, uncles and the other grandparents. They were drinking coffee and making predictions. "I am sure it's a girl. She carried so high." "It won't be long now," another old-timer conjectured.

Our wait was short. A beaming daddy bounced into the waiting room, "Come and meet Dylan, our beautiful daughter." When I saw Dylan, snug in Caitlin's arm, I burst into tears along with everyone else. There was our princess who would rule over our five yet unborn grandsons with a beneficent sense of entitlement. Then I ran back to the hallway to call my mother in Germany.

Three years later on the same day in April the Texas countryside was again decked out in glorious wildflowers. We barely had time for a glance at the abundance of it as we rushed to Dallas. Caitlin had been admitted for a C-section after the baby's umbilical cord was discovered wrapped around its neck. Our hearts danced with joy and thanksgiving when we arrived and learned that a rose-skinned

Nicholas had been safely delivered. Having been lifted wrinkle-free from the womb, I wondered, will he see life differently from others who have to tunnel their way out?

I delivered my three daughters with the ease of a cat birthing kittens. But I ceased advocating natural childbirth when our middle daughter Claudia labored for long, hard hours. From dawn to dusk we worried and paced the hospital corridor, interrupted only intermittently by the appearance of the obstetrician, "I admire your daughter's courage…. She's a trooper…. We're about there…." When Tommy, our son-law, brought us the good news we hastened to the bedside. Pale and still trembling under her sweaty gown, our daughter gazed at Zachary with the adoring look of Mary, the blessed mother of Jesus to whom Marie, Tommy's mother, had prayed throughout. Zachary's shining eyes were already fixed on his mother's face as if to say, "Sorry I took so long. Now I am here, 10 pounds strong and ready to protect you."

We try not to stray too far from home before the birth of a grandchild. But that winter we were on a dog-sledding adventure. There were no phones in our cabin. Anxious that I might miss the next birth, each morning before breakfast I hiked up a knoll where I could get reception and called Claudia. "Nothing yet," she reassured me. I had as my companion an old Inuit dog who silently followed me on my climb and then barked joyfully when I descended. He must have been a talisman because Alexander has an intense love of animals. Alex waited until the day of our return to make his entry. When we arrived at the hospital we came upon Tommy perched outside the newborn nursery in Joseph-like devotion, adoring his second-born son. I pressed a stuffed toy Inuit dog up to the glass partition.

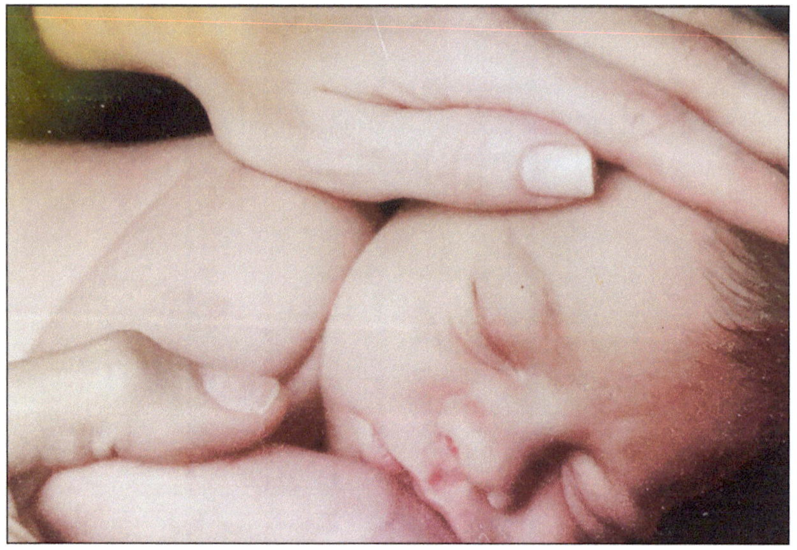

Our daughter Cecile and her husband Jeff had made beautiful plans for welcoming their first-born, including a hand-painted mandala and soothing music. But nature is unpredictable and one daybreak before the due date a vessel ruptured and Cecile was rushed to an Austin hospital. After the bleeding stopped, labor was long. Upon hearing of her distress, Caitlin and Claudia drove down from Dallas. We waited throughout the day. The doctor did not expect the birth before the next morning, so everyone decided to retire early. About 9:30 that evening, as I sent thoughts of comfort and speed to my youngest, I instinctively knew that the baby would come that night. I slipped out of the house, armed with my toothbrush and sleeping bag. Because I am not secure behind the wheel, I was frightened on the half-hour drive over hilly roads as irritated drivers honked at my grandmotherly pace.

Visiting hours were over and the parking garage was nearly empty. Not much movement on the maternity ward either except the clicking of my heels on the tile floor. I peeked into Cecile's room and found her dozing. Jeff slept soundly in a recliner. The staff, not overjoyed to see me, directed me to the waiting room where I pushed two chairs together and spread out my sleeping bag. I must have just fallen asleep when I felt a nurse's tap on my shoulder. I awoke, alert as a cat, and tiptoed barefooted to my children's room. A nurse stuck her head out of the door, "They are not ready for you." I sat down on my rolled up sleeping bag and waited. When Jeff called me into their room, I was the first, other than the parents, to hold Kaius and spin my web of good wishes around his precious being, grateful to be a witness to love and life flowing from one generation to the next. I had painted my fingernails a sun-moon yellow.

When our sixth grandchild was on its way, Kaius stayed with us. In the late afternoon he and I took a walk. We were sitting on a grassy incline when he asked, "When, Omi? When?" "Soon," I reassured him but had to ponder his second question." "How?" He was three-and-a half. The answer flew into view. "Look," I pointed. "A cardinal. See its red breast? It's coming toward us." "Really? Is the baby on its way?" I was not so sure of my reply but said, "Swoosh, and the baby will fly from your mommy's tummy into our arms." That seemed to satisfy him. He gazed up again. The cardinal had veered in our direction before touching down on a nearby tree branch. As soon as it had anchored its claws in the bark it puffed up its plumage and began preening its brilliant feathers. At that moment the phone rang with the good tidings that beautiful Lucas, who would became the delight of us all, had just made a soft landing.

Learning from Snails

My father was killed in World War II days after my birth. My mother remarried when I was four. An aunt stayed with me while the newlyweds went on their honeymoon. As soon as their coach departed I ran into our big, lush garden, sucking my thumb and crying. In the wet grass under a drooping lilac bush were my snail huts, built with moss and sticks. Carefully, I lifted one snail after another from its habitat and let it crawl across my hand and along my arm, leaving its silvery mucus trail. I watched with fascination as their raspy tongues cut tiny blades of grass. I touched an antenna with its pinprick eye and the feeler retracted, only to reappear when I pulled away. I counted the age of my large brown snails and of the smaller colorful ones by the whorls on their houses. Some had only a few rings, others up to twelve.

Most of all I loved the snails' ability to carry their houses on their backs, never having to reside in one location. My mother had given me a picture book about snails that described many of their habits which I then observed on my own. I learned that in the fall they closed their doors against the cold with a membrane made of calcium carbonate and protein. On the day of my mother's departure with her new husband my little companions were a great comfort to me.

I had rarely seen my stepfather before the wedding. He was a military man and had maps of Europe spread out all across his massive oak desk. I did not like him being with my mother but she explained, "You need to get used to your new father. Do something nice for him." When the couple returned from their trip I felt that my mother was not as close to me as before. Maybe if I did something nice for this stranger, everything would change back and, instead of being barred from their bedroom, I would be able to snuggle with my mother as before.

One afternoon when the two of them went for a walk I gathered a jar of my most beautiful snails and brought them to his study. When I placed them at the edges of the maps they began to march like soldiers. A web of glossy paths soon crisscrossed the entirety of central Europe. I was delighted with my surprise and eagerly awaited my stepfather's response. To his credit he did not scold me but instead sternly instructed me to gather up my little crawlers. "Snails are not pets." My mother praised me privately for my "good deed" and, even though we now snuggled less often, I felt reassured.

I have retained a love for snails as creatures. And over time, they have also taken on symbolic meaning. They are survivors, knowing when to retreat and when to advance, cautiously—at a snail's pace—probing, testing, learning.

A Secret Hiding Place

On his 7th birthday my grandson burst into tears. The excitement had been too much, a party at school where he was the center of attention and then the next day a birthday celebration at home. Still crying, he reached for pen and paper, began to draw a soaring Spiderman, and was soon rapt in concentration, calming himself through his art work. Watching his change of mood, I drifted back seventy years to when I turned seven and had to regain my equilibrium.

I had entered first grade midway through the official school year, having been discharged following several months quarantined in a children's hospital, gravely ill with multiple infectious diseases. It was postwar Germany in the winter of 1946, and I had never been away from my family. That separation would haunt me for decades. I either avoided relationships or clung to them fiercely even after they had vanished from my life.

During the year I convalesced, chaos was rampant in Germany. We lacked firewood and coal and the food shortage was severe. After the midday meal my mother rested with my one year-old sister while I began my chores. Wild berries needed to be picked, elderberries for soup had to be plucked from bushes, nettles gathered for a salad with carrots pulled from sandy soil to spice up the green mix. Sugar beets were also in demand so I rushed to overcrowded fields to compete with other scavengers in search of a stray beet here and there. Every household boiled sweet turnips to make molasses. Excursions with my father to the black market in town were routine. There we would barter for eggs or milk in exchange for a family valuable. Coal train spotting was a part of our daily lives. All neighboring families participated. When we children heard the hoot and steam-belching of a freight train, someone ran to fetch adults. As soon the train halted at the crossing signal, men and women jumped aboard the open wagons and tossed down as much coal as possible before the locomotive let out a long sigh and the train chugged on. We children busily picked up priceless lumps, stuffing them into burlap bags to be dragged home.

When I finished my tasks, I was free to roam until suppertime. My parents sternly warned me never to be tardy. I did not need to be reminded because I looked forward to evenings when my mother read and sang to me at bedtime, which was so comforting and reassuring.

We lived like that for two years in a dilapidated out-building located on a large estate where acquaintances from before the war had taken us in. In my spare time I had hours to myself. I made no friends after my companion Eric died in the hospital. His bed had been next to mine and I missed him with all my heart. I wanted no other friend.

But I did take care of a white rabbit with a black nose. I named him Snowflake and saved him several times from the knife. I carried him with me in a wicker basket with a lid, once even to school where I was forbidden to bring him again. One day, after subsisting on fruits and vegetables and watery soup for a long time, my father ignored my pleading and my rabbit ended up on the dinner table. But my father could not eat. We all sat silent and immobile, with tears streaming down our cheeks. Finally, no longer able to resist the allure of meat, we relented and our forks angled for the delicious chunks.

In my spare time, I also tended an animal cemetery which I had created in a nearby wood shortly after my release from the hospital. Mainly birds, some field mice, lots of lizards, and an assortment of spiders and flies slumbered under small mounds of soil. I decorated the graves with crosses made from sticks and piled flowers on top of the tiny hills. Nobody knew about this resting place, though my mother had secretly followed me there on occasion but never mentioned it.

Once while picking blackberries I came upon a hideout. A thick row of hedges separated two large meadows with a pond for ducks, geese and waterlilies in between. It had started to sprinkle when I spotted a small entrance beneath a thorny thicket. It looked as if an animal had used it as its burrow. I crawled inside where it was dry, a curl-up space with enough room for me to sit comfortably. I fell in love with that womblike place at once. A few days later I dragged a tattered blanket there which I wrapped around myself when it was cold. I escaped to my newly acquired den whenever possible and brought my teddy bear, Börle, and other valuable items with me. In a Care package from America were a coloring book with crayons and a fishing cap from Florida. A sweater my mother had knitted from leftover yarn stayed with me rain or shine. It could be rolled up and used as a soft cushion for my head.

As time stretched before me I was alone but never bored. I watched when the rain pattered down, unable to penetrate the thick cover of the hedge which I had fortified with branches and scraps of cloth taken from my mother's sewing basket. I loved the raindrops. They reminded me of my mother's pearls which she had worn in the air raid shelter. Large spiders helped me beautify my cave. Their fine webs resembled strands of my beloved grandmother's silvery hair. She had accompanied us on our flight from our home in Silesia to western Germany as the Russian army advanced. She was now stranded with distant relatives, miles from where we had found shelter. I knew that I would have taken her to my magical dwelling if she had visited.

I often daydreamed. Clouds were my inspiration. I saw shapes of bearded grandfather-like faces on misty days, and on bright ones my eyes followed fleets of sleek sailboats or herds of running deer. I imagined myself sitting atop a big billowy cloud, drifting away. Bird song put me in a trance-like state, and I learned to imitate birds' twitters and warbles. Every time a hare hopped across the grass in front of my crawlspace I believed it would befriend me if I held out one of my precious carrots. I giggled when the animal stopped for a second and then dashed away. Börle, my beloved companion, was an attentive listener. I told him countless stories. I spoke about the kind nurse in the hospital who, on the day my friend Eric died, carried me to a broad windowsill to watch the snow descending in fluffy cotton wisps. I talked to my furry bear about my parents and my baby sister. I painted a wonderful future when we would all live in a castle furnished with long tables sagging under the weight of apples and loaves of bread and even ice cream that I had glimpsed in my coloring book, and where not a single rat would scurry across our beds at night.

Through the slats in my hedge I could tell when the afternoon sun moved on and it was time to go home. I was never late because my mother had been ailing since the birth of my sister and the constant worry about food stressed her. I did not want to upset her or my father who, although university educated, now baled hay and helped with farm chores. After work he always slumped into the only upholstered chair in the room looking haggard and gray.

One day I fell asleep in my cozy enclosure. It was already dark when I awoke with a start. With Börle under one arm I ran as fast as I could and when I burst through the door I noticed a deep furrow between my mother's eyebrows. I knew instantly that she had been worried but she only hugged me tight. There was little privacy in our cramped domicile and that night I could overhear my father whisper, "Just let her be."

We moved two years later to a nice apartment in town where I skipped a grade to be with my age mates. I formed a deep friendship with a plump, brown-eyed girl in my class. In the third grade my very first essay, about Snowflake, was published in a nature magazine. The following spring I made a trip back to the cemetery which by then was overgrown with dense weeds and ferns. All traces of the animal graves were lost. And I searched in vain for the hedge around my magical sanctum. It had been cut down, no longer a habitat for birds, mice or a recuperating little girl. Only the pond still shimmered with bluish lilies as dragonflies danced over its sleepy surface.

As an adult I have often written about the war and the scars it left. But not until I observed my young grandson regain his composure by applying himself to his drawing did I think back to how I had once found repose in using my imagination to contend with early life experiences.

Nature

Ode to Water

I am a nymph.
I inhabit rivers, lakes and streams.
I sing to brooks and oceans.
I rise as a mermaid,
an aquatic creature,
mingle with the air,
drown fires,
and quench the earth's thirst.
The moon is my lover,
together we dance to
the rhythm of tides.

Last Chance for Pegasus

Life on our ranch centered on horses.

Fog hovered close to the ground, forecasting a hot day. A fragrance of clover and honeysuckle hung in the air. Two large milk drops glistened on the tip of Pegasus's udders. She was six weeks past her due date. While I groomed her, I had an earnest talk with her. I told her that she had been taxing our patience for too long and was beginning to worry us.

"I personally think Pegasus is having fun," Jacqueline told me. "She knows exactly when and where to foal. Where? Wherever she wants. When? As soon as we leave her alone."

Pegasus was my equine companion of many years. Her famous bloodline extended back to Sam Houston's horse stock. She conceived for the first time in old age. She was over sixty in human terms. In her youth she had never taken naturally and when she was artificially inseminated she miscarried. When we took in a common American quarter horse stallion, graying white, to retire on our ranch, he and Pegasus whinnied to each other. We saw no harm in letting two old animals graze together. They touched noses and shivered. Within a month Pegasus, our golden dun with the characteristic black stripe along her back and rump, was pregnant. Her mate's name was Chance.

Days before Pegasus was to foal Jacqueline and I began our vigil. Pegasus was out with the herd during the day but we stabled her at night. We camped in the back of our truck, equipped with flashlights, snacks and mosquito repellent. Jacqueline and I had made a deal. She was allowed to watch with me but she had to go to school each morning no matter how little sleep we got. We checked on Pegasus throughout the night, afraid to miss the onset of labor, so our rest was limited. Rachel and Isabel had been with me during animal deliveries, but this was Jacqueline's initiation.

We monitored all outward changes, engorgement of the udders, sunken flanks, relaxing vulva. But the preparations from within remained a mystery. Pegasus fooled us many times. We gingerly crooned our way within two feet of her, believing her to be dozing, and she bolted away in her fastest gallop ever. "She looks so funny," Jacqueline giggled, "ears forward, tail flying but her tummy bouncing like jelly."

Our mare had her own timetable. For us every symptom pointed to an imminent delivery but she kept us guessing. When she glanced at her sagging flanks and started to swish her tail as if there were flies, we called our vet. "Has the countdown begun?" he asked.

He was as anxious about the old mare as we were but he reassured us, "Nothing to do but wait." No one had witnessed the conception. Maybe I had misjudged the date.

One morning, I crawled out of the truck bed with a stiff back and cramped legs. I blew dust out of my nose. Jacqueline shook herself awake like a horse and ran home to shower and catch the school bus. I had plans to take my mother shopping, but first I did my barn chores. Our long-time helper Pedro had asked for part of the day off. Pegasus had been let out earlier and was now peacefully grazing at the pond with the rest of the horses. The dew moistened my boots as I crossed the pasture and picked the first blackberries, some ripe and juicy, others causing my lips to pucker. I got to Pegasus and moved my hand over her back, around her stomach. Milk streamed down her legs, her breath rising like mist. Then she peed, a long yellow stream, grunting with satisfaction.

I spotted a great blue heron, a greenish oily sheen on his feathers. He stood in the marshes near the pond, balancing on one leg, the other one tucked into the downy plumage of his underside. His neck feathers stuck out, a frayed collar. His beak snapped, a yawn? He released his hidden leg and stepped through the mud. With a slow beat or two he opened his immense wings and lifted up like a kite. He glided toward the herd. In mid-air over Pegasus's back he hovered a moment, spreading a protective shade over our mare's body. Was this glitter-winged bird our omen?

Later, returning from the grocery store with my mother, I said on the spur of the moment, "Let's swing by the pasture."

Scanning the horizon, I saw Pegasus stretched on the ground, surrounded by wildly snorting and pawing horses. What was going on? This herd had long known each other, and Pegasus, independent by nature, always stayed on the periphery of the group. However, during pregnancy she had reversed the pecking order. She drank first at the water trough with ears flattened back and the white of her eyes showing. She kicked when another horse tried to take possession of the hay. Pending motherhood had transformed our calm mare into a bossy matron.

The ice cream could melt and meat turn rancid in my trunk, for all I cared. "I need your help," I told my mother.

I had to get Pegasus to the safety of her stall. Her companions had gotten their wires crossed. Instead of forming a circle to defend her in labor, they charged. The geldings were confused, having never seen a mare in labor. Even Chance flared his nostrils. I heard a bird's mocking cackle. When I reached my mare, contractions pounded her belly in quick succession. A balloon emerged under her tail and she moaned like a woman giving birth.

My mother admired horses from afar, but at close range their size and unexpected movements frightened her. Still, I had no choice. I had phoned Pedro and Alan from the car phone but couldn't locate them. I handed my mother a lunge whip.

"Swing it…Swing it in a circle as high and wide as you can." She shooed and swished, slapping at the horses while I coaxed Pegasus. "You can do it, come on, and come on."

Pegasus pulled herself to her feet, wet with sweat, her breath steaming. She dragged herself into her stall, flopped to the ground panting with relief, her neck outstretched, veins large and pulsating under her soaked coat.

As if drawn by the urgency of the situation, Alan, Jacqueline and Pedro drove in. They arrived just as the contractions doubled in velocity. Then fluid gushed from the amniotic sac, the newborn's nose and front legs forging the way. The foal sucked in gasps of air with great slurping sounds. Within minutes, it struggled to stand. Its legs were tangled in the tough remains of the collapsed sac. Pedro gently pulled the rubbery scraps from around the legs and on the next try it was up, wobbly but on all fours. All the while Pegasus licked its damp coat. The foal's mane was matted like feathers glued together. The sun blinked through the cracks of the stall and as the light struck the mane, the strands sparkled like black gold. Pedro lifted the newborn's tail and looked under its belly. "It's a filly," he announced.

We named her Pandora.

No sooner was Pandora on her feet than her little red tongue came out in searching, sucking motions. She licked the stall walls and Pegasus's legs and belly until she found her mother's milk. With loud smacking sounds she had her first fill.

The umbilical cord had broken on impact when Pegasus stood up. Pedro cut down a Dixie cup and filled it with iodine. He placed the cup over Pandora's navel. In surprise she hopped sideways and the tincture splattered across Pedro's arms, staining the good shirt he had put on for his day off.

That May day evening, Jacqueline wrote in her diary.

"It's a girl. Goodness, I had expected a cute foal but this little filly is a beauty. She is mouse gray like Mommy had hoped for. She inherited that color from her grandpa, Pegasus's sire. She's also a dun. Everyone was surprised. A gray dun is very rare. She has long straight legs and tiny feet. Otherwise, she doesn't have any markings except for the white blaze down her nose, almost identical to her mother's."

We handled Pandora daily, paying attention to her moods. We cradled her with our arms around chest and rump to give her security and a sense of her boundaries. Soon she stopped jumping into the air like a little goat. She was halter-trained and willingly raised a hoof when we ran a hand down her fetlock. She overcame her fear of the unfamiliar when we lifted her into the dark interior of the trailer. She learned that the sizzling sound in the water hose was not a snake.

We colt-tailed her from the start. I would ride Pegasus and lead Pandora on a long rope behind her mother. As Pandora became comfortable, I shortened the rope until she could trot with ease at her mother's side. Pandora became familiar with our voices and trusted our touch. We mixed fun with discipline, repetition and patience. We observed her body language. Twitching a muscle meant she was questioning a command. When she was frisky, we knew she wanted to play.

Jacqueline did her homework under a tree so she could be close to Pandora. They had become inseparable friends. I watched with amazement as Pandora grew faster than Jacqueline, her caretaker. I would take Pandora through her daily paces, and then she would nurse and plop down or roll in the sand. She would shake herself, whinny and trot over to Jacqueline to inspect her notebook pages. Jacqueline waved them, causing Pandora to backtrack. But the curious filly would always approach for another look.

"Paper won't hurt you," Jacqueline laughed, cupping her hand over Pandora's soft black muzzle. I gazed at the two daughters.

Under the branches of a huisache bush near the pond the great blue heron avoided the noon heat along with a flock of egrets, white tufts on their heads like wigs. The heron stood motionless, opening and shutting its broad beak, snapping at a gnat or a fly. He emerged from under the umbrella of the bush on stilt legs and majestically unfurled his wings. He flew toward Pegasus and floated low over her back. Fall was here and soon the heron, the egrets and other birds would migrate farther south. As the heron soared along, his wings waved and rustled with soft applause. I wondered whether he was blessing our mare with more good tidings or whether he was telling us farewell until next spring when he would return to these nesting grounds.

Liebe Grosse Mietze Katze (Big Sweet Pussy Cat)

For my grandchildren

When I was a child I was crazy about animals. I made no distinction between the live ones and my furry toys. I took my dolls' clothes off to adorn my animals. Animals were my playmates, to be driven around in my doll carriage. Later on they slumbered in my backpack at school. Creatures great and small from the animal world were also the best listeners to the stories I wove from an early age.

My grandmother believed that animals attacked only when they were hungry, threatened or when they smelled fear. She was fond of telling the story of Daniel in the lions' den, and why he was not devoured because he was secure in his beliefs and remained calm in the face of great danger.

It was a warm May Sunday morning when I was 4 years old that my grandmother treated me to my first visit to the Breslau Zoo. There was birdsong in the air and monkeys scampering from tree branch to tree branch. I wore a sky-blue chiffon dress with a white bow in my braided blond hair. My mood was as chipper as my outfit. My grandmother hummed, as she was in the habit of doing when she was happy. I slipped my hand from hers and skipped along the pebbled paths, eager to meet as many animals as possible.

On a secluded sloping meadow with lush brush and a few stony cliffs, I spotted a large lion. I noticed his wild mane, tattered fur and his closed eyelids marked by dark brown lashes. He was stretched out along a chain-link fence, resting his heavy head on his tawny paws. In 1944 there were few barriers between the wild beasts and their visitors. I didn't need to cross a ditch or climb a fence. I easily reached through a gap in the fence and gently touched the lion's right ear which was flopped

across his cheek. The ear felt so soft, like velvet. I cooed to him "Du liebe, grosse Mietze Katze." My grandmother stood behind me and watched. Only when a woman passing by screamed "Child, get your hand out of there" did my grandmother gently pull me back. The commotion must have roused the lion. He shook his head as if to swat away a fly and yawned. "May I touch him again, "I whispered. "Another time," my grandmother answered as we ambled on in buoyant spirits. "We have many more of your friends to greet."

The Devil Runs Fast

They climbed over the stone wall of our gated community. During the day the thefts were minor, garden tools left in the yard, a bike leaning against a garage and even my denim jacket tossed on a bench. But after dark cars were the target and the ones with alarms sounded off through the night. The police increased patrols but never caught any of the stealthy burglars. We were fed up with missing hubcaps and broken car windows.

Terriers are fiercely loyal and ferocious in pursuit. Our gray Cairn, Princess, was no exception. She growled at strangers and tore after kids who took a shortcut through our garden. She was also fond of our old truck which had pulled many a horse trailer while she rode shotgun on the lookout seat.

We hatched a plan. One night we bedded her down in the truck before going to bed ourselves. As the moon was about to fade with the first light of dawn, her unmistakable yelping had us racing to the blinds. We peeked through the slats without turning on a light. There we saw shadows flitting by. One was clearly human with a bag slung over his shoulder. The other was a small gray ghost, close to the ground and running fast as a little devil. Neighbors flipped on porch lights as the barking chase continued. My husband laughed, "This time they broke into the wrong vehicle."

Our courageous warrior returned a few minutes later, a sandal in her mouth. She vigorously wagged her tail. We don't know if she had pulled the shoe off the frightened thief or if he just lost it as he fled. But Princess slept the remaining morning hours at the foot of our bed, her trophy between her paws.

Dem Herrgott Sei Skifahrer (God's Own Skier)

It was a perfect winter in Sölln, Tirol. It had been snowing for weeks and now frost glazed the soft ground and sunrays bounced off the slick surface in a myriad of golden ringlets.

Two dozen of us had traveled here in a minibus from the small town of Kirchheim in Southern Swabia. Although we were all members of a track team, only Angela and I were new to skiing. Our chaperon Ms. Schuster avoided the sport herself, but she had brought along her fancy new camera with extra lenses and attachments to photograph the week's events. We stood in front of a refurbished barn where cots lined the rooms under old rough-hewn rafters. Because it was pleasantly warm that morning I had wrapped my jacket around my waist and tied the sleeves. I smoothed my new sky-blue sweater down my 15 year-old flat chest. My mother had knitted the sweater and matching hat and gloves especially for this occasion. Angela and I waited to be taken to the nearby chairlift up to a hill for beginners. The more advanced skiers had left at sunrise to explore more challenging slopes.

At our departure from Kirchheim I had paid no attention to the skis which a kind old lady had lent me. They now seemed so heavy that I had to move them from shoulder to shoulder. My companions had picked up their skis with ease and were marching briskly ahead. Although I was in good physical condition, I soon lagged behind. An attendant gave me a funny look when I struggled to heave my skis onto the lift and said with a smirk, "Big boards, young lady." By the time we reached the meeting point at the first drop-off I was soaked in sweat. I inhaled the biting air deeply and soon the cold breeze began to dry my temples.

Our instructor looked Italian with his wild shock of dark hair and nut-brown eyes. His hands buried in his jacket pockets, he stood wide-legged before us. Latching on my skis was the first task and again I finished last. Our assignment was to turn around on the path heading in the opposite direction. Snowdrifts were piled high above our waists on both sides of the icy patch and as I tried to swing my right ski around I lost my balance and fell, landing on my back and making an involuntary snow angel with both arms and legs. I couldn't move. Nobody reacted until a roar echoed from our barrel-chested instructor. "Oh look," he bellowed, nearly choking on his guttural Tirolian brogue, "Dem Herrgott sei Skifahrer." Now the rest of the group turned to me in disbelief and started to giggle. "Get up," Angela hissed. I couldn't. After several failed attempts I managed to sit halfway up and flip the latch on my right ski so that my boot slipped out. While everyone stared at me I got my other boot untied, grabbed it by the laces, maneuvered my torso around and managed to get to my knees. Steadying myself on a pole, I got to my feet, picked up the skis and hobbled in the direction of the lift. Loud, unrestrained laughter trailed me as I left the group.

We were poor. My mother had just gone through a lengthy, painful divorce and as refugees from East Germany we were penniless. After World War II we had found shelter with relatives. I was a good student in high school and a valuable sprinter on the track team. I was quick out of the blocks and also a good finisher in relay races. When the plan for the ski trip was announced my mother searched for someone who might lend me a pair of skis. At first she came up emptyhanded. Then an old lady who lived next door to us announced that she had a pair in her shed from the old days. I was welcome to them. The skis were extra-long, made of oak with front tips curved upwards like sleigh-runners. They had probably been used for cross-country excursions. My mother and I knew nothing about skis, and we gratefully accepted the offer.

I can't remember how I got back down the mountain, only that I had to keep trying to swallow the knot in my throat. I spent the next few days wandering through fairyland Sölln with its gingerbread houses and quaint shops. One day I spotted Ms. Schuster leaning against a lamppost under an imitation antique lantern, her camera focused on the spectacular snowcapped mountain peaks above the town. I ducked into a side street. On another outing I stopped in front of a ski rental store but quickly hurried on after seeing the sleek modern skis on display. I often returned to my cot after the cleaning crew had departed. I always carried a book with me. My 17 year-old boyfriend Franz, a sensitive and caring person, met me each late afternoon at an après ski juice bar. He never asked about my day. His mood was as fiery red as his wind-burnt cheeks. He probably could not imagine anyone having anything but a marvelous day on the slopes. He talked nonstop about the gorgeous vistas he had seen from the top and breathlessly recalled the exuberance he felt while dashing down one black piste after another. Curiously, no one asked about my situation. Maybe they didn't realize that I had abandoned my group or, if they did, didn't know what to do about it. Angela questioned me as we lay in bed the night after the embarrassing incident, "Are you going to quit?" to which I spontaneously replied. "You bet, I'll quit."

We arrived back in Kirchheim in the late evening. Everyone wanted to get home and we hurriedly embraced as we said our goodbyes. I dragged my skis behind me and as it began to snow I felt a calm descending on my rage and hurt. I stacked the skis at the old lady's back door, attached a thank-you note in a plastic bag and ambled around the corner to my home. My mother waited with open arms, leftover Christmas cookies and hot chocolate. I hugged her with great intensity and went straight to bed. She probably attributed my tongue-tiedness to my tiredness from the long bus ride.

When our daughters were old enough, my husband and I took them on winter vacations to New Mexico and Colorado. We all enrolled in ski lessons. I became quite an accomplished skier and proudly regarded myself as "God's Own Skier" as I glided through dense forests where branches laden with snow thudded handfuls of white powder on my head. As I gazed around I felt such wonder at the beauty of nature and vicariously recalled Franz's exuberance those years ago as the wind now reddened my cheeks.

Goodbye Balmy Gulf, Hello Ice-Glazed Snow

A dog-sledding trip in Ely, Minnesota

O be self-balanced for contingencies;
To confront night, storms,
Hunger, ridicule, accidents....
                Walt Whitman

Shortly after daybreak on January 4th, 2006 the 49 Inuit dogs at the Wintergreen Lodge kennel serenaded us one last time with their eerie wolf-like howling. We would miss their communal chorus which would always stop as abruptly as it began.

We selected this New Year's Eve vacation partly to lay eyes and hands on this magnificent breed, one among the four remaining Eskimo dogs: the Malamute, the Samoyed, the Siberian husky, and our dogs, the Inuit or Qimmiq, the ones who were "born to pull." We wanted to personally experience these amazing creatures, described by ethologist Konrad Lorenz as "powerful and hardy, capable of bearing up to a hundred pounds day after day for as many miles as is required to reach their destination without as much as a whimper en-route."

It didn't take long for us to fall in love with these 100-pound bundles of fur whose bodies are firm as soccer balls and covered with thick insulating down under a layer of coarse hair which sheds water and snow. These canines fan their proud tails in the chilly air like feathery plumes. They exude a strong musky odor. Because I couldn't resist petting them with my bare hands, their smell penetrated the skin of my palms and remained there a week later as a faint memory.

Inuit dogs have not been domesticated. They are not pets but pack animals, and the social structure of packs is rigid. The dogs' personalities exhibit strange contradictions. They are affectionate with humans and ferociously aggressive with each other, but also playful. We learned that some animals bond deeply with their owners and each other. On an arctic expedition a team member was forced by illness to drop out and return home. His dog soon died, "having lost the spirit of pulling."

I had rather romantic notions about dog sledding. Visions of Doctor Zhivago whisking through a winter wonderland in a dark wooden sleigh, golden curlicues painted along its sides. I imagined myself snuggled in a fur coat, wearing an Eskimo cap and clinging to my loving husband. But things don't always turn out as anticipated.

We arrived on a clear night under a universe of bright stars and trudged from our car to Diamond Willow Lodge, our point of departure for the lodge-to-lodge sledding trip. Chris, a most personable guide, sprinted in sock feet across the crusty snow and heaved our luggage into a cozy room. Right away I realized that we had over-packed. My face started to burn, reflecting the redness of the flames from the fireplace. A couple about our age, Reva and Rick, laughingly greeted us in the lobby, "We also brought too much baggage!" Later, two young women, Molly and Leah, eager and vibrant as colts, traipsed into the lodge dragging heavy suitcases behind as if they intended to stay for months. Then we all exploded in a fit of laughter when Molly and Leah emerged from their bedroom with Hawaiian shirts instead of woolen sweaters. They had picked up the wrong suitcases at the baggage claim.

If I had to do this wonderful trip again, I would bring only a backpack with toiletries and a change of lounging clothes for dinner and fireside chats. Oh, and a bathing suit. I became a teenager again, rolling in the snow after absorbing the heat in the sauna whose temperature rivaled that of our Texas summers!

I would rent or buy everything else at the local Wintergreen store in Ely where garments are handmade in fashionable colors and are just right for this kind of adventure. Warmth is essential for such an outing and the store is stocked with everything needed to protect against the cold. Much of what I had packed, including my Texas boots and my make-up, was banished to the bottom of my suitcase until our return to the Minneapolis airport. I even stopped worrying about my hair, which was permanently blown about by the wind, looking as if tousled from sleep.

The atmosphere in the lodge was friendly and inviting. The evening meals were a luxury prepared by a French chef, Bernard, who not only has a most discriminating palate and impressive culinary skills but was willing to refresh my French as he chopped and stirred exotic foods for northern exposures. "Trés exquisite," I praised! And his bread, freshly baked each day, was a true giver of life.

Personal introductions and plans for the next days were made after dinner the first evening, and my romantic bubble about leisurely sleigh rides burst when I heard that I would have to stand on a sledge all day. For about five years, since turning 60, I had struggled with severe back pain. How would I be able to manage? Was it the excitement, the rush of adrenaline or my determination not to give in that enabled me to forget about the discomfort? Even after a long day on my feet, I was only mildly tired. Not until I curled up under warm bedding and relived the pleasures of a day on the trail did my body remember the aches and pains, and I reached for some aspirin.

The first morning, under a mild, misty sky, I stepped onto the porch and listened to the wind. It wheezed through the fir trees like heavy breathing. My pulse quickened when we were called to feed our dogs and harness them before trekking out across the lake and into the woods. Though I have been a horsewoman my entire life, I struggled with the harness. It looked so simple. The strapping goes around the neck and chest and under the front legs. From the neck, it extends to the base of the tail, finishing with a loop for the pull line. I fumbled and fumbled. At one point I was rolling on the ground with a playful young dog who must have taken my clumsiness for an invitation to play.

We were assigned the same sled and the same team of dogs for the three days of our adventure. Right away I had a favorite, Marina. She was not as gorgeous as her strapping male companions but she was smart. She was the only one who perked up her ears at the sound of her name, and whenever we stopped she would glance over her shoulder at us for instructions. She has very refined manners. While the other dogs greedily attacked their food, she sat in a regal posture, waiting. She also didn't like her dry food mixed with water. It had to be presented to her in a separate bowl while others just gulped down what was in front of them. She is different, a queenly Inuit dog!

The team consisted of three lead dogs, Marina and Moon and Blue, followed by Slobber and Clark, connected to each other by fan hitches. As we set off across the lake, sheets of ice below and a few soaring ravens above, I knew instinctively that my appreciation for these dogs would expand day by day. When we gave the command "Hike," the dogs clopped like draft horses across the ice, their chains clanging like bells. They do not bark while they are working. The desire to pull is innate. Their pride seems to lie in doing the task and pleasing their master.

Our guides, Chris, Mike and Nick were as muscular and physically fit as the dogs. They also mirrored the canine qualities of friendliness toward strangers and incredible endurance as they skied alongside us all day long. I was awed by their stamina. When dogs got entangled, they simply picked them up as if they were feather-light parcels and lifted them over the chains, correcting the flank-to-flank pulling order.

Maybe the credit is due to Paul Schurke, the owner of the Wintergreen enterprise who chooses his guides with precision. It may also be the work itself that shapes these men along with their intrinsic qualities of endurance and perseverance that bring them to jobs like these. They are a rare breed indeed. Seldom alone, they are often lonely. Outside relationships are difficult to sustain. "It takes a special woman to share this life," one of them commented, "and I'm still looking." The participants on a trip change about every five to six days and while they are together from dusk until well into the night, they bond. But then the visitors go home and the guides have to connect with new travelers. The empty nest syndrome repeats itself in a constant

cycle. Chris takes his canine companion "Buddy" with him on these trips, a black lab mix from the pound. Some continuous friendship there at least!

I was most impressed with the way the guides divide their attention equally among the guests. No one was left out or got special treatment. The guides are also quite knowledgeable about the environment, the wildlife and vegetation and they were eager to share. They showed us a beaver lodge where the wind had sculpted the snow into a rounded hill like a sand dune. But our guides also compared the beaver to human beings and lamented its power to destroy tree and dam. With our ears pressed to the powdery mass we hoped in vain to hear rumblings from these underground dwellers. It reminded us that life's sweet murmurs run like undercurrents even under the deepest snow.

I tasted a piece of lichen. Even though deer can survive on it, I doubted if I could. But I savored the mushroom-like flavor while it lasted.

Our guides took care of us when we fell off the sled and when we needed extra heating patches in our boots. They were the breakfast cooks. And when we were out on a trail, they grilled lunches over an open fire on one of the frozen lakes or in a clearing.

Mike stacked and layered sticks and then ignited them. The wood caught and began to crackle and pop in a blue flame. The smoke ascended like incense and the fragrance from the kindling wafted in my direction. I did not blow the fumes away but inhaled them. Soon the heat enveloped me and I was mesmerized by the magic of the flames as they leapt up and licked one snapping stick at a time. Around the fire stories were told. Chris recalled a camping trip when a girl's feet were so cold she didn't want to go on, "I placed them on my chest and in no time they warmed up and were okay." There is a naturalness in these gestures and easy physical contact without a loss of respect for boundaries. We all learned to relieve ourselves quickly in chilling bursts of air before freezing our butts!

Winter dreamed on when I came face to face with fear. My husband was the assigned braker on our sled. I am too light and even when I threw my full weight on the brakes, little happened. The dogs are trained to respond to voice command, more to the inflection or tone than to the words. When we said "hike" which means "go" and "whoa" which means stop or "haw" for left and "gee" for right, little happened until we used a different pitch, more demanding or soothing depending on the intended speed. But the driver of the sledge is in charge of the speed and the brakes are the only way to slow down. We had just trailed over icy ruts made by snowmobiles when we came to a steep downhill slope. A light snow was falling, pricking my cheeks. The cold quickened as we began to career downward past ghostly trees in the direction of a lake when my husband slipped and fell into a snow heap. "Stand on the brake," he yelled. As much as I tried, it was useless. Instinctively, I closed my eyes as branches and twigs slapped my face. I held on for dear life, trusting that the dogs would find their way. I had taken a deep breath when the sledge gained speed and now exhaled with a satisfying sigh as we rounded the corner into a clearing. We had arrived safely, my husband huffing and puffing his way back through snow drifts to me and the security of the sledge. We took the next down-hill with new confidence. This time my husband stayed on and was able to guide.

Even though every effort was made by our guides to keep us safe, there is some risk involved in such adventures. We all fell off the sled at least once or we slid and lost our balance. The snow is a soft cushion but you never know what lies beneath or when you might step through thin ice near the bank of a lake. The mood of the weather changes constantly. It can turn bitter cold. You can get frostbite. The list of warnings is endless. But we always felt secure in the knowledge that we would be taken care of if something serious were to happen.

Having exchanged the sight of bobbing sailboats for snowplows, we were transported from a balmy tropical climate to a harsh northern one where we were tested in strange new ways. Not only did we use muscles we had not used in years by standing all day on a sledge, we also pushed the limits of our endurance. At the end of each day we were filled with pride that we had been able to exert ourselves much more than we had thought possible.

We two-legged travelers had fun. We laughed at our follies. We bonded quickly—Riva, Rick, Leah, Molly and us—even though we came from different walks of life and knew little about each other's backgrounds. But while we shared this adventure we depended on each other and our guides. We looked out for each other. We worried when someone fell off, we stopped when a sledge broke loose or was just out of sight. For all of us time stretched. And after a day's outing we talked sparingly about our work or our families back home, recounting instead the day's events in all their exciting and trivial details. Boredom was nonexistent.

In our everyday worlds we tend to overlook or ignore the natural world. Stepping out of our urban environment meant a reunion with nature. The hands-on work with the dogs provided one kind of reaffirming connection. Shoveling frozen dog turds was quite another! But for the time being we were all steeped in nature, its harshness and its beauty.

The image of one day remains particularly vivid. Only for brief moments that morning did the sky shine arctic blue. The rest of the day the heavens were mostly overcast and the journey through dry marshlands, groves of ink-black firs and forests of blond birch trees with huge branches bending under the weight of snow, added a mysterious ghostliness to the countryside. There were fallen branches which cracked under the sledge runners and leaves, frozen and stiff, breaking like thin glass. The wind pried open the pores of my face and opened my heart, and when we picked up the tempo across a frozen lake or down a winding path, blood pounded happily in my ears.

The last morning finally arrived. The howling from the kennel had stopped and now it was as quiet as if we were back again gliding on sleigh runners across a wind-still lake. We all said our thank-yous and good-byes. When Chris hugged me, he suddenly picked me up as if I were one of the Inuit dogs and swung me into the air. It felt as if he was lifting me across an invisible fan hitch, a line that separated this vacation wonderland from my workaday world.

For the Love of a Horse

Children run away from home for various reasons, often neglect or fear. I was neither neglected nor fearful, and knew myself loved. There was no money. My mother would starve herself rather than let me go hungry. She was also a magician at crafting things. When I wished for a hobby horse, she made one from brown sackcloth with black buttons as eyes. Bridle and reigns were braided, the nostrils stitched so the toy horse could neigh. My stepfather was mostly jobless and a womanizer, and indifferent to me.

I was horse crazy. A stable where I helped with chores in exchange for riding lessons became my castle. I relished the scent of leather, manure and steamy hides. I buried my nose in the windblown mane of Sport, a spirited gelding that belonged to the wealthy sheepherding Harrison family. Sport become my first love. He was intelligent and responsive to my touch and soft voice. I was devoted to him and considered him my own. He was ridden by others only on weekends.

I saw Sport's owners from afar, a couple with young teenage daughters and a son who arrived at the stables in his sports car in elegant equestrian attire. I fantasized about the family, and when I got a lime-green bicycle with a Bismarck insignia for my 12th birthday I pedaled around the neighborhood to find out where they lived. The Tudor mansion with a blooming manicured lawn and two friendly German shepherds confirmed what I had imagined, a life without sadness and worries, and horses of one's own. When I saw an old woman rocking under a canopy, I thought of my grandmother whom I adored. Once, watching Mrs. Harrison join the grandmother with her fine knitting basket, I thought of my mother knitting beautiful garments with leftover yarn. On the spot I decided to move there.

I packed my rucksack with clothes and school supplies and rode out to the Harrison estate late one afternoon. I peeked through the thick ivy covering the wrought iron fence and when I was sure everyone was home, I rang the doorbell, "I have come to live with you," I announced. If they were surprised they didn't show it. I was invited to dinner. They made up a bed in one of the upstairs rooms with a view over a lush garden. They only made me promise that I would go to school the next morning.

We had no telephone, so one of the Harrisons must have driven over to my house to inform my parents. When I left school the next afternoon I ran and fell into the arms of my sobbing mother. There were no accusations, only a flood of tears. I became a frequent visitor at the Harrisons' and befriended them all. It was a friendship that lasted for the remaining 20 years of Sport's 32-year life.

Do Animals Grieve?

Although they couldn't talk in my terms, they had a language of their own that was easy to understand. Sometimes I would see the answer in their eyes, and again it would be in the friendly wagging of their tails. Other times I could hear the answer in a low whine or feel it in the soft caress of a warm flicking tongue. In some way, they would always answer.
Marle and Dalia Owens

Was it true or did wishful thinking mold the sounds of the night into the clopping, rhythmic hoofbeats? The light pounding on the ground grew more distinct as I called out repeatedly. Then his dark outline became visible and my favorite horse came trotting up to greet me on my return from a vacation.

Pet owners and animal lovers all remember such moments of joyful greeting and mutual recognition. Literature abounds in stories about the relationship between humans and animals, an animal's ability to learn, to perform tasks, and to remember places and people. What is the nature of animals' attachment to people and to each other? Do animals exhibit helping behavior? How do they learn to follow rules and carry out tasks? Over what time span do animals recall familiar places and people? Only if there is attachment that extends beyond instinctual needs and gratification does it make sense to ask whether animals are capable of grief. A corollary of attachment is separation and, following separation, a sense of loss. If animals love, they will mourn the loss of the one they love.

Most domestic animals adapt to new environments and new owners as long as they are well cared for. They recognize the person who gives them shelter and may purr or wag their tails in greeting or anticipation. This leads us to jump to the conclusion that surroundings do not matter much to animals and that owners are interchangeable as long as the animal's basic needs are provided for. Yet my cat, Easter, hides when I pack my suitcase in spite of the fact that she is always provided for by a competent "cat sitter." When Alex, the young owner of the black stallion, finds his horse in a herd of wild horses, the black stallion recognizes his former trainer and friend and shows his recognition by letting the boy mount and ride him. Through the trust he bestows on Alex and nobody else, horse and rider are able to accomplish unusual feats.

An old English cavalryman recalls returning home after a long absence and being greeted with a lick on the cheek by a horse he once saved from the slaughterhouse. Dogs spontaneously lick their owners, horses usually do not. But as the case of the cavalryman attests, there are exceptions. Animals can befriend people who are special to them and show their attachment in distinctive ways.

A striking example of bonding between big cats is related by Mark and Dalia Owens in their book, *The Cry of the Kalahari* (1985). Lion brothers Muffin and Moffet not only recognize each other, they show that animals are capable of attaching themselves, even in the face of instinctual needs that might be expected to drive them apart.

One morning... a rift developed in the male alliance when Blue came rambling into camp with the males in tow. She was in heat and doing her utmost to beguile her two brawny suitors. She slinked and swayed bewitchingly before them, dusting their noses with the tuft of her tail. When two male lions court a female, usually one gives way - or they share her favors. But it soon became evident that in this case the issue had not been settled.

After lying for several minutes near the plane, Blue began to move toward Mox's camp, and together Muff and Moff approached her hindquarters as if to mount her. Instead they bumped shoulders. With growls and snarls, the two males stood on their hind legs cuffing, biting, and clawing each other. Blue ran to the other side of the tree island and cowered behind a bush. Muffin reached her first and whirled to face Moffet. Again they fought, and this time Blue made for the thick bushes at the edge of the riverbed.

Muffin came away from the second round with his left eyebrow split and blood draining over his face. The two males snuffled through the grass, each trying to find the female first. It might have ended at this point if Blue had not chosen that moment to peer out from behind the bushes. Muffin saw her and began trotting toward her. But before he had gone halfway, Moffet charged in from the rear. They fought viciously, rolling over and over, uprooting grass and shrubs as they raked and battered each other with heavy forepaws. When they broke up, Muffin took final claim to Blue - by now thoroughly intimidated by the fighting - and lay down facing her in the hot sun. Moffet had gone to a shade tree to rest. Blue grew more and more uncomfortable in the heat, and she began to look toward the place where Muff was resting. But when she rose to join the other male, Muff curled his lips, wrinkled his brows, and growled menacingly. She cowered and was held captive all morning, panting heavily in the sun. The situation was finally resolved when Moffet sought more luxurious shade farther away. After that Muff allowed his lioness to rise and they both moved to the spot Moffet had abandoned.

For several days, while Muffin courted Blue, and for another week after that, he and Moffet were separated, even though before this, it had been unusual for them to be apart at all. Ten days after their scrap, we were awakened early in the morning by Muffin's bellows as he approached camp. After spraying scent on the small acacia tree in the kitchen, he moved north along the riverbed. Another lion answered his calls from farther up the valley, and the two moved toward each other, bellowing continuously. When Moffet emerged from the bush near North Tree, the two males trotted toward each other. They rubbed their cheeks, bodies, and tails together again and again, as if trying to erase the conflict that had come between them. Then they lay down together in the morning sun, Muffin's paw over Moffet's shoulders. It would take more than a rift over a female to break the bond between them.

Animals are capable of recognition, attachment and bonding. They can also learn. All pets adjust to simple household rules, but some rise to perform difficult, even extraordinary tasks. All animals use their senses in acquiring skills - dogs, the sense of smell when fetching a lost object or when hunting; cats, their eyes when spotting a fluttering bird; horses, their sense of touch, responding to the legs and hands of the rider. Learning comes with repetition and reinforcement, which, in turn, presupposes memory. For example, the domesticated horse has learned to jump over high and otherwise confounding obstacles, an accomplishment that is surely not in the horse's natural repertoire.

Animals learn quickly to distinguish between safe people and places and dangerous ones. A biologist doing a study at Lake Rayburn, Texas, reported what quick learners cormorants are. These migratory birds are protected from hunters by federal law. Biologists obtained special permission to selectively shoot birds in order to examine the contents of their stomachs. At first it was easy to drive a boat within range of the birds. They flew directly over the boats. After the selective shooting started, the scientists had difficulty getting within 200 yards of the cormorants. The birds flew away whenever a boat drew near.

Such behavior may be part instinct, part purposeful behavior. Beyond this, there are behaviors that have no serious purpose except sheer enjoyment. A young horse I once knew, after being trained to jump low hurdles on the lunge line, jumped the small course unattended, pausing to rip up a tuft of grass here and there. Our Cairn terrier Princess throws her ball up in the air, rolls from side to side, and catches it just for the fun of it.

Learned behavior becomes social behavior in Theodor Taylor's story *The Trouble with Tuck* (1983). When Tuck, a young golden brown, free-spirited Labrador loses his sight, his owner locates a retired guide dog named Daisy as a companion for her sightless Tuck. The owner trains the two dogs to become constant companions. It is a grueling task but a glorious achievement.

Wasting no time once I arrived, I knelt down to take off both dogs' leashes. This was it, I vowed. Freedom for Tuck day. To him I said, "Okay, no more leash. You're on your own, baby cakes. Put your yellow head against Daisy when she starts off, and don't you dare do otherwise." Those sightless eyes were riveted on me, and I think he understood. I added, "No more fooling around, Tuck. Today is the day." I had to be positive with him. Pity never worked. Maybe positive would. Daisy was watching us, and I simply said to her, "You know what to do, big mother." No question about that. Then I maneuvered Daisy up beside Tuck, so that his head was near hers. Without bothering to cross my fingers, which I'd learned gets you nowhere, I stood back and shouted, "Forward, Daisy."

She began to move, the little bell on her collar rang, and Tuck trotted after her, at last placing his head firmly against her rump. I let out another yell. I'd won. I'd finally won! If I'd angel wings and pearly toes, I would have taken off across the lake. Instead, I just ran after the dogs, a lot of sticky stuff suddenly in my throat. But it was certainly no time to cry.

They were truly a sight to see - Lady Daisy, her head high, ears up, and Friar Tuck Golden Boy, matching her step for step, guiding on her flank. That's the way we went jingling across the park, and the early morning onlookers applauded.

Helpful spontaneous behavior is also reported among the lions in the Kalahari.

As much as we hated darting, on one occasion, at least, it allowed us to learn something about the strength of the social bond between male lions. Having grown up with each other, Pappy and Brother had traveled large expanses of the Kalahari together as nomads, without having found a pride of their own to rule. Young males, often brothers, frequently stay together as adults, and these two seemed inseparable.

Immobilizing Pappy was a routine operation. After the shot he sagged to the ground and went to sleep on his side, the dart dangling from its needle just behind the shoulder. Brother, his head raised and his eyes wide, had watched intently as his partner had lost coordination and then consciousness.

He looked from Pappy to us, and back to Pappy again, as if trying to understand. Then, ignoring the truck parked just eight yards away, he walked to the downed lion and sniffed along his body until he found the dart.

Clamping it between his front teeth, he backed up and pulled. A cone of Pappy's skin clung to the needle and then finally popped free. After chewing the dart up and spitting out the pieces, he walked to his companion's side and licked the small wound made by the needle. He rubbed his head against Pappy's, cooing softly. Then, lowering himself on his forequarters, he took Pappy's neck gently in his mouth and began to lift. But the other's bulk was too unmanageable. After struggling in this way for more than a minute, Brother put his jaws over Pappy's rump and did the same thing; then under his neck again, while cooing. For fifteen minutes he went first to one end, then the other, trying to lift him with his mouth.

Was he trying to stand his companion back on his feet? It certainly looked like it, though we can't be sure. We know that elephants occasionally attempt to lift a fallen family member, and it does not seem unreasonable to suppose that lions might try to do the same thing.

We were greatly moved by this, but Brother was so persistent that we worried that his canines might injure Pappy's neck. I eased the Land Rover to Brother's side and maneuvered him far enough away so that we could ear-tag, weigh, and measure Pappy. Then we rolled the immobile lion onto a tarp, lashed the corners to the back of the truck, and dragged him to a shade tree, where he would be cool during his recovery. Brother followed and lay nearby until Pappy regained consciousness. Then he eagerly rubbed his head and muzzle all over his fallen comrade.

If memory is a prerequisite for learning tasks, it also plays a decisive role in relating to people, time and place. Our Princess starts pacing at the front door when the hour nears for our youngest daughter to return from school. At 9:00 a.m. she sits down before her leash because that is when we usually leave for the stables. I once knew an old schooling horse named Playboy that would proceed to the center of the riding arena and halt exactly at the close of a riding lesson. When I speak of "place," I have in mind not the drive of fish to return to breeding grounds or the migratory memory of birds. Instead, I mean the memory of places new and acquired.

Our cat Huckebein was born and raised in the country, and loved to roam. When we moved to a city and into an apartment building surrounded by concrete parking lots and busy streets, we tried to keep Huckebein indoors. He did his best to adjust to living inside, but each night he grew restless and began to paw at windows and doors. One night I said a tearful goodbye and let him out the back door onto a railed balcony, which was identical to all of the other balconies in the complex. Huckebein surveyed the scene, jumped to an outside staircase and, with tail erect, disappeared behind some garbage bins. A familiar meow awoke us before dawn the next morning. There he sat on the back railing. After being stroked and fed, he curled up and contentedly slept the day away. At dusk he grew restless again and demanded to be let out. This became his daily pattern. He was never late, always home before the morning traffic became heavy. Nor did he ever mistake any of the other identical apartments on our block for ours.

The Incredible Journey (1960) written by Sheila Burnford is a gripping children's story, a tale of three animals, an old white English bull terrier, a young red and gold Labrador retriever, and a Siamese cat, who travel from northwest Ontario, a vast area of deeply wooded wilderness, lakes and rivers, blanketed with snow half of the year back to their home in a small university town about 250 miles to the west. The three animals were boarded with a friend while their owner and his family were away on a lecture tour. They were well cared for but they pined for their real home. When the friend left for a weekend, the trio set off on an unbelievably hazardous journey. They stuck together through every imaginable adversity, though they got separated temporarily when the cat nearly drowned and was rescued by a kind-hearted country girl. As soon as the cat was strong enough to leave the shelter and pick up the trail of the two dogs, she caught up with them in two days.

It would have been impossible to find three more contented animals that night. They lay curled closely together in a hollow filled with sweet-scented needles, under an aged, spreading balsam tree, near the banks of the stream. The old dog had his beloved cat, warm and purring between his paws again, and he snored in deep contentment. The young dog, their gentle worried leader, had found his charge again. He could continue with a lighter heart.

The trio had started their travels during the warmer days of an Indian summer and arrived 12 weeks later at their owner's cottage on Lake Windigo, exhausted and nearly overcome by hunger, cold, and other perils of the journey. The dogs and cat had taken an almost perfect compass course due west from start to finish. The welcome was emotional.

Hurtling through the bushes on the high hillside of the trail a small black wheaten body leaped the last six feet down with careless grace and landed softly at their feet. The unearthly, discordant wail of a welcoming Siamese rent the air.

Elizabeth's face was radiant with joy. She kneeled, and picked up the ecstatic, purring cat. "Oh, Tao!" she said softly, and as she gathered him into her arms he wound his black needle-tipped paws lovingly around her neck. "Tao!" she whispered, burying her nose in his soft thyme-scented fur, and Tao tightened his grip in such an ecstasy of love that Elizabeth nearly choked.

Longridge had never thought of himself as being a particularly emotional man, but when the Labrador appeared an instant later, a gaunt, starve-coated shadow of the beautiful dog he had last seen, running as fast as his legs would carry him towards his master, all his soul shining out of sunken eyes, he felt a lump in his throat, and at the strange, inarticulate half noises that issued from the dog when he leaped at his master, and the expression on his friend's face, he had to turn away and pretend to loosen Tao's too loving paws. Down the trail, out of the darkness of the bush and into the light of the slanting bars of sunlight, joggling along with his peculiar nautical roll, came - Ch. Boroughcastle Brigadier of Doune.

Boroughcastle Brigadier's ragged banner of a tail streamed out behind him, his battle-scarred ears were upright and forward, and his noble and pink and black nose twitched, straining to encompass all that his short peering gaze was denied. Thin and tired, hopeful, happy - and hungry, his remarkable face alight with expectation - the old warrior was returning from the wilderness. Bodger, beautiful for once, was coming as fast as he could. He broke into a run, faster and faster, until the years fell away, and he hurled himself towards Peter. And as he had never run before, as though he would outdistance time, Peter was running towards his dog.

Lassie (1840) and *Black Beauty* (1877), too, are filled with accounts of dogs and horses remembering old familiar places and faces, and readers can probably add a favorite tale of their own.

Queeny, a cocker spaniel, was Mr. Cardwell's dog. Mr. Cardwell, a neighbor, was known to family and friends as a man with a special affinity for animals. From puppyhood on, Queeny was Mr. Cardwell's constant companion. Even though Queeny's primary attachment was to Mr. Cardwell, he was used to other people, and he possessed a friendly disposition toward kids and even strangers. Queeny was six years old when he was stolen. Stopping at a local café for a cup of coffee, Mr. Cardwell had left his dog in the truck. When he returned, his companion was gone. The owner of the filling station next door to the restaurant reported that a man had just walked up after getting gas and lifted the dog from Mr. Cardwell's truck and put it in his own. For three long years Mr. Cardwell was on the lookout for his lost friend, crisscrossing Texas in search of him. A hint provided by a Gulf Oil credit card receipt led to a dead end, as did several attempts to locate the thief through forwarding addresses. One weekend the Cardwells were invited to a wedding in Huntsville. They arrived to discover that they had confused the dates and that the wedding had taken place the previous week. To make their long drive worth their while, they decided to attend Huntsville's famous prison rodeo. Mr. Cardwell stepped out of his car, and hearing a faint, familiar sound, he bent toward the ground. The yipping grew louder and louder until, from three blocks away, a dog came running, crazy with joy, and with a thump he jumped into the middle of Mr. Cardwell's chest. After three long years, Queeny had found his master again. We know that vibrations on the earth's surface are picked up by animals through their footpads, and possibly through the nails, and transmitted through the limb bones to the brain. Queeny's yelping expressed his tremendous joy at locating his master and old friend.

A heartwarming story of trust and attachment between a blind stallion and his trainer circulated in the media in Texas a few years ago. A successful Arabian show horse suffered a severe head injury in an accident in 1985. The optic nerves in both eyes were destroyed and in spite of valiant efforts by veterinarians at Texas A&M University, the sight of Bask Elect could not be restored. His performance career seemed to have ended. But his trainer, Martha Murdoch, was not ready to release him for breeding. Instead she tried riding him. Not only was Bask Elect still ridable, he was also capable of moving from easy arena appearances to more and more difficult shows. All the while the judges were unaware of his blindness. Until, that is, after Bask Elect won the Open English Pleasure Championship in Katy. Winning that event is a formidable accomplishment for any horse, but for a horse with such a disability it required total trust in the rider. The eyes are one of a horse's most complicated and vulnerable sensory organs. To be deprived of sight must be extremely frightening for a horse. Bask Elect was so confidently bonded to his trainer that he was able to overcome his instinctual fear and flight reactions and take his cues instead from Martha Murdoch's subtle voice and hand commands.

A story of a wonderful friendship between a boy and his two dogs is told in the unforgettable book *Where The Red Fern Grows* (1996) by Wilson Rawls. It is the story of a bond between two animals that is stronger than their loyalty to the boy and in which the dogs' mutual devotion reaches beyond death. Billy's boyhood dream "I want hounds - coon hounds - and I want two of them" was fulfilled when he finally earned enough money to get two pups, a male, Old Dan, who is muscular, bold, and aggressive, and a female, Little Ann, who is small and timid, more cautious and more sure of herself, and smart. "I knew I had a wonderful combination. In my dogs I had not only the power but the brains along with it." Billy trains his dogs to tree raccoons. During adventurous nights of hunting, he also acquires a knowledge of his animals and develops a deep bond of love and friendship with them. Right from the start, he notices a connectedness between the two dogs. Dan, for example," would not hunt with another hound other than Little Ann, or another hunter, not even my father. The strangest thing about Old Dan was that he would not hunt even with me unless Little Ann was with him."

Not only will they not hunt alone, but food is eaten only when shared, as when Old Dan retrieves two biscuits from the back yard, trots around to the doghouse, and with a beckoning growl announces his find to Little Ann, whereupon they each eat a biscuit.

The dogs' mutual loyalty is cemented when they come to each other's rescue. Billy tells of a near-fatal accident which occurs when the dogs are pursuing a raccoon in winter. The clever prey leads them through the fog out onto the ice-covered river and leaps the trough, where the ice is thinnest. Little Ann slips and falls into the icy water. Old Dan quits the chase and runs for home, fetching Billy with "a pleading cry for help... his tail... between his legs and his head... bowed down."

Billy rescues Little Ann by making a hook of his lantern handle and attaching it to her collar, pulling her back onto the ice. "As gently as I could I dragged her over the rim of the ice. At first, I thought she was dead. She didn't move. Old Dan started whining and licking her face and ears." Little Ann revives after Billy builds a fire and works on her body. "Old Dan washed her head with his warm red tongue while I massaged and rubbed her body. I could tell by her cries when the blood started circulating. Little by little her strength came back. I stood her on her feet and started walking her. She was weak and wobbly but I knew she would live."

In return Little Ann comes to help Old Dan when he is caught up in a bad fight with another dog. And after a vicious attack and a successful killing of several raccoons comes an unforgettable scene in which Old Dan stands perfectly still with his head bowed while Little Ann licks his ears: "'She always does that,' I said, 'if you watch when she gets done with him, he'll do the same for her.' We stood and watched until they had finished doctoring each other, then trotting side by side they disappeared in the darkness." Billy and his dog team became known as the best in the country and together they win a challenging coon hunting competition. But the story does not end in triumph. Instead, the final chapters are filled with sadness and loss. Ordinarily hunting dogs avoid confrontation with mountain lions, and Old Dan and Little Ann would probably have done so had the wild cat of the Ozarks not attempted to attack Billy. "I never stayed with my dogs when they got between the lion and me but they were there; side by side they rose up from the ground as one. They sailed straight into the jaws of death. Their small red bodies taking the ripping, slashing claws meant for me." With Billy's help the ferocious dogs finally kill the lion, but they pay dearly. Little Ann is cut and scratched though not seriously. Billy's life is saved but Old Dan is badly injured, his entire body a mass of deep, raw wounds. His belly has been clawed open and the loss of blood is fatal. Old Dan dies on Billy's lap. "Old Dan must have known he was dying. Just before he drew one last sigh and gave a feeble thump of his tail, his friendly grey eyes closed forever."

Billy, overcome by grief, holds a vigil after his father carries Old Dan onto the porch to be buried the next morning. Sitting there, he hears what sounds like a whimper. He goes to the door and discovers Little Ann lying by Old Dan's side, as they had always slept. At daybreak Billy buries his beloved friend on a hillside at the foot of a beautiful red oak tree. Being so caught up in his own grief, Billy does not pay much attention to Little Ann. She disappears, and Billy finally finds her under a blackberry bush in the garden. She is listless and her eyes are dull. Billy springs into action, frantically trying to revive her, not yet comprehending that she is heartsick. He offers her food and water but she will not take it. He checks on her all through the night. The next day he mixes eggs and warm milk and force-feeds her. But nothing avails. Slowly Billy realizes, "My dog had just given up. There was no will to live." That evening, when he returns from the fields, Little Ann is gone. Billy discovers her lying dead on Old Dan's grave.

Imaginative literature has given us an account of the love between two animals. They could not survive without each other. The following story is about loyalty of an animal to a man. My friend, Claire Cardwell Donovan, tells it. It is the memory of a dog whose selfless devotion to her owner goes beyond the instinct for survival and whose love for him remains beyond death.

Mr. Cardwell and Queeny are already known to us. For eight years an unsightly black and white off-brand terrier, Eeyore, was Mr. Cardwell's constant companion. She was given to him as a three month-old puppy by the local veterinarian who had rescued her after a poisoning. Eeyore slept at Mr. Cardwell's feet, rode with him to work every day, and enjoyed many hunting and fishing outings with him. Eeyore was four years old when Mr. Cardwell had a heart attack. Rushed to the hospital, Mr. Cardwell was separated from his animal companion for the first time. When Mrs. Cardwell and daughter Claire returned from the hospital, Eeyore could not be found. A moaning, whining sound prompted Claire to look for the dog who was cowering under the house. No food would coax her out and Eeyore, until now always good-natured, growled menacingly at Claire. After a second day with food left untouched, a snapping Eeyore was forcibly taken out by the veterinarian. The vet diagnosed a heart condition. A dog with no history of any ailment, Eeyore was put on digitalis just like Mr. Cardwell. The two women struggled to get Eeyore to take her medicine but she spit it out, whining and pining for Mr. Cardwell. He missed his dog. His first request was that Eeyore be brought to the hospital so that he could see her from the window. Mr. Cardwell was released following a two-week stay and an exuberant reunion took place. All at once giving Eeyore her medicine was no longer a struggle. Instead it became a comical and playful spectacle. Mr. Cardwell commanded, "Eeyore, time to take your medicine," and she came running, settled between his legs, rolled over on her back and eagerly opened her mouth while onlookers laughed in disbelief. When Mr. Cardwell retired, he and his dog spent even more time together. Not even church attendance separated the pair.

One morning Eeyore and Mr. Cardwell set out on a fishing expedition. Twelve miles from home an accident occurred. Neighbors were alarmed when Eeyore returned home, crawled under the house as before, and started whining. Mr. Cardwell had died at the wheel of his truck. Now nobody could coax Eeyore from her hiding place. Rescue attempts by family and friends and volunteers from the humane society were fruitless. Eeyore would interrupt her moaning momentarily at the sound of Claire's familiar voice but she would not let her come near. She had retreated into a dug-out hole deep under the house where no one could reach her. After one-and-a-half weeks of grieving, Eeyore died.

Cognitive ability in animals is not highly developed. There are in the animal kingdom no creators of cultures, inventors of tools or problem solvers. Wild animals are sufficient unto themselves but domestic animals are dependent on humans for their bare necessities. It is doubtful whether animals are conscious of death. When I had to put down my beloved horse, he kept rubbing his muzzle on my shirt and munching his carrot even though I told him tearfully that he would soon die. As the lethal injection was being administered, he trustingly nibbled on my sleeve. But through experience animals learn to identify danger, as for example the cormorants did. They had no foreknowledge of death but they learned to identify death by association.

In Ditha Holesch's book *Der Schwarze Hengst Bento* (1974), a cowboy tells how his experienced mare "perceived" death. For years the two of them had driven cattle over rugged countryside. Time and again a calf or an aged animal with a foot caught in the cleft of a mountain trail would have to be put down on the spot. One day the old mare tripped and broke an ankle. The pain numbed her for a moment. Then she looked at the cowboy trustingly but her eyes widened and filled with fear when he pulled his revolver. The cowboy had to blindfold his old companion before he could bring himself to shoot her.

There is other evidence that animals may sense impending death. In *Die Strasse der Elefanten* (1949), William Quindt describes a scene in which ailing elephants travel to a particular swamp which served as a resting ground for injured and dying elephants, known among local tribesmen as the elephants' cemetery.

We move in murky waters when we speculate about animals' knowledge of death. But we do know that animals are capable of binding themselves and that they miss an animal companion or a human friend. They pine for a lost home or a caretaker, and their memories are long. In some instances, animals mourn a loss to the point of relinquishing their own life. When they try to tell us how they feel we have to look beyond verbal communication. The language of their bodies gives us clues, as does their behavior. I once read an obituary of an old man who shot himself two weeks after his wife's death. His children and grandchildren ended their sorrowful statement with the remark, "Without her, his life no longer had any meaning." Meaning is partly cognitive, and animals do not think. But meaning is also a matter of perception, feeling, and memory. When Billy looks into Little Ann's eyes and sees them dull and cloudy, with no fire, no life left in them, he knows that her will to live has departed from her. This will to live must depend, in some measure, in animals as in humans, on a sense of loving and being loved, of needing and being needed, and of joy given and received. When this sense is absent or interrupted, animals grieve.

Vanished

Civilization collided with nature the day the deer got hit.

A small herd dashed across a busy highway causing cars to swerve and brake. When a frantic youngster slipped on the pavement, its front legs were clipped by the left rear tire of a truck and bloodied. The driver pulled over and dragged the motionless creature off the road into high grass. He was sure it was dead.

Darrell could not rid himself of the image of the deer. That evening he asked his wife Carolyn to ride with him to the scene of the accident. To their great surprise the deer was up, standing next to a boulder, protected by leafy bushes. Hope flared like the white flag of the yearling's tail. As they approached, the frightened creature hopped rabbit-like on its hind legs into deeper brush. Carolyn uttered an incantation for a quick recovery, and the two vowed to return.

When they came back the following evening, the deer had moved again and was stretched out on a bed of moss in some tall weeds. Because the day was steaming hot, the couple had brought along a bucket of water and a few pieces of lettuce. As they crept toward the deer, its amber-colored eyes widened and it perked its velveteen ears, sensing danger. At arm's length Carolyn was able to sprinkle drops of water on the animal's nose which it eagerly licked off.

The next evening looked less hopeful. The deer had crawled away and was now camouflaged by heavy branches. It looked up as the dry ground crunched under Darrell and Carolyn's cautious footfalls. It did not seem frightened but dazed.

A decision had to be made. Carolyn had called animal control and was informed that the neighborhood was overrun by deer. Half of the present population was scheduled for culling. The workload was heavy, but they would come as soon as possible to euthanize the deer, "humanely of course." They asked Carolyn to call back if she wished.

The couple talked about what to do next. Because no predators had attacked on previous nights and the yearling was hidden from sight, they decided against any further human intrusion. Carolyn prayed for a peaceful natural death.

When they visited a couple of days later their hearts sank. There were tire marks. The brush had been hacked back toward the secret place. The deer was gone. There was no evidence of a struggle, only a soft indentation in the nest of undergrowth.

The couple held hands as they made their way back to the truck. Tearing up, Carolyn whispered, "I hope it died before animal control got here." "I hope so too," Darrell agreed.

They were startled by a white vehicle parked on the path. Two guys jumped out. "Seen a dead deer? We got a call to pick one up?" "No deer around here," they answered in unison, and smiled.

Horses Are a Valuable Part of Police Work

Steel-reinforced and supercharged, a squad car is built for speed, needs minimum maintenance and is virtually impregnable. A horse has a depletable energy reserve, needs daily feeding and grooming, and is vulnerable to physical attack. The two seem beyond comparison. And yet studies of crowd management and reports of the pursuit and apprehension of individual troublemakers show that the comparison is valid. In fact, in some situations the horse is the superior choice. The reasons are deeply rooted in our fascination with horses.

Toddlers love a rocking horse, and children gravitate toward horses on a merry-go-round. Mythological horses are endowed with wings, and the chariot of the sun is drawn by horses to announce the dawning and passing of each day. In ancient religions, horses bear the dead through the gates of heaven. Horses carry knights into battle and saints through vision-filled forests. The horse suggested supple strength and grace to the French painter Degas, who portrayed the same qualities in his better known ballerinas. For his countryman, Gauguin, the horse was a figure of gentle beauty, affectionate and self-assured. Countless stories explore relationships between horses and humans. Everyone knows Black Beauty.

People tend to be of two minds about horses. They admire them and they fear them. The sheen of the coat, the ripple of the muscles, the flow of mane and tail, the elegant gaits and the speed all evoke admiration. The rumble of galloping hooves, the flaring nostrils, the rearing, kicking and bolting imply danger and inspire fear. What do these images and emotions have to do with mounted police work?

A beautiful animal on a city street is an appealing sight. Tourists want to touch the horse and have their picture taken with it. Horses remind us of life lived closer to the land. As a mounted officer remarked in a recent news article, "City kids are startled by the fact that horses eat grass."

People are drawn to horses for the same reason that urbanites keep pets. They are a vital connection to nature. And just as nature can be gentle or ferocious, a police horse can nuzzle a passerby on the street or pursue a terrified robbery suspect down a narrow alley and pin him against a wall.

Cars and motorcycles are indispensable tools in police work, but horses are companions. Horse and rider are a team, and their effectiveness depends on mutuality and cooperation. A police horse must be well-trained, disciplined and responsive.

But every rider knows, even the best-schooled horse remains deeply instinctual. Sensing danger, a horse's basic instinct is that of flight. A car backfiring, an empty plastic bag sent sailing by a gust of wind, a hastily unfurled umbrella can cause a horse to panic. Good riders take pride in anticipating their mounts' reactions, but they also remain alert to the unpredictable and maintain a healthy respect for the potentially explosive power beneath their saddles.

The police horse is an image builder. In a car, an officer is protected but also isolated, whereas from the high perch of a horse's back, the mounted officer is at once imposing and accessible. In a crisis, he or she is always within earshot and can quickly spot trouble. He or she can be called to by voice and can respond in kind. The very sight of a horse can soothe an anxious crowd. And a hostile person thinks twice before attacking a thousand pound animal. Police horses build bridges of understanding between law enforcement officials and the community. They break barriers of mistrust and correct misconceptions. It's hard to think of a mounted officer as a cop.

Images of the horse are alive in all of us. They influence the excellent work of mounted patrols. But of course without the horse sense of the officers who are skilled riders, the work would not get done.

Three Coins in a Fountain

As Hurricane Rita drew a bead on Galveston, we followed the advice of our farsighted mayor, filled the tanks of our two cars, secured the house, took jewelry, photo albums and old LPs and headed north. We had already had our two horses transported off the island. Our trek started at 5 a.m. with a packed lunch and water. We expected it might take all day to get to Austin in heavy traffic. Our children, Cecile and Jeff, had come down from Austin to help us load and be of assistance on the way. None of us knew what awaited us.

The exodus began smoothly with a misty sunrise, followed by a flaming fireball from the east foretelling what lay ahead. Once we arrived at the 290 junction our confidence flagged. That's when we realized that all roads ahead were clogged, restaurants and gas stations closed. The call for evacuation had worked like clockwork but left a highway horror in its wake. State authorities had opened the contra-flow lanes too late and fuel tankers arrived only after tens of thousands of people were stranded on the banks of the freeway and in parking lots. A peaceful, courteous departure turned into chaos as motels filled to capacity, food and drink ran out, and gas needles plummeted.

When stripped to bare necessities our humanity mirrors colors and shades in strange configurations. So it was with the travelers fleeing Hurricane Rita. Human behavior was topsy-turvy.

Like a dragon spewing fumes, half a million cars crawled at snail's pace. Drivers turned off their air-conditioners and opened their doors, as they inched forward on the pavement sizzling in 100 degree heat. Back in Galveston, before we left, an 87 year-old black lady with an indomitable will defied the odds. Her deeply furrowed face was as calm as the surface of the Gulf before the storm. She sat on her porch and rocked to the rhythm of the wind. "I'm stayin. My mind is in this house. I won't go to no shelter," she insisted. Thinking of her, we had moments when we regretted our decision to evacuate.

General frustration mounted as drivers cut in and out of lanes and criss-crossed the median. There was honking and swearing at fellow drivers through open windows. Serious incidents occurred. People collapsed from heat exhaustion. One man had a heart attack and the ambulance could not get through to him in the stalled traffic.

But we observed a lot of spontaneous helpfulness as well. As we came to a standstill in the snarled traffic, a dog collapsed by the roadside and people rushed to its aid with wet towels. A middle-aged woman got out of her loaded truck and walked along beside her family caravan, pouring water over the heads of her youngsters. At one point an old man leaned through a car window, tilted his head forward like a graceful gander, his bountiful gray hair cascading down over his face. He too got a good dousing.

Eighteen hours later, we arrived at The Woodlands, outside Houston. We had driven 86 miles. It was time to pull into a parking lot and sleep a few hours. "No Availability" signs loomed large at every motel where entrances were locked and manned by security guards. For a fleeting moment, panic gripped my growling stomach. Any minute it could storm. A riot could break out and people would demand to be let into the barricaded motels.

Cecile asked a deputy where we might fill our empty water bottles. "You're on your own" was his gruff reply. "Find a spigot." We retreated quietly, remembering that after Hurricane Betsy President

Johnson had asked local soft drink bottlers to make their inventory available to the thirsty and they did. So far we had had no luck. Our throats were parched and our bottles were empty.

We needed something to drink soon. In search of water, we came upon a bucolic scene. Two old trucks with their hoods up were parked nose to nose in a V-shape on the grassy median. A group of Mexican-Americans sat in a circle, talking quietly. Between them, on outspread quilts, several babies and children lay curled together, all fast asleep. In the midst of veiled panic, the comfort of rest reigned there.

Necessity generates ingenuity. Jeff collected our quarters and found a boarded-up service station where he was able to get water from a hose used for replenishing overheated radiators. We drank our fill. Our stomachs would have to wait for something solid!

"All I want is a room somewhere," I hummed as we returned to our cars and stretched out as best as we could. Mosquitoes attacked my bare feet, dangling out of the open car window. A full moon, like a pockmarked pumpkin, illuminated the humid night. Memories of camping under clear, star-filled skies in my youth must have lulled me to sleep. When my daughter woke me three hours later, she teased, "You were totally out, Mom." I glanced at my husband beside me and for once his snoring filled me with tenderness.

Running on near empty as the sun rose, brilliantly forecasting another steaming hot day, we arrived in Huntsville. And joy of joys, Walmart was open. There was still some canned food on the shelves. It would be a treat to eat green beans out of a can. And they were expecting a fuel delivery!

Just then my husband spotted a little boy swinging a beat-up gas canister.

"Want to buy it?" the boy yelled.

"How much?"

"Ten bucks."

"You got it."

The boy grabbed the money and skipped off. Jeff laughed, "We would have given him even more if he'd asked for it."

Wal-Mart was a beehive of activity. And there were bathrooms. I waited patiently for over an hour in line when a large wheelchair-bound white woman rolled in and begged, "I need to go number two and I can't straddle the toilet. Can someone help?" Most of the toilets were clogged. A smartly-dressed black teenage girl in low-cut jeans and a fancy silver-buckled belt offered to steady her and hold the broken door shut. Modesty had long gone by the wayside on the road, but here one woman provided help and privacy to another.

Politeness did not triumph everywhere. There were scuffles at the pumps. After the first several rows of cars had pumped the reserves dry, the rest had to wait again. Tempers flared and people on foot with containers pushed and shoved. Hard words were exchanged. But then one man with a full five-gallon container shared with a fellow traveler holding an empty gallon milk bottle, and it caught on. No different here from anywhere else in everyday life. "Lovely Rita, meter maid...". She empties the coins and, different in shape, design, wear-and-tear, heads or tails, they fall into the fountain of life, unpredictable as fortunes.

We were lucky to find a motel with an available room just outside Austin where the beds and the shower felt the way heaven must feel. But not everyone had a place to lay their heads and many could not have afforded a room if they had found one. Disaster makes the discrepancy between haves and have-nots more glaringly apparent. Privilege glitters like a diamond in the desert. Life shortchanges the multitude under good conditions and bad.

Hurricane Rita reminded us that we are social creatures. We need each other, and can take care of each other if we have the will to try. Before we left the island a curious incident brought that truth home to me. A horse transport arrived to pick up the four remaining mounts from our pasture. Spunky young Romeo and my middle-aged mare, Pandora, loaded without a hitch. Next in line was my 36 year old mare, Pegasus. She had trouble steadying herself on the ramp but we managed to get her aboard with the help of two tough, kindhearted cowboys. Poco is Pegasus's shy, adopted grandson. Even in the pasture he gets nervous if she is out of his sight. But Poco is terrified of trailers. On a previous occasion, Poco's owner had to ride him to a safe pasture because no coaxing or whipping could convince him to venture into that monster of a trailer. This time he acted up as before, rearing, kicking, snorting. Suddenly Pegasus whinnied once, twice and then again, softly. And Poco jumped right in behind her, shaking uncontrollably. He had taken a leap of faith to be with his trusted older companion.

It was a stressful odyssey but we learned a thing or two. We had arrived in Austin without injury, found a place to stay and could recuperate. All three of our lucky coins had come in handy.

Life Choices

The Quotidian

The roulette of fate does not let you choose
the circumstances of your birth,
nor are the traits embedded in your character
of your own making.
But you can decide when and where
to step off the carousel of life
and take life in.
I descend at the quotidian stops,
not the tedious everyday places
but there where I glimpse an ordinary stone
glowing in the moon's beams.
And then I get back on.

Lessons from a Food Thief

We had arrived in the West after fleeing from the Russian troops. Safe at last. Spring eased in as warm as a lagoon, with trees leafing out and meadows starred with anemones. The Second World War was nearly over. But the post-war chaos was about to begin.

My father had been killed at the beginning of the war. Two years later, pregnant with my sister Karin, my mother remarried. Her second husband was a Count who had spent his youth on the battlefront. On leave, he searched for a mate and found my mother, but he was not prepared for a pregnancy and even less for me, a vivacious five-year old.

"I need my freedom, not more obligations," he shouted at my mother when she gave him the news of her pregnancy.

But Count Friederich had been raised in a family where the code of *noblesse oblige* still held sway, so when the war ended he dutifully married my mother and adopted me.

The nobleman and I were thrown together by necessity.

"Come on, you little shit," he told me. "If I'm going to have to put up with you, you'll have to help me make ends meet."

And that's why I began to steal.

I became a thief, a lavish thief, a food thief. My stepfather was my instructor and I his eager pupil. I was by then no longer a toddler but a little girl of six.

It started with raids on coal trains. On the outskirts of our town, the loud-squeaking trains had to slow down and were often halted completely by a red and white signal before moving on to a single track leading into the train station. Whenever a coal train stopped, the word spread like wildfire from house to house. "Coal train—coal train." The Count would sprint away and I'd be right behind him armed with several burlap sacks. He had already jumped on a train car by the time I arrived, wishing for grasshopper legs so I wouldn't lag behind.

The Count threw coal down in my direction, using his hands like huge shovels. I gathered the chunks as fast as I could and filled the bags. Together we dragged the coal home and hid it behind the bushes in our garden where I stood guard until nightfall when the Count would empty our loot down the coal chute into the cellar. Once in a while a policeman caught us and confiscated the coal. "He"ll keep every bit for himself," the Count grumbled. "You can't tell me he hands it over to the authorities."

The Allies were the new authorities and they were baffled by our strange wheeling and dealing. Without coal we could not keep warm, and there would be no fire for preparing food.

Mint tea leaves which once grew abundantly along streams or brooks became a rare commodity to be traded. Wearing old winter gloves, we also harvested nettles and boiled the leaves to make soup. We were experts in gathering edible mushrooms from cow dung and from the soft moss along the forest floor. I learned to distinguish nonpoisonous ones by color, shape, the texture of their lamella and by an acid, foul or sweet-sour smell. I also became skilled at plundering elderberry bushes, reaching for a low branch and pulling it down to my level. I could then scoop the white blossoms into my basket and later my mother boiled them into a delicious sugary brew. From the elderberries themselves we squeezed an ink-blue juice. Everything was used. In the fall acorns were cracked open and the soft contents eaten or pressed into cooking oil. After the wheat had been brought in from the fields, women gathered fallen husks into their aprons and later shucked and ground them into flour. If carrots were a little rotten, I smuggled them away for my pet rabbit Snowflake.

But the natural harvest was limited and the sites of these foods were soon swarming with people quarreling over the diminishing supply. So we stole!

Fields and gardens were our first forbidden targets. I did my best there. I climbed on fence posts where I could survey the terrain, then gave an 'all clear' to the Count. Sometimes we stuffed our mouths so full we had chipmunk cheeks as we plundered a raspberry bush or pilfered strawberries from a patch.

This is when I learned to whistle through my fingers and learned to fight. My basket was filled with pears one day when a boy, pretending to amble by, reached over and dumped the basket. He started grabbing handfuls of my fruit right in front of me. I whistled sharply for help. The Count was already watching. "Don't let him do that." "Stay out of my way," the boy snarled. I lunged forward and shoved him back. He reached for my sweater, the one my mother had knitted from leftover yarn and I saw it begin to unravel. I pulled back, he tore at the sweater. So I punched him hard in the nose. He put his hand up as a guard over his bloody nose, left the pears and ran.

During the post-war era farmers fared best because they raised their own produce and also kept poultry as well as livestock. When we heard that a pig had been butchered, we took an heirloom or a piece of jewelry to trade for some liver, a kidney or that rare delicacy, bits of the brain. My mother fried them with scrambled eggs.

A dead pig was strung up by its hind feet in the open entrance of a barn, then sliced down the middle and swung back like the sides of a door. The blood was gathered in a pail, vital organs were carefully removed, and chunks of meat were gingerly carved from the body, each worth its weight in gold.

I hated the sight of a slaughtered pig and usually squinted up into the clouds where I imagined it alive and well. Some clouds were puffed up like feathers, others stretched along the horizon like elephant trunks, and others resembled the forelocks of sheep.

One night the Count and I sneaked up to a pig that had been butchered that evening, cleaned and stripped, the carcass hanging out to dry with flies taking their share of the leftover meat. With one deft stroke the Count cut two long slivers from a thigh and stuffed them into the front of his shirt. He wiped the blade of his pocket knife, snapped it shut and we ambled home, nonchalant.

There were no colorful outdoor markets after the war. But the black market flourished, especially with food. My sister Karin was born late that fall and my mother pumped extra milk. I remember tears dripping from her eyes onto little Karin's face as the baby sucked on cracked and swollen breasts. My mother stimulated her milk production by nursing Karin for a while and then pumping extra milk. Often Karin was put back in her crib still hungry. She only whimpered though, having adjusted to post-war scarcity like the rest of us.

The Count and I made daily trips around town to sell the precious ounces of breast milk. He found his customers, often women short on milk for their own babies. Many of the women lacked attention as well, and I became a witness to the Count's frequent stopovers. I was told to wait in a foyer among umbrellas in metal stands and winter coats reeking of moisture and stale sweat, or in a kitchen where I slumped into a chair, dozing after our long outings. Sometimes a dog or a cat would streak by my leg, and I got to play for a while. When the Count reemerged, I was often given a treat by the women, a peach, fuzzy as little Karin's head, or a slice of freshly baked bread smelling of yeast.

"Now, don't tell your mother about our stops," the Count warned me. "It might upset her." I was confused but decided to keep these secret visits to myself since my mother was so sad all the time as it was.

In the broken-down shed behind our house the Count kept his prize possession, a rusty, rattling woman's bicycle with crooked handlebars and no lights. Bakeries began to operate again before most other shops reopened. And as before the war, shopkeepers set out their baked goods in large baskets first thing in the morning. I straddled the bent handlebars as the Count pedaled us to a bakery around the corner. There I slipped down and bolted past the store quick as a weasel, grabbing a roll or two without missing a step. At the end of the street the Count would swing me back onto the handlebars, his right arm hooked under one of my armpits. Because the shop owners were quick to shout for the police and ready to chase me with a broom, we pulled this trick on only a few occasions.

On the other hand, like the fox in the fairy tale, we often raided chicken coops for eggs, and when we felt extra lucky, we would catch a squawking hen or duck. While I looked away, the Count would twist the fowl's neck. A catch like that would fill our cooking pot for weeks. After the meat and skin had been consumed, my mother boiled the bones, extracting rich nourishment from the marrow.

I saw my first black man, an American soldier, in a chicken coop. He was gathering eggs in his helmet. He offered me chewing gun which I was afraid to touch, not knowing what it was. The Count said it was safe to take, so I grabbed the gift and stuffed it into my pocket.

We invited friends and neighbors to a special Christmas meal. On the table decorated with fir branches, pine cones and candles stood a steaming roast, spiced with thyme and caraway seeds. Before we sat down, I rushed outside to feed Snowflake whom I had raised on spinach leaves and carrots. The hutch was empty. I knew immediately that the "duck" my mother had so lovingly prepared was no duck at all but my pet rabbit. I said nothing as I plopped down next to our neighbor, Mr. Martin, who was asked to say grace and complied with a long, heartfelt prayer, his crippled arthritic fingers laced together. But I burst into tears when the Count started carving. Then my mother said she couldn't eat. I felt the Count's eyes on me. After a few bites, he too pushed his plate away. Was this thieving stranger becoming my father?

Our guests filled their stomachs until they could eat no more, then held their sides with clammy palms and let off satisfied puffing sounds, like steam escaping from the engine of a coal train.

Once we were caught stealing sugarbeets. Boiled beets, stirred into molasses, made a spread as tasty as jam or honey. That evening a policeman surprised us just as my stepfather was saying, "Let's quit. We have enough."

The Count could usually talk himself out of any situation but that evening his clever tongue deserted him and we were booked. The Count's face turned lobster-red with embarrassment as he stumbled over his words. "Officer—it won't happen again—please." But we had been warned before.

The night in the jail was a humiliation for Count Friedrich and an adventure for me. I had been parted from my family before when I was hospitalized for several weeks, so I took the separation lightly. I was taken to a cell where four women were curled up on bare mattresses. They got up and fussed over me and gave me their only blanket. The jailers served us split pea soup that we slurped with relish, watery broth with flour lumps swimming on the surface.

"Get that damn mouse," a woman squealed while on the way to the toilet pail. She had slipped on the furry paw as the tiny thing headed for her shoes. I tried to catch the soft, gray creature but had no luck. How could anyone make such a racket over a little mouse? I had once spotted a rat as big as a cat carrying off one of little Karin's socks.

Count Friederich and I were released the next morning without breakfast. He seemed glad to see me and put his hand on my shoulder as we walked away together.

When we arrived back home my mother was inconsolable. "I just knew something terrible had happened to you." I waited until she calmed down to tell her about the marvelous soup.

Having once experienced the scarcity of food, I know few boundaries. "Please help yourself," is my attitude. In my childhood food separated the satiated from the hungry. Christmas dinner was a communion even if the roast was my rabbit. And food served as a bond between two thieves, a Count and his little accomplice.

But I am frugal to the point of stinginess. My lean years as a youthful thief are long gone but not forgotten. My present plentitude has made me want to share, even though I realize that I can't feed all the starving people. But also, in small measure, I do what I can not to be wasteful. I scowl if my dinner guests leave a morsel on their plates. I take along plastic containers whenever we dine out, be it at McDonald's or the Ritz. I eat moldy bread, week-old leftovers, and seldom throw away a scrap. My family wonders why I have never gotten food poisoning.

I gladly gave up my thieving to become a paying customer at Kroger or Safeway. But I never acquired the conviction that stealing is wrong. I know we can't live together without respecting each other's property, and I do enjoy my material possessions and want to protect them. Still, I never developed a moral stance against stealing. Even when I look at a picture in an art exhibit and consider buying it, my first impulse is simply to take it off the wall. I especially have trouble passing my neighbor's flower garden when the vases at my house are empty and his roses are in bloom. I have learned to ask, but I would have no qualms about just picking one or two without his permission. Two years ago my childhood bicycle was stolen, an antique with a "Bismarck" insignia. When the police recovered it and asked me if I wanted the thief booked, I replied, "No, I've been there. Just help me straighten the spokes."

The Wife and the Piano Teacher

A True Philadelphia Story

The story did not start in Philadelphia but on a prosperous estate in the province of Silesia in the Kingdom of Prussia.

It was 1829 when Clara, then 29, sat for her family portrait. Her eyes were dreamy, fawn-like, and unruly ringlets dangled along the sides of her face. Only her full, pouty lips hinted at her bottled-up determination and unconventional spiritedness. She was perched on the arm of a divan, ready to sprint away.

Clara was the daughter of Baron and Baroness von Thielau who had brought up their seven children to be independent, giving them free run of the bountiful grounds and woods surrounding their impressive manor. All members of the family rode horses, the women sidesaddle in those days. The children were schooled by an English nanny, a French tutor and music teachers. As a teenager Clara was a sufficiently accomplished violinist to perform at family soirees. At the time the portrait was painted she had married and borne three children.

Her husband, Rochus Baron von Lüttwitz was sixteen years her senior and owned an estate a few kilometers to the east. He was a decorated officer in the Garde du Corps of the Johanniter, the Knights of the Order of St. John, a quiet man, prone to melancholy. And he preferred hunting to his wife's lively social gatherings. Though he adored her, he often dozed off in his high-backed overstuffed chair while listening to her play the violin.

When their first child, a boy, turned seven, Clara hired a piano teacher who had just arrived at a neighboring country home from Russia. Stanislav Rosen was young and talented. The only thing we know about his looks is contained in a letter from Clara to her parents, "His slender fingers fascinated me from the first time I saw him play. They glide across the keys like spiders, beautiful and a bit uncanny."

The course that Clara and Stanislav's relationship took and the tragedies that followed are shrouded in mystery. All we know comes from rumors and early warning signs. A maidservant told of watching Clara and her husband ride out one leafy fall afternoon to their favorite family picnic area by a lake covered in sky-blue water lilies. To the servants' surprise Clara later rode home alone and spent the next several hours in the stall, grooming and talking to her beloved mare. That evening she called for the coach and was driven to her parents' home.

The devastating news seeped out. Clara, who had delivered her fourth baby a few months before, declared her love for Stanislav. Divorces were rare in those days and Rochus was not given to outbursts. He showed no emotion upon hearing his wife's confession. Instead, he had his belongings moved to a separate wing in the mansion and told inquirers that his wife was in the process of making profound choices which would affect them all. The couple agreed that Clara would stay at the estate for one year before finalizing her decision. If at that time she was certain that she desired the piano teacher as her companion, he, Rochus, would set her free. Stanislav was asked to leave, and soon thereafter departed for America.

In the months that followed, Clara was often seen on trail rides with her husband. Everyone hoped for a change of heart. Time would surely move Clara's mood for the good of the family and reunite husband and wife.

But the stars did not align that way. There are no records of Clara's deliberations. Was she pining for her lover? Or did she simply tire of the comfortable but predictable life aristocratic ladies lived during those years on remote landed estates? Was she a spirited person trapped by her sex and circumstances? Or was it true love? And was music the lure?

The mansion was decorated for Christmas and Rochus had forgotten that the year of waiting had elapsed. A week before the holiday festivities were to begin Clara brought her youngest child to her parents' home. The following morning she was seen slipping through their portal, making her way on foot to the road where the daily stagecoach would come by. She was clad in the long, hooded plaid cape she always wore on country outings. It was rumored that she had a small bundle tied around her waist containing a few personal belongings and jewelry. No one knows how long her travels lasted from southern Silesia to the coast, then onto a ship bound for America.

As soon as Clara disappeared, Rochus ordered all likenesses of her taken down from the walls of the mansion and forbade her name to be uttered by anyone. The children, except the youngest, remained with him and were not allowed to correspond with their mother as long as Rochus lived. All contact occurred via the von Thielau family.

It often took months for letters to cross the ocean. The first letter to her family from abroad seems to have been written in response to the tragic news that had reached her of the death of her youngest child, a girl, who died several weeks after Clara's departure. The child's gravestone bears the mournful inscription: "Died of a broken heart." Clara's note to her parents was brief and revealed nothing about her circumstances. It stated simply, "God does not punish us, LIFE does."

The next letters are few and far between. Clara had borne two sons by the time tragedy struck again. A custodian at the music school on the outskirts of Philadelphia where Stanislav taught described the scene. Stanislav was sitting at an open window. Piano chords rippled through the spring air. A young girl was standing next to her teacher rehearsing an aria when two unsavory characters slipped into the enclosure of the school, climbed through the gaping window, and dragged Stanislav away with them. Search parties were sent out by the authorities but there was no trace. The von Thieleau family had grown accustomed to receiving unsettling news from their truant daughter, and they recalled that an earlier letter had contained a brief mention of a large gambling debt. Stanislav was never heard from again.

As the initial shock over Stanilav's disappearance faded with time, Clara's letters reassured her parents that she was well. She had found work as a language tutor and was giving piano lessons. Eventually she was able to support herself embroidering pillowcases, tablecloths and cloth napkins in her own distinctive style. Clara wrote of the satisfaction she found in her work and described in detail her trademark embroidery featuring sky-blue water lilies. She was proud of her sons, who were growing up to be fine young men.

Clara died in 1860 at the age of 60. The trail might have ended there, and was lost from view for nearly a century.

In the bitterly cold late spring of 1945 my great aunt Baroness Vera von Lüttwitz returned to war-torn Germany from her position as a war correspondent in Denmark. She had no children and many of her family and friends had been killed. She found temporary refuge in a shabby attic room in a small town near the Danish border. One frosty day she was lugging twigs, branches and a few solid chunks of wood up to her tiny stove, which stood next to a mattress on the floor, her sole furnishings aside from some makeshift kitchenware and utensils. A knock interrupted her bustling to and fro. It was probably the distraught tenant who regularly begged her to share a bit of kindling.

Instead, a middle-aged American officer stood at the door. He greeted her warmly in broken German, "I believe you and I are relatives." Aunt Vera had heard too much during the last terrible months to be taken by surprise by anything. She simply straightened her faded apron and, as there was no place to sit, the two stood facing each other. She listened, noticeably shivering, and was pleased when the officer himself stoked the fire and piled on a few sticks. He did not stay long but spoke in detail about the lengths to which he had gone to locate her through the embassy in Copenhagen. He assured her that he was eager to learn more about his German family and, if she had no objection, he would like to visit again. Aunt Vera was touched but also tired. She accepted a bundle of letters from him, along with his name and address and his winter coat which he discretely placed on the mattress without a word.

A few days after this visit Aunt Vera was picked up and interrogated by the American military about her work in Denmark. When the authorities realized she was innocent of cooperating with the Nazis, they released her. Soon thereafter she moved to the outskirts of the city of Kassel, the center of which had been severely damaged by Allied bombers.

Although a copy of the von Lüttwitz family portrait had been prominently displayed in my grandfather's study, as a child I had shown no interest in the ghostly figures in strange costumes who stared down at me from Grandpa's walls. But in my late teens my curiosity about the woman who fled to America was piqued.

When Great Aunt Vera was in her mid-eighties, I visited her in hopes of learning more about Clara. Aunt Vera seemed a bit annoyed by my questions. "In our family in those days one did not leave one's husband," she said adamantly. "And those poor children, one still a baby." When I wanted to know if she read the letters she replied curtly, "Yes, I did. They are full of descriptions of embroidery. Grandmother should have left it at that." When I told her that I longed to see the letters Aunt Vera seemed to blush. A little scarlet wave appeared along her hairline. "They are gone. I had them in a box without a lid and one of my cats used the thin sheets of paper to cushion her birthing place." My aunt had always been an animal lover but had gone overboard after the war, adopting strays in her old age when she could once again afford food for herself and her feline friends, thanks to a generous government pension. The name and address of the American officer who had paid Aunt Vera that surprise visit also disappeared along with the letters.

Fate had given our family a chance to connect the dots of the saga of Clara von Lüttwitz but the trail was once again covered for posterity. Unless, of course, some distant family member reads this story and is curious enough to retrace the footsteps back through time from Philadelphia to that Silesian estate where a mystery woman will not let me rest. Was she simply ahead of her time, courageously following her heart? Or was it heartless of her to leave husband and children behind in search of personal fulfillment?

I am haunted by Clara. She was my great-great-grandmother.

The Freedom to Be the Woman of One's Own Choosing

If I bear burdens
they begin to be remembered
as gifts, goods, a basket
of bread that hurts
my shoulders but closes me
in fragrance. I can
eat as I go.
>Denise Levertov

Taking stock of a movement-in-progress is an arduous task. This is no less true of the women's movement of the 1970s. Pessimists among us point to all the unfinished business, remind us of the discrepancy between laws passed and lived realities, and, with some justification, lament the return of a certain acquiescence in the status quo now that the initial battles on personal fronts and in the political arena have been won. Optimists count their good fortune and concentrate on those places where the struggle of women has opened new paths which are ready to be walked on. They show how a general awareness of women's worth and their knowledge of their own rights has given them confidence and the capacity to choose a novel way of living.

As a contribution to this general assessment, I want to look at three traditional role models in which women have been portrayed: woman as life-giver, the independent woman, and woman as lover. With reference to a few literary works I will make some observations on how these roles and our images of them have changed. Evidence points to the need for contemporary women to combine several of these roles which traditionally have been either exalted or suppressed. The desire to unite several capacities into a fulfilling lifestyle is many a woman's laudable goal but it also lays bare her unique dilemma. It is my conviction that the choice of one role will necessarily involve compromises, that any choice has consequences in that any gain brings a loss. But the novelty of our time rests in the fact that more choices are available. This essay tries to show why the departure into a particular way of life necessarily bypasses, even if only marginally, other desirable roads not taken. There are many ways of being a woman today, but the multitude of possibilities does not take away the anguish of choosing. My argument will be that there is no longer a single "right way" but that as we contemplate choices we can confidently assert that an individual life can now be *led* rather than lived out in a predetermined way.

Woman as Earth Mother/Life-Giver

Can nothingness be so prodigal?
Here is my son.
His wide eye is that general flat blue. He is turning to me like a little,
                       blind, bright plant.
One cry. It is the hook I hang on.
And I am a river of milk, I am a warm hill.
                     Sylvia Plath

Images of woman as life-giver, as the great mother, can be traced to ancient mythology. The central symbolism of the feminine originates from the body which is the vessel that is inclusive of the world and extends into all of nature. From its beginnings that image combined contradictory elements. As elementary character we designate the aspect of the Feminine as the Great Round, the Great Container which tends to hold fast to everything that springs from it and surrounds everything like an eternal substance. Everything born of the Great Mother belongs to her and remains subject to her; and even if the individual becomes independent, the Archetypal Feminine relativizes this independence into a long essential variant of her own perpetual being.

Ambivalence is present in that image because the Great Mother is provider of life as well as procurer of death. Being part of Nature women are seen as wheels in the great cycle of life and death. Women bring forth life but also usher in death. Being conscious of the two-pronged character of that role, one of the two usually becomes dominant and the Great Mother image drowns out the darker one. In spite of the doubts about the role of fertility, the transforming, sustaining, protecting qualities gain the upper hand. In motherhood we seek fulfillment as organisms, we *are bodies*, not just *have them*.

A profound uncertainty about the possibility of reconciling womanhood with artistic endeavors as well as work outside the home runs through Sylvia Plath's work. But in her poem "Three Women" she shows women in their most elemental ways. She teaches what pregnancy and birth can mean.

First voice:
I am slow as the world. I am very patient,
turning through my time, the suns and stars
regarding me with attention.
The moon's concern is more personal:
She passes and repasses, luminous as a nurse.
Is she sorry for what will happen? I do not think so.
She is simply astonished at fertility.
When I walk out, I am a great event.
I do not have to think, or even rehearse.
What happens in me will happen without attention.
The pheasant stands on the hill;
He is arranging his brown feathers.
I can not help smiling at what it is I know.
Leaves and petals attend me. I am ready.

Here is woman not as an individual but as all Women. She is a part of nature, passive and repetitive. Death is part of the natural cycle, as is fertility. Giving life is the great event. The body has a life of its own, the woman follows its destiny without control. And through this experience of pain and blood a woman learns something no man will ever know—what resources the body holds and how through the work of her body woman can cry out "I am reassured. I am reassured" about herself as well as about life. The experience of birth culminates in rejoicing, "A red lotus opens in its bowl of blood... what did my fingers do before they held him? What did my heart do with its love?"

Pregnancy and birth are events a woman shares with every other child-bearing woman. They are also experiences of herself. With the arrival of a child a woman has to consider another human being besides herself. Out of the wonder of unity between mother and baby grows the awe of gazing at a separate human being. Decisions have to be made. The agony of trying to combine several roles begins. Caring takes time, and if we believe that a constant mothering figure is essential to the growth of an infant, other options are limited for the time being. Priorities must be set. The "quality over quantity" time argument may apply to an older child but not to an infant, for whom constant availability of and recourse to a mothering figure provides the basis for trust and learned responses.

Full-time motherhood may entail fears that reentering the professional world at a later date opportunities may have vanished. Worry sets in with the realization that society still does not provide part-time positions for both men and women so that child care and housework can be shared. Even if some women do not regard motherhood and housework as negative, they still might pause at the thought that those roles may have shaped them imperceptibly. Doris Lessing lets her main character, Kate, express it this way in *The Summer Before The Dark*: "What he [the boss] was good at was to be the supplier of some kind of invisible fluid, or emanation, like a queen termite, whose spirit (or some such word as electricity) filled the nest, making a whole of individuals who could have no other connection. This is what women did in families—it was Kate's role in life... . It was a habit she had got into. She was beginning to see that she could accept a job in this organization, or another like it, for no other reason than that she was unable to switch herself out of the role of provider of invisible manna, consolation, warmth, 'sympathy.' Not because she needed the job, or wanted to do one. She had been set like a machine by twenty-odd years of being a wife and a mother."

The nurturing mother role has made many women adaptive and put them at the disposal of others. And they in turn crave to be needed. Thus more and more women have realized that while being a caring and providing mother, they must not lose sight of the need for self-fulfillment. It is important to have other interests to avoid being consumed by motherhood.

Women are caught in a dilemma. Motherhood is not, as Margaret Mead called fatherhood, a social invention, but a biological condition out of which grows a psychological need. If we decide not to have children, "the valuable inner space" as Erik Erikson calls it, remains empty and all our lives we may experience a vague sense of missing. If we opt for motherhood, we may be able to keep our sense of self intact by continually feeding on old interests. But in our competitive world the consequences may be that we will have to take second place to men when, after years of intermission, we want to reenter the professional arena.

Women as Artists and Workers/The Independent Woman

Women do know something as women
not entirely different from what men know
but in a different way.
In speaking of women as knower
I refer to her potential for possessing
insight and wisdom.
                Robert Lifton

Traditionally independent women have been envied their freedom but pitied their insecure and lonely way of life. But that has been changing. More and more women embark on professional roads, sometimes with, sometimes without a steady partner, and derive their sense of fulfillment from the task they are engaged in rather than from personal relationships. It has been rightly argued that the suburban housewife in her isolation can be lonelier than a single woman living in a big city. Sylvia Plath, Virginia Woolf, and Anais Nin have reflected on the imaginative and intellectual work women produce from three very different points of view.

The second voice in Sylvia Plath's *Three Women* is that of a secretary who has just had a miscarriage. She reflects:

I watched the men walk about me in the office. They were so flat!
There was something about them like cardboard, and now I had caught it
that flat, flat flatness from which ideas, destructions,
bulldozers, guillotines, white chambers of shrieks proceed,
endlessly proceed and the cold angels, the abstractions.
I sat at my desk in my stockings, my high heels,
and the man I worked for laughed: "Have you seen something awful?
You are so white, suddenly." And I said nothing.
I saw death in the bare trees, a deprivation.
I could not believe it. Is it so different
for the spirit to conceive a face, a mouth?

For this secretary the world of men is terrifying and if a woman is not able to bring forth life, she is in danger of being infected by a deadly emptiness. Ideas and infertility go together, and in comparison to the abundance of nature the world of work and ideas will always be found wanting. The woman who works and produces works of art is always only second-best to the woman who gives birth to a child. Men, who are flat, are envious of woman's abilities, but the woman who is unable to bring forth life is even worse off and feels a greater lack since she stands between two worlds: "I see myself as a shadow, neither man nor woman," says the secretary. Work can be no more than a substitute for woman, according to Plath. An atmosphere of sterility pervades the lives of those women who derive their identity from dead objects rather than living realities.

Not so for Virginia Woolf. In her writing, concern with the woman's nature takes two contradictory forms. One is with women in their relationship to men and society, and the other with the development of women as individuals and artists. Woolf's first concern has to do with the roles women can play in society, and her view on that is quite conservative. Again and again she stresses the contrast between the two natures, female and male. Wanting women not to emulate men, she insists however on their right to have "rooms of their own" to which equal education and living space belong. Foremost in her mind is the individual development of a woman rather than her political or economic rights. In a work of art woman rises beyond her femininity.

For Woolf the literary mind is androgynous. She lifts the question concerning women's creative powers above and beyond gender. For her any creation of the mind cannot be interpreted as special to the particular sex of the artist. In Woolf's novel *Orlando*, the main character is a writer and poet. He starts his journey through four centuries first as a man who, just before the beginning of the eighteenth century, is changed into a woman who then marries in the nineteenth century. Here is an excerpt from the encounter between Orlando and her fiancée. It describes their amazement at recognizing in each other an androgynous mind. "'Oh? Shel, don't leave me!' She cried. 'I'm passionately in love with you,' she said. No sooner had the words left her mouth than an awful suspicion rushed into both their minds simultaneously. 'You're a woman, Shel!' She cried. 'You're a man, Orlando!' He cried. Never was there such a scene of protestation and demonstration as then took place since the world began. "

Because, according to Virginia Woolf, we are all part man, part woman, we need the qualities of the other sex for creation. For that reason woman should engage in works of the mind or with her hands as freely as man and should no longer feel bound to develop her creativity in just one way. Since the work stands on its own merits, it is of no importance whether a man or a woman produces it.

At the other end of the spectrum stands Anais Nin, arguing a most radical point of view. She encourages women to creative work other than childbearing and rearing, but she also insists that women use the gifts they have acquired through long centuries of being mothers and wives. Every work a woman produces is, according to Nin, sex-linked. In her diary she writes: "Woman's creation, far from being like man's must be exactly like her creation of children, that is it must come out of her own blood, englobed by her womb, nourished by her own milk. It must be a human creation of her own flesh, it must be different from man's abstractions."

The concept of the body being one's destiny takes hold in Nin's art and writing, except that channels heretofore closed now open up. A woman must create children as well as other works in this world in her uniquely feminine way, and her uniquely feminine way is her "close identification with organic life and its perpetuation." For centuries, Nin suggests, women have been nature only and therefore unable to communicate what they know or translate it into practice. "Women lacked the eye of consciousness," she asserts. Nin believes that a woman is in position to create a feminine art because of her connection-making ability and because of her organic knowledge, which Lifton has defined as "the personal participation of the knower in the knowledge he believes himself to possess and which transcends the disjunction between subjective and objective." As Nin herself is creating works in which she realizes her feminine potential, Lifton urges women to expand their knowledge into all areas of life. He writes, "It would seem that women have a special relationship to them [problems of the human situation] that we may do well to explore... a relationship based upon her nurturing function and upon her particular capacity to bridge biology and history."

These are rudiments of a hopeful and challenging future for the independent woman.

Women and Their Bodies / Woman as Lover

In life as well as in literature a new type of lover and temptress is emerging. The claim of woman to an enjoyment of her body without shame or remorse, even if that enjoyment runs contrary to social obligations and expectations, can be found in much modern literature. It is based on the rebirth of the body and its passions. Relationships between men and women are founded on sex, not affection or intellectual companionship. Madame Bovary, as well as novels by D.H. Lawrence, Willa Cather and Kate Chopin come to mind. In these novels women long for and achieve sexual fulfillment, and female sexual powers are praised, acknowledged and used.

But fulfillment is not always achieved without commitment and emotional involvement. The heroine Sabina, in Anais Nin's *A Spy in the House of Love*, moves through one affair after another, to end up not liberated as she desired but fragmented and lost. At first she had hoped to reach independence and anxiety-free connections by moving in and out of relationships. "She opened her eyes to contemplate the piercing joy of her liberation: She was free, free as man was, to enjoy without love. Without any warmth of the heart as a man could, she had enjoyed a stranger." But after many such encounters she realizes that "all her seeking of fire to weld these fragments into one total love, one total woman, had failed."

A sense of failure also runs through Erica Jong's book, *Fear of Flying*. Unable to free herself from dependence and security on a man, Isadora returns sadly to her estranged husband. Her dream is to live out her fantasies with an anonymous stranger with the quickest of transitions from entanglement to detachment. Her journey is one of lonely self-gratification, and the men she meets are either robots like her husband or desexualized anti-heroes like her lover who is potent only when he transgresses taboos. They lend each other their bodies but even in their spontaneous actions they experience nothing but desperation. When Isadora reflects on her 31 year-old life, she sadly admits, "I see all my lovers sitting alternately back to back as if in a game of musical chairs. Each one an antidote to the one that went before. Each one a reaction, an about-face, a rebound." She calls her longings her "hunger thump, her ravenous appetite for experiencing everything," but whatever else she gains from her adventures, it is not liberation. For Jong, sexual experiences with men no longer count in a woman's life. The most important thing is putting those experiences on paper, becoming a writer and poet, being the independent female artist.

Works of literature also point to an identification of woman with woman and love between the opposite sexes is displaced by love for the same sex. Maybe it is because relationships between men and women are often portrayed as in disarray that a move toward someone of one's own sex brings security and fulfillment. These connection-making qualities in women seem to hold in relationships between women. And what comes easier than understanding and identifying with someone more like ourselves. A moving example of the faithfulness and exclusive devotion of one woman to another is found in Sarah Orne Jewett's story, *Martha's Lady*.

What choices, then, are open to sexually liberated women? Personally, we can, without being banned from the midst of our friends or expelled from our jobs or ostracized by society, indulge in loving ourselves. We can learn that love relationships are inclusive and not limited to the opposite sex. And we can try again to sing a love song with a male companion and mate. Literarily, the novel of a strong independent woman in love with herself and her man still waits to be written, a novel in which a man and woman find each other in their sexual lives and shared goals.

"If you want to be me, be me... if you want to be you, be you. There are a million things to do... to be free" goes the theme song from the movie *Harold and Maude*. More ways than ever before are open to us, and we may want to travel as many of them as possible. We will find that not every way is right for us. There will always be the "unattainable other." Some of us may have to admit that we only partially succeeded in the task of motherhood, others that we did not quite measure up to the success of our male colleagues or that we are still a few orgasms short of being a super-lover. But whatever we choose to be, it is now possible to take pride in having become accomplished in our own right.

Notes

Denise Levertov, "*Stepping Westward,*" from *The Sorrow Dance* (New Directions, New York, 1966)
Sylvia Plath, *Winter Trees* (Harper and Row, New York, 1972)
Erich Neuman, *The Great Mother* (Princeton University Press 1955)
Doris Lessing, *The Summer Before the Dark* (Alfred Knopf, New York, 1973)
Margaret Mead, *Male and Female* (Penguin Books, 1950)
Erik Erikson, "Inner and Outer Space: Reflections on Womanhood," in *The Woman in America,* Robert Jay Lifton, ed (Beacon Press, Boston, 1967)
Robert Jay Lifton, "Woman as Knower: Some Psychohistorical Perspectives," ibid.
Virginia Woolf, *Orlando* (Signet Books, 1950)
Anais Nin, *The Diary of Anais Nin*, Vol. II (Harcourt, Brace, Jovanovich, New York, 1971,
 Anais Nin, "Prolog" to *Ladders of Fire* (Dutton, 1946)
Anais Nin, *A Spy in the House of Love* (Swallow Press, Chicago, 1959)
Erica Jong, *Fear of Flying* (Signet: New York, 1973)
Sarah Orne Jewett, *Martha's Lady*, (Doubleday Anchor Books, New York), 1956

Here I Stand

Maria was a shy 8th grader. When called upon to read aloud, her throat turned dry, her stomach queasy. Going to the blackboard in front of the whole class terrified her. She was a good speller but when asked to write on the board, her hand would shake and the letters would tumble all over themselves. Maria was happiest bent over her blue-lined notebook earnestly composing stories about rabbits and horses and the antics of her puppets.

Maria's small body was topped with a head of full brown hair which her mother harnessed into two thick braids and, when time allowed, then coiled them around her head. The braids were a temptation for many of Maria's classmates and when someone ran by her, a quick yank was inevitable. Maria's dreamy dark eyes filled with tears when the tugging was too harsh. "Please don't do that," she would plead.

Classroom seating was arranged so that the tallest pupils sat in back. Tiny Maria ended up in the very front row. Short, chubby Heinz sat right behind her. He was smart and, as an only child of wealthy parents, spoiled. He believed he could get away with any prank, and nobody seemed able to curb his nonstop talking.

Physical punishment was permitted in German schools in the 1950s, though not all teachers used it. Mr. Bankwitz, a history and gym teacher, was the exception. When a girl misbehaved Mr. Bankwitz had her stand at her desk with outstretched fingertips which he smacked with a slender reed. The boys he took to the hallway and gave them a stinging lash or two across the bottom with a leather strap.

Maria grew up in a loving family. Her parents had repeatedly petitioned against corporal punishment in the school. "It's simply wrong," her mother exclaimed. Maria had never even been spanked, and she winced every time she saw the swollen fingers of her girlfriends. When a boy received a whipping, the sound of the strap made her recoil. She leaned very close to her notebook, her nose touching the pages, and covered her ears. She disliked having her hair pulled but knew that if she reported it, she would have to witness the perpetrator's punishment. Being bullied was bad but the whippings were worse.

Heinz got a laugh out of the class every time he pulled Maria's braids. When she let out a plaintive "Ouch" he beamed triumphantly and turned to his approving audience. But he tormented Maria only before the start of class or after the closing bell had rung.

Mr. Bankwitz was a canny observer who often arrived early on the school grounds and then lingered in the hallway. Several times he had watched Heinz from afar. One day when Maria's hair was fluttering loose like a horse's mane Heinz had more fun than ever wrapping a few strands around his fingers and squealing, "Snagged you!"

When Mr. Bankwitz entered the classroom everyone scrambled to their seats. Slowly, he put his briefcase on his desk, then took out the book for the day's lesson and placed it face down. Peering over his glasses, he said firmly, "Heinz, do not do that again."

About halfway through the hour, Mr. Bankwitz, while writing on the blackboard, glanced over his shoulder momentarily just as Heinz took a quick pass at Maria's hair. Without a show of emotion he put the chalk down, walked to the cupboard, and retrieved the strap. "Heinz," he called out in a stern voice, "Step outside."

Heinz, who was unaccustomed to being disciplined, could not believe what he heard. He tried to explain, "I only brushed Maria's hair aside because it was blocking my view of the blackboard."

"Step outside!" Mr. Bankwitz was clearly irritated.

Suddenly the situation seemed serious. Heinz began to shake, "I will never do it again, Mr. Bankwitz. I promise."

Mr. Bankwitz was not a patient man. "For the last time, Heinz, outside!"

Heinz lost his composure and sank to his knees. "Please, please don't."

Mr. Bankwitz got hold of Heinz's shirt and lifted him like a limp kitten, steering him into the hallway. Heinz howled so loudly and pitifully that other teachers emerged from their rooms to see what was happening. When Heinz returned to the classroom he hung his head and did not even wipe the tears from his cheeks.

Witnessing Heinz's humiliation, courage surged up in Maria's fearful heart and her mother's words echoed in her ears. Before she had merely been an observer but now she was implicated.

Mr. Bankwitz opened his book and was about to pick up where he had left off when Maria's faint voice made him spin around. "I ha…hate spankings," she stuttered haltingly.

"What did you say, Maria?"

"I hate spankings," she repeated, her voice quivering.

Mr. Bankwitz was incredulous. "Apologize, Maria," he demanded.

"I can't," she said and stood up. Her words were clear, her voice steady.

"You can't? Then take your seat and be quiet." Mr. Bankwitz's ears turned red with anger and he seemed to lose his bearings. That a pupil—especially a girl—would dare to question his authority!

"I can't do that either, Mr. Bankwitz." Maria was composed now, confident.

Mr. Bankwitz took several steps toward her in a failed attempt to intimidate her, then suddenly turned, gathered up his book and briefcase and left the room without a word, slamming the door behind him.

A pencil rolled off a desk and clattered to the floor. Ordinarily someone would have picked it up. Instead the pencil rolled and rolled until it bumped into the far wall. Nobody moved a muscle. Maria remained standing, immobile as a statue until the bell rang.

Everyone rushed out except Heinz. He approached Maria. "Wow," he whispered and then touched her hair ever so gently before running outside with the others to spread the word.

Nothing But Snake Oil?

After completing my hypnosis training, a physician friend teased, "nothing but snake oil?" That comment came back to me recently following an oophorectomy. As a privileged 66 year-old patient I had a superb team of doctors, excellent nursing care and was released the same day as the surgery. Following a speedy recovery, I felt it had all been a piece of cake. Modern medicine is amazing but what about the "snake oil"? More and more patients and health professionals are asking questions about alternative therapies.

In 1998 Eisenberg, et al published the results of a follow-up national survey on alternative medicine use in the United States in the Journal of the American Medical Association. They concluded that "estimated expenditures for alternative medicine professional services increased 45.2% between 1990 and 1997 and were conservatively estimated at $21.2 billion in 1997, with at least $12.2 billon paid out-of-pocket. This exceeds the 1997 out-of-pocket expenditures for all US hospitalizations." Astin reported similar results that same year and the trend toward alternative medicine is still rapidly rising.

What's going on?

Maybe my recent experience can shed some light on this question. My physicians and I had tracked bilateral cysts on my ovaries for several years when in October 2006 we discovered that the right cyst had changed shape. My doctors recommended immediate removal of both ovaries and my uterus as "standard medical procedure," the second most common surgery for women in this country. There are over 600,000 hysterectomies each year in the United States and one in three women will have had a hysterectomy by the age of 60. I asked for a reprieve. Dr. Taylor, my gynecologist of many years, is a wiry man who speaks first with his eyes. They darkened by the moment. Furrowing his eyebrows, he voiced his dismay, "You are playing Russian roulette." I admire him for his dedication. His focus is on prevention. But he often frets when a dark spot in the road is not a sinkhole but only a shadow. I stood my ground against hasty invasions. I needed to investigate the shadows.

I sprang into action using the tools of my trade, hypnosis. I also employed Reiki healing touch methods. I balanced my chakras with my color (all matter has a unique frequency which vibrates to one of the colors in the color spectrum, and mine is yellow). A crystal with its electromagnetic properties helped. So did my friend Debra, an energetic screener who put me on nutritional supplements. I uncovered some psychological reasons for my physical symptoms. I reread old mythologies. I was bent on restoring my ovaries to their original functioning. All approaches that are snake oil to skeptics!

During the wait I was not immune to anxieties and doubts. I remembered my first hospice patient, a young woman who died of ovarian cancer. Ovarian cancer is stealthy. The symptoms usually do not surface until the disease has spread in deadly abundance. But the greatest challenge is that of fear itself. When I went back to the doctors in early December and my ovaries had not changed for the better, the pressure mounted. Why did I ask for still more time? My own beliefs were at stake, or so I thought. I was still asking the wrong question, "Were my tools just snake oil after all?" When the next ultrasound showed no improvement, my surgery date was set for the end of February. Now I shifted from disappointment to a search for meanings. They thundered in like an avalanche.

Many people, including doctors, are poor listeners when the body speaks. They have difficulty deciphering and trusting bodily symptoms with their own senses. How often can doctors still make a diagnosis from a whiff of urine? As Abraham Verghese, writer and physician notes, "I was taught to tap and thump my patients and listen for the sounds of sickness and health. But this is fast becoming a lost art." By not knowing the language of our bodies, we unnecessarily relinquish much control and neglect our innate powers.

If you can't see it, it's not real. I too fell under that fallacy. Intuitively, I felt that I was not afflicted with cancer. I could have been wrong. I had been wrong before. I became like the doubting Thomas who needed to touch Jesus' wounds to believe in his resurrection. If only we could reclaim our bodies as trusted allies!

Most of us no longer know how to mine the wisdom of nature either, for instance using flower essences and herbal remedies. Ongoing long-term studies of natural compounds like one being done at M. D. Anderson Cancer Center using curcumin as a complementary therapy for pancreatic cancer and multiple myelomas are rare.

With my affinity for alternative healing methods, I was haunted by the question, "Why is the use of these obvious tools missing from medicine's miraculous technologies?" A partial answer may lie in our view of the body.

Modern Medicine versus Ancient Medicine

Doctors often see the body as a complex machine. Medical scientists dig deeply into the minutest body parts, down to the DNA of a cell, the better to be able to remove a diseased growth or replace a faulty part with great efficiency. What this view ignores are not only the emotions and environmental influences on health but also the vital forces which breathe life into each organism. The ancients knew about that energy, be it called Chinese Chi or Hindu Prana. We sometimes call it Spirit but then place it at a distance, outside of our bodies, instead of seeing it as the moving energy which swirls through and around us. Present-day medicine wages war on diseases, aggressively manipulating organs and cells. But there have always been other ways to heal. Vibrational medicine, for example, takes a different path. It is based on attunement, adjustment and harmony, rather than a fight with the body's ills. Health and illness are examined from the perspective of energy fields. This healing method works by rebalancing disturbances of structure and energy flow within the context of multilevel interactive energy fields. Not a single cell can be disturbed without having an effect on every other cell in the body. Not Newton but Einstein! Can these two ways of thinking be linked or are they irreconcilable? Is snake oil just greasing a complicated machine?

Let's return to my operation

My gynecological surgeon, Dr. Angeles has impatient hands and dexterous fingers. Her beautiful first name is Concepcion. I was taken by the symbolic connection between that name and her profession. I liked Dr. Angeles immediately. When my daughter explained to my three year-old grandson, Zachary, about my operation and that Dr. Angeles was my surgeon, he said, "Tell her to do a GOOD surgery." She would indeed perform a perfect laparoscopy while respecting my wishes to minimize the invasion as much as possible. Of course, she could not predict the outcome. She had to wait and venture inside my abdominal cavity before she could weigh the options. Ovaries are risky to biopsy. If cancerous cells spill into the bloodstream, the disease can spread. I had to trust her judgment. For me even organs that have limited function never lose their symbolic value. Since ancient times ovaries have represented creativity in its kaleidoscopic forms and the uterus symbolizes motherhood in all its beautiful ramifications.

Unsure of its contents, Dr. Angeles removed my right ovary, maneuvered it into a small sack, and pulled it out through a tiny incision. The cyst on it turned out to be benign. My left ovary and uterus, which had grown into each other in a curious embrace, she left intact. Had not my creativity always been intertwined with my feminine intuition?

My witty anesthetist, Dr. Whale, is cut from a special mold. He spent much time on the phone discussing my concerns and answering questions. When my surgery was over he whisked in and out of the recovery room for two hours until he was sure I was alright. Safety is his highest priority. Dr. Whale's surname is symbolically linked to the largest mammal in the sea. According to Ted Andrews these animals possess ancient knowledge of how to use breath for a variety of purposes. They can conserve oxygen under water by decreasing the blood flow to areas in the body where it is non-essential. Could I withdraw from the surgery just enough to help myself survive but also recover speedily?

The operating room or OR is an unfamiliar place to me. Since I had declined a pre-op sedative and asked to use self-hypnosis for relaxation, I was able to take in my surroundings. The equipment is astonishing. Inflatable warm blankets, wrap-around leg massagers and tables with blinking, clinking instruments, blinding lights and a masked staff. They looked like they belonged to the raccoon family.

When I entered the OR I was enveloped in a cocoon of love, flowing from my husband, my children, grandkids, friends, clients, readers. I had a well-made plan in mind but the unconscious had its own ideas. As my team assembled around the operating table, Dr. Angeles placed a reassuring hand on my arm, Dr. Taylor's eyes flickered, "You asked me to be present. Here I am." I blinked back a thank-you. Dr. Whale was humming, rhyming. Whales have a great sensitivity to sound, a form of sonar, echo-locator. They sing. I was not in enemy camp but among professionals who meant well, and I knew they would respect my wishes while performing their expert tasks.

Grateful thoughts spread positive vibes. All anxieties evaporated and the room became crowded with healing energy. A line from Mary Baker Eddy that my friend Natalie had sent the day before flashed by, "Divine Love always has and always will meet every human need." Just before I started to inhale life-giving oxygen through my mask and send it to all my cells, my eyes fell on a silver cross vibrating along the indentation of the attending nurse's throat. She was not yet gloved and an old-fashioned ring, red-gold with tiny rubies, reflected the artificial overhead lights. I felt grounded. All would be well. Dr. Whale calmly instructed the team to give me time to center myself. He assured me I would not be rushed. He would wait until I had put myself to sleep. Hushed voices hovered in the cold air. A snake-oil ritual?

When the natural energy flow of the body is compromised, we can harmonize our chakras with our color, unblocking the pathways. I never have trouble stepping into a yellow circle and then allowing that color to travel through me. But this time I could not visualize any colors at all. In retrospect I realize that circumstances prevented me from balancing myself. That's when my unconscious helped. In hypnosis I have often gone to a safe place in my childhood and, when I failed to see colors, I decided to take myself there again. But to my surprise I was whisked to Abaco Island where years ago my husband and I had spent a romantic week in a rented cabin, doors open day and night to the roaring music of the ocean. Now I found myself again on a big brass bed, listening to the murmurings of the sea when, as if through dense fog, Dr. Whale's instructions rolled in, "Ute, Ute...," sounded like a far-off echo. I didn't hear what he said next, nor did I feel the chilling, then burning infusion of Propofol which sent me into deeper regions of slumber.

Awakening from surgery can be fraught with anxieties. When my husband whispered the good news I felt like crying. The cyst had been only a "worry" cyst. What a name, especially in medical circles. I have been asked how I would have reacted if instead of a joyful recovery a struggle for survival had been my fate. The tears would have been tears of sorrow, but I hope my outlook on the future would have been the same, enabling me to activate all the dormant healing powers my body has in store. As soon as my sentences were coherent again and I was back in my room, I repeatedly asked nurses and helpers, "How do people cope?" To a person the answer was, "If they have a positive outlook, they recover better—no matter the medical condition." Positive attitude? What kind of snake oil is that?

Pain is our body's alarm. I wanted no pain medication except what had already been given during anesthesia. I had little discomfort in my abdominal area, only a delayed shoulder ache due to escaping carbon dioxide bubbles trapped under my diaphragm. But for several days my urethra burned like a flame from the catheterization. Easy explanation. Despite my conciliatory demeanor, I was pissed! A warm sitzbath helped.

I was voiceless after the intubation. I coughed when I tried to talk and my throat was sore. The enforced silence sent me inward to reflect. Two weeks later I was still detoxing my body and my liver was working overtime to get rid of all the poisons. But I was gratefully on the mend.

A New Paradigm

"Nothing but good can come of this," Debra said. That's what I hope. High-tech medicine is here to stay and can be of great benefit when we use it wisely and sparingly. And sometimes expediency is not only desirable but necessary. My only wish is for more awareness and acceptance of other therapeutic approaches. The common goal is to ease suffering, and there is more than one way to reach it.

Many doctors know about invisible forces, have seen them at work, and on occasion used them themselves. Both Dr. Whale and Dr. Taylor shared their stories. Dr. Taylor had witnessed a hypnotist helping with a difficult delivery and Dr. Whale told how he once promised a colleague to be his wife's substitute liturgist. He chanted all through the operation, "You will heal quickly... You will not hurt... You will not bleed excessively... You will fight infection... You will be up in a chair today... You will be walking tomorrow." The attending surgeon thought Dr. Whale had lost his mind. But the patient recovered swiftly.

The ways of healing work differently for all manner of people and vary under diverse circumstances. I became a zealous advocate of natural childbirth after three very easy deliveries. I was chastened by an experience of one of my daughters who, only after hours and hours of strenuous labor and considerable pain, delivered a ten-pound boy. She was not only exhausted but nearly delirious. Maybe she should have had a C-section.

Medicine has the caduceus symbol of two snakes which heal through wisdom, a knowledge that moves from past to present to future generations. Because of a very flexible spine the snake can slither back and forth with speed and agility. In ancient ceremonies snake poison was intentionally injected into the body through venomous bites. People who survived had succeeded in transmuting the poison within their bodies and were then believed to be able to convert all poisons, physical or otherwise.

Snakes have been seen as symbols of rebirth because they shed their skin. When the molting starts their eyes cloud over, giving them a trance-like stare. The eyes clear as soon as the skin is shed, enabling them to see the world with fresh eyes. I too gained a new perspective.

Ten days later I had my follow-up appointment. My old vitality was back and the three incisions were now faint lines like thin pencil marks. "You are doing fantastic. You look like you never had surgery." Dr. Taylor, ordinarily a reserved man, was exuberant. I felt like hugging everyone. But my privileged treatment, outcome and recovery will be an obligation to share and a commitment to help others heal themselves. Snake oil has more than one ingredient. Some I used for myself. There is plenty to go around.

Notes:

1) Eisenberg D, Davis R, Ettner S, Appel S, Wilkrey S, Van Rompey M, Kessler R. "Trends in alternative medicine use in the United States, 1990-1997; results of a follow-up national survey," Journal of American Medical Association, 1998; 280:1569-1575.

2) Astin, J A. "Why patients use alternative medicine: results of a national study," JAMA, 1998; 279:1548-1553

3) U.S. Department of Health & Human Services Office on Women's Health. The National Women's Health Information Center. Available at http://www.womenshealth.gov. Accessed August 13, 2007.

4) Verghese A, "Bedside Manners," Texas Monthly, February 2007; vol. 296, p.70.

5) Stix G,"Spice Healer," Scientific American, February, 2007, pp. 66-69.

6) Andrews T, "Animal Speak," St. Paul, MN, Llewellyn Publications; 1993.

Lightning Over Kaufman

I was not to speak or look directly at any person for 10 days.

The countryside quivers in the July heat and the atmosphere is laden with moisture. Thunder rumbles in the distance. Steel-white streaks zigzag across the flat Texas horizon. Some of them traverse the entire length of the night sky, others pierce big-bellied clouds with quick golden stabs. A flash encircles a cluster of smoky billows near me like a fire-ring, followed by a loud clap. Lightning has struck here. I stare in awe, faintly trembling. Suddenly the energy is released into a pelting rain, falling in coin-sized drops at my feet, forming swirling, gurgling pools in the dust. Just then frogs start a joyful concert.

This is my fifth day at the Vipassana meditation center, a 15-minute car ride from the small farming town of Kaufman. Of the six centers in the country, this is the only one in Texas. After days of silent introspection, my eyes magnify the outside world into dazzling clarity. Time is no longer predictable, and the day of my arrival seems long ago.

My daughter, Claudia, had driven me to the retreat site. It took us just over an hour from downtown Dallas to reach the bucolic setting. Nestled among meadows sparkling with wildflowers and dotted with grazing black, brown and white cows, the buildings are surrounded by clumps of dark green live oaks and flat-topped mesquite trees. A still pond lies at the edge of the property. Sparrows flutter to and from nests under the eave of the main building, and cats stalk through the high grass in search of mice and lizards.

Men and women are housed separately at the center, and there is a free-standing meditation hall between them. For the women there are three dormitories, furnished with hard bunk beds and thin mattresses. I brought along my sleeping bag. Each bed is enclosed by a canvas curtain for privacy, and ceiling fans whirr softly overhead. We are treated to sumptuous vegetarian meals, cooked and served by volunteers. There are no washing machines or dryers. Towels and underwear and socks galore flutter on a clothesline in the lazy summer breeze. Claudia watched me unpack and store away my few belongings, and then departed. I felt like a kid left at camp. I had a fleeting urge to run after her. What was I doing here at age 62? Right away I knew this would not be a vacation.

I had learned about Vipassana in yoga class, an ancient Indian meditation practice whose symbol is the ever-changing wheel. The practice differs from other healing techniques in that it is neither verbal nor visual. Vipassana uses the breath, common to all life, as a tool to observe the sensations of the body as calmly and attentively as possible. Human misery is universal, and Vipassana bases all unhappiness on two principles: craving and aversion. Craving causes clinging, the desire to hold on. Aversion produces frustration, negativity and anger. To reach harmony and enlightenment in life, Vipassana teaches mastery over these two negative reactions. During meditation the breath scans the body, never lingering at pleasant or unpleasant sensations, only observing them. Respiration also builds a bridge between the conscious and the unconscious mind. With the breath, old mental conditions (sankharas), which manifest themselves mentally or physically, rise to the surface and then dissolve, eventually replacing strife with harmony. The approach seemed full of contradictions. Would it work for me?

Day 1:

It is 4 a.m. when a gong wakes me from deep slumber. The gong will become my signal to rise and assemble for a meal. I soon come to love the reverberating sound of the gong, linking me to centuries of cloistered, peaceful lives.

I wiggle out of my sleeping bag, yawn and stretch. I slip into my beige jogging suit in total silence. I hear only faint rustlings from my neighbors as they dress. Speech fell away easily last night like shedding a worn-out coat. Even though I do not look at or talk to my fellow students, currents of life sweep through the dorm. Someone snored. Someone called out in her sleep, and female odors reach my nostrils long before the day's breathing drill begins. After the wake-up call, I can go to the meditation hall, but I decide to meditate on the rug next to my bed. At 6:30 a.m., I devour my breakfast of hot oatmeal and fruit and drink green tea. At 8 a.m., we are summoned for an hour of group meditation, followed by private meditation until 11 a.m. Lunch is ready, and the dishes are labeled "Vietnamese Salad," "Vegetarian Texas Chili," "Indian Curry." I am well-nourished. The lunch break lasts until 1 p.m. It gives me time to shower, take a stroll and rest.

Throughout the course, the teachers remain remote, sitting like immobile statues on their thrones, watching their muted flock. Teachers serve as guardians of the regulations. Though most people are determined to stay the course, a few don't last. Rule-breakers are asked to leave. Teachers are also available for consultation, but only questions relating to the practice are permitted. Because I have too many intellectual "whys," I decide to forgo an interview.

We have an hour of group meditation again at 2 p.m., then private meditation until 5. For the last meal of the day newcomers can eat plenty of fruit and have a choice of hot or cold drinks. Those more experienced in the practice are permitted only tea. At 6, it's more group meditation, and then we listen to a video lecture by S.N. Goenka who rediscovered Vipassana. We are dismissed around 9, with just enough time to amble briefly outdoors before we retire to our quarters. Lights out at 9:30 p.m.

Lying in bed, I am discouraged. My first day was nothing but discomfort and anguish. I'm not used to sitting in an upright meditative position for a total of 12 hours. My body aches, my ankles are sore from crossing them and my legs are dead wood by the time I plop onto my bunk. As hard as I tried to pay close attention to my respiration, banishing gently any distracting thoughts, my mind didn't just wander, it ran wild. Will I last 10 days?

However, in spite of my misgivings my mind caught some sparks. Knowledge here is not imposed but experienced, and this knowledge is not abstract. I heard my breath as it streamed through the nasal cavity and felt it as it touched the wings of my nostrils. This is about my body, my sensations. It is about Me. Breathing in and breathing out places me right in the present moment, no retreats into the past or speculations about the future. In daily life, I often revisit the past or plan for the future. But the present is in the Now, in every precious moment.

I curl up in my sleeping bag and practice the conscious relaxation that I learned in my yoga class at home. My mercurial mind must have dozed off because I did not stir until the gong roused me before dawn.

Day 2:

Much easier! I sink into the daily routine. Yesterday I questioned the strict rule forbidding even the use of my notebook and pencil, but today I see the purpose of the regulations. No longer do I think about household chores or whether my husband fed the cat and took the dog for a walk. No phone calls interrupt, no television diverts me from the one activity: observing my respiration.

On entering the course, all participants took five vows: to abstain from killing or harming any being (even the pesky mosquitoes), from stealing, from sexual activity, from telling lies, and from all intoxicants, even sleeping pills. We are also not allowed to communicate with each other through speech, direct glances or physical contact. But soon I notice people by their footwear, open-toed sandals, scuffed-up tennis shoes or flowery flip-flops. I distinguish walks, shuffling steps and light, short strides.

Only sometimes do I catch my thoughts scattering to old concerns, everyday preoccupations. I fidget less in my cross-legged position. Drowsiness, as much an enemy as a wandering mind, is held at bay, and I am able to perceive bodily sensations without reacting to them. Respiration is neutral. I do not crave for more breath, nor do I dislike my breath. I try only to observe and to sustain the awareness of the present from moment to moment.

Day 3:

The focus of the breath is narrowed to the place under my nostrils, above my upper lip. I am to concentrate on that tiny notch to sharpen my mind, to purify it. Calmness sets in, and more insights are ablaze as my breath enters my right nostril and goes out the left, then jumps and reverses the order. Sometimes I feel my breath in both nostrils. I also sense cold when I inhale, warmth when I exhale. Then I notice a tingling on my upper lip, and tiny beads collect as if I were sprouting a wet mustache. I try to be patient, and words from the evening lecture drum through my mind: "Start again, start again." My little grandson Nicholas has his first swimming lesson today. I push away the distraction and begin anew. "Everything rises and passes away. Anica-anica-anica-everything is impermanent, everything is changing." In spite of myself, I think of my recent hot flashes before I can return to my task "A bird needs two wings to fly. You need awareness and equanimity," I hear the instructor. Balance is like a scale, and I try to weigh both sides equally. I am getting to know my breath.

Day 4:

Each time I enter the meditation hall I feel as if I am descending into the darkness of an underground cave. The light is weak, the walls are veiled. Every object is covered with sky-blue cloths from the elevated chairs of the teachers, to the television set, even the speakers. No candles light up my dim vision, no calming incense is burning. We sit on our assigned velveteen blue mats, and I think of the blue hues of air and water, two fluid elements. The hall is air-conditioned, and I wrap my black woolen shawl around me, sitting mummified as in a shroud. I feel protected, at ease. Group meditations lend solidarity in a supportive atmosphere. No one moves. Only an occasional cough, clearing of a throat, and the air-conditioner turning on and off interrupt the silence. I start to swallow and on reflex have to swallow again and again.

This is a difficult day because we move from the familiar place of concentration around the nostrils to scanning the entire body. It is as if my breath illuminates me. This is the only time during our stay when we are required to sit in a meditating position for two hours. After an hour the yoga position becomes an endurance test and I lose all concentration. Silently I curse to myself, and for the second time since my arrival I harbor thoughts of flight. But as soon as I get over my frustration, the scanning runs smoothly. I let my breath escape through the fontanel of my head, a thrilling sensation, and I realize how much I want to hold onto that pleasant feeling. But I move on and my breath crawls over my face and then from limb to limb, back and front, over bony bumps, through soft crevices. Energy flows easily through some parts of my body. Other parts hurt or burn my knees, and others are numb like my lower back. I try not to linger, but continue my mental walk, just observing, only observing. My mind becomes lucid, it stays dispassionate, no longer flutters about. So simple! So difficult!

Days 5 through 8:

I have been shown the rudimentary steps of the Vipassana practice. Now all is repetition and training. The success, I am told, is not how easily I scan my body, but how calm and objective, yet alert, I can make my mind. My task is to learn how to act instead of blindly reacting. I am bursting with this helpful insight. Back in the outside world I will try to cultivate a tranquil, detached attitude in the face of life's vicissitudes, its impermanence. Learning to be calm in all situations should make me more tolerant. And I see how valuable it is to seek answers in myself and not blame others for my troubles.

My body is heavy, my mind is buoyant. More light has been cast and I am fulfilled. I sleep without dreams.

Day 9:

After meditation this evening the precious silence is lifted. We swarm toward each other and crowd into the hallway. Talk buzzes as if it's coming from a bee-hive. We are, after all, social beings! We feel gratitude. And we want to share. We have survived a challenge, and now we are full of questions: What did you experience? What was difficult for you? Did you ever consider giving up? Why did you come here in the first place? What will you take back with you to your home, your workplace?

Our conversations spill into the late night hours. I am surprised at the variety of problems people carried with them. They range from eating disorders, concentration impairments and the effect of childhood traumas, to recent losses. Many now feel less burdened.

People come from all walks of life. There is the graduate student from India whose colorful sari I admire, who grew up practicing Vipassana and now devotes 10 days each year to a silent meditation retreat. I learn that my bunk bed neighbor is a Vietnamese-American computer expert from Houston. There are teachers and housewives and hordes of young people, many college students searching for meaning and truth. There is even a safari teacher from South Africa.

In Buddhism there are no chance encounters, and I wonder about mine. We are squatting on the floor in a large circle telling amazing animal stories. I contribute one about our 18-year-old Cairn terrier who postponed death, surviving on just a few drops of water a day, waiting for our youngest daughter, Cecile, to return home for the holidays to say good-bye.

A young woman wearing a flaming-red bandanna and intricate tattoos of butterflies and flowers on her arms and legs bursts into tears, "My dog died a few weeks ago." "I'm sorry," I say. I have to get used to talking again and feel a headache coming on. A walk seems just what I need.

The sky is loaded with powerful gray clouds as the daylight sinks slowly over the peaceful countryside. I smell a threatening fragrance of rain and hustle along the dusty rutted lane. I hear long clipping strides catch up with me. "Sorry I cried," a sweet girlish voice says. "Suddenly I had this lump in my throat, and I couldn't stop myself." She glances at me with fawn-brown eyes, now clouded with more tears. Her lips tremble. "I have not cried the entire stay. Why now? I can't fit it in with a calm mind and all that." I slow my walk and say, "It is perfectly all right for you to cry. I am glad to be here to listen to your story." Then Melinda speaks about her feelings of loss, finally telling me, "I also lost my mother three months ago."

It is getting dark, and peals of thunder roll in the distance. Yet, at this moment a full July moon still peeks through the indigo sky. I take Melinda's hand. It is warm, and, as if embarrassed, it responds shyly to my gentle squeeze. "Look" I point to the branch of a live oak. A barn owl is perched there, silhouetted against the creamy yellow disc. "And it's not even Halloween," I chuckle. Then a single bolt of lightning radiates the horizon, and an earsplitting explosion breaks the stillness. We hurry back to the house.

Day 10:
The last morning is fair and clear. The retreat is not over. We are supplicants, thankful for what we have received. Now it is our turn to give. Not just a donation to this nonprofit organization, but also something of ourselves. So we sweep, wash and scrub the center until the place is as clean as we found it. Then we change back into our worldly attire and stare at each other. I put on makeup, don dangling silver earrings and slip into my suede suit and high-heeled shoes. The transformation complete, the recluse of 10 days turns into a lady of the world again.

What do I take away with me from my journey inward?

Ingrained habits do not die in 10 days. I crave my pen and paper, a glass of red wine and my husband's embrace. But in a world noisy with activities and distractions, calmness and peace have set in. Fresh insights have dawned, and I see things more clearly. Maybe by controlling my mind I can master my actions with equanimity.

I pass my first test at the airport by shutting out the intrusive cell-phone conversations that usually annoy me. And when my flight is delayed, I smile at the attendant and sit down without protest. I close my eyes and concentrate on my respiration and the words echo through my mind: Observe, observe, only observe. And other lines from the retreat return:

"Feeling the entire body I shall breathe in," thus he trains himself.
"Feeling the entire body I shall breathe out," thus he trains himself.

Pali Passages (Maha-Sattipatt Sutta, Diga Nikaya, 22)

The Hand that Feeds Us

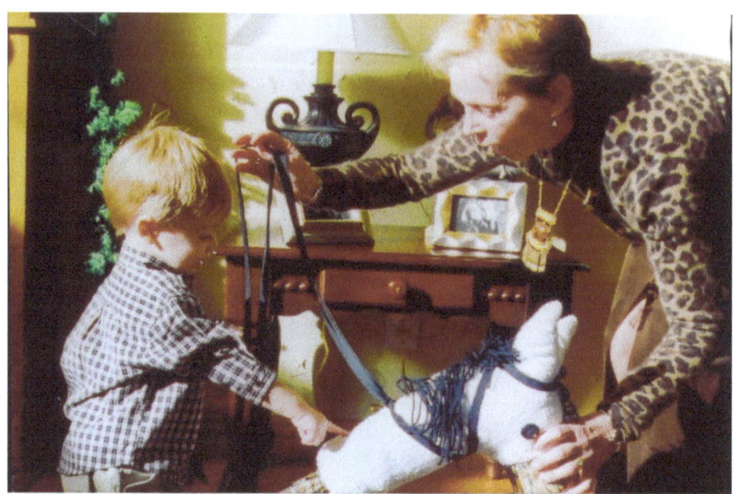

It's the week before Christmas. I sit cross-legged on the floor, stuffing fiber-fill into the pelt of the hobby horse I am making for my youngest grandson, Alexander. I have made equine play companions—brown, gray and dappled ones—for all the grandkids. This horsey is velveteen black, sleek with startled, heart-shaped eyes. The flowing mane, made to look like a mighty wind, is of wooly white yarn and the bridle and reins are braided clay-beige ribbons. I still have to stitch the nostrils so that this little animal can neigh. Then I am ready to wrap my surprise in glittering green paper.

As I work, memories become vivid of my final Christmas on Silesian soil where I had spent my first five idyllic childhood years before World War II forced us to flee from the advancing Russian troops. In our castle overlooking a snaking, wildly roaming river, it was a child's fairytale Christmas. I knew nothing of the approaching troubles. The cannon fire rumbled far off like familiar rolling thunder. The huge fir tree bathed in candlelight stood in the wide-open living room. Though most household help had already escaped over the snowy mountains into Czechoslovakia, a loyal family servant had managed to cut and bring in this majestic tree from our forest. My mother and grandmother decorated it with delicate glass ornaments that would soon be buried beneath the rubble of war along with the Persian rugs and the breakfront filled with fine china. Food supplies were already scarce, but for a child a polished red apple and cookies made with molasses and spiced with ginger were feast enough.

I had a single ardent wish that Christmas for a lamb like the one I had seen born in our blooming meadow last spring. My mother was a magician when it came to surprises. With my hair done up and caught in a golden bow, I knelt in my light-blue chiffon dress under the canopy of branches, unaware of the wax dripping from the flickering candles and the many brightly wrapped presents strewn about. I saw only one thing: a toy lamb. I swooped up the soft bundle and, overwhelmed with joy, cradled it in my plump little arms. My mother had made the lamb from fluffy terrycloth. It had soft pink ears and a moveable tail, with an invisible wire inside. When I was put to bed that evening, I clutched my cuddly new friend tightly to my chest. From then on I never let go of that precious gift, not even during the sudden exodus that followed only a few days after we had extinguished the lights on everything familiar and evergreen.

We relocated to western Germany. There were hungry winters after the war but happy laughter resounded when my mother, sister, brother, grandparents, an aunt and an occasional neighbor or friend gathered in the darkening hours of the late afternoons during each Advent season. Although most nights were sharp with cold and the days clear and still, the atmosphere indoors was welcoming and warm thanks to the big tiled corner stove and the deep red flames of four Advent candles that decorated a wreath. The sweet pungent fragrance of fir sap emanated from its branches. In that cozy room we began to make presents, an activity which became a lesson in disguise, a lesson I was to understand only much later in life.

My siblings and I had small wooden chests which, like secret caves, held our treasures and kept our gifts out of sight. Depending on our age, we decorated the chests with stickers, painted or colored the sides and top boards. We lined the insides with fabric. When I was in my early teens, I adorned my chest one last time with colorful squares, rectangles and circles Mondrian-style. My brother, who was less ambitious in his desire to decorate, was content with the plain pine wood of his treasure chest. Inside the lids of the chests we pasted pictures of our family, friends and favorite animals. My sister Lisa glued a photo of Clark Gable onto the lining of hers and I pinned a picture of my first boyfriend close to my chest's outer rim so it wouldn't be seen at first glance.

As the snow descended, piling up in thick, milky-white layers on the window sills, we made our presents. There were potholders in multiple colors and long scarves winding around necks like snake tails. We made picture calendars using pressed flowers and leaves. We glued tiny stones, polished with spit and feathers onto small wooden boxes designed for jewelry, and strung necklaces of beads and painted noodles. My mother had sliced, then ironed, shafts of straw into long flat pieces. We cut them to different lengths and bound them together with golden yarn into straw stars. My brother, who liked to whittle, once even carved a figure out of a bone. Lisa had a child's loom and wove beautiful miniature wall-hangings. I enjoyed making covers for coat hangers. All coat hangers at that time were wooden with removable wire hooks. We crocheted long, narrow sleeves which we slipped over the hangers, then screwed the hooks back in. They were the forerunners of today's padded hangers. As we grew older we knitted sweaters of every size, shape and color.

My boyfriend was the first recipient of a sky-blue pullover which he proudly wore on ski outings.

We labeled our presents with a name tag as soon as one was finished. "For my dear Mama, the best in the world," "Brother, I adore you," "Grandma Maria, I couldn't do without you," and "I love you!" written last minute on a folded piece of notebook paper to my boyfriend Wolfgang. I sealed it with a lipstick kiss.

During the activities our voices hummed like whizzing fans. We nibbled on homemade cookies of such delicious flavors no childhood palate could ever forget. The adults drank hot spiced wine. We were allowed sips of a watered-down version but mostly contented ourselves with cider. Our grandfathers reclined on the sofa and easy chairs and smoked pipes whose vapors mingled with the rest of all the other good odors. Once in a while grandmother started a Christmas carol and we all joined in. We sang the

traditional songs over and over again, and even though some hymns had four or five verses I still today remember every one of them by heart. During the singing our minds wandered, letting our fantasy roam. We daydreamed about our friends and the upcoming outings to the snowy mountains for sledding and skiing. But I am sure that the older generation flew on wings of nostalgia back to better times in their beloved faraway homeland, now no longer in German hands.

It was my mother who was the puppeteer behind all this craftsmanship and the protector of the Christmas spirit. I see her even now flitting from person to person, her small firm hands busy at catching a loose stitch here, a missed loop there, her lips wet from threading yet another needle. She also smoothed many a wrinkled brow, foremost for us children who used our handiwork to play out our sibling rivalries, "How come your star is much prettier than mine?" "I wanted that purple yarn. Give it to me!!!" But she also calmed the elders who easily felt neglected, a glass not filled, a favorite cookie snatched just when Grandpa Rolf was reaching for it. She always intervened when my Aunt Paula had started to recite a poem and we children kept whispering.

Besides my mother's industriousness and warmth certain character traits of the rest of us came to light as well. My sister's perfectionism which led her to unravel wall-hangings she didn't like, my brother's fine workmanship but lack of artistic sensibility, my aunt's procrastination and her dejection over never finishing a project, and my reluctance to part with gifts that I found especially pleasing. I also recall the gentle suggestions of both grandmothers when we were at an impasse in our creative endeavors, "Have you ever thought of...?" Although my grandmothers were totally different in appearance and personality, on this they spoke in unison. And then there were the grandfathers who participated mainly by their presence and their huffing and harrumphing.

My mother was also the reader. When she finally sat down and let her hands rest, she picked up our favorite book, *The Travels of Nils Holgerson*, by Swedish author Selma Lagerlöff. Darkness pressed against the windows and falling snowflakes as white and soft as the belly of my toy lamb blinked off and on like lightning bugs, illuminating the moonless night. That's when we flew away with Nils. Securely positioned on the broad, cushioned wings of his snow goose, we traversed dense clouds, glided by blazing sunsets, over snowfields and above houses the size of tinker toys, swept through lush green valleys and soared high above fog-veiled mountaintops. We were timeless. Leaving our familiar places, we rose into the air and, resisting the pull of gravity, floated freely, borne up by the buoyant power of the imagination.

With Nils we wondered about the sleeping people below and, during the day, watched them at work in their fields, factories, kitchens and schools. We saw children on the playground kicking a ball or tipping on a teeter-totter. We spied into peoples' rooms, felt bad about their meager meals, or giggled when a fat man belched, and heard lovers quarrel and then reconcile. We became treasure hunters with gold diggers in California. We urged on Indian ponies galloping across the prairies of Wyoming, and gasped when fishermen killed a baby seal on the shores of Finland. From our lofty wing-thrones we appeared as princes and princesses at fancy balls, and we cried with the orphans and beggars in the slums of London whose plight saddened us so much that we wished to leave our safe flying carpet and descend to comfort them. But as my mother turned yet another page we remained persistent onlookers. And since there were no boundaries, we spun our minds around myriads of unknown lives. We continued to observe unflinchingly what flashed before our eyes on the fleeting land far below. And thus in the end, we made a home in our imagination for the accumulated impressions and gathered them into ourselves.

During my shared journey with little Nils, the seeds for my poems and stories were sown. On one of the Advent nights, snug in bed, I reached for my flashlight under the pillow and started my very own notebook of stories and poems. What I write today is the harvest.

And then finally it was the morning of Christmas Eve. One last time we trailed our fingers over each present before covering it with star-spangled paper. Our cheeks glowed from the efforts and our palm lines glistened with sweat as we feverishly finished the last boxing up and wrapping of presents for this day's deliveries. And then, bundled up in warm coats, woolen caps and mittens, we became caroling elves walking from house to house, ringing doorbells. As soon as we heard footsteps approaching, we ran. Sometimes we bumped into a couple of eloping friends who were also on secret missions. We pretended not to notice.

Hours later, back home with cold, red noses and stiff fingers, we ate more cookies and pressed our hands against the tiles of the warm stove until the blood flowed freely again through all our limbs. Then we waited with bated breath to see what we might receive in return, especially surprises from friends. My excitement rivaled the happiness over my toy lamb when one Christmas my boyfriend left a collection of Rilke poems on my doorstep.

Christmas Eve is the time at which German households exchange gifts among themselves under candlelit Christmas trees. We all knew that by nightfall church services and private celebrations would begin and no more gifts would be delivered. We had retreated only partially from the outside world while busy with our secret activities. Then we reentered the wider community with our gifts, a movement reminiscent of the rhythm of butterflies opening and shutting their wings. There was never a sense of quid pro quo in our gift-giving, only the silent hope that others would feel like we did, finding joy in giving and receiving.

The making and giving of presents created a magical sensation for me during my childhood and youth that has kept its hold over me during my adult years. My mother taught me that what feeds us needs also to be fed by us.

The Calf-Skin Notebook with Rose-Colored Lines

Experiences may be forgotten but they are never lost. The unconscious, our curious guide, stores them forever. Sometimes memories sink into shallow waters, other times they sleep deep underground. We live our lives largely on the surface. Then one day when we least expect it, one or another experience is released from slumber and we remember.

Lately, I had come to my weekly writers' meetings complaining, "I'm all out of fresh ideas." "Try hypnosis," my friend Lisa suggested one evening. "It did wonders for me." I took her advice. The next day I made an appointment at *Tranquil Thymes* with Lady Fatima, a hypnotist whose psychic powers are legendary. I was struck by the flaming red hair that streamed behind her like a comet and by her corpulence which she claimed protected her from too much empathy.

Lady Fatima told me in a deep, rumbling voice, "Make yourself comfortable."

She gently pushed me onto an overstuffed moss-green sofa. I was already drowsy with anticipation when I sank into its soft folds. It was as if I were putting down roots. Then Lady Fatima told me to close my eyes and turn inward. Soon her incantations soothed and relaxed my body and mind and I drifted into an altered state of consciousness as easily as when I went to sleep at night. "Now imagine three houses, Maya." She spoke directly to me. "One is the House of Knowledge, another the House of Silence, the last one the House of Healing. Go into one and remember."

I did not hesitate but followed an urgent inner tug toward the House of Knowledge, a silvery, transparent glass temple. "How long have you been writing?" my internal guide asked once I was seated on a cool marble bench in the center of the temple. Sunrays spilled through a skylight onto the crown of my raised head.

"Forever."

"Who inspired you?"

"Many people. But I have forgotten most of their names."

"How did you get started?"

"I don't know."

I was often asked that question. But though I had sifted through my memory for the answer, I always came up empty.

Then suddenly, with a whiff of magic, I was transported back to my childhood in Germany and I found myself in a classroom, probably third grade. Wooden desks with scratched and ink-spotted retractable tops, were lined up in rows, children's heads moved from left to right over open books, golden pigtails bounced off ruddy necks and fingers traced the words. The idle hand had to be placed next to the book, on the side of the desk, into a groove worn hollow by past pupils. I knew I'd be scolded if I cupped my chin in my palm.

A lady, dressed like all German middle-aged ladies in the late 1940s, wore a cheerless blue suit with a frilly white blouse buttoned all the way up to her throat. Her shoes were a sensible dark color with square, plump heels. She smelled a bit of leather and shoe polish, with a sprinkle of *Kölnisch Wasser* mixed in. Her hair was parted in the middle, exposing a line of pale scalp, and gathered in a bun. I can't remember if she wore any make-up other than lipstick, poppy-red, the same kind my mother used to touch up her lips. Whenever my teacher turned to write on the blackboard I noticed the seams of her hose zigzagging up the back of her calves like bulging, menacing veins.

Each day our pencils made tapping sounds on smoky-gray sheets of black-lined paper like woodpeckers attacking a tree. We worked hard at writing sentences and subtracting numbers. Then as predictable as the hourly striking of the school clock, our efforts ended. And we were rewarded with a story. Before starting, our teacher smoothed the pleats of her skirt with her right hand, lifted her slender hips one at a time onto her desk, and faced us. Both of her legs dangled just off the ground, one longer than the other, the ankles crossed like scissors. Then she slipped the heels of her shoes from her feet, a daring gesture. I had never seen a lady do that.

"Children," she would say in a hushed, lilting voice, "Give me a hint, anything, a frog, a leaf, your papa."

"A nose, a crocodile, a pumpkin," we giggled.

Then the words poured out of her mouth like the ink from the blue fountain pens that we were allowed to practice with on Fridays only. Magically, our teacher wove the story around our promptings. Without ever breaking the flow of words she also entrusted something to the soft-skin notebook she balanced on her left thigh, something she kept to herself, something mysterious.

I was sitting in the front row, and one day I leaned forward so close that her words tickled my hair. That's when I glimpsed the rose-colored lines. My teacher blew on them, now topped with her words. Afterwards she screwed the top back on her shiny black fountain pen. I wondered why hers was black and ours were blue. At the end of a week, a month, a year when her stories were patched together in a quilt-like pattern, she would start a new notebook.

Slowly, I opened my eyes. Lady Fatima stood silently observing me. Her hair was still a wild tussle and her flowered dress touched the tops of her feet. She smoothed out her dress with gentle strokes like silky caresses and, leaning against the wall, slipped out of her left sandal. The gestures seemed curiously familiar. Just then her voice reached me as if coming out of a dense fog. She instructed me,

"Go back to sleep at once." Again I slipped into a trance as if sinking into warm, soothing water. And suddenly, with a click, my grade school teacher's name sprang to mind: Frau Klinck. But her name was just a tag. I felt again the strain in my scribbling fingers as I sat on a hard, marred desk chair, setting tiresome letters and numbers down on paper. And then a quickening joy seeped into my heart as Frau Klinck treated us to our daily story. Her voice traveled through the air like a current, and as before, I drank in every word, absorbed every image, followed the storyline and mulled over its meaning. That day, after school, I didn't linger at the gurgling brook to set my papers asail, but hurried home. It had come to me.

"Mutti," I panted, barely through the door, "I want to tell stories like Frau Klinck."

Then I confessed that I had craned my neck during story time until I could spy into the book Frau Klinck was holding.

"Mutti," I whispered excitedly, "The notebook's lines were pink!"

My mother, my wondrous witch with a magic wand, listened but said nothing.

The next day I dawdled after school, as was my usual way. But when I got home, there on the kitchen table was my very own soft calf-skin notebook. I cradled it in my hands and stroked the cover front and back. It was so pleasing to touch. Then I thumbed through the pages to see if it had rose-colored lines like my teacher's. It did! I sighed happily, took out my blue fountain pen, the one I was only allowed to use on Fridays, and wrote on the first line: Maya Halle - Writer.

One raindrop follows another until it becomes falling water. As I unlocked the memory of my German grade school days, I began to conjure up the atmosphere upon first entering the imaginary world of stories, and the ideas began to flow. "Give me a hint, a frog, a leaf, your papa." I had all the fresh ideas I needed.

Substitutes Are Not Supposed to Smile

"For all the trouble we have given you, we sure love you." These were Peter's parting words as he dashed out of the classroom to catch the school bus. I was left behind, sorting through stacks of papers, writing notes where lesson plans ended and generally clearing the desk for my colleague, Mrs. J., who would be returning next week from two months' maternity leave. Overwhelmed by feelings of farewell, I had no room for reflections.

Monday morning I luxuriated in my private time, swimming laps during the morning hours when only a few days before I had been conjugating verbs with the third period class. I was surprised to find my mind wandering back to the classroom. Would Jim have taken his make-up test yet? Would David have studied to get his grade average up? Was I hooked on teaching again, or just not yet free of the experience. The parties the students had given me had taken me completely by surprise. The cakes, the special treats, Eric playing the guitar, the goodbye wishes on the blackboard had made me feel good and grateful. But that was the last day—a special day. What had it really been like to substitute teach at a high school in Gainesville, Florida in 1982?

The experience had been manifold and I knew that I could not draw a picture that would speak to all substitutes at all times. What I tried to assemble were impressions and attitudes which I wanted to share.

Called on short notice to fill in for Mrs. J., I had been ready to throw in the towel before the first week had passed. Too many new faces and over 50 names to remember, and hardly anybody paying attention while I struggled to continue where Mrs. J. had left off. I asked myself whether it was at all worth doing. Would I ever succeed in keeping the class attentive enough to learn or would all my efforts have to go into being a disciplinarian, gaining their respect by sitting on them? A gentle, reasonable approach might work with the willing, polite student, but would never reach the one who didn't care about an additional failing grade. And enforcing discipline drained me of my energy. I had to learn that some students can't be reached, that no matter how often I sent students to the guidance office or kept them after school, they would continue to float through the system untouched by my efforts. It troubled me that a considerable number of high school students would remain drifters, waiting to get out, to go where? They were the ones who were bored and slept in class, who fought in the library, and cheated and lied.

Upon confronting a student I suspected of cheating on an exam, he denied any wrongdoing. On my last day I found a note from him with a palm tree as a symbol of peace drawn on it. The note read in part, "I did lie to you. Will you please forgive me? I won't ever do it again. Please forgive. Love, T." I could never bring myself to give up on the students completely but realized that I had to limit my efforts in order to teach those who needed and wanted to learn.

A temporary teacher is never a sufficient substitute for a permanent teacher. That's what makes substitute teaching a difficult and sometimes trying task. It's not the difference in teaching styles, even though on the surface it may appear as such. "No, that's not the way Mrs. J. does it." "Mrs. J. would like for you to do more grammar than conversation." If it were only a matter of style, shifting the emphasis would solve the problem and a firm reply ("I'm not Mrs. J.") would do the trick. The underlying conflict is over a breach of loyalty. Students are committed to their permanent teachers. The newcomer is viewed as an intruder, a foreigner to be tested, to be kept uncomfortable, so that when the regular teacher returns, things can continue as before. This loyalty to the teacher is the linchpin of all good teaching. It also takes tact to avoid interfering with the students' attachment to their permanent teacher. Two weeks after Mrs. J's return I was invited to a student banquet where I received flowers and a standing ovation from the students. I had apparently gained their affection without destroying the old alliance.

A substitute has to prove to the class that she respects its priorities. But she can't just hang back. In order for the teaching to be effective she must establish herself as distinct and separate from the regular teacher and gain affection on her own terms. Should she succeed in that delicate balancing of loyalties, the students will have learned that two different, yet simultaneous, attachments are possible. Conflict as well as success were evident in Sonja's and Jim's comments, "I have just gotten used to you," Sonja protested, "and now you are leaving." Jim solved the problem by suggesting spontaneously, "Can't we petition the school board to hire both you and Mrs. J. as teachers?" At the banquet, after the farewell speeches and applause for me, Steve toasted Mrs. J's return, which sparked a second round of applause. The transition was complete.

I remember students for a variety of reasons. I fondly recall the helpfulness of Erika and Melissa and Randy when I could never find anything the first week. I remember Jim's humorous greeting the first day on the job,"If you are our new substitute, I hope you like jokes." And Brad, who broke the newness by introducing his girlfriend to me, and Nathan feeling confident enough to tease me the last day, "Please call me Nathan," he announced, smiling disarmingly. I have not lost my German accent and my "th" still sounds like "s." I repeated Nathan's name with the proper pronunciation whereupon he retorted, "For once you did it right. Thank you, Mrs. Carthon."

Human experiences bring people together, as did the skit the students and I rehearsed. After the group had performed for orientation, they burst into my class, bubbling over with details about which parts had gone well and which ones had failed. And I recall the innumerable interactions that occurred during the lunch hours, after school and between bells. I sympathized with Donna's concern about how to be a friend to a boy and still be able to say "No," and I felt for Jim when he plopped down on a chair next to me, depressed about everything, exclaiming, "It's no fun being 16." I liked hearing about Robert's interest in cars. and shared a love for horses with Kim. I responded with pleasure to Kirk's probing questions about history.

It is this human interest that will ultimately make or break substitutes. It goes without saying that they have to be qualified in their subject areas and that their teaching abilities and standards should be scrutinized and reviewed, but interest in the students will determine the atmosphere in the classroom and shape the interactions. It will even usher in each new day. The negative image of the substitute has a long history and everyone has to battle it anew. There are many pitfalls to watch out for. How to be the students' friend without being their buddy? How to allow their personal hobbies and concerns to enter into the classroom without turning learning into bull sessions? How to guide and set limits to student behavior without pushing students to the wall where their only way out is confrontation? And finally, a word of advice to teachers who at times must substitute in areas in which their knowledge is spotty: never fake it. When in doubt, fall back on something you know well.

Students need models, men and women who are experts in areas of knowledge, but who are also examples of how to live one's life. When I entered the classroom, I brought with me not just my knowhow but my personality and my background as a mother, a writer, and a wife, as well. It takes time to establish relationships and here substitutes are again at a disadvantage, especially if they are filling in only a day or two at a time. But like a regular teacher, a substitute must be permitted to fail as well as to succeed. There will be times when she is drained and when she feels that nothing much was accomplished. There will be other times when the day is a joy.

On my way to class the morning after a holiday, I heard a voice shouting across the courtyard, "Did you miss us, Mrs. Carson?" It was Tom, one of the lovable troublemakers. "No," I shouted back, "I didn't miss you one bit, but it does feel good to be back here again this morning." "Substitutes are not supposed to smile," he shot back, and that's how we started the new day.

The Device

During the sweltering summer of her 75th birthday the horizon of Florence Delano's world in Elkhart, Indiana began to close in. Up to that point her life had flowed like a tranquil river with the satisfactions of work, her bountiful flower garden, gratitude from her patients and her only intimate companion, Snowy the cat. Snowy's name was a stretch for a calico cat with white feet and stockings. Florence figured it must have been the large white tip on his fluffy tail that fanned out like a silky paintbrush which earned him his connection to snow.

Florence had known Edward Vicosa since his rotation as a medical student when she had taken him under her wing on visits to hospice patients. He was a doctor with long, twisted fingers which had probed much flesh rarely touched by the sun during his twenty years in practice. As always, when she entered his office Ed hugged Florence with a gentle intensity that went through her many layers of clothing right to her heart. Then he led her to a chair and took his seat behind his sturdy wooden desk. He looked at her with sensitive, fawn-like eyes.

Florence pulled her sweater tighter and slipped her hands, small but strong and callused from work in the garden, into the openings of her sleeves. She was a tiny woman with matchstick arms and legs who wore sweaters over sweaters to make herself look bigger. She also strained after the sun.

"It's freezing in here," she smiled at her friend.

"Old age thins your blood."

"Then I must have always been old."

Florence was comfortable with growing older. She looked at age as a force that was gradually taking away what life had gradually given. She had seen much shrinking, withering and wilting in her patients and she did not fear decline or endings. She knew why Ed had called her in. "Your heart, Florence. It's your heart." Florence smiled. But when Ed's frown lines deepened, her smile froze. She took a breath. Surely, it was no surprise to Ed that of all her organs her heart would fail. Hadn't she always led with her heart? She concluded that it was Ed's reluctance to convey bad news which made him somber.

"How serious, Ed?"

"No way to know. Your faithful old pump could give out any day."

"No rest for the wicked. What do you have to offer?"

"The usual. We tried the pacemaker. We tried medication. Nothing new."

Then he leaned back and wrinkled his fine eyebrows into a crooked line.

"We have a new device, an IVD, an intraventricular cardiac device. It shocks your heart back to life every time it stops."

"And?"

"Well, that's the benefit and the problem. It can keep you alive for several more months, maybe even years, but it also makes it difficult to die. Your heart will be shocked back into action every time it quits."

Now Ed was on a roll.

"And it's very expensive. Not just the implantation. There can be postoperative complications, not to mention the medical maintenance." He caught himself. He had gone too far.

"But Medicare covers the cost of the device and the surgery. And of all people, you are entitled to this one!"

When Ed was breathing calmly again, Florence asked, "How much, Ed?"

"Two hundred fifty thousand dollars."

Florence could feel her heart speeding up as she heard that figure. She was about to say something when Ed added, "But if you decline the device, you're eligible for a generous cash payment. Or, if you're of a mind to, you could donate the money." Again he caught himself. His attempt to advise Florence about her options and this incentive plan backfired. His well-known kindness which was stamped all over his face turned into blood-red embarrassment.

"Maybe the device is just the thing for you," he added hastily.

Florence rose slowly. "I'll call you. Life-and-death decisions take time."

"Of course, of course." Ed hugged her again, this time with a mixture of guilt and relief.

Florence landed in Rome, took a bus to the train station and departed for the city of her ancestors whose anglicized name she bore. Snowy was panting in his cage. Once in their compartment, she took him out, stroked him and then stuffed him inside her outermost sweater. They were both jetlagged and anxious. Florence had made a life-changing decision, leasing her house to another hospice nurse, cashing in her savings and the incentive money for declining the IVD. Before leaving, she had phoned and informed a stunned Dr. Vicosa, "I am going on vacation. To Italy." She had snickered behind her tiny free hand.

Next to the entrance to the Florence train station, on a tobacco shop window plastered with announcements and want ads she couldn't understand, Florence peeled off the address of a small hotel. The taxi driver took them to a wooden building held up by large beams which seemed to have battled against erosion for centuries. There was even romance in all the decay in and around the old building. The early signs of fall were visible as dead leaves drifted into ridges and spirals. An ample-bodied lady welcomed them both with a wide-armed gesture. Florence paid for six months in advance.

She liked her room immediately. It was so small and crammed with furniture it reminded her of a rabbit hutch overstuffed with hay. The wallpaper was peeling but had a pleasant flower pattern and the forest-green linoleum floor was covered with overlapping faded yellow rugs. Exhausted, she plopped onto the cozy quilted comforter and even under her feather weight the bedsprings immediately began to bounce and squeak.

The window was wide open and car horns blasted from the streets beyond the small courtyard below. She inhaled the sweet fragrance of bougainvillea and wondered if she would find any of her beloved asters and marigolds in the garden. The windowsill was packed with flowerboxes sprouting sage, mint and basil. Snowy relieved himself in the soft dirt. An hour later the moon sent its enchanted beams over a woman and a cat curled up together in peaceful relaxation.

Once Snowy had learned to balance himself along the edges of the flowerboxes, climb down a knotty olive tree and venture out of sight for awhile into lush grapevines, a new hope was born in Florence. For the first time she wanted to live for herself alone, without the obligations of work and caring for others. Her health back home had been declining, but here she would set out on a journey with full sails. She forgot all about her heart and instead began to explore Florence with the zeal of an adventurer. When she became short of breath, she would stop and take in the ancient atmosphere of mortar and brick and lives past.

Soon she discovered that every cobblestone street, every park, every bridge, even the sluggish River Arno which gurgled along under the Ponte Vecchio, seemed somehow familiar. It was as if knowledge of the city circulated in her blood. Both she and the city were old and both had their dents, pockmarks and scratches. She was not interested in Florence's artistic wealth or its architectural treasures. No Stendhal syndrome for her! She never set foot inside the Uffizi Gallery but instead ambled through crowded markets where myriads of odors vied for the attention of her nostrils. She inhaled the scent of fresh mangroves and fingered crisp lettuce leaves. She stopped at steaming food stalls and bought her favorite chunks of skewered roast pork, spiced with rosemary. Then she walked up and down narrow streets and alleyways where the wind played with debris and tossed paper in the path of her sandals. She inspected name plates on houses, tracing the colorful letters with her fingers. She found several Delanos. She meditated in many dim-lit churches permeated with incense and spicy candle smoke.

Florence had been on her feet all her life, tending patients, bending over to pull weeds from flowerbeds, and now her feet were like wheels effortlessly carrying her to the remotest parts of the city. She never tired. She listened to Italians talking and suddenly recalled long forgotten phrases from her youth. It amazed her that she soon loved the sound of this foreign tongue more than English. She believed and rejoiced in gardens and growing things, so she visited a different park each day. Her favorite was the Boboli Garden where a copy of Cosimo's well-known dwarf is displayed astride an unhappy turtle. She immediately liked the plump little fellow, and soon she had put a few pounds on her own fragile bird-bones. She had a taste for pasta.

As the city revealed itself, Florence herself opened like a garden. She began to shed layers of clothing and within two weeks she was wearing a blouse with only one light sweater over it. She let her untamable mouse-gray hair tumble down her shoulders and, in memory of her maternal grandparents, she bought a large leather handbag. Her grandfather had come to Elkhart as a skilled leather goods merchant. She stowed her knitting and her English-Italian dictionary in the new purse.

Her landlady asked if she would volunteer in a soup kitchen twice a week and she accepted with joy. She also visited the animal shelter regularly and soon gave money for many strays. She felt useful in both places and learned more Italian. She also made a friend, Camilla. There was nothing special about plump Camilla but she was kind and had green eyes flecked with gold. The two women met in the Boboli Garden with their knitting on warm afternoons and Sunday mornings. So much for Florence's desire to be alone!

Florence had arrived in late summer, and now lived through a damp fall and a chilly winter that had spread a coat of frost on the ground. With the advent of spring Snowy went missing. The rain wasn't much but the wild wind delayed her search for several days. Once the rain let up Florence hurried through the neighborhood, calling Snowy's name. For the first time since her arrival her heart felt heavy. It was as though a sack of sand was weighing on her chest. She realized that it was time to return to America. The months had been exhilarating, full of freedom and new discoveries. She had sent Ed a few joyous postcards but she had never thanked him for giving her such an unexpected choice. She would write him that letter tonight. This vacation was all she could ever have dreamed of.

Florence eventually found Snowy curled up in the unchecked brushwood of a lush grapevine. She buried him in Camilla's small garden. The same day she made out a large check to the shelter, nearly depleting her bank account.

It was a balmy Sunday morning. Church bells pealed throughout the city. There was a lilac and lavender fragrance in the air. She had gone early to the Boboli Garden and upon entering had picked a crimson bougainvillea bloom from the vine cascading over the old stone wall. She inhaled the pungent aroma and was reminded of her first night in her small quarters with Snowy in the window box. Nostalgia and gratitude filled her heart. She sat down on her familiar bench and carefully bent back the fragile petals hiding the center of the flower. Gently she put her lips to the blossom's heart. The shadow from her face fell over the tiny calyx and tears light as raindrops wetted its crown. Did she miss her little furry companion that much? Or was she homesick?

As she sat remembering Snowy and waiting for Camilla, she noticed a hole in her Italian mohair sweater. It was a large tear, too big to mend. She would need to find a soft patch, matching the colors of the lapis lazuli yarn. She was attached to this pleasing garment which she had bought on one of her first strolls through the city. Suddenly she grew hot under the caresses of the gentle sun and felt heat rising from her skin. She removed her sweater and undid the top buttons of her blouse. The front of the blouse jumped with each breath. Florence tilted her face skyward like an animal taking a scent, and briefly wondered what might be growing in her Indiana garden. Then she heard steps approaching along the gravel path. Camilla was at her side.

"Are you alright, dear?"

"I'm having the most wonderful time. Is it about to end?" Camilla patted her arm.

At that moment Florence's heart began to thud like thunder and each beat sent jolts of sharp pain through her body. Her hands fluttered up like nervous birds.

"I need to go back home to America."

"You are home, dear."

Camilla continued to stroke her friend's arm. An angelic smile played around Florence's lips. She stifled a moan followed by a childlike giggle, "The IVD must not be working. I knew it. I'll have to tell Ed." She had trouble getting the words out. She felt such pressure on her windpipe.

A gust of wind buffeted the crowns of the gnarled olive trees and shook some bougainvillea blossoms off the branches. Suddenly Florence let out a yelp like a puppy, and sweat started to trickle down her face. Then she slumped forward as Camilla tried to catch her. A moment later everything was absolutely still. The spirits of Florence's forebears hovered around her on silent wings.

The Old Should Be Explorers

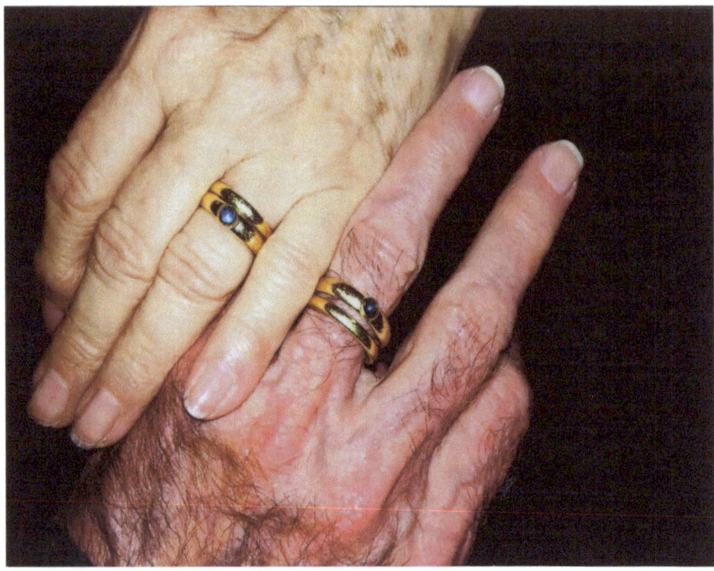

The night clouds had drifted away and the morning broke silver-gray. Little had disturbed Eva and Mike's breakfast routine since their retirement from Rosewood High School three years ago. The atmosphere in the kitchen was warm and friendly and the pair sat next to each other like two contented cats with their tails entwined. The water kettle whistled until Mike turned it off and poured Eva her first cup of coffee, so strong the silver spoon threatened to stand up.

"I need my jump-start," she said, her face bent into the vapor of the mug.

The coffee aroma was almost too much to bear as it overwhelmed the smell of fresh bagels and an alluring fragrance arising from the marmalade homemade from overripe strawberries. Eva twisted the halves of a bagel apart, handed Mike the bottom half and then began to nibble on a piece of crust. They chewed calmly while listening in companionable silence to the ten-minute news roundup on the hour.

"Joe Schreiber celebrated his 75th birthday by swimming the English Channel." The information boomed from the radio as if the announcer had performed the feat himself.

Mike ran a dreamy hand across his ample stomach, popping out of his shirt, and with a deep and earnest voice, slightly lifted, said what he always said when hearing of amazing adventures,

"Old men should be explorers."

"You've said that before," Eva reminded him.

"I snitched it from T.S. Eliot."

Mike pushed his chair back from the table and made his way to his study where he spent the next hours thumbing through travel guides, perusing maps and tracing his right index finger along roads and across mountains. He frowned at the volume of information until he found their next destination. A historic spot. Mike had not taught history in vain.

Eva, a fragile-boned woman who had shrunk and furrowed with age, ambled into her bountiful garden where flowers with round, sunny faces and the scent of damp grass gave her daily sustenance. Her garden made her feel alive. Here time did not stand still. Eva used to teach photography, "time-catching" she called it. Even now she sometimes tried to capture the miracles of nature with her camera, an orange black-speckled butterfly flitting like a sunbeam from one blossom to the next or a yellow brown-spotted bug climbing the dizzying heights of a grass blade.

As the day turned to dusk, Mike and Eva often retreated again to their kitchen and talked over the day's events. That evening their conversation needed to be brief because they had an invitation to a party. Mike shot his long-time companion a quizzical look, yawned and said, "Let's call and cancel." He was surprised at Eva's quick retort, "Yes, let's."

The years of teaching had created strong bonds with colleagues and they had celebrated family events as well as holidays together. On those occasions they enjoyed the verbal bantering, the cheerful camaraderie and the high spirits that flowed from the bottle. Parties were a welcome escape from the stresses of work. After retirement the gatherings continued with more frequency and had become more boozy and rowdy. Emotions kept under wrap in professional alliances now erupted, inflamed old jealousies, uncovered weaknesses. Too much leisure time led to infidelities. Mike and Eva had become increasingly reluctant to participate.

Now Mike gazed questioningly at Eva, wondering how she would take to his latest plan. "We're flying to the Bahamas. Little Exuma, a small island. I found a deal at the Cove Inn. If we stay two weeks they'll throw in an extra night." Mike was always finding deals.

Mike could read Eva's reaction by the shape of her eyebrows. If she was pleased she'd draw them up into perfect arches. If she bunched them together caterpillar-style, he was out of luck. Today he got the desired response. Eva not only beautifully arched her eyebrows, she also curled her long auburn, silvery-tipped hair around two fingers and said, "Sounds great. When do we go?"

The sky did a color-changing trick from velvety purple to glossy pink. Each day Mike and Eva woke up to the heartbeat of the ocean. "Let's see where the morning takes us," was their vacation motto. Little Exuma was idyllic. They rented bicycles and rode them to the rugged tip of the island where waves moaned with hopeless abandonment against exposed rocks. Hand-in-hand they strolled along an uncluttered, dazzling white beach, and collected shells for their grandchildren. Seagulls flew loops around them and then sailed down, kissing the sea foam with the tips of their wings. On sun-baked afternoons Eva and Mike roared over the swells of the water in a powerboat. They ignored their healthy dietary resolutions and enjoyed sumptuous meals in restaurants with a welcoming atmosphere which cozied up to the sea. And they indulged in long naps after leisurely lovemaking.

Fog rolled onto the island and clouds scurried past the sun. Lulled by a warm, dancing breeze, Mike and Eva carried two chairs onto the porch of their cabin. A sand dune placed them out of earshot of their neighbors and the roar of the waves muffled everything but the sound of their own voices. They spread provisions from the village store onto a small stone table, a long loaf of crusty bread baked in a clay oven, juicy papayas, a variety of cheeses, and a bottle of Sauvignon Blanc. After Mike uncorked the wine, they toasted the end of another marvelous day and settled in to watch a veiled sunset. A golden mist glazed the crimson disc. Slowly the evening air wrapped itself around their bodies, squeezing them into a cozy cocoon.

Eva got up and went inside to spread towels over their bed sheets and set their favorite massage oil on the night stand, a balsam of rosemary, the love charm herb.

"Making preparations for a special bedtime treat," she called to Mike.

"I'm for that."

Then Eva joined him again and asked for more wine.

"Old women should be explorers," she said with a fetching smile.

"Said who?"

"Says I."

She unfolded a piece of tinfoil revealing two bluish-white pills. The pill faces were inscribed with butterfly logos.

"What's that?" Mike's voice came from deep within his throat. He was obviously dubious.

"Ecstasy."

"Are you crazy?" Mike said, shocked. "It's illegal! I don't have the money to bail you out."

"Just an idea. Don't get all riled up."

Mike rubbed his eyes and coughed twice.

"Where did you get these?"

"My physical therapist. Try one, you'll like it, she said."

"You trust her?"

"I did my own research. But Liza uses X with rape victims."

"Rape victims!"

"Or the old and decrepit."

"The old and decrepit. Have mercy!"

"You don't have to take one."

"We have fun...always have fun...without shit like this."

"I want to explore...shit like this. You can just stand guard. I'll go ahead."

"The hell you will. Not without me."

That night woke them to another world. A feathery, mild-mannered rain muffled the air and its wetness deepened the tone of all things. The moonlight, just a splinter like a night candle, submerged the inside of the cabin in bronze-colored mystery. The light bulbs on the night stands shone like little, unnatural suns.

Mike and Eva placed the pills on their tongues and carefully swallowed as if chewing might spoil the effect. They sprawled naked on the bed for maybe twenty minutes before adrenaline shot into their fingertips and toes and a fire raced through their veins. The light stroked their skin like scraps of lace. Their breaths, sweetened with wine, mingled and their hands moved gently over each other as the pounding of their hearts filled their ears. They felt weightless, on upward winds. Eva trembled as Mike's hot fingers began to knead her dewy body. Mike's face was flushed and sweat poured from him and mixed with the oil he began to rub on their bodies. They slithered in and over each other with the smooth grace of snakes. Several times Mike reached for the water glass. Eva chilled and snuggled into Mike's warmth, unable to wrest her hands from him. Endlessly their tongues crawled along familiar places, dipping into crevices, hollows and indentations, marking territory in the bend of a knee, the tender elbow curve, legs spread in delight. Desire brimmed in their glassy eyes, dark as blackberries. As their pupils dilated, the whites around the irises glowed. They stared at each other with such rapture. It was as if they were seeing each other for the first time. Their bodies were singing with ecstasy as if life itself flowed through their veins. Mike and Eva were overtaken by this passion that blossomed like a crocus in the winter of their lives. Their minds opened like window shades and they were attuned to each other's emotions, constantly asking, "Does this feel good?" "And that?"

Mike sighed with contentment and Eva purred like a happy cat.

They were keenly aware of each other, yet they were both afloat. Not out of control. They could have reached for the phone, done what was necessary. But an oceanic feeling united them with everything and everyone. Time was an accordion. What seemed like five minutes was actually five hours. The door of the cabin gaped into an endless night and the waves crashed on shore like Wagnerian music.

What had brought them here was a longing for a perfect moment. It was granted. Mike did not hallucinate, but Eva did. She gazed at objects and wondered, "Am I swinging from the ceiling?"

"You are in my arms. It's the fan moving," was Mike's reassuring reply. Mike also couldn't see the purple birds flying out of the tapestry behind the bed. And when Eva cooed, "Now the birds are juicy grapes… plump to bursting," Mike gripped her earlobes with his teeth and nibbled on them as if they were grapes, all the while shaking with laughter.

The next morning on Little Exuma, light nudged Eva and Mike awake and rays from the amber crown of a rising sun drew them from their bed and sent them running to the beach. The wet sand sucked at their feet as they waded into the waves. The water rose above their waists, tickling their navels. They squealed with delight like children and vowed forever to remember that the old can be explorers.

In Defense of Wrinkles

After reading an op-ed piece that painted a gloomy picture of what awaits women in the mid-life stretch between 40 and 50, I decided that this wasn't the whole story. A disconcerting outlook awaits the traveler who thinks of herself as over the hill and on the decline when she reaches a certain age. What became of the respite that awaits on having reached the mountaintop after a strenuous climb?

The paunch protruding just below my waistline is evidence of my having borne three children. It has been under assault for years. But no matter how often I ride my bicycle or how many leg lifts I do, I can't seem to win the war against the paunch. So I accept it, smilingly. No longer do I bounce back elastically when I touch my toes. Instead, my muscles stretch sorely and my joints creak. Did I remember to take my calcium supplement?

I have to squint at the small print when reading the morning paper. And I get no consolation from my ophthalmologist friend's best efforts to persuade me that this is normal at my age. I do see well enough to notice my puffy eyelids. Yet, I can live with diminished vision. I also wonder whether it is always advantageous to see so clearly. And then there are those little lines that appear around our eyes that may inhibit a smile or a laugh if the lines become pronounced. But I like to laugh, even at myself.

Who would not want to slow the physical decline of aging? But are lotions and potions and facelifts genuinely useful means to "retard aging," or merely clownish attempts to fool ourselves and others? And can our face communicate under the cover of makeup? The German poet, Rilke, wrote of our inability to face our own mortality as long as there are "unlived lines in our bodies." And who is to say that the smooth surface of a baby's face, unblemished but also not engraved by time and experience, is more beautiful than the wrinkled and creased face of a Katherine Hepburn or a Glenda Jackson?

When my youngest daughter was eleven, she and I, both avid horsewomen, participated in a cross-country obstacle event that meant something different to each of us. She was thrilled to have mastered an even higher jump, proud of having surpassed her previous record time. Joy radiated from her face as she successfully coaxed her young mare to trot through a forbidding gully of water for the first time. I, meanwhile, relished feeling comfortable back in the saddle after a lengthy hiatus, taking in the fall foliage as I rode. I had no stake in winning, or even placing. Doing a known thing well gave me the satisfaction my daughter derived from meeting a new challenge. When my daughters were teenagers I marveled at their ability to sprint through life. But I also witnessed their struggles as they pushed against the ties that bound them to family and home, seeking independence and searching for their own identities.

I have not achieved everything I set out to accomplish. Not every road taken ended in success, and on some roads I stumbled, even fell flat on this once seamless face. But now in mid-life, I know who I am and what I expect (and don't expect) of life. And I have myself off my hands (most of the time!).

Middle age can be depressing if we regret missed opportunities. If we continue to test the limits of life, we may bridle at our own shortcomings and remember our youth nostalgically. But if we are lucky, we may have learned a thing or two by middle age. There is still time to savor past accomplishments and explore new opportunities. Being over 40 (or 50, or…) is a stage in life and a state of mind. We don't write the script, but we can act the part—or not.

Loss

Crying is a Gift

I dislike sentimentality

and have always thought

that tears should be shed sparingly.

Then our 8 year-old grandson uttered

these simple words of wisdom:

"I don't like my friends to laugh when I cry.

How can I be happy again if I don't cry?"

Tears are our release

from joy and sorrow.

Like a stream

they gurgle over small stones

or gush down ravines,

ending in the universal maelstrom

of oceanic lament and solace.

Death Rehearsal

I collapsed after a strenuous hike in the wilderness of the Whitefish Range of the Rocky Mountains in Montana. I had fainted once years ago, first feeling lightheaded, then dizzy. This time it was different. It occurred without warning. I was struck with the speed of lightning before an unexpected thunderclap and dropped to the ground unable to break my fall. When I regained consciousness I was disoriented, only dimly recognizing my husband's worried face. Then I could make out other people peering down at me. "What party is this?" I mumbled. Slowly, normal awareness returned and I realized that this was no party. Emerging from total darkness, the light blinded me and I was changed.

Had I not awakened I would have known nothing about my dying. No going gently into that good night. My loved ones would have been vexed, grief-stricken, and I would not have been there to comfort them. Where the soul goes in those moments remains a mystery but certain is that my body would have been stone dead. I was startled at having been taken unawares. No red flags, no flashing ambulance lights, nobody crying, "Look out!"

The lessons from my fainting spell seem obvious. They are life-lessons. There are no second acts in death. It's too late for words of forgiveness. A tender touch can no longer be felt. An entry in my diary lamenting frustrations with a dear friend could no longer have been erased. I would have left this world unprepared.

There are few death rehearsals. But if the opportunity arises, take it to heart. Don't put off apologies, love letters, good deeds—or a gorgeous day on Glacier Mountain. Carpe Diem!

A Child Loses a Pet

Acquiring a pet in our household was never for the purpose of providing a "learning experience" for our children. We like animals and whenever the request came, "Oh, please, can we take this little kitten home," our response was, "Let's do." We always expected our children to share responsibility for taking care of the animals. When our bird Peter was given to us, it was understood that Caitlin and Claudia would take turns changing his water and bringing him fresh seeds. Without needing to be told, our one year-old Cecile found out that kitty's response to having his fur pulled was to take off in a dead run. Sitting on the floor beside him she learned to run her fingers gently through his coat cooing, "Oo-oo."

One day our girls came home from school in excited spirits, spewing out the words, "Our teacher's rabbit had babies and we are getting two." "Hold it," I interrupted. "Who said you can have rabbits? We already have a cat and a bird that we have to keep in separate parts of the house." "Mrs. B. said we could have rabbits," was their stormy reply. "Oh, please, Mommy, can we? We can put them in the garage. Mrs. B. told us all about it." "Did she?" I sighed. "Next time ask your parents first before you agree to another animal." "Okay, we will." The girls jumped up and down. "Can we go and get them this afternoon?" "Let's tell Mrs. B. in a few days and ask Dad tonight if he can build a hutch this weekend."

Building the hutch turned into a family project. By Sunday night it was ready to be put on cement blocks safely off the ground, and the girls laid on the finishing touches by painting the new roof a barn red. We even drove out to a nearby farm to purchase some bushels of hay for cooler days. The rabbits had a glorious reception in their new habitat. Even after the initial joy of owning rabbits wore off, Caitlin and Claudia would faithfully feed their animals after school, watch them graze (so they would not nip all the leaves off my blooming plants), and clean the hutch on weekends. On school days that task fell to me.

We were not sure how two males would react to each other, but they seemed content together and grew quite tame. They came running at the sound of their names. No amount of argument could persuade our 7 year-old Caitlin not to name her gray rabbit "Snowflake." Our 5 year-old Claudia insisted on calling her white rabbit "Kathy." My husband and I never discovered how the girls had chosen those names.

It was a brisk fall morning when I went out to do my daily cleaning chores. Off from school that day, the girls accompanied me with rakes and paper bags to get busy cleaning out the hutch. "Come here quickly," Caitlin called, "the rabbits have worms. Something pink is moving in the hay." "Those are not worms," I informed them, looking in, "Kathy and Snowflake have had a litter." "Oh, really!" The girls jumped up and down with joy. Caitlin had already reached in and was holding a naked, squirming baby rabbit in her hand. "It looks like a mouse," Claudia commented. "When will it open its eyes? Do they grow fur like Kathy and Snowflake?" While answering, I was contemplating what to do next. All of a sudden Caitlin cried out, "Look, Mommy, one has fallen out. It is all covered with ants. Get the ants off, quickly." In no time she was busy cleaning the baby rabbit herself. Her next concern was to get that one back with its mother. We called the rabbit pair back to the hutch. Any other day a cabbage leaf would have done the trick. This morning we had to chase them through the yard. Once inside the hutch they pushed vigorously against the door in an attempt to get back out. Caitlin was horrified to see that Snowflake seemed to trample her babies. "How can she do that to them?" she screamed. "Isn't she supposed to take good care of them?" I could calm her down only by convincing her that she was probably doing that because of all the excitement around her. It was time to leave her alone with her little ones. Being new to the experience of rabbit breeding, I decided to call the veterinary clinic. Armed with professional advice, I returned a few minutes later to determine who was the father and who was the mother, as the couple needed to be separated at once. Claudia's small white "Kathy" turned out to be the father. She solved the name problem quickly by changing Kathy into Katho but was less able to adapt to the fact that her rabbit had to be put into a separate makeshift home.

As our rabbit saga unfolded, both girls projected events occurring in our backyard onto our family situation. For Claudia that process started with the removal of Katho into his new habitat. "Won't he miss his babies?" she queried. "Wouldn't Daddy be sad if we had sent him away when we were born?" To restore her confidence in the importance of fathers in the life of the young, I did two things. At bedtime I pulled down a book on animal fathers and selected a few stories in which fathers take part in caring for their offspring. In an attempt to make the connection to our Dad I recounted the time I had gone to the hospital to have baby Cecile. Only after I came back had Daddy started to help with the caretaking. I explained that some mothers have to do the tasks first before their mates may join them. The thought that her Katho would eventually be allowed to return to his family comforted Claudia greatly.

Meanwhile, night had come. For extra protection against the cold we had covered the hutch with blankets. Throughout the evening the girls urged me to check the rabbits one more time. Caitlin worried aloud whether the ant-bitten baby would get extra milk. "Snowflake will take good care of all her babies, won't she?" she tried to convince herself. "That's what a mother is supposed to do," she emphasized one more time.

Full of excitement over the unanticipated arrivals and eager for their Daddy to return from a business trip, the girls finally dropped off to sleep. I had my own worries about the baby rabbits. The veterinarian had warned me that the mother might not accept her litter. There was a possibility that the presence of her mate had undermined her interest in her young brood. I also suspected that the damaged newborn would be thrown out of the nest. But I was still pitching for the rest. I stalled in the morning when the girls wanted to check on the babies first thing. "Let's wait until after school to look at them," I told them. It's still too cold to take the covers off. With some reluctance I looked into the hutch shortly after I sent the girls off to school. Snowflake was eager to escape into the yard. I could detect no movement in the hay and on closer examination found all the babies to be dead.

I put them in a box for burial and decided to await the girls' return from school. I had to call a friend to cancel an outing we had planned with our children that day. I explained why we couldn't go. "If I were you," she counseled me, "I would bury the rabbits now and just tell the children about their deaths. Seeing the babies dead might upset them unduly." I began to vacillate. What motivated me to carry out my original plan and wait for the children was the memory of my own childhood experiences. I, myself, had several pets that died. And I remembered well the little cemetery I had constructed for them. That they had died had saddened me, but burying them had helped me through the grief.

It wasn't easy to tell the girls the sad news. A stormy outburst of tears and rage was Caitlin's response. "I don't want them dead," she howled and then she started furiously to ripping the leaves off one of my rubber plants. Claudia stood silently, staring at her untouched snack. "I want to call Daddy," Caitlin interrupted her sobbing. And so we did. He was called to the phone from an afternoon meeting to hear a quite unexpected story. I have often wondered why they turned to my husband at that point. Both children always want to share events that are happening to them with the absent parent. That was part of it, but in this case they also expected help from my husband, as a later comment by Claudia revealed. "If you had been here, Daddy, you could have been the rabbits' doctor." One of their early beliefs was that someone, or something, must surely be able to restore the rabbits to life. The children also perceived me to be emotionally upset. I had conveyed my concern about the rabbits to them. They wanted and expected my concern, but they clearly didn't want too much involvement on my part. As Caitlin explained to her dad, "I didn't want Mommy to be sad, too." Days later she told the whole story to a friend, saying, "I could see what had happened from the look on my mother's face." A realization dawned on me. If part of a child's stable world breaks, it is important that the rest of that world remains intact. The task of the adult, I learned, is to provide answers to troubling questions and to give practical guidance. Empathizing with the distraught child is required. Since the child is not yet equipped to master many problems, she must be reassured of the adult's ability to cope.

Only after I had convinced the girls that we could not make the rabbits alive again, did they consent to the burial. "They look alive," Caitlin insisted. Even after she had touched them and felt how cold and stiff they were, she asked, "Couldn't I warm them?" We selected a spot in the corner of our yard. I handed them each a spade and we all dug a shallow hole. Caitlin interrupted her crying for the first time during that activity. Earlier I had urged Claudia to talk with her dad on the phone, but she only repeated to me in a monotone "the baby rabbits are dead… the baby rabbits are dead…" Now, shoveling the sand back into the grave, she spoke for the first time. "I'm glad their eyes are still shut," she commented, "so the sand can't get in."

The girls decorated the grave with pretty stones and pine cones and then fetched our elderly neighbor lady to show her their work. She admired the burial place and told them that sometimes out of sadness something beautiful grows. Our girls took to that idea right away and insisted on planting a rose bush on the grave. Mrs. Worthington also told them that maybe the rabbits were much better off now, being with God. At bedtime Caitlin whispered to me, "I don't care if the rabbits are better off with God, I would rather have them alive and with me."

Conflict situations of this magnitude are seldom resolved on the spot. They must be worked through over time. Our girls asked many questions in the days following the episode. Caitlin visited Mrs. Worthington repeatedly, inquiring about her dead husband, and as Mrs. Worthington related to me later, she was very interested in whether they loved each other and how often she thought about him and why anybody ever had to be taken away from people and places they love.

Children react variously to the loss of a pet. Personality makes a difference and so does age. Caitlin's outward expressions of grief elicited immediate responses. It would have been easy to overlook Claudia's silent mourning. The two ways of dealing with the same event demanded different responses from the adults. Some encouragement was needed for Claudia to express her feelings. She held them back until nighttime when I sat down at her bedside. All of a sudden she began to sob uncontrollably, and no amount of coaching from me produced any verbal explanation.

At last she was able to speak, "I'm glad I am only five. You only die when you are old." But she added, "Daddy once said that babies also die." She recalled a story my husband had told about a premature newborn. Her two assertions were only apparently contradictory. They show both her attempt to deny the fact of death by pushing it far away into old age and her identification with the rabbits. If rabbits can die and babies can die, so can I. Her first concern was for herself, the fear that death could happen to her. Caitlin, being older, was more worried about the durability of relationships, as her questions to Mrs. Worthington show. When she saw the film version of Bambi, she was inconsolable over the death of the fawn's mother. Fear of the loss of or separation from a parent seemed of primary concern to her. Both children showed an increased need to be physically close to one of us during the days following the death of the rabbits.

The teacher who had given the girls the rabbits now gave them some advice. "There is renewal in life," she told the girls. "Your rabbits can have little ones again." For the coming weeks that is what we hoped and prepared ourselves for—the next litter! Unfortunately the story did not have the happy ending we anticipated. In spite of all our careful preparations, Snowflake would not accept her young.

We went through another burial and more explanations. Help finally came from an unexpected source. A student learning to become a zookeeper persuaded the girls to give him their rabbits. It was hard for them to bring Katho and Snowflake to their new home, but to our amazement they parted from them after the student told them he would find out for them why Snowflake had not been a good mother. "I'll get to the bottom of the problem for you," he reassured them.

Katho and Snowflake are not forgotten by our girls, and the story of the death of their babies is told again and again. But comfort came from the assurance that parents, teachers, neighbors, even incidental acquaintances, took children's puzzling questions seriously and tried to come up with answers to them.

Turn Down the Lights Gently

Funerals in Germany draw large crowds. Maybe it's because we're summoned by mail. A black-bordered envelope alerts us. We take a deep breath and open it. The name and dates of the deceased, a Bible verse, lists of family members and information about the funeral are engraved on ivory-colored stationery. The rim of the paper is black.

When my mother died, it was as if an international bird sanctuary had opened its gates. Such a mixed lot, our family. Neighbors, friends and acquaintances, too, heard the call. It was, after all, not an ordinary funeral, but the leave-taking of a Countess. A parliament of owls was already present. They lived in the same assisted-living residence as Mother and had shared in her illness, watched her decline. They were wise to grieving.

A detachment of ducks and a gaggle of geese flocked to the funeral. They knew Mother from the grocery store, the pharmacy, the knitting circle, the Titled Ladies Auxiliary. From America and Africa casually dressed foreigners drifted in, conspicuous among the black-clad local crows. The strangers were like a flock of birds blown off course at the *Inn on the River* with no televisions in their rooms and with keys that made scraping noises in the rusty iron doorlocks.

Old, old friends, some with feathers missing and others wearing dark suits with frayed cuffs and shiny elbows, patches of skin showing through the down, arrived at the train station with large hats and small suitcases. The two taxi drivers on duty were out of breath from flitting back and forth.

Nieces and nephews fluttered in, perky hens and red roosters, squawking and flapping their wings. There were even a few curious magpies in search of shiny hand-outs. Only I knew that there would be no leftovers. Mother had willed everything to her beloved American grandchildren, including the gold-framed, gloating ancestors who, I suspected, might step from behind the glass and join the company. They had seen it all before.

Within this aviary were the truly bereft, my children among them. They resembled awkward fledglings, unaccustomed to sadness, new to loss. The first lines, fresh tiny wrinkles, appeared around their innocent eyes, their smiling mouths.

Whatever the ilk, they all came. They stayed and witnessed and listened to the story of a gentle death befitting an aristocratic life. Mother died the way she had lived, a Countess.

She had looked regal. She walked straight-backed and held her head high as if in stern reproach. She always donned hats like the Queen of England and dressed with graceful elegance in sedate tones of deep greens, blues and browns. She was a prim, old-fashioned beauty with real blond hair before it turned silver-white with a single stroke. Her eyes were dazzling like the sun she worshipped, and blue like the cornflowers she adored. She extended the cigarette she always had lit in an ebony holder between fine-boned fingers, showing off her ring, a ruby set high in spikes of white-gold.

Mother should have been given a medal for grooming, for I never saw her unkempt. Even in the World War II airraid shelter, she wore pearls. Her given name, Maria, was used by intimates only. She was affectionate with the ones she loved and comfortable with her body, but she detested informality and bad manners. She understood why the English would take tea under a merciless sun, never shedding their black gloves with white-stitched seams, to dab beads of perspiration from their brows with monogrammed starched linen handkerchiefs. Appearances reflect attitudes. Mother kept up appearances and adhered adamantly to family rituals. "Tradition endures like a hardy desert plant," she once said, "it will survive in the most inhospitable terrain."

Mother endured grave losses. Men adored her and she took advantage of her natural beauty. She flirted shyly and dated with reserve. But no men stayed. Life is blind to personal charms. Loneliness was to be Mother's lifelong companion. Her father, whom she adored, left the family when she was seven, and she lost two brothers and two husbands in the war. Today they look out from yellowed photographs in pressed uniforms, with confident smiles, joining the ancestors, forever young.

At 27, Mother was driven from her estate in Silesia during the Russian invasion to settle in West Germany, a widow with two young daughters. She endured mostly in private and kept her thoughts in clouds of proper silence. But occasionally there were outbursts when she would blame the world and her children for her fate, with a wail of woe, a flood of tears. She was never able to build a new life. Like a sandcastle, her dreams crumbled and washed away. But at all times she clung to our hearts.

Mother was brought up at a time when women were well educated in private boarding schools but were expected to become wives and mothers. She felt betrayed by her daughters' independence, moving to Africa and America, becoming professionals, living with different partners. Mother earned some money selling needlework, but her scant funds were supplemented by contributions from her children and wealthy relatives. All the while she stiffened her back to fate and held on to a vanished lifestyle, her elegant wardrobe, her classy furniture, her refined manners, and many an ancestral cobweb.

And babies. Babies, her own, mine, my sister's and then the grandchildren and great-grandchildren, always fitted perfectly into the shape of her life. All children slept peacefully in the cradle of her ample arms, and holidays in Mother's Germany were fairytale adventures. Children were Mother's bridge between the generations, her hope beyond life's disappointments.

Mother was a victim of an unfair fate. But as a magician of appearances she became the master of her death. As far as I know, she never contemplated suicide but she determined the course of her dying. She had a simple belief in a heaven above, her reward for enduring earthly troubles. And she did not fear death, "Death is not evil or frightening, just the end of a difficult life." And Mother hoped there would be some use for her knitting in the beyond! Despite being of high birth, she had no intention of resting her nimble hands.

Mother used to come to America for extended stays. "It doesn't pay to travel so far for just a few weeks," she insisted. She made her last journey to this country one July for her 80th birthday. Bone cancer had invaded, deeply tormenting her, and she had lost her mobility to a wheelchair. But she celebrated like the proud matriarch she was, demanding everyone's full attention.

That December I began making yearly visits to the historic spa of Bad Arolsen where Mother lived in a retirement community. I relished my homecomings. It was the time of the Nikolaus Markt when the aroma of Lebkuchen, Advent wreaths, spiced wine and dripping candle wax wafted from the street market right into her apartment. Mother loved this festive season as much as I do. But she was in pain and had no time for the sorrow she saw in me as I watched her suffer. Her decline dragged on for three long years. Our relationship had been wracked with omissions. These last years allowed for second chances. It was 1999. The cancer had spread to her spine and she was on a morphine drip around the clock. She was delighted to see me and kept me busy buying and wrapping Christmas gifts. For long hours I sat at her bedside, knitting, talking. We moved entirely in the moment, looking neither forward nor backward. Those were full, warm days.

The time came for me to return home. Mother was in good spirits, but reduced to eating morsels. By now she was so thin, it was as if she had been diminished to her essence. One morning she asked for her hairdresser to have the "dullness washed out" of her hair. The ordeal left her wrung out and bone weary. It was then that she gave me a shopping list and some unusual instructions, "I'd like you to make potato pancakes tonight." My mouth watered at the thought. When I was a child, my mother had taught me to whip up batter from raw, grated potatoes, then fry the pancakes in butter until crisp, sprinkle them with cinnamon and sugar, and top them with applesauce.

Mother cheered up under the influence of crispy potato pancakes and smooth, soothing champagne. We talked quietly, mostly about the children and grandchildren. But when she held the chilled champagne glass to her left temple, I knew her terrific headaches had returned. Several times she licked her lips compulsively. Then she sank into her pillow and drew a deep breath that was almost a sigh. With a voice now brittle as a hollow egg she whispered, "No diapers. Do you hear me? No diapers. And turn the lights down gently." I swallowed. The insult of being treated like a baby had always worried her. It took me a minute to find my words but then I promised to do my best. I hoped I didn't sound as transparent as I felt.

Mother was at odds with my sister, a nurse. But she instructed me, "Call your sister. You'll need her." Then she deliberately set her jaw, gumming her lips together. Her eyelids fluttered like tiny bird wings, and then they shut down. She never opened her eyes again. Distressed, I called my sister and Mother's personal doctor. They both arrived within hours.

"Your mother and I talked about her dying," the doctor said calmly, and turned up the morphine drip.

For the next ten days my mother's breath was a rattle, then a flicker. Her strong heart opened and closed like her firm, dappled hands, fist, palm, fist, palm. Finally she curled her fingers like a flower about to rest for the night. My sister and I massaged her bluing feet, then slipped on woolen socks. We watched over her as people came and went, relieving us for a meal, a breath of fresh air, a couple of hours resting on the couch. It was time to turn down the lights, light the candles, play music from the old days. Her plump cat "Tiny" who once had been a scrawny orphan kitten, used Mother's chest as his cushion and slept.

How long had it been? A couple of minutes? My watch ended at 2 am. I woke my sister who emerged slowly from deep slumber. Then I curled up on my sleeping bag. I had not been there long when I heard a thump as Tiny jumped to the floor and meowed. Startled, I leapt up, rushed to Mother's bedside and placed my ear to her lips. No quivering. Not a single puff. She lay still, as though carved. My mother had slipped away within minutes, between watches, silently and alone. For the duration of a just a few flutters of my heart, I cocooned her body in mine.

Then I woke the rest of the family. My daughter Claudia had arrived the previous night. My sister led us through the ritual of washing and dressing. We chose a white silk dress with lace and ruffles, luxurious as any bridal finery. Claudia had bought it for Mother for her 80th birthday in America. Preparing my mother for burial was an act of love, a farewell that yielded the comfort of ancient practices. When we were ready for the funeral director to be called, I went to the windowsill and cut all the orchids she had so lovingly grown. I placed the bouquet, a scented crucifix, under her folded hands.

It snowed, had been snowing for days. The winter wind was moaning and downy flakes kept drifting down. For a while I kept my eyes on the window and the snow beyond. As the first sun rays pushed back the starless night we began to notify Mother's acquaintances among the other residents. They arrived with rolls, eggs and freshly brewed coffee, passing by Mother, kneeling a minute, touching her hands, murmuring good-byes, hugging us. The in-house nursing staff paid their respects. We had done their work and I couldn't tell whether they felt left out or pleased with us. Our doctor completed the death certificate after probing Mother as gently as he had handled her when she was alive. Then he joined us for coffee. "No diapers," I announced proudly. "Sometimes, just sometimes," the doctor told us, "the body shuts down cleanly. Your mother must have willed it." I heard admiration in his voice.

Life was still, as in a painting. The elegant furniture in the apartment had faded beautifully over the years. Even now, Mother was an integral part of her peaceful surroundings. As we ate, we looked at her resting on the daybed, formidable and serene. Our conversations floated in her direction and we reminisced about her life. This breakfast made the room foreign to sadness and death. Yet death was solemnly present. Death gave dignity to our wake. When the funeral home director and his assistant entered wearing masks and sterile gloves, they quickly removed them before picking my mother up.

There are no beautiful deaths. There is always a vacant seat at the table, an empty place in the heart. But this was a chosen death, a gentle death, a death that did Mother proud.

That night, about to take a bath and searching for some talcum powder, I opened the medicine cabinet. There were my mother's morphine injections, another month's supply. I slumped down on the toilet seat and cried. A dear voice forever silent, a familiar face now vanished.

Mother had planned every detail of her funeral and we followed her instructions to a T. We put her favorite pillow, embroidered with tiny pink rosebuds, in her plain cherry wood coffin among a profusion of colorful flowers. "Contributions to worthy causes are fine. But I want flowers, plenty of them," she had said.

For the service she had requested summer songs, flower songs and a song about the sun. Only her authority as a Countess persuaded the stodgy pastor to allow such lighthearted singing. Mother had asked my husband to deliver the eulogy. The two had grown fond of each other, though choosing an American had been a cultural faux pas on my part. Two granddaughters sang a popular love duet. Then I had to invoke the spirits that hover in the realm between the visible and invisible worlds. As we shed tears, the newest great-grandson made sucking, smacking sounds, sweet music to my mother's ears. And as Mother had predicted, the crowd was huge, standing room only in the chapel.

The cemetery lay in deep winter sleep. It snowed as Mother was dying, it snowed during the service, and now wispy flakes tumbled down from heavy clouds as her grandchildren carried her casket from the chapel to the gravesite. These pallbearers glimmered like moving ghosts as they wound their way under white powdered trees up the path, the soft ground muting their steps. The snow was calming, mystifying. There was a mellow odor in the winter air like clean linen. The snow settled in silver-gray layers over each grave, blanketing the entire cemetery. Mother certainly would have liked the pristine orderliness of her resting place.

A traditional meal followed the burial. At the threshold to the restaurant, we shook off the snow clinging to our coats and hats, stomped our boots and wiped melting snow drops off noses and cheeks. Then we walked into a hazy curtain of heat. Plumes of steam from the round, tiled stove in the dining room obscured our faces and soaked through our garments into our hearts, drying, soothing. We consumed the rich food heaped on hot plates like hungry hunters. And we drank amber-colored schnapps in crystal tumblers. Our eyes moistened in the sea of warm bodies. We had accomplished what we came for. We had given Mother a proper escort on her final journey.

As the evening wore on we huddled together in small groups. The wise owls, the yapping geese, the curious magpies and the awkward fledglings nibbled on sweets and drank more schnapps. And we told stories about Mother. That was her obituary. We all relished these moments. Was it harvesting memories? Or reaffirming connections, some spanning several generations? Or was it the joy of being among the living? Whatever each of us felt or thought, we knew that we were honoring a tradition that transcended our individual needs.

"Turn down the lights gently," Mother had said. And so we did.

Stalingrad, a Lifetime Later

In memory of my father Gert, my uncles Hubertus, Heio, Eberhard,
my stepfather Fritz, and their countless fallen comrades.

I belong to the post-Second World War fatherless generation. I remember many roll calls in my German primary school classroom: "Father's Occupation?" "Killed"… "Missing in action"… "Disabled"…"Gone"… "Gone."

The city of Stalingrad was destroyed during World War II and rebuilt as Volgograd in the gray cement-block style of the Stalinist era. On a high hill just outside the city a statue of Mother Russia, a massive woman with outstretched arms, one hand menacingly wielding a sword, towers over town and country beyond. As we mounted the steep steps, martial music boomed out over loudspeakers from behind massive rock and concrete battle scenes, as haunting as Wagnerian Valkyries. Halfway through the climb, next to one of the numerous fountains, stands another female figure carved in stone, cradling a wounded soldier in her arms. Both statues are firmly grounded in Mother Earth but while the first signals might and fight, this one suggests comfort and sympathy, all important parts of the legendary Russian soul. Throughout our journey we were confronted with both sides of her character.

Many of our preconceived notions were confirmed during our stay in Russia and Ukraine. Or was it that, as spoiled westerners, we were most aware of the contradictions? While Moscow brims with high-priced stores, elegance, and entrepreneurship, the countryside shows signs of the old regime, sullen attitudes, resentment of foreigners, corruption, and the black market which deals in everything from human flesh to drugs, displayed in broad daylight. Even good hotels are shabby beneath touched-up surfaces. Delicious meals are served in a wide choice of restaurants, but there is no water pressure in the shower and the toilet handle comes off in your hand. In the first-class train compartment from Kharkov to Kiev which boasted of (non-existent) airconditioning, businessmen stripped to their underwear and then stood alongside us at the open windows in the corridor, only to reemerge from their compartments at their stop in jackets and ties, with traditional briefcases and new Blackberry phones in hand. The young were outgoing and helpful, and eager to try their English. But they also seemed skilled in black market dealing.

Although we were not on a cultural tour, we did visit the lovingly restored churches and monasteries which survived Stalin's purges. But the main purpose of our trip was a pilgrimage. A long time ago I promised my beloved maternal grandmother that I would find the burial grounds of Uncle Heio and Uncle Hubertus, her sons and my mother's brothers, Germans who were killed in 1943 on the Russian front. Hubertus was 21 when he died, Heio 19.

Between 1992 and 1999 the "Deutsche Kriegsgräberfürsorge," a German organization founded to maintain cemeteries of fallen soldiers in foreign countries, built a memorial at Rossoschka for the victims of the Battle of Stalingrad.

A nine-foot high wall 30 yards in diameter and bearing the names of identified soldiers, encircles the resting place of the estimated 11 1/2 million Germans and Russians lost in the winter of 1942-43. The official Russian cemetery lies across the road but as we were told, "bones from both sides mingle at Rossoschka." A mass grave, equalizer of age, ranks and nationalities. For the countless unidentified soldiers, massive granite blocks with names and dates in black lettering stand all around the circle in an adjacent open field.

We had travelled from Texas to Moscow, now making our way to Volgograd with high expectations, armed with maps, letters and old pictures. But when we asked at our hotel, and then made the rounds of several others, no one could tell us anything about the location of this cemetery. We had no luck with taxi drivers and people on the street. Even with the larger-than-life monument looming over the city, the reality of World War II seemed to have been forgotten.

Sitting in an outdoor cafe and watching fashionable young couples amble by, we felt in pursuit of a lost cause. Before giving up, we stopped one evening at *The Intourist*, a leftover from the Soviet era, the one hotel in town our guidebooks advised us to avoid. But there we met Vasily, fluent in German and English, who was well-acquainted with the site we sought. In the past he had taken German veterans and their families to these burial grounds. "Nobody has been here in a long time. Those who knew have died and the young ones don't remember." We hired him on the spot. We had found the needle in the haystack. The next morning Vasily was as punctual as the church chimes on the plaza. He brought with him a vast knowledge of the history of Stalingrad and its environs and a driver in a late-model Toyota.

What's in a name? I traced the lettering H E I O with my index finger along a deep dark groove on the hot stone. My uncle had been listed as missing and therefore his name was not on the wall but on one of the large square blocks in the meadow. I had to stand on my tiptoes to reach the top. I don't know whether it was the burning June sun or my imagination heating up but suddenly over this large field of the dead, images from old stories and faded photographs of Heio's life swirled through my mind. They blew in with the hot breeze along with the soft kites of gray-haired dandelions.

Heio was the youngest of three, my grandmother's "Sunshine." He, along with my mother Gerda-Maria and his brother Hubertus, grew up in carefree abandonment on the estate of his ancestors, Silesian landed aristocrats. He was popular in school, not so much for his grades as for his winning personality, his leadership potential, and his great sympathy for the marginalized. One of his teachers later told about the following event. Heio was on his way to school when a much younger schoolmate, wearing blazingly the yellow star on his jacket sleeve, was attacked by a gang. As they started throwing stones Heio crossed the street and without a word put his arms around the little fellow's shoulders and led him safely inside the school. Dumbfounded, the gang stood back. Heio was also known for his sense of humor. He disliked marching to war songs, so as the leader of a small company en route to the Russian front he taught his men to whistle or sing love songs instead.

When Hitler began shutting down "Jewish schools," Heio was attending a private one in Berlin. The headmaster decided to relocate to Switzerland and asked Heio to accompany him there to help

establish a new academy. Among the many friends Heio made there was Louis Guigoz, son of one of the owners of the Nestle company, and his sister Cecile, Heio's first love. The Guigozs took Heio in as one of their own. In that atmosphere of camaraderie and future promise Heio heard that Hubertus had been called up in the war draft. Hubertus had no love of war. He was a quiet and reserved man, my mother's favorite. As children they had played house together and tried their hands at cooking. Hubertus like my father had begun to study ancient languages, and also had a serious girlfriend. Despite urgings from his adopted family in Switzerland, the tears of his devoted love Cecile, and my grandmother's fervent pleas, Heio returned to Germany. "I can't let Hubertus go alone." He was soon called up too and sent to the Russian front.

Hitler was under the illusion that General Paulus's Sixth Army could prevail over the Russian Army. The German troops had entered the city of Stalingrad without much resistance. They had no knowledge of the Soviet commander Marshall Zhukov's tactical brilliance and determination to defeat the Germans. Heio's reserve battalion set up camp about an hour outside the city during the late summer of 1942, encountering a hot, dry season on the steppe. By the time the Russian winter arrived with subzero temperatures, the German troops were surrounded by Russian tank divisions and were desperate. They lacked warm clothing, food was running out, and their supply lines were cut.

When Heio was killed in January 1943 his personal belongings disappeared with him. When Hubertus died the following May, near Kiev, my grandmother received his iron cross, several of her last letters to him and a photo of his girlfriend in a small silver frame, all neatly tucked into a checkered handkerchief tied together at the corners.

At the sound of Vasily's voice I emerged from my ruminations. "Every man is first a baby, suckles at his mother's breast and then grows up with dreams, only to encounter the horrors of war. It does not make sense," he said. "Thinking about all the deaths that occurred here makes me ill," I replied.

Vasily had a plan. "Do you have more time?" he asked and when we nodded, he told the driver to speed away. Vasily knew that one of the final battles in the Stalingrad campaign had taken place near the village of Baburkin. Burned to the ground in the fighting, the village had never been rebuilt. Decades later now, its ruins lay overtaken by nature. My grandmother had received Heio's last note from Baburkin, dated New Year's Eve 1942, "Nobody will come out of this hellhole alive," he had written. "Only the memory of my idyllic childhood keeps me sane." Few did survive, and General Paulus surrendered soon thereafter in early February 1943.

We rumbled over rutted, washed-out roads, through dry ravines, along waist-high meadows. The driver got nervous and started to argue with Vasily. Until recently Russians were forbidden to travel beyond their towns of residence without a permit. We too had to share our passports to check in at hotels and carry identification in case we were stopped by the police. Vasily urged us on. Finally we halted next to a vast field of tall grasses running up to a deep gorge. The driver parked and we started to walk. Vasily pointed straight ahead, "This deep riverbed was once the demarcation line. The Germans were here, the Russians on the other side. During the night of the final battle layers of solid ice covered everything."

When we had taken only a few steps we were startled by what lay before us. Nothing had prepared us for what we saw. Rusted chunks of artillery, small piles of shovels that were used for digging foxholes, remnants of hobnail boots— distinctive German issue. And then a sea of bones. It was surreal. I stumbled over a thigh bone. Long. It must have belonged to a very tall man.

There were pieces of skulls, fingers, feet, all weathered but not gone. Over a lifetime the sands had swept through the looming grass, covering and uncovering the remains as once the snow had carpeted the footprints left by terror.

I swayed with the thick grass blades and an echo from the past resounded through the still air. The wind seemed to blow in from the four directions and the dry bones began to jostle and rattle as in Ezekiel's prophecy. And before my inner eye the bones grew layers of sinews, and flesh connected to bones and skin covered the muscles, and an army of men rose around me with shrill moans and loud howls like the lone wolves who once patrolled the tundra on bitter cold nights. I began to shiver, though it was unseasonably warm. And then I heard Heio's voice.

I am snuggly dug into my foxhole but can no longer feel my feet. I wrapped my boots in burlap before leaving the tent. My fingers are pressed around the gun barrel. They too are numb. I wonder if I can even pull the trigger. Gerda-Maria sent knitted woolen mittens. She must have patterned them after her own hands because they barely stretch over mine! I like them though. They are sky blue, not the usual mouse gray color. It's snowing softly. The flakes seem to multiply as I stare into the powdery veil. I feel like I'm in a trance. The night stretches on and I whistle to Helmut who is in the hole nearest to mine. No answer. He must not fall asleep. How can I keep him awake? I whistle again and then swallow several times. My mouth is dry but I can still almost taste the snow soup we had on New Year's Eve, which was seasoned with the last of our horseflesh. The snowflakes look like froth on the broth.

There! The first sunrays. They glide over the glaring surface and light up the nebulous haze. I have no physical sensations in my legs or arms. Am I frozen? It's quiet at Helmut's hideout and I can only just see his helmet sticking up. No movement. Without the cover of darkness I am not allowed to whistle. My eyelashes are stuck together. I can hardly make out the shapes creeping toward us. Huge turtles with feelers. Suddenly I hear crunching. These things are driving over our foxholes! I want to scream at them. Russian tanks? Why am I suddenly afraid? There must be a way to escape this moving menace. Why do I feel like laughing? This is hilarious! Opapa is having one of his famous dinner parties and Hubertus and I have been busy wrapping all the toilet seats in the castle in garlands of ivy. We worked hard all afternoon and now are hiding in a hallway closet watching the first guests enter and then quickly leave the bathrooms. Here comes Opapa to check things out. Now he is storming in our direction. He catches us by the shirttails. He has never spanked us before, but we can't stop laughing. Hubertus and I are still smirking as we hold our painful behinds. I drop my weapon and raise my arms to greet the glorious morning.

"God must have left just before the massacre at Stalingrad," Vasily brings me back to the present. "Yes," I concur, "he seems to make a habit of that." Icy rivulets of sweat streamed from my hairline down the front of my chest in the midday heat.

When Hubertus heard of Heio's death he was incredulous. "Not Heio," he wrote from the Ukraine, "not him." The brothers had met by chance only a few months before at a briefing in Kiev after having been without mail contact for weeks. Heio could always be recognized by a distinctive white lock at the neckline of his otherwise dark brown hair. Hubertus had instantly spotted him sitting in the front row of the briefing room. "Stay strong, brother," Heio had encouraged. "We *HAVE* to survive!"

Swallows fluttered like cupids over the quivering warm May landscape. The earth was melodious with birdsong and blanketed in wildflowers. Bluebells swayed dolefully in the morning breeze when Hubertus emerged from his tent, stretched toward the rising sun, and was instantly felled by a sniper. Hubertus was buried in a small cemetery in Romny and his remains later moved to memorial burial grounds on the outskirts of Kharkov.

It was not difficult to locate the German soldiers' cemetery because it is specially designed section of Kharkov's City Cemetery. Stanislaus, the hotel concierge, and his driver friend were eager to earn some extra money. Like all cabbies we encountered on our journey, this one drove with the speed of an unimpeded whirlwind. Oncoming traffic was an opportunity for a game of chicken. I closed my eyes every time we swerved from lane to lane. Accidents were common and fender-benders a frequent occurrence. Safely arrived at the cemetery, the two men stood next to the taxi, smoking. But when we set off in search of the monument where Hubertus was memorialized, they ambled along.

Maybe tracing a dead man's name calls forth magic forces. As before, the spirits started to encircle me like a dense fog. Hubertus stood tall and lanky, his bemused smile wrinkling his nose just as I knew him from pictures. Was I hallucinating again? He seemed pleased that we had found him. But his voice sounded sad:

If only Heio had lived! He was the hopeful one. He gave me such courage when we last met. I am despondent. Even the thought of my loved ones at home, my dear mother, Gerda-Maria, and Elsa can't pull me out of this slump. They have their hardships with wartime rations and worries about us and all the personal losses they have had to bear, but they cannot imagine the conditions out here. Their letters are full of love and concern but they read as if we are living in different worlds. And indeed we are! When Karl was evacuated after his legs were blown off, my tears were a mixture of relief and sorrow. Would I want to survive as a cripple? So many of our comrades have already died and we take more casualties daily. I dreamed about one of Heio's childhood pranks the other night. He always had something up his sleeve. Aunt Emma often visited at teatime. We noticed that she carried an umbrella into the drawing room into which she secretly deposited the cookies that were not to her taste. One day when her coach arrived to pick her up, and she had finished covering our faces with sloppy kisses which we could barely wait to wipe off, Heio announced at the door "It's raining." Not hesitating to notice that the sky was blue as blue can be, Aunt Emma opened her umbrella and was showered with cookies! Heio laughed and laughed. I also found it funny but stood by rather awkwardly. I am not Heio, could never be Heio. But I could live if he had lived.

When I blinked, our driver was wiping his eyes. "He was younger than I am," he said quietly. "Yes," I replied and only then did I notice that he had been reading the words of Albert Schweitzer etched into the memorial stone: "Soldiers' graves are the best advocates for peace."

We had brought plenty of film with us. But that day we had left our spare batteries behind. When our camera stopped working, Stanislaus spontaneously began to take photographs with his phone. Back at the hotel I asked if he could send prints of the pictures. An hour later he was at our door with a disk of the photos. He accepted our thanks but courteously declined our offer of payment. A shared emotional experience had transformed an event from a lifetime ago into a moving personal encounter between representatives of former enemy countries.

On our flight back to the States I resolved to tell this story of understanding across cultures which is also the story of my beloved uncles who died more than a half century ago, nearly half a century younger than I am today. The stories of the dead must be told lest they vanish like shooting stars.

He's My Brother

That was only prologue.
When books are burned,
eventually people will be
burned as well .
      Heinrich Heine 1820

The autumn air had deepened and thick mist was drifting through a Swiss valley near Lausanne. Biting winds whipped over the mountains. Madame Juliette, a slender woman, wearing tan slacks and a blue mohair sweater, her gray hair pulled back into a chignon, sat on a flower-patterned sofa in her oak-paneled study. A sturdy cardboard box stood next to her. It was crammed with loose photos, family pictures, landscape shots and vacation mementos. A fire crackled in the large stone fireplace.

Juliette's former teacher, Dr. Schreiber, was visiting from America. With bushy white hair and a mustache he bore a certain likeness to Mark Twain, but he had shrunk in stature since they last met years ago. He rocked calmly in his chair, his eyes sharply focused on Juliette. Under his steady gaze she felt like the shy student who had been dazzled by his lectures and intimidated by his kind but demanding demeanor. Dr. Schreiber had come to assemble a collection of stories and articles about his former school in Berlin and its pupils.

As they talked, Juliette's small hands rifled through a pile of photographs. With squirrel-like dexterity she picked up one picture, then another, discarding them until her face twitched with recognition. "Here," she whispered. Dr. Schreiber reached for the photo and studied it at arm's length. Then, uncharacteristically emotional, he said, "Oh, I remember Heio well. It seems like only yesterday." But it had happened a long time ago.

Dr. Schreiber began to reminisce. "Following the 1933 book burning on the Bebelplatz at Humboldt University my worries about the National Socialist regime mounted. I considered accepting your father's offer to fund a new school for me here in Lausanne, but I could not bring myself to dissolve my beloved school in Berlin." "What made you change your mind?" Juliette interjected. "It wasn't that I changed my mind. I simply waited too long and the Nazis closed me down."

Dr. Schreiber then recalled an incident involving Heio that occurred a few days before the Kristallnacht in 1939. "I was standing at the window of my study watching students cross the street on their way to the school when I saw an SS officer shove Jacob Bernstein into the gutter. Heio ran to the boy's side, lifted him up, exchanged a few words with the officer, and escorted Jacob through the door of the school. When I questioned Jacob about what had happened he told me that Heio had witnessed the incident as he jumped off the streetcar at our stop. He ran over to help Jacob up. As Heio brushed Jacob off and straightened his cap, the SS officer turned on him. 'Judenfreund,' eh? he demanded menacingly. Heio replied, with his disarming smile, 'I am Baron von Lüttwitz, officer, and this is my brother.'" Dr. Schreiber pondered Heio's remark momentarily before continuing. "The boys did somewhat resemble each other. Both were trim and had chiseled profiles. However, Jacob had begun to affect a slouching and shuffling gait whenever he spotted black jackboots or men in dark uniforms. Fear had seized him after his epileptic brother was forcibly institutionalized by the Nazi "health authorities" and he had witnessed his father, a respected jeweler in town, being roughed up by a street gang shouting anti-Semitic slurs. Jacob admitted that he was astonished that, after hesitating for a moment, the SS officer had let the matter lie and walked away." "It is curious, don't you think?" Juliette asked. "Yes and no," Dr. Schreiber explained. "The Nazis both loathed and admired aristocrats and still handled them with kid gloves in those days. It was in the wake of this incident that I contacted Heio's mother, a Christian Scientist and pacifist, to seek her permission to ask Heio if he would like to join me in establishing a new school in Switzerland." Dr. Schreiber mused, "Heio was a born leader with a sunny disposition and compassion for others. He was always eager to help but never ingratiating. I knew he would set a perfect example for my school."

Juliette knew this part of the story well and her cheeks flushed as she broke in. "And Heio accepted your invitation and came here for a few carefree years. We studied together, rode our horses through meadows at dawn and dusk and, wonder of wonders, we fell in love. Heio was in my older brother's class and was often invited to our home. My parents sometimes interrupted our adolescent conversations with their worries about what was happening in Germany. But we were young and optimistic about life. They also often opened their mountain chalet to us and a group of friends from school on weekends. It became Heio's favorite place in Switzerland. He was always full of vitality and good humor at the chalet."

"Were there ever signs of a change in his mood?" Dr. Schreiber asked. "Not at first," Juliette replied. "He did make regular visits home to Germany. He had a married sister and an older brother there. Upon his return from those visits he sometimes seemed distracted and gloomy. Then, when his brother-in-law was killed in France in 1940, he began to question whether it was right for him to remain in relative safety in Switzerland. We were startled. We knew that Heio's older brother Hubertus had been drafted when he graduated from boarding school at Castle Salem. Serious and reclusive by nature, he was not cut out to be a soldier so was initially assigned to a desk job.

Heio described his brother to me as quite different from himself. But he asserted that they had been very close from childhood on. Heio was the gregarious one and full of mischief. I remember sitting around a campfire near the chalet one evening as he told us stories about how he often coaxed his brother into various fooleries. Once, while guests were arriving for an elegant dinner at their grandfather's estate, Heio took Hubertus with him to cut long strings of ivy from the walls of the manor house which they then proceeded to wrap around the guest room toilet seats. Their grandfather dearly loved the two boys but that night he gave them a whipping with his riding crop." Juliette laughed as she recounted this story. "Heio often had some such prank up his sleeve".

"While Heio wrestled with his qualms of conscience," Dr. Schreiber interjected, "I was getting ready to leave for America. Your father had it all arranged. I now loved my school in Lausanne and stayed as long as I dared. But Switzerland no longer seemed safe in 1942. Late that summer Heio was sitting in front of me, stooped forward, his head buried in his hands, telling me about his decision to return to Germany for good. Hubertus had been sent to the front. 'He is my brother,' he sighed, 'I cannot abandon him.' Heio did not even respond when I implored him to emigrate with me to America."

Juliette was now in tears. "We all tried. My parents even attempted to bribe him by holding out the possibility that he could join our firm. We reminded him that he would be drafted as soon as he crossed the border but he only shook his head. 'I must go, Juliette, I simply must.' A single weekend remained before his departure. I can't describe it, it's too personal!"

"Please, Juliette, do try. It is very important. My editor, that youngster Jacob who is now a successful publisher, is waiting for Heio's story which will appear in print along with a few other recollections soon after I return."

Juliette let the moment pass, then took a long breath in and out and began to speak as though in a kind of reverie. "In late summer our forest teems with delicious wild blueberries, and bluebells sway in the balmy breeze in the meadows. The days are pleasant and the nights refreshingly cool, often crisp enough for a fire in the cast-iron stove. We had hiked up to our hideout, my parents' chalet. Heio was splitting wood for the evening fire when I snapped this last picture of him, shirtless, his blond hair tousled, axe swinging high above an upturned block of wood. In retrospect an awful omen, but at the time I could only admire the well-sculpted body of my first love. After a simple supper with milk from the fat meadow cows, bowls filled to the brim with blueberries we had picked that afternoon, and crusty brown bread with chunks of cheese, he brought a bottle of wine to the steps of the chalet. As we sipped the wine, bells from the village below began to ring. Like wedding bells, I remember thinking. We listened and held each other tight until the sounds no longer echoed through the mountains, and night enveloped us."

The rest of the story is a sad memory. Heio left Juliette and Switzerland and, as was foreseen, was drafted soon after he reached his homeland. Like his brother before him he was deployed to the Russian front. By sheer coincidence they met one last time. Their units had been stationed in proximity to each other near Kiev for a short reprieve from the fighting. In the mess hall Hubertus spotted Heio from behind by the white lock of neck hair that had marked him from childhood. Flinging their arms around each other, Hubertus gasped, "What are you doing here, Heio? I believed you safe in Switzerland." To which Heio replied, simply, "I could not leave you here alone."

As their separate companies moved deep into Russia during the extremely cold winter of 1944, their supply lines severed behind them, both brothers were killed. Hubertus was 21, Heio, 19. Heio's comrades discovered a photo of Juliette and a letter to his mother (my grandmother) in his shirt pocket. The letter contained a single message, "If it had not been for my idyllic childhood and carefree youth I could not survive this hellhole."

Evening had dimmed the study. Silence lingered until Juliette stood and walked over to the fire. Dr. Schreiber also rose and stepped to her side, gently placing a hand on her shoulder. "I thank you, my dear, for this painful, beautiful look back. May I borrow this photograph? I promise to return it to you with a copy of the book." And with that, the old teacher took his leave.

Teachable Moments Occasioned by "Small Deaths"

WHEN TO TELL, HOW TO TELL, AND WHEN TO BE SILENT

Children experience "small deaths" at all ages through separations from toys and pets and people. When life presents these situations to children, they develop ways of coming to terms with them. In the intimate family circle, as well as in a classroom setting, children need help in making sense of experiences of loss. Children need guidance but without the imposition of an adult point of view. Children often perceive a loss quite differently than we do. They are ingenious at finding channels to work through a hurtful event. It is important that teachers have their own perceptions about death, are comfortable with the subject, and are able to answer questions honestly. But even more important is listening carefully to what children tell us about a particular experience. It is our task to hear children out and to interpret for them and for ourselves what they are going through.

Children differ in their responses to loss. Some are curious, others are timid or frightened. Children also react according to their level of maturity. Anna, seven years old, and Lisa, twelve, have just listened to their mother read them a story involving a death when the conversation turns to the possibility of their own mother's death. Their mother reassures them that although she hopes to live a very long life, that death can occur at any time. Lisa breaks into tears and throws her arms desperately around her mother's neck. "No," she sobs, "you must never, never die, even when you are very old." After Lisa's outburst Anna smiles proudly at both and declares, "Mommy, when you die I'll bury you under the lilac bush in the garden. Won't that be a pretty place?" Lisa is no more sensitive a child than Anna but being at a stage of development where breaking into adolescence and independence is accompanied by the need for strong support, she cannot bear the thought of ever losing her mother. Anna, still anchored in a firm mother-child union, is not yet threatened by the possibility of separation.

Teachers must be attuned to children's emotional development. On the subject of death it is important to listen for hidden questions, uncover buried fears, and clarify misconceptions. It may also be appropriate, on occasion, to leave children alone if probing seems unsettling. Children need to learn to mourn and to find ways to recover, but the way is not always straight and there are temporary forms of denial which need to be respected.

Aunt Hannah is known to me as a person who has weathered many losses in her life and has given comfort and strength to others who were bereft. Her story may exemplify the importance of letting children guide us in deciding how much to tell, when to tell, and when to be silent. Aunt Hannah was born in a farm community early in the last century. Babies were delivered in the home and people died there as well. A farm worker was hit by lightning during harvest time, a boy killed by a runaway horse, a mother died in childbirth. Numerous small gravestones told of the early death of children. Pets died and farm animals were slaughtered for consumption. Rabbits were hunted in the fields. When death occurred, the body was laid out in the parlor for three days. Aunt Hannah recalls the odor of decomposition mingled with the fragrance of flowers surrounding the deceased. "The smell stays with you," she tells me, "like the sight of blood gushing from a butchered pig."

Aunt Hannah was ten when her grandmother died. It was customary to view the body and for the community to participate in a feast following the funeral. Children were not asked whether they wanted to take part. It was taken for granted. When the time came for the immediate family to take their place at grandmother's coffin, little Hannah refused. She had already wet her pants and been scolded by her mother. "Let the child be," counseled the girl's visiting aunt. And since there was no opportunity for lengthy discussion, Hannah's mother dropped the matter. She grieved, too, but for her the loss was not unanticipated. She would miss her mother in many ways, not least as an extra hand around the house. Grandmother had helped with many household chores and done all the darning. That's how they had found her, slumped over in her armchair. Death had interrupted her, knitting a pair of woolen socks.

Hannah's aunt took her for a walk the day of the funeral. They talked until Hannah's tight little fist finally relaxed under the gentle pressure of her aunt's hand. It was weeks before Hannah's aunt returned to the farm. When she set out to pay her customary visit to the cemetery, she asked Hannah to come along. "That child hasn't been to her grandmother's grave once," her mother commented. Later at the burial place Hannah and her aunt set about pulling weeds, straightening tendrils of wild ivy. "I know you can't hear me down there, Grandmother," Hannah suddenly burst forth with anger, "but I don't like it at all. Now nobody tells me stories, and I have to feed the chickens all by myself. "Hannah frequented her grandmother's grave weekly from then on. One day she was near tears. "I do miss you, Grandmother," she mumbled and went on, "but Mr. McNeil said, if there are too many deer they will overpopulate the forest. Maybe it's the same with old people. It would be too crowded if everybody lived forever. I'll just come and visit you here."

Several elements of denial as well as the beginning of a slow healing process are evident in Hannah's recollections. Eventually Hannah came to terms with the finality of her grandmother's death. However, what helped her at this early stage was that she was neither confronted abruptly by facts nor pushed into a resolution of her grief by adults. Her aunt intuitively sensed that Hannah needed time to work through the loss on her own terms.

To help children understand losses which they experience as they grow, it is important to discern their perceptions before guiding them. Books, films and television, as well as children's own experiences, can be starting points for discussions and, to some degree, tools in shaping opinions. There should be no taboos on subject matter. What matters is the approach.

THE IMPORTANCE OF FANTASY FOR SMALL CHILDREN

In his book, *The Uses of Enchantment*, Bruno Bettelheim takes the fairy tale as the art form which best helps children to deal with problems of growing up and interpreting the world. "The child," he writes, "intuitively comprehends that although these stories are unreal they are not untrue; that while what these stories tell about does not happen in fact, it must happen as inner experience and personal development; that fairy tales depict in imaginary and symbolic form the essential steps in growing up and achieving an independent existence." Bettelheim captures here some important meanings of fairy tales for children. We have learned from Piaget that the child's worldview remains animistic until puberty, and from Freud we know that it is the inner life that confronts the child with basic human predicaments. Only slowly, step by step, is the world outside incorporated and understood as a separate entity. Children need suggestions in symbolic form which help them transform their inner needs and struggles into thought and action in the outside world.

According to Bettelheim, several characteristics of the fairy tale make this transition easier. The fairy tale presents a conflict situation briefly and in simple terms. Since children are not yet equipped to handle ambiguity, the fairy tale simplifies dilemmas. Characters in a fairy tale are always either good or bad, beautiful or ugly, lazy or industrious. Choices are clear-cut, nothing is ambiguous as in real life. "Presenting the polarities of character permits the child to comprehend easily the difference between the two, which he could not do as readily were the figures drawn more true to life, with all the complexities that characterize real people." The child can thus identify with a character in a fairy tale and learn to make simple choices which are based on the child's like or dislike and not yet on right versus wrong. The fairy tale is an art form tailored to the needs of children. Children will choose one particular story again and again over all others. Or they will choose the fairy tale which corresponds to their inner conflicts at a particular stage of development. Children do not themselves know why they are fascinated by a certain fairy tale because the struggle is carried on at an unconscious level. Bettelheim warns us repeatedly not to interpret for the child by pointing to hidden meanings. In doing so we risk destroying the enchantment the child derives from the story.

Fairy tales deal with the problems of life but they do it in a way that permits the child to cope and grow and not be unduly frightened. Problems of sibling rivalry are depicted in Cinderella, the changes of adolescence in Sleeping Beauty, and separation from parents in Hansel and Gretel. Themes of marriage and old age and death are also dealt with in fairy tales. A fairy tale always has a positive ending. This strengthens children's budding ego and encourages them to take on the unavoidable difficulties of life at a time when a more realistic viewpoint might undermine their still shaky self-confidence. It assures the child that everything will turn out alright in the end.

Adults may be troubled by what seems to them the "unreality" of fairy tales. What is the difference, they ask, between a fairy tale and telling a lie, such as "The stork brought the baby?" Bettelheim responds that the problems of the inner life are timeless for children and that we are not lying when we allow them to develop according to their timetable. Children do not begin with an abstract understanding of things and acquire objective thinking over time. The emotions and the unconscious dominate the perceptions of childhood, and the world is experienced only subjectively at first. Allowing children to cope with unconscious pressures in a childlike way will enhance, not diminish, their chances of developing a rational explanation of the world when the time is ripe. Fairy tales often begin with the death of a parent and almost always end with the line, "and they lived happily ever after." An uninformed view of the fairy tale sees in this type of ending an unrealistic wish fulfillment thereby missing the important message it conveys to the child. These tales tell children that forming other personal relationships can assuage the separation anxiety which they are experiencing.

"THE WOLF AND THE SEVEN LITTLE GOATS"

The following fairy tale was told to a class of three and four year-olds at a preschool. It was also told to a kindergarten class, a third grade class and a fifth grade class. Because it is not well known to English readers, I will recount it here.

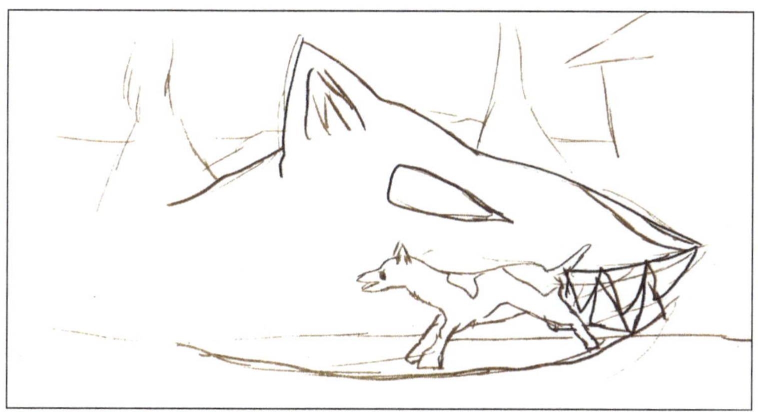

A mother of seven goats leaves them alone at home while she runs an errand. She warns the little goats to play nicely and not to open the door to anyone except herself. After she leaves, the little goats occupy themselves contentedly until a wolf comes to the door and asks to be let in. Twice the goats reject his overtures because he cannot identify himself as their mother who has a soft voice and white hooves. The wolf's voice is gruff and his paws are brown and covered with coarse hair. The wolf seeks a disguise first from a druggist who gives him chalk to soften his voice, subsequently from a baker who sprinkles flour over his paws. When he comes to the door the third time the goats mistake the wolf for their mother and let him in. He swallows six of the goats. The seventh one, the youngest, hides in a grandfather clock. Seeing the door open upon her return and discovering none of her children inside, the mother goat despairs. The sound of the voice of the smallest goat revives her hope. She fetches the little one and together they search for the wolf whom they find sleeping under an apple tree. The mother goat cuts open the wolf's stomach and rescues her children. Together they fill the stomach with heavy stones. When the wolf awakes he goes to the well to slake his thirst and the heavy stones topple him into the well where he drowns. Mother and children dance around the well, singing merrily.

Many of the symbols which appear in this story are discussed by Bettelheim. The figure of the wolf, as portrayed in *Little Red Riding Hood* and *The Three Little Pigs* is multi-dimensional. It is the stranger who beckons the goats to the door, the seducer, the world outside the self and the home, the externalization of evil the child feels when it does not obey. The wolf is the animal in all of us and, most important for our purposes here, the wolf is the bringer of separation from the parent. It is the one who tempts the goats to try independence and who finally brings death. That death is not final here corresponds to the child's understanding. Factual death is not yet comprehensible.

What is experienced by the child are forms of death, separation from parental security, and steps toward independence. The reunion with the mother at the end shows that independence is only slowly achieved and, if entered prematurely, can have grave consequences. The parent is still necessary as a shield and support in the maturing process. Death is seen here as a part of growing up. It is not the end of life in this story. Being cut out of the "womb" again, this time by the mother out of the wolf's stomach, means being reborn, entering a new stage in one's development. The wolf is punished at the end by drowning. In this way children can externalize the guilt they may feel over their efforts at separation.

The mother figure can also be understood at various levels. Suffice it here to say that she is a bridge for the child. She leaves the children because she knows that separation is necessary, but she also returns and lends her assistance as long as the children are small and need her. The youngest goat holds a special place in the story. Its example shows the child that even if it is small, it can avoid the worst fate by being smart. It also shows the child that older siblings have to endure growing pains first. For the very young, the close tie to the mother is sanctioned. Equipped with this "adult" interpretation of the story, I set out to test Bettelheim's assertion that "the 'truth' of fairy stories is the truth of our imagination, not that of normal causality" by telling the story, first, to the three-year-olds. I wish to stress that I am discussing the responses of school children to "small deaths" and not children's reactions to uncommon tragedy or the loss of a loved one.

The children listened attentively even though no visual material was used. Upon finishing the story I asked the following questions. Did you like the story? Was it a funny story? A sad story? A scary story? The answer most often given was that it was a bad story. Why? Because "the wolf came," or because "the wolf ate the goats." Whom did you like best in the story? All shouted, "The little goat." Why? "Because he is hiding." Could the wolf come to your door? This question brought the greatest reaction. All children said "no." When asked why, one child answered, "there are no wolves in Florida." Where are they? "They are way downtown." Another said, "We have two doors in our house. The wolf would come to the other door." Or, "we have a big, big house.

He couldn't come in." Or, "we would lock the house up."A final answer was, "my father has a gun, and my brother would shoot him." The children had no cognitive awareness of dealings with separation or any of the other meanings of the wolf. All was denial and defense against the wolf.

The pictures the children drew afterward tell a different tale. To the question, "Do you think that the little goats did something wrong in letting the wolf in," there was an unequivocal "no." "We don't open the door to anybody." "A stranger might give us some poison candy." "We play nicely." "We do what mommy says." "My mom always stays with us and watches us." "We are with our mom." Children who stay with sitters gave similarly reassuring answers. There was no apparent awareness of guilt. Divided answers were given to the last question. "Should the wolf have drowned?" "Yes, because he eats goats." "Yes, because he is bad." Others felt, "no, because he was thirsty." Amplifying this last answer, one little girl burst forth, "I'm getting a stomachache." There was no mention of cutting open the wolf's stomach and filling it with stones.

Figure 1

Fourteen children drew pictures after answering the questions. Two could not remember the story well. Five children, all boys, painted pictures with the wolf at the center (Fig. 1). The importance that separation seems to play at this age, particularly for boys, is overwhelming. Only one boy drew the wolf in the water, which suggests that he has come to terms with the problem. At the other extreme was a boy who drew squares all over the page and pointed to every square saying, "There is the wolf, and there he is too."

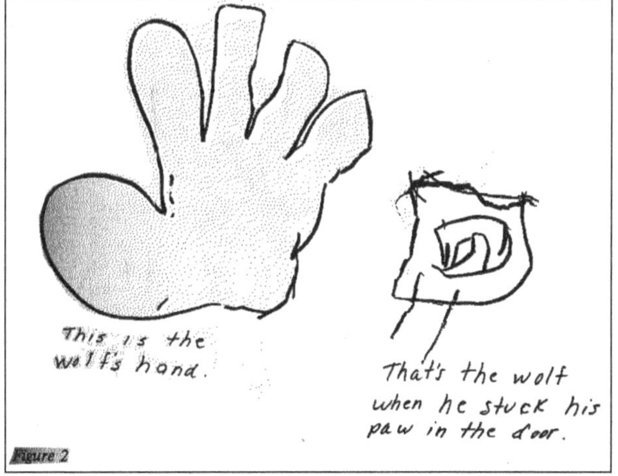

Figure 2

The most sophisticated picture was done by Josh (Fig. 2). Drawing the wolf's paw covered with flour and extended through the door opening shows that Josh unconsciously perceived the disguises a symbolic figure can assume.

The other children, all girls, had the mother goat and/or baby goat and the wolf as their theme. Girls at this age seem much less threatened by separation and still quite secure in the parent-child relationship.

Jennifer's picture (Fig. 3) shows her to be bound to her mother in a secure way but unaware of the wolf. She drew mother and baby goat. Another girl drew only the baby goat, that is, herself. Two children drew the wolf and the goats, which indicates the theme of being threatened and swallowed. Lara drew the wolf inside the house with the baby goat looming large above the scene. No mother goat is in sight (Fig. 4). As I learned later, Lara is going through the trauma of adjusting to the presence of a new baby sister. Cecile drew all three characters (Fig. 5). The picture shows the drowned wolf in the well (mastery of the conflict), as well as mother and baby goat.

Figure 3

Figure 4

Figure 5

There was some overlap in responses when I told the story to the four-year-olds but the older children gave more detailed answers. The discrepancy between verbal responses and the pictures was greater too. The children tried to outdo each other in answering the questions regarding how they themselves would handle the wolf, while in their drawings they concentrated on a variety of subjects. A slight, but interesting shift occurred in that the children came up with very active defenses against the wolf, ranging from "Putting a mask on," to "going boo!" to "I would chop his head off." Some of the four year-olds also responded to the question regarding their (the little goats') own collusion in the wolf's gaining entry by admitting that "The goats shouldn't have opened the door so wide," "they should have just peeked out," "they should have checked the wolf's paw more closely."

Guilt first becomes conscious here. When I came to the question, "Were you surprised that all the goats were alive?" the children turned the question around and asked me "How did the wolf eat the goats?" or "Why were the goats not chewed up?" Regarding the question, "Should the wolf have drowned? Should the goats have put stones in his stomach?" they asked, "How did the wolf drown?" "Why didn't he swim?" And after coming up with answers themselves, connecting the drowning to the heavy stones, one girl volunteered, "The wolf should have used his sharp claws to scratch the stomach open and get the stones out."

Questions about the father goat came up in this group. In one of the drawings a boy placed the father goat inside the house with the little goats and the mother. Another boy said, "Father goat is at work." I learned that his father is away on business a lot and that the family spent a recent vacation on the beach without him. In all the answers and the drawings, reality (as the world outside) is incorporated into the fantasy world of this fairy tale. One boy began, "The mother goat told all the little goats to get into the space ship to get away from the wolf" (Fig. 6). Another boy shows a police car waiting to pick up the wolf (Fig. 7). In another picture the well is a boat that tips over, drowning the wolf.

Figure 6

Figure 7

Details are mentioned and included in the drawings. The stones appear frequently in the pictures, as does the grandfather clock. One little girl insisted on having white chalk so that she could portray the mother goat accurately. More children at this age use all three figures, the mother, the goats, and the wolf. One boy used three devices to overcome the wolf problem (Fig. 8). There is the hiding place (the grandfather clock), the well water (which he wanted labeled "hot"), and the stones in the wolf's stomach. This is a child who had considerable difficulty adjusting emotionally to preschool and has only lately (midyear) come to like it.

The next groups to hear the story were in elementary schools. The kindergarteners gave answers not fundamentally different from those given by preschoolers, though the details become ever more elaborate as the children grow older. The discrepancy between the verbal accounts and the drawings also continues to widen. Verbally, the children in the early grades (through approximately grade three) jump on the bandwagon against the wolf, outdoing each other in their attacks on the villain. In their drawings, however, many children returned to the mother

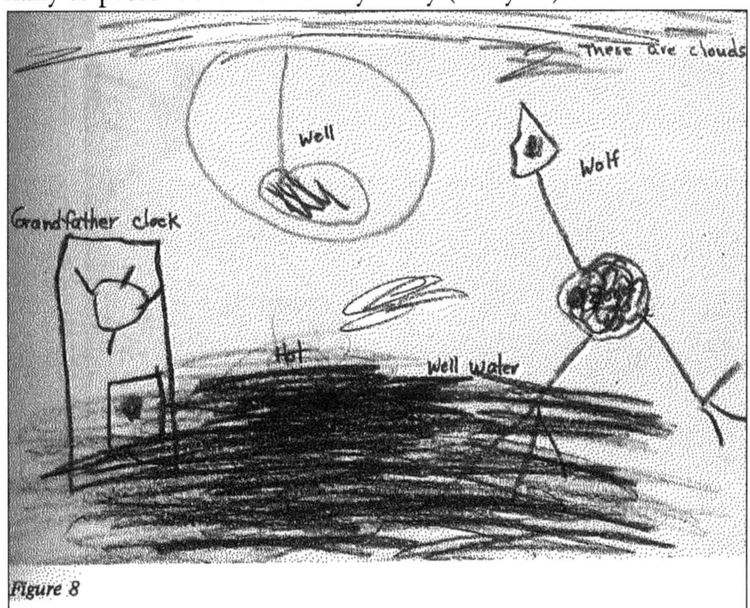

Figure 8

goat and the baby goat symbols. One kindergartener named the baby goat after herself and had the mother goat call that name repeatedly. The wolf gets drawn more and more expressively. Another girl showed the wolf's mouth full of big teeth. Means to frighten the wolf from the child's environment are used again and again. Matthew had his dog chase the wolf away (Fig. 9).

Figure 9

Children are convinced by this age that the wolf must be punished. They are as concerned about his disguises as they are about his devouring the goats. They also are more ingenious regarding ways in which the little goats might have identified the wolf. As one girl suggested, "They should have seen the flour dripping from his paw." Affections are divided between the littlest goat ("because he is smart") and the mother goat ("because she put stones in the wolf's stomach").

A big change in perception is noticed with third graders. I added a question in my discussion with this group, asking them to describe what the wolf did and then to tell me what the wolf means. Most said simply "a wild animal" or "he's like a fox." Only three of the twenty-five children attempted to translate the symbol into reality. One girl thought "the wolf could be a person dressed up in fur for Halloween." Two others likened the wolf to a stranger coming to the door.

No child expressly identified the wolf as the bringer of death, but the wolf clearly meant for many the tempter, against whom mother has erected rules and commands. One child's picture was a sequence of the deceptions the wolf used, followed by the admonishments of the mother (Fig. 10). No child said the wolf is not real or does not exist.

Figure 10   "The little goats make a mistake by opening the door to the wolf."

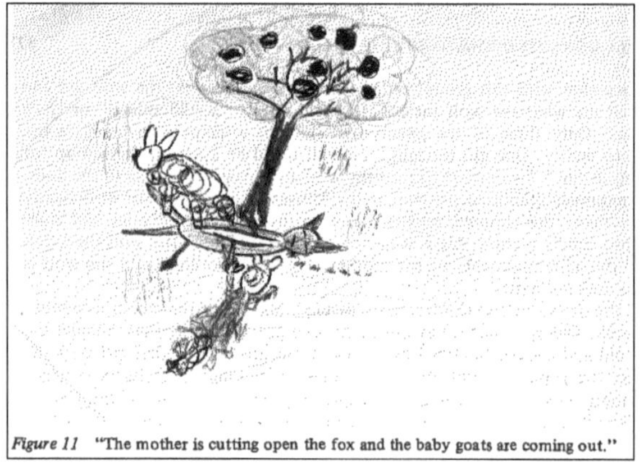

Figure 11   "The mother is cutting open the fox and the baby goats are coming out."

About the drowning, the children were divided. Many saw the stones as punishment enough. Old age came up at this point, one girl suggesting that "maybe the wolf was old and needed food and had to catch the goats." Another girl drew the wolf under the apple tree with its stomach opened, the mother (scissors in hand) standing there while one of the goats escapes (Fig. 11). I inquired of the teacher about this girl's apparent preoccupation with death and rebirth and learned that her grandfather had died only a week prior to my visiting the class. A happy ending was important to most third graders. "The story was sad, but I'm glad it had a happy ending," one boy commented. "The wolf ate the goats, but in the end they all got out alive."

After these conversations about the wolf and related matters I was most surprised when I saw the pictures. Fourteen children of twenty-five drew neither the wolf nor the mother nor the baby goat but the grandfather clock where the little goat is hiding (Figs. 12 and 13). One boy showed the little goat hiding in the television. A strong identification with the baby goat suggests that the self at this age has gained enough strength to overcome the close familial ties and is no longer totally dependent. "The little goats make a mistake by opening the door to the wolf." And later, "The mother is cutting open the wolf and the baby goats are coming out."

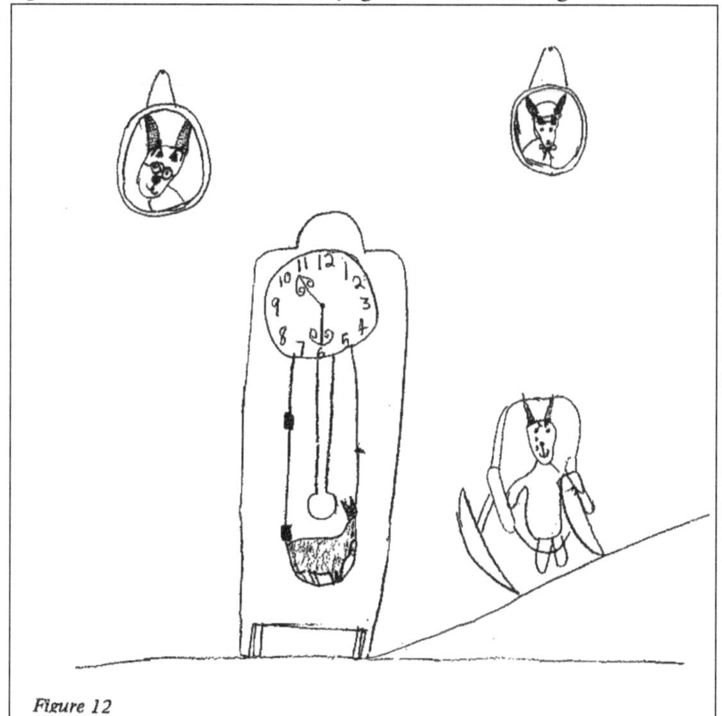

Figure 12

Figure 13

Being in charge of the situation overpowers of the threat of separation. The outside world gets explored and takes on new importance. Friendships provide an alliance against being overwhelmed by the world. The little goat suggests to the child that he can master the challenges of the world, and that the wolf—danger, loss, temptation, and separation—can be outsmarted. Tears may be shed over the death of a beloved pet, but even greater sadness is experienced when a close friend moves away. The child is still vulnerable and needs protection (grandfather clock, or another friend), but death is not of primary concern when all energy is directed toward strengthening the self and establishing a secure place in a small community (classmates, friends) outside the family. By this age, the child is also beginning to comprehend the problems of others, as one girl's picture suggests in portraying the little goat comforting a crying mother goat with the words, "Don't cry, Mommy."

As I moved up through the grades, the fifth graders exercised increased control over the story. For example, they preferred to work with a pencil over crayons in doing their drawings. Otherwise, there was little change in the responses except that they were reticent to talk about the story. I had to press them for answers. At this age peer pressure is very strong, with the result that the children fear giving a "wrong" answer and appearing foolish. There was, however, unanimous agreement that the goats were careless in admitting the wolf to their house. One boy cited the fact that a wolf does not have hooves like a goat and claimed that the little goats were negligent in not noticing this. For the first time a boy identified the wolf as evil, not just a stranger or a deceiver. Of the twenty-one children, six identified with the little goat, as shown in their drawings. Two girls drew the little goat outside the protection of the grandfather clock. One drew it outside the house. Both girls, I learned, had recently had to work through the breakup of a friendship which had left them quite vulnerable. All other pictures show the wolf very much at the center of things.

The wolf is the tempter and the wrongdoer, as shown in Andrea's picture (Fig. 14), where the wolf knocks at the door of the peaceful home of the little goats.

Or he is the deceiver, as shown in a picture of the wolf with a white paw (Fig. 15) and in another of the wolf entering the house (Fig. 16).

Figure 15

But the comment on this drawing is also revealing. Even though the wolf is present and eats the goats, the smart mother punishes the wolf by putting rocks in his stomach. In one response "The wolf knocks at the door of the peaceful home of the baby goats and gets his punishment."

"I thought the part in the story where the mother goat put the rocks in the wolf's stomach was pretty smart."

Figure 16 "I thought the part in the story where the mother goat put the rocks in the wolf's stomach was pretty smart on behalf of the author."

Figure 17 "It was nice to listen to a fairy tail instead of a composition."

In another picture the mother goat is an ally. She arrives at the sleeping wolf's side with a pair of scissors ready (Fig. 17). Birth and death symbols are mixed in several of the pictures.

Figure 18

The wolf (the bringer of death), slumbering in the shade of the apple tree, looks quite pregnant (Fig. 18). This symbolic ambiguity reminds us of the perceptions of the three-and four year-olds for whom the wolf first played a central part in their attempts at independence. Here, as there, he is the severer of ties, but now in a different disguise and inhabiting a more complex world.

MOTHER MOUSE IS DEAD

The unconscious and the emotions govern a small child's life, but reality does exist even if separated only in part from the inner world. The older the child, the more reality gains the upper hand. Mrs. Lenox did not intend that the little book, *Year In and Year Out with Pixie and Mouse*, should turn into a lesson about death for her kindergarten class. Each day Mrs. Lenox reads aloud to the class about a particular month of the year. January is about snow and an underground burrow for the mouse family. July brings a harvest of apples and peaches. About November she read:

What does this mean
the autumn crocuses ring
Mother Mouse died today.
Did she have a stomachache
or did she catch a cold
so late in the year?
The animals of the meadow mourn
and the mouse child shudders
because she is without her mother
everybody cries.
The November fog is damp
let's light our lanterns.

When Mrs. Lenox begins to read about December and Christmas, Jennifer interrupts, "Read us about Mother Mouse is dead" again. The rest of the class crowds around Mrs. Lenox and demands the same page be read again and again. The children are drawn to the subject but there are no questions at first, only the repeated demand that the poem be read. Recess brings some help. Stephen finds a dead beetle and starts poking it with a stick. The children congregate around. "Ooo," someone yells. "Leave it alone," another interjects. "It's dead." Cheryl curls up her nose, "Look at all the ants eating it." The children are simultaneously repelled and fascinated.

"It's time to come in," Mrs. Lenox calls to her class. The dead beetle and the poem about the mouse elicit a variety of reactions from the children. "Mrs. Lenox, what is 'dead'?" Erica asks. Before she can answer, Eric mumbles, "Don't be stupid. When ants eat you, you're dead. " "Is the Mother Mouse dead?" Erica continues. "Yes," Mrs. Lenox confirms. "But when will she wake up again?" "She won't, Erica." "Did she eat something bad?" It is still Erica, pressing. "Yes, perhaps she ate something that made her very sick." "But now the little mice are without their mother." Erica becomes agitated. "That's right, Erica, and that is very sad. But it doesn't happen very often. Most mothers die only after they are very old."

"How long?" John wants to know. "Until their children are grown up and can live without them, maybe even have children of their own." "How will I know when I'm dead?" Linda whispers. Mrs. Lenox explains, "Your heart will stop beating." She puts her hand over her heart. "Now," she instructs the children, "Put your right hand on the left side of your chest. Feel it? It goes thump, thump. That's your heart." She goes from child to child, helping them feel their heartbeat. "When your heart stops beating, you are dead." The class is excited. "How does my heart beat?" Eric is back with his down-to-earth questions. "Let me show you." Mrs. Lenox goes to the basin and fills it with water. The group gathers around her. "Your heart is a big strong muscle about the size of your fist which opens and closes. The water is like the blood that is pumped from your heart throughout your body." "Even into my toes?" Eric looks quizzical. "Yes, Eric, into your toes and into every other part of your body." Mrs. Lenox squeezes the water out of her fist and opens it, letting water flow back in, then presses it out again. She lifts her hand from the water. "When your heart stops pushing the blood in and out, you are dead." "Like Mother Mouse?" asks Erica. "And like the beetle," Eric chimes in. "Death is disgusting," he adds. "When you are dead, you look like a beetle." Erica seems exasperated with everyone, including Mrs. Lenox. "But I am asking you, when does Mother Mouse wake up again?"

The lines about Mother Mouse stimulated the children to ask questions about death. The subject aroused their curiosity, but the reality of death seems at best partially understood by most and pushed aside by others. Most important, the subject of death was discovered by the children and carried by Mrs. Lenox as far as the developmental stage of the children permits her to go.

FACTS VERSUS EXPERIENCE

Mrs. Douglas likes to garden. Living in Florida she finds that she can grow vegetables and flowers all year round, so she starts her school garden during summer vacation. One of the projects for her first graders is a unit on health foods, good eating habits, and balanced meals. She is pleased to have peas ready to be picked by September, and the tomatoes are also ripe. When it comes time for the tasting party, her pupils are thrilled to harvest the vegetables themselves, and even the finicky eaters taste the pea that pops out of its green casing.

The garden serves many educational purposes. The children learn the parts of plants, they press leaves for their art collections, and Mrs. Douglas explains the natural cycle of living things from birth through growth to decay. She points to a rose on her desk. "The rose is wilting," Mrs. Douglas tells the class. "Losing its petals is the beginning of a dying process. Later the leaves will dry and their edges will wrinkle." She crumples the dry, fallen leaves in her hand. "What do these leaves look like?" she asks the class. "Like Grandpa's tobacco," Raymond observes. "Like ashes," says Monica. "Exactly," Mrs. Douglas concurs, "And if we spread these ashes over some dirt, soon they will all be mixed together and we are back where the plant started, with the soil in which a new seedling can grow."

When Mrs. Douglas plants her garden again the following year, she waits until classes have begun. She realizes that the children need more involvement from the start and more responsibility for the maintenance of the garden. The children derive satisfaction from digging in the soil and sowing seeds. They faithfully water and weed and are thrilled when the first seedlings peek through the earth. Again this year the harvest proves to be the high point for all the little gardeners. Mrs. Douglas shows them the discoloration on the leaves and explains how the plant prepares for cooler times by withdrawing moisture from all exposed surfaces and finally sheds its leaves. The children have raked together a small pile. Following a rainy weekend the leaves have a strange odor and are matted together. Mrs. Douglas tells the class about decomposition, about the elements breaking down the structure of the leaves and the growth process coming to an end. She also assures the children that the bare bushes will bring forth new growth in the spring.

At home in the evening Mrs. Douglas looks through the pupils' notebooks. She ponders one drawing which bears this label in neat handwriting: "This is a dead plant." She is pleased at how much the children have learned about the life cycle of plants, but she cannot explain a feeling of slight dissatisfaction with her garden project. Clearly, the children have understood how a seed is put into the soil, grows, bears fruit, then wilts and decomposes. The children can all distinguish between a living and a dead plant. Why does she still feel something is missing? A chance incident clarifies her puzzlement. After the vegetables are harvested, Becky brings some sunflower seeds to class. "Sunflowers," she tells Mrs. Douglas, "are my mother's favorites because they really look like the sun. Can we plant them?"

A spot in the garden is readied. After all dead plants have been pulled and the soil turned over, Mrs. Douglas draws a line about two inches deep. Each child deposits a few seeds several inches apart in the furrow along the line. They cover the seeds and sprinkle water over them. As the sunflowers come up, the children watch over their plants with great devotion. Green and ready to bud, the sunflowers are greeted each day by the expectant youngsters. Then one afternoon the sun shines mercilessly on the fragile plants and by evening their crowns are drooping, their shafts bent sideways. Becky comes running in the next day. "Our sunflowers are falling over," she cries. "They are all dry." She grabs a paper cup and runs to fill it with water and bring it to her plant. Many other children follow suit. But it is too late, the damage has been done. Mrs. Douglas stands before a disappointed group, explaining how the sun, which makes plants grow, can also kill them by beaming down on them too long. "No," she reassures the class, "it was nobody's fault. You watered enough. It was an accident. The hot sun destroyed your plants and your work." The children remain listless the rest of the morning, and after school many a child glances at the devastated little plot.

To restore faith in life's continuation, Mrs. Douglas starts a new project the following day. She hands out small flower pots and new seeds. Together they begin again, and soon the enthusiasm for planting and gardening returns. Mrs. Douglas discovered that death, even in its smallest form, must be experienced if it is to have an impact. To learn the facts of the life cycle is one thing, but to live through and experience the loss of a plant into which effort and concern have been invested is quite another matter.

THE BIRD WITH THE BROKEN WING

"Mrs. Nelson, Mrs. Nelson, it's a bird. Come and look!" Peter's breathless outburst leaves little room for a reply. He is off, running back to the track field where he has spotted a sandy plumaged bird with a black crescent around the back of its neck, the right wing dragging like an anchor adrift. Mrs. Nelson glances at the power lines spanning the athletic fields before she clasps both hands around the bird whose attempts at freeing itself are feeble but frantic. "Peter, run ahead and get a cardboard box out of the front closet. Amy, Sue, Mike, help him cover the bottom of the box with Kleenexes." She follows slowly, trying not to loosen her grip but careful not to squeeze. "It's a ringed turtle dove," she instructs the class while placing the bird in the box. Amy hands the teacher her loosely knitted sweater which she spreads over the box. The dove is unusually docile. The children take turns bringing it water and dip its beak into it. The bird becomes frantic again and flutters around for a few seconds. To fill the remainder of the hour Mrs. Nelson tells the class about different kinds of doves and pigeons, which are the larger members of the same species. But she cannot hold the class's attention for long. Again and again the children want to look at the dove, and they bombard their teacher with questions. "Can we keep it?" "Will the bird get better?" "Do you think it will fly again?"

Mrs. Nelson decides to stop at the veterinary hospital on her way home from school. She tells the class that the dove seems to have broken its wing when it struck the power line above the track field. She hopes that Dr. Anderson can set the wing and tell them how to take care of the injured bird. "In any case," she instructs the class, "bring some seeds tomorrow. Maybe we can start feeding it." "Let's name it," suggests Peter. "'Little Dove'," Amy calls out. "No, let's call it 'Dovey'," is Sue's proposal. "Could it be 'Sandy' because of its color?" asks Mike. Mrs. Nelson writes the suggestions on the board and brings the decision to a vote. "The name of our little bird is 'Sandy'," she announces to the class. She is relieved when the school day has ended. The children, still in a state of high excitement, reluctantly prepare to leave for home.

Dr. Anderson is not able to offer good news about Sandy's condition. "It's not the wing alone, I'm sorry to say, Mrs. Nelson. The bird has suffered internal injuries as well. The kindest deed I can perform is to put it out of its misery." Mrs. Nelson, feeling miserable, nods her consent. "There will be no charge. I'm glad you brought it in." Dr. Anderson looks up questioningly. "I need the bird back, when it's dead." Mrs. Nelson says this as someone who has made a decision which has not yet come fully to consciousness. Dr. Anderson's puzzlement about Mrs. Nelson heightens. He has treated many of her pets in the past and she always seemed a reasonable young woman to him. "Yes, I need the dead dove back," Mrs. Nelson says more steadily than before. "I left my class with the expectation of having a wounded animal to nurse back to health. I must not rob them of the only way I know to get them through their disappointment, and that is by having them take part in Sandy's burial." "It's up to you," Dr. Anderson replies. "If you'll step out into the waiting room, I'll hand you your box back in a moment. Remember, the bird will be stiff by tomorrow. You'll have some explaining to do." "I know. Thank you, Dr. Anderson."

It was not easy to face the class the next morning. Mrs. Nelson waited until everyone was seated before bringing the box containing the dead bird into the room and placing it on her desk. "Children, our bird had been hurt inside its body and it was suffering a great deal. It is dead now, and I know how sad this will make you. But if you try to think of Sandy first and then your own feelings, I think you will agree with me that putting the bird out of its misery was the kindest thing we could do for it." After a moment of stunned silence Peter bursts forth, "Couldn't the vet have given Sandy a shot? Why did he have to kill it?" "Don't be angry with Dr. Anderson, Peter. I know that if there had been a shot that could have saved Sandy, Dr. Anderson would have given it. A veterinarian has chosen his profession because he cares about animals. He wants to help them get well. But he can't always do that." Heads sink to desktops, and a pin could have been heard dropping. "Would you like to see Sandy before we find a place to bury it?" Mrs. Nelson asks the children. They all file past the little box and glance inside. Amy asks, "May I touch?" "Of course," Mrs. Nelson replies, "that is a kind way to say goodbye." Amy's fingers glide over the dove's head and wings. "You expect it to move any minute, don't you?" "Yes, you do," is Mrs. Nelson's response, "but Sandy won't move anymore." Sue burst into tears. "It won't be able to fly again."

It is time to find a gravesite. Mrs. Nelson realizes that continuing to talk at this point will only heighten the tension and deepen the sorrow. The children walk out silently, but at the fence of the schoolyard they begin to argue over where the best place for Sandy might be. Mrs. Nelson wants to involve as many children as possible, knowing that participation will help them work through their sadness. One child holds the box, another digs the grave, another places Sandy in the excavated hole. Several sprinkle dirt over the box, and then they are dispersed in several directions to find pretty objects such as flowers and stones to decorate the grave. "We won't forget you, Sandy," Mrs. Nelson closes their little ceremony. "Even though you were with us just a day, you made it a day that all of us will remember for some time to come."

The story of the bird with the broken wing does not end here. The bird's death stirred many questions in the minds of the children. The following morning Peter kicked over a box of study sheets standing next to Mrs. Nelson's desk. It was the kind of box the children had buried Sandy in. "I don't like it that Sandy is dead," Peter mumbled. Mrs. Nelson guessed that other children also felt this way and decided to devote some time to their concerns. "Write something, anything you would like to say, about Sandy," Mrs. Nelson instructed the class. "If you want to go to the library and look up details about the pigeon and dove family, you may do so."

There were many moving accounts of Sandy's death, but Peter's story is representative. "Sandy was a dove that flew into our schoolyard and hit a high wire and broke a wing. I found it. I wanted to keep it and love it. Doves are birds of peace. In the dictionary it says they are gentle and pure. A dove is the emblem of the Holy Spirit. Sandy was a pretty bird. Its color was like sand. If I were Sandy I wouldn't want to die. I am glad I'm not Sandy. I believe Sandy still flies through the sky." The children want to hear each other's stories and listen with great interest. Mrs. Nelson comments and explains, reassuring them that, for them, death lies in the distant future. Whereas she had previously found it necessary to convince the class that it was merciful for Dr. Anderson to put Sandy to death, she now had to shift attention back to Sandy and away from the children's identification with the bird.

Two other small episodes occur. Mrs. Nelson customarily observes the children at play and it comes as no surprise to her to see Rachel and Sarah acting out Sandy's death. Rachel, spread out in the sand, holds her fingers in a cramped position much the way Sandy's foot had looked. Sarah walks around her, gently straightening her arms and legs. When she succeeds, she exclaims joyfully, "You can move again." Watching the two girls, Mrs. Nelson is glad she did not suggest role playing, as she had contemplated.

Children will act out events that are unconscious or too painful to express verbally. Or, as we noted earlier, they may draw pictures of what they cannot yet say. In playing out a drama, conflicts are externalized and, once external, they become less threatening. Young children, who have difficulty putting themselves in someone else's place also play out fantasies in numerous ways. Mrs. Nelson remembers her own five-year old daughter stuffing a pillow under her play shirt and acting out fantasies of pregnancy and birth. The initiative for acting out inner events at an early age is best left to the child. Adult suggestions such as, "You be Dr. Anderson" constricts the child's imagination.

At about the third grade level children begin to identify with others, close friends or a grandparent. But even such identification is still largely a projection of self. The other person is primarily a support and buffer. At about fifth grade level, children are capable of working through events by role playing suggested by adults. By this time children are able to empathize, to imagine someone else's experience for themselves.

When Mrs. Nelson catches Richard and Scott digging up Sandy's grave several days later, she can hardly hide her anger. Taking the two scoundrels by the scruff of the neck, she trots them back to the classroom, plants them in their seats and asks, "What were you two up to?" The rest of the class is suddenly very attentive. Wrongdoing creates an atmosphere of excitement. "What were you doing?" Mrs. Nelson becomes insistent. The two conspirators look sheepishly at each other, unable to suppress a smirk. "We wanted to see what Sandy looks like now," Scott confesses. "Ooo, gross," several disapproving sounds echo through the classroom. "You guys should be ashamed of yourselves," Amy admonishes. "And what did you find?" Mrs. Nelson asks, having regained her teacherly composure. "Goofy stuff and lots of tiny bones," Richard blurts out. Pride resonates in his voice at the discovery that has been made, and Mrs. Nelson does not fail to register the contentment in his look, a satisfaction that comes from pursuing one's curiosity. "I could have brought some in, but you wouldn't let us finish," Richard continues, "The bones are smaller than chicken bones."

By now it is clear to Mrs. Nelson that the two boys did not perceive digging up Sandy's grave as a defilement, as an adult might. She sees her role as teacher in two ways.

First, she must respond to the children's curiosity. So she gives a short talk on the durability of bones and how explorers sometimes find the bones of people of bygone ages in their excavations. "It is our bones and teeth that survive longer than any other parts of our body." She also has to explain a custom to the children that has been invented by society to protect the grave against the curious. She tells of grave robbers who wanted the jewels that had been buried with the dead and of bodies exhumed for medical study. She tells them about the sacredness of burial grounds in societies where people believed that the spirits of the dead inhabited graveyards. "And even today," she continues, "the cemetery can serve people otherwise busily involved in everyday activities as a quiet place where they may go to remember someone who has died. Not that we should not think about the person wherever we may be, but the graveside is a special place at which to think and feel." "I know, I know," interrupts Becky, "we often visit my grandmother's grave. She made fresh brownies when she was alive." "Yes, Becky," Mrs. Nelson wraps up her little talk, "we remember people by the things we did with them or the things they did for us. Graves are just one possible place to recall them. We might think of Sandy when we see a bird flying, but it is also comforting to have a place where we know it lies buried." "Where its bones lie," Richard mumbles, a remark which Mrs. Nelson graciously passes over.

THE INSTRUCTIVENESS OF IMAGINATIVE LITERATURE

The Yearling by Marjorie Kinnan Rawlings, is a book about relationships which range from little Jody's ties to a particular place in rural Florida, his attachment to his parents, especially his father, interactions with neighbors, his friendship with the crippled and demented boy, Fodderwing, to his bond to the foundling, the fawn Flag. It is also a story about growing up, and the title refers not only to the young deer but to young Jody as well, as a remark by the father to his son at the end of the book reveals, "You've done come back different. You've taken a punishment. You ain't a yearlin' no longer". For Jody, growing up means working through those many relationships and assessing their meaning. He experiences the value the land holds for him through hard, satisfying labor. He learns from his father through imitation, and their relationship goes through tests of trust. After a year of painful maturing, Jody is able to take his ailing father's place on the homestead. Through living and working with his neighbors Jody sees that even uncouth and rowdy folk are stricken by sorrow and hardship. Twice Jody must deal with the breaking of an important relationship, the death of Fodderwing, and the killing of his beloved fawn.

The tone of the friendship between the two boys resounds in the joy of one of their meetings. "Jody saw Fodderwing hurrying toward him. The humped and twisted body moved in a series of contortions like a wounded ape. Fodderwing lifted his walking stick and waved it. Jody ran to meet him. Fodderwing's face was luminous". Jody, who does not find his friend's body repulsive, is able to enter into Fodderwing's strange, wondrous world. Sharing a love for animals, they tend and play with the various pets Fodderwing has acquired. Then one day, when Jody comes to show Fodderwing his new fawn, his friend is dead. "Like as if you blowed out a candle", an older brother informs him. The sudden news numbs Jody. He feels nothing at first, "no sorrow, only a coldness and a faintness. Fodderwing was neither dead nor alive. He was simply nowhere at all." When he confronts his dead friend, laid out on a bed, he is frightened. He wants to escape the terrifying scene, because that waxen face does not belong to his Fodderwing.

Three experiences help Jody over the shock and sorrow. Fodderwing's brother encourages Jody to say something to his dead friend. "He'll not hear, but speak to him." Jody whispers "hey," and suddenly the paralysis is broken. Jody understands that "death was a silence that gave back no answer." But Fodderwing has become familiar again. Next, he is given a task, to care for Fodderwing's pets. Even though he does not feel the joy he felt at sharing the task with Fodderwing, he derives comfort from doing what his friend is no longer able to do. He is also instructed to help Fodderwing's mother with her household chores. The best comfort comes, however, from his fawn to which he briefly returns and for which he asks when it is his turn to sit the night vigil with Fodderwing. Once again Jody is near panic when he is left alone at the deathbed, but Flag keeps him company and Fodderwing is not so frightening to look at when an image occurs to Jody. "When he leaned far back, Fodderwing looked a little familiar. Yet it was not Fodderwing who lay under the candlelight. Fodderwing was stumbling about outside in the bushes with the raccoon at his heels. In a moment he would come into the house with rocking gait and Jody would hear his voice. He stole a look at the crossed crooked hands. Their stillness was implacable. He cried to himself soundlessly."

After the burial, Jody is given "Preacher," the lame redbird, as a remembrance. The death of Fodderwing is a sad experience for Jody, but the death of Flag evokes an existential crisis. Flag is Jody's companion from the day he finds him, and even at night the fawn is at his side. As Jody put it, "he and Flag were free together." To Jody's mother, Flag was always a nuisance. Full of curiosity, he had often come to her table uninvited. As a yearling he is forbidden to enter the house because he has grown too big and restless. Jody tries to keep the fawn out of mischief, but one night Flag tramples the tobacco seed bed. He swears to his angry parents that it will never happen again. Then one morning when Jody inspects the young cornfield, he sees that all the delicate sprouts have been pulled up. He detects Flag's sharp hoofprints and knows who the offender is. After a fearful debate, Jody's parents give him one last chance. Jody is allowed to build up the fence around the field and plant again. But after all the hard work, Flag clears the new fence without trouble and again pulls the shoots up by their roots. Jody's father tells him to take the yearling out into the woods and shoot him. It is a choice between that and going hungry. All day long Jody thinks of alternatives to killing his beloved deer but none are workable. He returns at night, having been unable to carry out his father's order. His father, who is bedfast, tells Jody's mother to shoot the deer. She aims, fires, and wounds the animal but does not kill him. Flag topples into the sinkhole, a familiar rendezvous point with Jody in happier days. Jody has to finish the botched job so that his fawn will not suffer. The deed accomplished, "Jody threw the gun aside and dropped flat on his stomach. He retched and vomited and retched again. He clawed into the earth with his fingernails. He beat it with his fists. The sinkhole rocked around him. A far roaring became a thin humming. He sank into blackness as into a dark pool."

Jody feels that his father betrayed him. Nothing matters now but getting far away. His odyssey on the river is an exhausting one. He encounters loneliness and discomfort and terrifying hunger. Found unconscious from starvation, he is brought back to the shore of his island by a passing boat. Seized by homesickness, he makes his way back and is welcomed with relief and joy by his father, who knows what a despairing road his son has traveled. "I've wanted it to be easy for you. Easier'n 'twas for me. A man's heart aches, seein' his younguns face the world. Knowin' they got to get their guts tore out, the way his was tore. I wanted to spare you, long as I could. I wanted you to frolic with your yearlin'. I knowed the lonesomeness he eased for you. But ever man's lonesome. What's he to do then? What's he to do when he gets knocked down? Why, take it for his share and go on." In his exhausted sleep the first night back home Jody answers his father, in a way. "He did not believe he should ever again love anything, man or woman or his own child as he had loved the yearling. He would be lonely all his life. But a man took it for his share and went on."

It all depends on the relationship. Animals are not more important than human beings, but in this story the most significant relationship for Jody was with his deer. For the child even a small loss can be painful. This should stand as a warning against adult judgments such as, "It was only a pet." Whatever binds us most deeply is worth being mourned when lost.

A FIFTH GRADER IS KILLED

Most children relegate death to old age or at least to a distant time in the future. To have a death occur in their school, striking close to them, is a shocking experience for most. Thinking back on our own early school years, we tend to remember our friends but find that most other faces have faded from memory over time. Those few who died young are, by contrast, usually remembered clearly.

If you enter a school on a normal day and there is neither laughter nor mild mayhem, and every pupil walks the corridors silently, you know something out of the ordinary must have taken place. The news of Doug's death has preceded Mrs. Wright into her fifth-grade classroom. She has not yet heard when she stops in at the library to check out a book before going to her room. Miss Rex hands her the book without engaging her in the usual small talk. "What's happened?" Mrs. Wright inquires. "Doug Murphy, in Pat Smith's class, got killed in a car accident this morning. The sitter was driving a carload of children to school when a truck didn't stop at the intersection of Main and Fifth and hit the car broadside. All the children were injured, and Doug was killed on the spot." Mrs. Wright had not known Doug personally but she had seen him play ball occasionally. He was a strong looking boy with a mane of blond hair, a kid with a reputation of being a nice guy, an average student, good at sports, and not very well known around the school, except by his fellow soccer players. The atmosphere of shock that has swept through the school affects Mrs. Wright too as she stands at her desk sorting through her notes for the morning's first class period. She stacks the notes to one side and watches the children come in and quietly take their seats. "You all, by now, have heard the sad news of Doug's death," she finally breaks the silence. Tears run down her cheeks, not because of any personal association with Doug but simply because, like everybody else, she feels a deep pain at the thought that so young a person has been killed. The teacher's tears bring release to pent up emotions, and several students begin to weep. Mrs. Wright sits down. There is nothing more to say or do except to allow time for sorrow's expression.

Mike approaches Mrs. Wright's desk. "May I have permission to ask the class something?" "Of course," Mrs. Wright nods. "The funeral," Mike begins, "will be in a few days. I think we should all go." "You should give that suggestion some thought," Mrs. Wright agrees. "Talk it over with your parents. Don't feel obligated to be there, but if you decide to attend as a class, I will of course go with you. How many of you have attended a funeral before?" Only three hands go up.

The principal announces over the loudspeaker that all students and teachers are to come to a short assembly. Students will be dismissed for the day on account of Doug Murphy's tragic death. Buses will be prepared to depart the school ten minutes following the assembly. Accompanying her class down to the auditorium, Mrs. Wright overhears several conversations. Students have turned to reconstructing the accident, to the details of how it happened.

The class's decision to go to the funeral was unanimous. Mrs. Wright studies the faces of the students as they listen to the eulogies and file by the closed casket, but she can only guess at some of the hidden emotions. At this age children guard their feelings. After the day of Doug's death, no more tears are shed in public. Only Pat Smith's class goes from the funeral to the graveside. They carry flowers. The other children get into waiting cars to return home. The students that Mrs. Wright drives home are silent. She prefers that herself. The last stop is Marsha's house. Marsha slouches in the front seat and hesitates to get out of the car. "He was just a boy," she bursts forth, "just a boy like Mike or Bruce. It could have been my brother, or a friend, or me. It scares me to think of it, but death can hit anybody out of the blue. A few days ago Doug was playing ball. Today he was buried. How can anyone be safe?" Mrs. Wright touches Marsha's arm. "Death is unpredictable and often, as with Doug, we are unprepared for it. We have no warning. But we cannot live our lives in fear that death might strike us or someone we love. There would be no joy in playing or working if we were that fearful all the time. A death reminds us that we will all die, but its presence must not make us so timid that we are afraid to live. We can only be grateful to be alive. And, dear Marsha, one way of expressing that gratitude is to stand by those who suffer the pain of loss. See you tomorrow. We'll talk about this some more."

Mrs. Wright starts her class the next day with a reminder of the day past. "I'd like to have your thoughts," she addresses her class, "on how we could be most helpful to Doug's family. They have suffered a deep loss and need our support. Does anyone know the family? Who was on the soccer team with Doug?" They tell each other what they know about Doug's family, about his working parents and his two smaller brothers. "His two little brothers are on the Little League team. I played with Doug. I could be like a big brother, look out for them in a way," is Raymond's contribution. "I could just drop by and visit with his mother in the evenings. The Murphys are practically neighbors down the street from us, and she likes to garden. "Suggestions such as these spur other helpful ideas. "You see," Mrs. Wright says, "it will be important to keep up the help over the weeks to come. Right now, everybody feels for the family. Soon we will all be concerned with our own daily affairs and we'll think less and less about Doug and his family. But, for them, healing will take a long time." "I have an idea," Bruce seems excited. "Each first Monday of the month we'll talk about new ways to help Doug's family." The class nods approval. "Great suggestion, Bruce," says Mrs. Wright. "Let's make that a promise, and I'll be responsible for holding us to it. But now we have to get to work. Get your workbooks out and begin the composition on pages forty and following."

LEARNING TO LIVE WITH LOSS

Children have the capacity to love another person through their early attachment to the person who mothered them. This early bond provides them with what Erik Erikson has called "basic trust," that is, the ability to relate to the world in a positive, affirmative way. The parent-child relationship establishes a pattern according to which children later model their relationships. Children who are fortunate enough to experience such a relationship start out with the confidence that life will be good and with the assurance that they can master the world. The roots of deep and lasting attachments lie in childhood. Young people who acquire an attitude of basic trust will not only be able to attach themselves to others, they will, generally, also be capable of living through the loss of a loved one and of establishing other relationships once mourning is over.

In his work on separation anxiety, John Bowlby makes a convincing case for attachment behavior being the corollary of separation anxiety. The fear of losing the mother figure or her love begins in childhood. Every mother knows that from about eight months through five years of age children show clinging behavior, ranging from a refusal to be put to bed at night to the demand, often following a joyful outing with playmates, "Pick me up, Mommy." Running back to the mother's open arms after exploring the outside world is a familiar pattern among small children. If the child does not find adequate assurances against anxieties and also experiences the loss of parental love, personal development can be severely dislocated. Bowlby describes three phases of separation anxiety: protest, despair, and detachment. Protest is characterized by outward distress—crying, searching for the lost person, accompanied by the strong expectation that the loved person will soon return. Despair is a slow withdrawal by the child who makes few demands on others but mourns the lost person. Detachment is an expression by the child of renewed interest in his surroundings with, however, diminished interest in making new attachments. Breaking through the wall of protection children build around themselves during the phase of detachment requires both love and skill, and time must pass before they can regain the confidence to attach themselves anew.

In our study of the reactions children had to the story of *The Wolf and the Seven Goats* we learned that the basic anxiety of being separated from the source of love and security permeates every age level and is more or less well-handled at different stages of growing up. How a particular child will master the death of a friend or relative depends largely on how much anchorage his family and school environment have provided. The sorrow will not be less for such a child nor will there be a cushion against sadness, but he or she will not ultimately lose trust in life so easily, even when confronted with death.

REFERENCES

1. Bettelheim, B., *The Uses of Enchantment: The Meaning and Importance of Fairy Tales.* New York, Vintage Books, 1977, p.73.
2. Rawlings, M., *The Yearling,* New York, Charles Scribner's Sons, 1967 (1938).
3. Bowlby, J., "Separation Anxiety." *The International Journal of Psychoanalysis,* 1960, 41; "Grief and Mourning in Infancy and Early Childhood," *The Psychoanalytic Study of the Child,* 1960, p.15; "Processes of Mourning, "*The International Journal of Psychoanalysis,* 1961, p.42.

The Dark Room

Four steps down from the buckling floorboards of the living area and I was engulfed in darkness. Here the room had no window, no door to the outside. It was unusual for a Florida cottage to have a space on a lower level from the main building. Like a mole I adjusted my eyes, groped for a dangling string and switched on a dim lightbulb. A mattress heaved up on its side on an iron bedframe revealed what looked like blood spots. The accordion-like partition to a tiny wardrobe gaped open and drawers were pulled from a bureau and stacked next to it. A shower stall was visible at the far end of the wall where a floral curtain dangled to the floor as if someone had grabbed it while steadying herself. The place smelled damp and desolate. Here my friend Rose had moaned through agonies of her late-stage stomach cancer before the hospice staff intervened and transferred her to a nearby hospital.

Rose was a Christian Scientist who believed that the body would heal itself. When it didn't, she clung to the idea that she was merely an earthen vessel for her eternal soul and that she would pass from this world with ease. At first she refused most standard medical treatments and even shipped back the soothing coca tea I had sent her from Peru. She meditated on devotional texts and read selections from Mary Baker Eddy's *Science and Health*. Only when she could stand the pain no longer did she allow the hospice nurse to give her morphine injections.

I wanted to rush to her side when the cancer became unbearable but I was rudely rebuffed. "I want to do this my way. Alone." "And, if you can't do it alone?" I queried. "Then I will ask help from strangers, not friends." She had an exaggerated fear of imposing on others. She was generous to a fault but resisted accepting even a morsel of kindness from others.

Rose and I met in Montana at a training center for seeing-eye dogs, and I had often visited her and her dogs in Florida where she worked as an accountant at a local college. There I observed her rich community work in a small impoverished section of St. Petersburg where she lived among retired people. She was their go-between with doctors and chauffeured them to various activities. She was the hub in their wheel and much loved. Neighbors told me how they enjoyed watching her run by with a dog or two toward a nearby beach.

When I emerged from the starless night and climbed the few steps back up to daylight I was stalked by despair. Most of Rose's furnishings were gone. After her illness was diagnosed she invited her neighbors to take whatever material possessions they could use. Reluctantly at first, a few items were accepted. When Rose became bedfast people helped themselves more freely. What remained of her possessions? The couch, chairs and bookshelves were gone, even the table where we had enjoyed having coffee together. The floor was barren of all the throw rugs, the heavy brown drapes taken down. Incongruously, white enamel stove covers sat undisturbed over the burners in a kitchen bereft of cook ware and dishes. And a few photographs still hung next to smudged rims where colorful paintings of roses had once decorated the walls. There was a favorite of mine, the picture of an old man leading a horse to a water trough, another one of dogs pulling sleighs through snowdrifts.

Suddenly a flash of sunlight washed over me and my gaze rested on the black upright piano. It had not been moved and stood erect in the corner next to a window. I approached. Mouse droppings littered the top, and the keys were gnawed at the edges. Rats, maybe? When I pressed a key an eerily dissonant sound escaped. The piano stool swiveled round and round as before but one leg had sunk into the rotting floorboards. With no air-conditioning in the cottage, a mossy green fungus was crawling up the piano legs. Then from far away, flooding through my memory, I heard Rose playing and singing "I feel the earth move under my feet." I saw her jump up, rouse one of her sleeping pets and twirl around and around in a joyful dance.

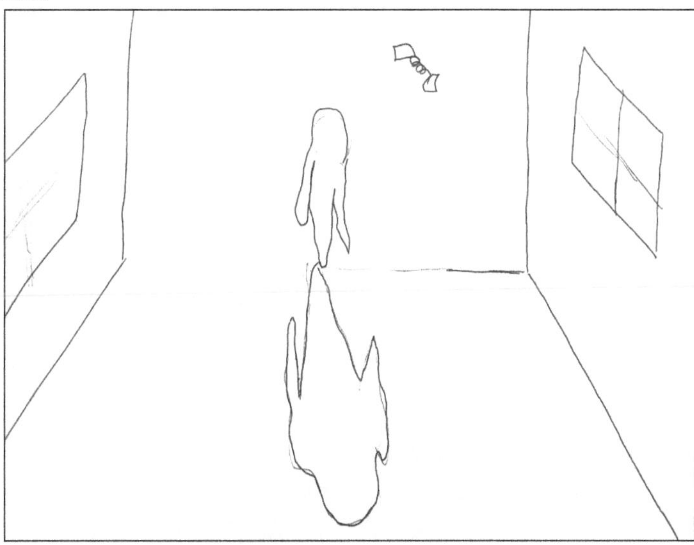

The house had stood deserted for over a year. Rose had willed it to the guide-dog society but her estranged sister was contesting the will. A NO ENTRY sign dangled from the chain-link fence surrounding the property. The rusty gate creaked when I trespassed into the overgrown garden from where I entered the cottage through the unlocked back door. Now I retraced my steps and sat down on the stoop. The sky was overcast, rain was in the air. Here Rose had rested when she was still able to move about and had written short notes in reply to my pleas to come and lend her a hand. "No thanks, just tell me about the birds," was her reply. "They are singing and I close my eyes and listen to their wondrous morning duets."

I complied with her wish and sent books and tapes about birds, mainly of the Florida variety, egrets and pelicans and herons but also finches and sparrows, even mockingbirds.

Under the heavy foliage of unpruned bushes I spied the burial site of Rose's ashes and the ashes of her beloved last canine companion, Buddy. On the small gravestone for her dog was chiseled: "To Buddy, my beloved friend." Rose's stone was even smaller, the size of the palm of my hand and inscribed with only her name, not even a date. She had planted her favorite roses in a circle around the tiny plot. At the periphery of the garden swung a clothesline, a pair of torn jeans clipped onto it blowing in the breeze.

And then it happened. I was still haunted by the gloom of her bedroom, the deserted living area, her lonely dying, unwavering in her refusal of friendly help when through the sinister clouds a picture revealed itself in sudden bright sunshine. I was struck with wonder. Three seagulls landed on a branch of a live oak tree, swaying as if on a high wire and making cooing, whirring noises. Rose loved seagulls. During walks on the beach her dogs had chased them, coming within snapping distance of their tempting feathers. We would laugh at their hapless pursuits and often run along with them. It was as if these birds had come now to comfort me. I had once asked Rose why she favored these birds above all. "Seagulls are known for their independence, their free spirit," she replied. Maybe Rose was now among them, twirling, pirouetting, and flying free.

Love

Cradling the Heart

Chocolate hearts,
cut-out paper hearts,
hearts of gold,
all symbols of the one heart,
sweet, malleable and strong,
pulsing through a life's years.
But beware!
Unless you take tender care of it,
it will wither and die.

Gypsy Spirit

The palm of my right hand stung as I swatted three mosquitoes on the splintered windowsill, leaving a trail of fresh blood streaked across the peeling white paint. The suckers had been full to bursting. With my blood! I propped my feet up on the sill with the soles pointing toward the smudged window and wryly looked at the carnage, sighing, "All dead. Like my marriages."

Nestled in the hills of Wisconsin, my cabin was only a five minute walk from the campsite where I taught art in the summer. The sparse interior of the cabin had exposed beams and buckled planks. Each time I took a step, gray dust particles flew up and tickled my nose. When my son Jack heard that I was stepping out on my own again, he gave me three braided oval throw rugs to soften the floor. Opposite the door that always jammed stood a wrought iron bed, a round wooden table and a rocker. My portable radio found a spot on the windowsill. I'd brought my favorite tapes, gypsy songs from Hungary.

I was ambivalent about the lone portrait of two women on the wall. Framed in ornately carved rosewood, the picture both unnerved and attracted me. The woman in front wore a cornflower-blue dress, printed with wavering wisps of white, like clouds. The fabric was tight over her broad hips and square shoulders, and her back was rigid as if stiffened in opposition. She clutched a velvet handbag, parishioner style. Over her shoulder peeked the other woman's finely chiseled face. Tar-black strands of hair draped over her forehead like a bridal veil. Her tortoise shell earrings glittered. The rest of her body was hidden except for her hand holding a single tiger lily and her gracefully curved throat which seemed to pulsate slightly. The glass over the picture welled up with air-bubbles like blisters on skin as if to disguise the two figures.

As the light dimmed, fleeting sunrays stretched across the floor like streaks of gold. An evening mist rolled in, enveloping the hills in privacy. The silence in the room slipped into my mind. I sat a long time and tried to return to that place inside myself where everything was calm. But my soul was uneasy, and an abyss of remorse was opening up. My body, like my life, was showing deep wear and tear. Even my dreams were tattered.

A month ago, with only a day's notice, I had left my third husband, Melvin. Even after he'd implored me, "Give us time, we can work it out," I had not listened. Once a certain restlessness gripped me, I was like a ship tossed high by the rising tide, my anchor torn from its moorings as I rushed toward the open sea.

Mel, who helped me raise my children from my previous marriages, was the kindest of my three mates, patient and long-suffering. This short, balding pediatrician with protruding leaf-like ears and gentle, darkly veined hands had heard the patter of tiny feet for over 30 years. Though well-acquainted with poopy diapers, runny noses and bruised knees, he lacked insight into the dark recesses of grownups' souls where fears lurk and passions hide. My recurring agitation baffled him. How could he keep a hold on a centipede that scurried off at the slightest provocation?

As before, it came over me at a fancy dinner party. Suddenly the food tasted too rich and moldy odors from overstuffed furniture clogged my throat. I felt caged among the well-dressed, well-fed bodies, and a single desire drove me: the need to escape. A craving for mud between my toes and the perfume of pine needles overwhelmed me. In mid-conversation I tuned out and disconnected myself from my surroundings. The lure of an unattached life drew me like bait draws a fish.

My parents died when I was three. My grandmother raised me. In her gabled gingerbread mansion in Germany, I never lacked for physical comfort, good education or lively company. But I was shortchanged on emotional nourishment. Grandmother Ursula was like an ancient oak tree. Her roots reached deep into family soil, and her limbs and branches protected everyone under their wide-spread umbrella. Potatoes, always still in their skins, were the staple of her diet and she served them at every meal. "A potato is a woman's best friend. It soothes the stomach and keeps appetites grounded," was her motto. I hated potatoes, with or without the tough skins. They settled in my stomach in heavy lumps.

As far back as I can remember, Grandmother Ursula tried to ground my appetites. As I rushed excitedly from one activity to another, she ordered me to sit still, "You are not a raggle-taggle gypsy, do you hear?" Her lips were pinched together like the edges of an oyster shell. She grew tall and erect whenever she reprimanded me. But she was fiercely proud of me as long as I toed the line. Grandmother Ursula tried to keep everyone together in one house, one town, and one country. "Stay with one mate, always," she warned sternly.

Her sister-in-law, my unmarried Aunt Vera, on the other hand, reminded me of that gypsy I was not supposed to be. Her long, flamboyant dresses with no pants or bras underneath swished loosely around her lanky body. She smelled of wildflowers and chamomile tea, her gold chains and wrist and ankle bangles jingled and clinked musically as she moved barefooted through her house, which was always in marvelous disarray. A child's paradise.

Every year Aunt Vera took me to a traveling circus. Once, she paid for a palm reading. The psychic cackled, "You'll roam the world, little tiger. Your spirit is restless and wild. But don't forget your camouflage, little tiger, for escape." Aunt Vera nodded approvingly.

Like warring adversaries, my rooted Grandmother Ursula and my footloose Aunt Vera fought to gain dominion over my soul.

Wayne was an American enlisted man, strong and dashing in his uniform. He was starved for sex and I was ready for adventure. When he asked me to marry him, I said, "Let's give it a whirl." And a whirl it was. We left Germany for the United States on a military transport. I spent most of the voyage leaning over the rocking ship's guardrail, trying to get my rebellious stomach under control, while Jack's strong heartbeat was thumping away in my womb.

Life on the army base in Georgia was dreary and monotonous. The match flame of pleasure which had attracted us soon burned low. Boredom and disappointment spread through me like poison. When Jack was two and Wayne was away on a six-week assignment, I packed our bags and, with Jack straddling my left hip, placed a note on top of the chipped fake-wood dresser that looked like all the other chipped fake-wood dressers on the base. "I can't stay any longer. I'm becoming part of the furniture, the broken blinds and the green plastic sofa. Jack will be fine with me." Wayne never came after us.

Jack and I drifted across country with the wind. It was during the late sixties and we survived as members of first one commune, then another. I helped with household chores, threw pots and made macramé shawls to sell at flea-markets. Eventually I also added my paintings to my sales booth.

I met Ted during a raid on our compound. The police found the usual stashes of marijuana and enough cocaine to arrest a few group members. When Ted flashed his blazing blue eyes at me, I was vulnerable. As he questioned other people, he stood very close to me and fiddled with his tie knot. His words brushed past my ears, "You don't belong here."

He had broad hands with tapered fingers, the nails yellow and hard. But his mouth was full and smelled pleasantly of peppermint gum.

Maybe I attracted solid men. Ted was solid. He promised me that I could get rid of my Salvation Army clothes and eat fresh peaches and raspberries year round. When I told him I was pregnant, he said, "I'm gonna teach you to shoot." He gave me a 9mm Glock, saying, "You want a weapon you can trust. You carry a weapon to protect your life. You don't want click, you want bang." But besides target practice together, there wasn't much to the relationship. The dynamics changed after we were married. Soon I felt roped like a calf at branding. Ted tried to alter my lifestyle. He grumbled about my colorful clothes, disapproved of my purple nail polish, and wanted Jack's brown curls cut.

Three months before Madeleine was born I moved out. This time I told Ted in person. He turned away from me as I spoke, his back ramrod straight, "I saved you and your son," he growled. He shot me a look from those eyes and said, "Get lost before I lose my temper."

We bolted out the door like horses from a burning barn. Jack and I giggled, then laughed the liquid laughter of relief.

Melvin bought six of my paintings while my little son clung tightly to my legs. We could have stayed at the YMCA for a whole year on that one sale. He was not only interested in my pictures. After carrying them gingerly, one at a time, to his car, he returned and asked, "Would you like to have dinner with me?"

"Can't you see I'm about to have a baby?"

"Well, I'm a pediatrician."

When Mel asked me to move in with him, I agreed without a moment's hesitation. I had glimpsed some unusual kindness in this small man. Jack, and later Madeleine, quickly learned to love him. The bond we formed was as tough and flexible as an umbilical cord.

My firstborn and I were joined from the start. Whenever we were together, we sat on opposite ends of a couch, our bare soles flat against each other. Our mutual understanding flowed best that way. Jack was a nature guide on rivers, and also taught survival skills to the more dedicated. When I moved into the cabin, he told me to sprinkle drops of citronella oil on my bed and other warm hiding places to repel spiders and other insects. He lived half a day away in a cabin like mine. From there he watched for poachers and worked to preserve certain endangered species, including his favorite, the Timber Rattlesnake.

Fog had settled over the countryside. I felt snug in my cabin. While gently rocking, I noticed my breath laboring. A draft made me fetch my macramé shawl. Then I heard humming, like power lines. The wind became angry and a light rain muffled the air, splattering against the window. A shadow of change cast itself across my mood.

Suddenly I smelled something like the odor given off by musty clothes. Then I spooked when a hand crawled slightly over mine like a tiny bug, and a breath slid across my shoulders like a snake. At that moment, hairpins flew into my loose hair, braiding it into a threefold cord, and pinning it to the chair. I heard a crackling like ice splintering. Reflected in the window, I saw a zigzag line bisect the picture, and two figures stepped from the rosewood frame, Grandmother Ursula and Aunt Vera. They glided across the floor until they crowded me like two bookends. My knees knocked together. "You are not a raggle-taggle gypsy." I knew that voice. "Go. Go," urged the other. Then the room was so still, it was ghostlike.

My heart was speeding and my mind was needle-sharp as I grabbed my bag, pulled my shawl closer and left my seductive solitude. I cut a swath through the brush and felt the wet ground beneath my bare feet. The jeep at the camp was unlocked, the keys on the driver's seat. I adjusted both mirrors and started the engine. As dawn spread its bright halo, I reached Jack's slumbering cabin, steeped in witches' smoke.

I stepped in and saw Jack dozing, his head leaning against the headboard of the bed. His right foot was bandaged and propped up on a pillow. My eyes burned as if I had stepped through a brushfire. "Are you all right?" I nearly choked on my words. His eyes opened slowly and he slurred his words, "I'm all right." His irises were dilated big as pennies. He blinked and asked, "How did you know?" "Your great-grandmother and your great-aunt returned as smoke and wind, a humming insect and a hissing snake. They told me." I was so relieved that Jack was okay, I started to cry. Then I sat on his bed and listened.

"Of all snakes, the rattler bit me," he explained. "I had come upon this beautiful female. She rested on a rock, the rattle on the tip of her tail absolutely still. Her head was only an arm's length away and for a moment our eyes met. I didn't want to disturb her, so I stepped back quietly. Snakes have babies in August. I should have figured her den was near. A baby got me right above my boot." Jack's entire face grimaced, remembering the pain. "Luckily I got only a small amount of poison. Hazards of the trade." He paused, giving me a meaningful look. "I'm so glad you're here, Mom. When I called Dad, he got here right away, disinfected the wound and gave me a shot of anti-venom." I pulled back within my inner walls and then placed a hand on Jack's arm as if to anchor myself. "Mel is here?" And then, a moment later, "You know snakes symbolize transformation." Jack reached for my hand and pulled it close to his chest. "Maybe this was a sign, too, like the smoke and wind and all...now go find Mel."

Mel was sitting on the back stoop of the cabin. Without speaking, he patted the spot next to him for me to sit down and then looked up with his sad, longing eyes. I worked my mouth but no sounds came out. He said, "you don't have to run away. We can travel whenever and wherever you want." He glanced at my bare feet, muddy from my dash to the jeep, and added, "even with mud between your toes. Please, just...." There was little room in his steady voice for me to refuse. He sat there aglow, his face flushed with expectation. Then I saw something in Mel's eyes that I had missed before. Acceptance? Understanding? He would hold on to me but not hold me back.

My heart took an unexpected turn and my entire body burned hot under his glance. I dropped my defenses like a wilting flower, for I knew then that I had come home and that factions, however incompatible at times, could merge within my soul. I extended a naked foot into the dirt, drew a magic circle there and said softly, "We could try again. Gypsies never lose their wanderlust, you know. But they do take on fellow travelers."

The Adoption

There had not been such a brilliant autumn in recent memory. Even though it was already September, a month that usually brought dense fog and rain to the port city of Hamburg, this year the temperature was deceptively mild and dry. Margret and I had the door to our balcony wide open. The row houses where we shared a flat were shoulder-touching close and noises from neighboring balconies drifted in. It was the beginning of the fall semester, our second year at the university. We were architecture students, a field that promised plenty of opportunities in the early sixties. We lay stretched out on the floor on our stomachs, drawing.

A knock at the door surprised us. We were not expecting visitors, and our watchful landlady usually screened all callers.

"May I come in?" An elderly man pushed his skinny frame toward the door. He looked like a detective, wore a long gray trench coat, was bald, and balanced horn-rimmed glasses on his beak-like nose. He carried a battered briefcase with big brass snaps which he pressed to his chest as though it contained something very valuable. "May I have a word about a matter of importance to one of you?" Too startled to say no, and not wanting to seem impolite, I gestured toward the battered green hassocks in the corner of our common room. They were laden with books and papers which were tipping toward the adjacent white-tiled stove, still silent for the season.

Margret jumped up, pushed the stack of materials off the hassocks and said, politely, "Please sit down." I remained on the floor but sat up straight and pulled my short skirt down over my bare thighs. The prune-like man lifted the back of his coat as if it were a frock and placed himself squarely on the closest hassock, facing us.

"Dr. Schwarz…Dr. Schwarz…Dr. Schwarz," he introduced himself in a soft, dreary voice three times as if to make sure we got his name. All the while his fingers drummed on the top of his briefcase so that the letters of his name seemed to engrave themselves into the brown leather. We sat quiet, expectant. "Which of you is Countess Ute von Hardenberg?" His gaze flitted from me to Margret and back to me. Even beneath his smudged glasses his eyes were prying. "I am Ute," I said. "This is my friend Margret." The stranger hesitated and then pronounced with much gravity, "Please, Miss Margret, could you give us some privacy." "No," I blurted out a bit too loudly. "She can stay." I had no intention of being alone with this hawkeyed stranger.

He seemed to be trying to take my measure as a slow smile lifted his sallow cheeks and he continued, "You no doubt honor your father's memory." I still had no idea what this was about but my suspicion was now aroused. "Yes…of course…but how do you…?" He interjected, "Good, good, I presumed as much. I have been apprised of the circumstances of your childhood. I am aware that your father was killed in action early in the war and thus was robbed of the opportunity of watching his only daughter grow into a beautiful young lady." He seemed to be pondering my growing puzzlement. "But you can make it up to him. I will get straight to the point of my visit. I have come to encourage you to take back your birth name." I must have looked dumbfounded but before I could speak he continued, his voice more subdued than before. "Because your adoption was never finalized, your mother has lived throughout the postwar years on fraudulently acquired income and you are the bearer of a false identity."

"Now, wait a minute!" I stood up, incredulous. "Who *are* you? And who is making these foul accusations?" "Please, please, I am only the messenger," he said in a whisper. "You may not be aware that your mother is under indictment for lying under oath. You and she have reaped the benefits of Count Franz's inheritance while your half-sister Helga, her father Richard and her poor Aunt...." "Which Aunt?" I interrupted rudely. "Why, Richard's sister, the Countess Beate, who feels that you have disgraced her aristocratic family." My mouth dropped open. "Count Richard and my sister have shared our inheritance from the beginning." As I stepped toward him, Dr. Schwarz got up quickly and began backing toward the door. "No need to get exasperated. I am only here to introduce myself and to inform you that I am representing them in a lawsuit being brought against your mother and you." As swiftly as Dr. Schwarz had entered he now exited, leaving the door ajar which drew a gust of wind through the balcony door and scattered our papers across the floor.

As soon as the door closed, Margret started to giggle. "Did you hear his accent? Russian? Or maybe Polish?" But I was in shock and for a while said nothing. For some reason I had focused mostly on his boots, dull and scuffed. They had clearly seen better days. After regaining my composure I sighed and turned to Margret. "I wish I had your family history. No deaths, no money worries, your parents are not divorced and you even have a grandmother who still lives with you." Margret got up, patted me on the shoulder and walked toward the little kitchen. "You need a glass of wine."

I certainly did have a complicated family history. My mother Gerda was born into an old family of the Silesian landed aristocracy, the Barons von Lüttwitz. Her mother Maria too came from royal stock and always boasted of having taken tea with the Queen Mother of England before World War I. When she was twenty-one, my mother fell in love with my father Gert who was the oldest son of an affluent upper-middle class family and an aspiring academic. When the war started in 1939 he was drafted, posted to France, and was killed two weeks before my birth. I became the talisman of my parents' passion. Until her death in 1999 my mother placed a fresh flower on her nightstand next to my father's photo every week.

Three years after my father's death, my mother married Count Franz von Hardenberg who was the adopted son of his Aunt Sybille and heir to her gorgeous vast estate near the town of Liegnitz. A military man, he rose to the rank of Staff Officer with the Army High Command. I knew nothing of his politics except that on one occasion he had used his influence to save my grandmother Maria, who was an outspoken opponent of the Nazis, from being sent to a concentration camp. Like so many of her compatriots in the resistance she had naively signed the guestbook at a clandestine gathering on a neighboring estate and was subsequently arrested by the Gestapo. Count Franz adopted me shortly after marrying my mother. I was four years old at the time, and I bore his name from then on.

Soon thereafter, as the Red Army swept into Silesia, my mother and grandmother fled westward with me, taking all the winter clothing they could carry and their jewelry sewn inside the lining of their coats. Everything else was left behind, and all family documents were lost.

In the early 1950s the German government began to reimburse former landowners for their losses in the eastern territories. Thousands had to vouch for the validity of missing birth certificates, marriage licenses and in my case, adoption papers. Thereafter we began to receive monthly checks which allowed us to move from the rat-infested shelter where we were housed after the war to a spacious apartment in which we lived comfortably. I was even able to afford tuition fees and living expenses at the university.

In 1945 Count Richard, Franz's brother had brought my mother the news that Franz had been killed flying back from a staff meeting with the generals on the Russian front. Bereft for a second time, my mother turned to Count Richard for comfort and soon became pregnant with my sister Helga. Count Richard married my mother and became the only father I ever really knew. He lived with us for ten years until the marriage ended in divorce.

Not long after the strange encounter with Dr. Schwarz, Count Richard paid me a visit. He was now married again and helping his sister Beate with her thriving dog grooming business. She gave him the responsibility of walking the boarded canines. Count Richard and I had bonded in an unusual way. He came into my five year-old life after the war and though he did not particularly like children, he taught me to be his useful accomplice. Times were hard. He was unemployed, and all we had to live on was the family jewelry and my mother's breast milk, which we sold on the black market.

Count Richard was also a womanizer. I had to accompany him on his forays to the market which he combined with clandestine stops at various houses along the way. I was always amazed at how many ladies eagerly awaited him. We never left these rendezvous without an extra piece of warm clothing or some needed food. On our way home I stole vegetables from crowded market stalls. While Father distracted the stall keeper I slipped some eggs into my pockets, all the while stroking the heads of clucking hens in their straw baskets. We pilfered fruit from orchards and potatoes from unattended fields. These thieveries created strong ties, strengthened by the secrecy I was sworn to. Count Richard was shrewd and looked out first and foremost for himself. But these early days together had led to a lasting fondness for me, which never extended to his own daughter, my sister.

The Count was his charming self as he swept into our student apartment in his rumpled clothes, embraced me and Margret, and exclaimed, "You two look lovelier every time I see you." He was all sincerity and smiles as he went straight for the glasses on our coffee table, still unwashed and sticky from the previous night. Acting as if he were at home, he uncorked a pocket-size bottle of fine French cognac he had brought with him and poured himself a stiff drink. "Santé!"

"Did Dr. Schwarz unnerve you?" He grinned at me. My face turned beetroot red with anger but I was at a loss for words. He instantly lowered his gaze and turned into the shape-shifter I knew him to be. "I feel a little bad, Ute dear," he began. "You have always been like my own daughter but things have turned nasty in recent months. My sister has discovered a deception. And you know how she is, she will get to the bottom of any falsehood. She has found out, quite by chance I should add, that your adoption by my brother Franz was never finalized. Your inheritance deprived her of hers." "But not yours and Helga's," I interrupted. "No, but you see, my circumstances have also changed. I have new responsibilities, and your mother can no longer help financially." "So it's all about money, right?" "Oh, no," he protested and immediately resumed his dissembling. "It's about honoring the dead. You see, we never fully considered your father's feelings. I mean, what his wishes might have been. I am sure he would have liked his surname to pass on to his daughter." The Count topped up his drink. "I am not pressuring you, only appealing to your sense of fairness. I have known you always to be very fair-minded. This is your chance to make up for our thoughtlessness toward your dead father." "And the money would go to whom?" It seemed too transparently obvious. "I'm not sure, really. We would of course see to it that you and your mother are provided for. Please, just think about our request." Then he placed the half-empty bottle on the table and with a generous swipe of his hand announced,

"I'll leave this for you to enjoy. I must be off. I know, Ute dear, you will make the right decision." And with a flourish, he vanished.

"It's all about money, disguised as honor," Margret trumpeted once the Count was out of earshot. Then suddenly we heard pounding rain on the roof, an unanticipated downpour.

I was torn. I had blissfully lived with my adopted name and its privileges and never considered what my biological father might have wanted. The following day I sat through lectures with a knot in the pit of my stomach. Later that evening I decided to pay my paternal grandparents, Aenne and Karl Köhler a visit.

They were waiting at the train station when I arrived, bent slightly forward at the waist like twisted branches laden with snow. It was not age that had crippled them but the burden of a destiny I could not imagine them bearing day after day, the terrible sorrow they continued to shoulder. They were a tolerant, educated couple who had resided in a small town near the Baltic Sea before the war where my grandfather was a judge. My grandmother wrote stories, poetry, even a play that was performed in the local community theatre. Before the Red Army stormed their town, they abandoned their home, changing location again and again as troop movements shifted until the war ended. In the ensuing years as the country slowly rebuilt, they settled in western Germany and despite their advanced years started a new life. My grandfather joined a law firm and began to attract a small clientele. But tragedy had already done its damage.

My grandparents had five children, four boys and then a daughter. On a walk with her nanny, the toddler was fatally struck by a motorcyclist who lost control of his bike and careened off the road. My father, the eldest of the five siblings, and a second son were killed in the war, and the third son returned home shell-shocked and soon died. The youngest boy was sent to Sweden where he was taken in by relatives and survived unscathed. He became a Swedish citizen and never returned to Germany. No wonder I was doted on as the only remaining jewel from a trove of lost treasure.

As was customary, the main meal of the day at my grandparents' house was taken at noon and light snacks were offered in the evenings. My grandmother had lovingly prepared slices of apples, a variety of cheeses and cold meats served with crusty brown bread. A bottle of white wine whetted our appetite. I ate fast, then delved into my story. My grandparents listened intently and without interruption, though when I described Dr. Schwarz I noticed my grandfather's nose twitch. After I finished, circling back once or twice to fill in a forgotten detail, grandfather responded first. "Your mother nearly did not survive the news of your father's death. They were very much in love. So when, three years later, she met Count Franz and brought him to meet us, we were relieved and happy for her. I supported your mother's intention to have you adopted. We wanted you to be integrated into your new family, of course not knowing that death would strike again. Count Franz's own adoptive mother was a refined but rather simple-minded lady who took to your mother and you with one reservation. You were not of the aristocracy, and your mother, as she put it curtly "had strayed by marrying a commoner." Here my grandmother smiled and broke in, "Your mother adored your father but if she could have changed one single thing about him she would have turned him into a Count." Grandfather picked up where he had left off. "I went to Seidorf to inspect the adoption papers, and found them in order save for a few typographical errors. Franz planned to sign them during his next furlough from the front. I know he returned once before his final fatal flight. But owing to all the turmoil at that time, nobody can know for sure if the papers were ever actually signed."

It was my grandmother who surmised my unspoken quandary. She had left the table and come back with a thick art book. She fingered through the index and flipped to a page with a picture of Uta, Duchess of Naumburg. "Look at his picture. On a visit to Naumburg your parents stopped at the cathedral and saw there the statue of Uta. Your father, who was convinced that you would be a girl, decided on the spot, 'We'll name our daughter Ute, only change the spelling slightly to give her name a softer sound.' Your father marveled at the beauty and self-contained expression of this lady. He would have liked for you to keep that name forever. As for the surname, he would not have cared either way." I was so relieved. I loved my given name and would always bear it proudly.

But I was not finished. "What is this about, this lawsuit?" I queried. "Money, of course," my grandfather bellowed. Countess Sybille left a curious stipulation in her will. Upon her death the estate would pass to her son Franz, then to his children, only then to his siblings, Beate and Richard, and finally to your mother. She expected of course that your parents would have several children. But Countess Sybille preceded Franz in death. She vowed to remain in her castle come what might and was murdered by the invading army. So she never knew that he died in the war, without having any children."

Matters were beginning to fall into place. "Why did you make a face when I mentioned Dr. Schwarz," I asked. Grandfather grimaced as he always did when caught off guard. "I must reserve judgment and investigate further but he may have been the Polish clerk who worked at the office in Seidorf. My stay there was brief but I do recall a young man who fits the description of Dr. Schwarz. He volunteered to me at that time that he intended to enter law school."

I did not sleep well under the comfortable featherbedding that night. Half awake, half dreaming, vague memories bubbled up. I recalled a morning when my parents were in their bedroom during Count Franz's last leave at home. I had run into their room and jumped onto their bed. Swept up into my new father's arms, I giggled pleasantly, then disentangled myself and, glancing back teasingly, ran into the hallway to play. There I overheard my mother say, "I am so pleased you will honor my request to adopt Ute. You two seem to get along so well." "She is a sweet little girl and I will certainly keep my promise. But be patient, dear. My mother has to warm to the idea of the adoption. There is no rush, right? I will be back soon and never leave you alone again." I heard my mother sob, whether from joy or fear I could not tell.

A secret abides, a secret wants to be revealed. What really happened?

A letter from my sister awaited me upon my return to Hamburg. She is six years younger than I, and when she was a baby I had treated her like one of my dolls. Later on as our interests diverged, we shared little of our lives. But like Aunt Beate, under whose influence she had come, my sister always felt that she had been shortchanged. In her eyes I was the more beautiful one, favored by my grandparents, had more friends and better schooling…. The list was endless. As often as I tried to right the balance between us, Helga always had a new agenda. She felt neglected and disadvantaged no matter what. I was nevertheless sympathetic to her feelings. I *had* been dealt a fortunate hand. My fiery, passionate Grandmother Maria favored and protected me like a lioness. I had stayed with her when my mother was ill or being courted, which in the years after Gert's death was not infrequent. I, in turn, loved Grandmother Maria fiercely. My sister never had such a bond with anyone in our family. I was closer to her own father than she was. My mother tried to share her affections between us, but I was, after all, the child of the great love of her young life.

My sister's letter was brief and calculating, clearly dictated under Countess Beate's auspices. "Sister," it began, "I have always admired you but you have never requited my feelings. Everything in life has gone your way, and I have had to content myself with being second-best. Can you not at least leave me my name? My father is not your father, and your father is dead. I am the only *real* Countess. Please do me this ONE favor and I will never ask you for anything again. Take back your Köhler name and let me be the Countess von Hardenberg. I beg you." I wanted to weep. Instead I crumpled up the letter and threw it into the wastebasket.

My mother was the most beautiful woman I had ever seen. Her svelte figure matched the pearls she always wore, even in the air-raid shelter. She had an understated poise and style that elicited caring protectiveness in most men. She was the real Countess. I loved her, though my feelings for her could not rival those for my Grandmother Maria. Mother sensed this, which must have added sadness to her life, already much burdened by loss.

My mother stayed with Margret and me the day before the hearing. I gave her my bed and I shared Margret's. That night we went to a neighborhood Italian restaurant and had a good time. Mother studiously avoided any talk about the hearing. Every time I subtly broached the subject, she became strangely evasive. "Everything will be fine. Let's just enjoy ourselves." And so we did. But her calm outward demeanor belied her underlying anxiety. I knew that she would stand her ground against any false accusations. I also knew that for my mother, honoring a promise was a token of love.

Next morning in the courtroom, Count Richard arrived in his usual disheveled attire, hair uncombed as if he had just bounded from bed. His stout sister Beate, wearing a white ruffled blouse and looking awkward without her aristocratic pet dachshund, sat stiffly on the hard bench with an air of righteous self-assurance. My sister Helga, also in a white ruffled blouse, flicked her long brown braids through the air menacingly from time to time. The three sat like birds on a wire, facing us. Dr. Schwarz, looking even more hawkish than I recalled, crouched at their side. As it turned out, he was not their lawyer but a witness. When my mother spotted him, she exclaimed, "Why, that's Max. What is he doing here?" I could not answer her because we had just been ordered to silence. In the following cross-examination our accusers spoke on script, like parrots.

The judge, twirling a black fountain pen, had each of them tell the adoption story which was further embellished with each retelling. My mother swore that the adoption papers had been signed and duly notarized. Not a single bead of perspiration was visible on her brow. When she finished, Dr. Schwarz had his moment of glory. He carried his well-guarded briefcase to the bench, snapped the brass locks open, produced a single piece of paper, and held it up triumphantly. "There is no signature on this document." His cheeks paled to yellow under more questioning. How had he come into possession of this document, the judge wanted to know. Dr. Schwarz did not hesitate. He gestured toward to Beate. Dr. Schwarz continued, "before we took flight from the advancing Russian troops, the Countess instructed me to gather her documents. It was all very last minute but I fetched them, to my own detriment. I did not even have time to locate my law school degree." Our accusers glared at us, sensing victory.

The judge called a recess in the hearing during which Dr. Schwarz's document was examined. Then my mother was called to the stand again. In a calm, firm voice she told the judge that she knew Max from the office in Seidorf. "Max was absent on the day of the signing. A young woman named Doris witnessed the signing in his stead."

No one could have foreseen the sudden appearance of my former nanny. Doris approached the bench, toothless, her lips curling over her gums like a rabbit nibbling a carrot. She began her testimony, rising to her unaccustomed role. "I was there that day," she started, her eyes ablaze. I had come up to the castle because we had promised Miss Ute a party with girls from the village the day she officially became our new Countess. To me she was always a Countess, such a sweet little thing. Max was out of the office and could not be found. So I was called to witness, and I did. Right afterwards Count Franz left to return to the front. Later in the week I trekked westward with the women. I now live in a nursing home in Kassel." Unbeknownst to us, my mother had summoned Doris. Across from us the three parrots sat speechless, knocked from their perches.

When the judge reentered the courtroom to announce the verdict, my skin prickled. I tried to catch my mother's eye but she turned away. The judge stated that the date on Max's document did not match the date on the alleged adoption papers. "Dr. Schwarz's document appears to be a declaration of intent, composed long before the preparation of the official adoption papers." He continued, "Many unusual things transpired in those war-torn times, and much remains uncertain to this day. Some things are simply not ascertainable. Case dismissed." He then gazed admiringly at my mother. It was as if he had come under the spell of a true Countess—and a devoted mother.

Suddenly we all shuddered as a clap of thunder ended the proceedings and the courtroom went dark. I jumped up and hugged my mother, then turned to see the reaction of our accusers. Beate and Helga were incredulous and irate, parrots with their feathers plucked. Count Richard blew us a kiss on his way out. He still had not tucked in his shirttail.

That evening Margret and I took Mother and Doris to dinner at Hamburg's exclusive Fürstenhof Hotel. My mother had called my sister and pleaded with her to come along, but Helga declined, saying "Aunt Beate has bought tickets to the ballet. I'll visit you soon."

Over dessert I asked, "Did I ever have that girls' party?" Doris busied herself with her chocolate mousse. My mother leaned over and tenderly caressed my hand. "No dear, the Russians were already burning down neighboring villages to the east. We had to leave in a hurry and were lucky to get out alive." Did I notice a conspiratorial glance flit between my mother and Doris? Or did I just imagine it?

When we left the restaurant the night was balmy and a myriad of stars twinkled in the sky as though they were dancing. A promise had been kept but the truth would remain forever hidden.

Cruel Pleasures

As a child pulling a cat's tail delights in its squeal, our stepfather Walter enjoyed watching others squirm.

It is a few days before Christmas and we are at a holiday fair. The lights and smells dazzle us but we have no money to purchase trinkets or have fun on the merry-go-round or the Ferris wheel. To our surprise Walter offers to buy my sister, Erica, 6, and me, 8, pink cotton candy. We nearly wet our pants at this delicious prospect. Walter flattens out a dollar bill and hands it to the vendor in exchange for two fluffy balls. Slowly he swishes them through the air, then deliberately swipes them under our noses. We swallow with anticipation. Walter looks intently at us as if we were salivating dogs and then drops the candy into a snowy slush pile next to the stand and ambles on, grinning as we lunge for the treats. We eagerly lick the sugary puffs, ignoring the grit between our teeth.

Another holiday ten years later. It is Easter. My mother possesses an heirloom pendant with a sapphire surrounded by a crescent of tiny diamonds. "You should wear that to church," Walter entreats her. But when she goes to fetch her treasure the jewelry box is empty. "You lost it?" Walter exclaims as he storms out of the apartment. On hands and knees we search high and low, even the dust-filled storage room. My boyfriend, who is wise to our family dramas, and I venture downtown to the grungy pawnshop where Walter is known for covering his gambling debts. There amidst glittering earrings and shiny bracelets we find the lost pendant. "We hate him, don't we?" my sister and I agree when Walter plays his cruel tricks on us.

When I wonder why my mother does not leave him I recall seeing them strolling along, his arm snaked around her waist. They are laughing and talking. And I remember Walter building Erica and me a treehouse from leftover lumber he had found at an abandoned construction site. We were happy as clams!

Years later, at my mother's pleading, I visited Walter in the hospital where he was near death. His broad smile told me that he was pleased to see me. I pulled a chair to his bedside and he fixed me in his gaze like a hunter eyeing his prey. As we spoke, he sneakily slipped the IV needle from his arm. As fluid dripped onto the bed sheet, he shouted, "Call the nurse. Look what you have done." Half expecting one of his shenanigans, I calmly replied, "I'll call. Shall I tell her what *you* have done?" As the mischievous expression on Walter's face softened, he reached for my hand and held it tight. I felt an unexpected warmth flowing between us. "You were always on to me, weren't you?" Words failed me and tears welled up, prompted not by what had just happened but for what might have been.

Forever Love

From the Gulf, the fog rolled over the island in dense billows, enshrouding the houses of Galveston. Inside Barbara's home the windows had steamed up. She drew on the windowpane, peepholes to the outside world. Her finger was tracing a heart with the inscription "Love Forever" as her mother approached and admonished, "Are you daydreaming about David again?"

David had learned the carpenter trade in the Army. He was a quiet, reserved man whose talent was concentrated in the skill of his hands. Barbara was a bouncy fireball, cute and at ease with people. Her parents had high hopes for her. Maybe she would become a nurse or a teacher and would provide for them in their old age. They never foresaw her marrying. But when David returned from the service, the childhood attraction was revived. Barbara told her parents she was going to marry him. They calmly consented.

David built their first home, a bungalow, from scratch. Barbara was at his side assisting whenever she could. They enjoyed working together and got great satisfaction from building their own domicile. Soon after its completion, Barbara's parents constructed their own cottage right behind the bungalow. From the kitchen, Barbara's mother could see her daughter's window blinds being lowered at night and raised at dawn.

Together the two women sowed seeds, and the morning glories stretched their tentacles along the sideyard fence, tying the two households together. When David tinkered with his car in the driveway, Barbara's dad ambled over to advise. The foursome often listened to ballgames together on the young couple's radio, and Barbara's mother always brought a bowl of popcorn.

It was the time of the Great Depression, and David had trouble finding steady work. He and Barbara spent many late night hours mulling over how to get ahead. The decision to go north to look for a job in Michigan came as a surprise to Barbara's parents. Their disapproval took the form of long silences and a slow withdrawal from daily contact. "Your parents are just pouting," David assured Barbara. They'll snap out of it. Take my word for it." Barbara trusted David's judgment and overlooked her parents' brooding and detachment.

The young couple headed north with high hopes. Barbara's parents remained taciturn. Her letters home went unanswered and she worried. David, too, was changing. Jobs were as scarce in Michigan as they had been in Galveston, and at times David's reserved temperament bordered on depression. Barbara had not felt well in weeks. Maybe a visit home would break the worrisome silence and dispel her own gloomy mood.

Through the pane of the bus window, David couldn't see a tearful Barbara making him signs, drawing hearts in the air, while whispering, "Forever." He was solemn, assuring himself that he had done the right thing in letting her go home. "It won't be for long," he had told her each time. He waved to the bus pulling out, flailing his arms wildly in the air as if that gesture could stop the inevitable. Only when the taillights had diminished to tiny stars did his arms fall limp to his sides.

Barbara's parents were overjoyed at their daughter's homecoming. Having her to themselves again reminded them of her childhood years. They welcomed her back with open arms, which soon tightened into a protective embrace and then to an imprisoning clasp. Barbara too rejoiced at being home again, being cared for and pampered. Soon it become clear that her ill disposition was due to the fact that she was pregnant.

David's industriousness and diligence paid off when he found a job with a cabinetmaker. After his first day at work, he began to scour the city for an apartment. He rented one. After work and on weekends, he scrubbed and painted and repaired it. Soon the place looked like a home awaiting only Barbara's feminine finishing touches. He wrote Barbara of the good fortune and asked her to return right away.

Being welcomed back by relatives and friends eased Barbara's longing for David and distracted her from the fact that the weeks were passing quickly. Every day she checked the mail in vain, but she knew David was busy trying his best to find work. He would send for her, of that she was sure. She trusted David, and she trusted her parents. Never would it have occurred to her that they were intercepting David's letters and returning them unopened, nor that they never posted Barbara's letters to David.

Hands that always hit the nail on its head, hands that smoothed rough wood into soft surfaces, hands strong and secure, lining up parts and fitting joints together, these hands fluttered like tethered birds and let the letter from Barbara's father, read a dozen times, tumble to the floor. The letter informed David that Barbara was pregnant, that she was no longer interested in rejoining him, and that she was filing for divorce.

David's strength of character abandoned him. He behaved not the way one would have expected under the circumstances. He did not jump on the next bus to Galveston to reclaim his love, his wife. His reserved, quiet nature allowed no raging fury, no hasty action. Instead, he wrote again and again questioning, even begging, for explanations. When, after months, none came, he granted the divorce. Dismayed and unable to understand, he buried himself in his work. His success was partly due to his single-minded devotion to his job. The years passed, he remarried and had a family.

Bitterness never crept into Barbara's heart. Believing that God works in mysterious but always rightful ways, she waited. Only in the lonely hours of the night did she let herself go and cried her heart out over the loss of her beloved David. Never did she say, "Why did this happen to me?" Only, "What could have happened to him? What could have caused him to abandon me?" She had not become a teacher or a nurse but instead found a job in a flower shop. Once, before Valentine's Day, she was arranging bouquets, adding a balloon here and there to the flower arrangements. Gold letters were embossed on one red balloon saying, "Forever." Barbara cupped the balloon in both hands, pressed and burst it. The bang sounded like a release of pent-up grief and longing, but it frightened Barbara's co-worker who scuttled in, "Dear, you scared me! And, you've popped the prettiest of our balloons."

When the baby was born, Barbara named her Felicitas, the happy one. Barbara was overjoyed with her baby daughter. She knew David would have been, too. Barbara's parents were also delighted to have a granddaughter. Their love and protection were lavished on her, as they unconsciously relived Barbara's own childhood.

Over the years, Barbara's relationship with her parents began to change. While they concentrated on Felicitas and saw her grow to young womanhood, Barbara took on a different, caring role. When, in old age, her father developed lung cancer, Barbara reluctantly moved him to a nursing home where he died. She then stayed with her mother for the following two years until her death, tending her as her health failed and she grew frail.

In the years between the death of Barbara's dad and the death of her mother, David buried his second wife, who had succumbed to an incurable terminal illness.

Hearing the news of the death of Barbara's mother, David decided to call Barbara to express his sympathy. This was the first time they had heard each other's voices in 32 years. At their first reunion, they both confessed that they had never stopped loving each other. Initially bewilderd beyond belief that Barbara's parents had conspired so heartlessly to keep them apart—and never acknowledged the harmful role they had played—eventually Barbara and David vowed to move beyond resentment and to fan the still glowing embers of their love.

On the anniversary of their marriage, David and Barbara exchanged vows again, with Felicitas by their side. The officiating minister placed his hands over the joined hands of the kneeling couple and blessed them with these words, "How mysterious and wonderful, O Lord, are thy works, revealed in the lives of those who trust and believe in Thee. How marvelous, too, the human heart that has its reasons and secrets accessible only to those who respond to its prompting."

For Old Time's Sake

Once more she opens her handbag to let the reflection in her pocket mirror tell her how to smooth a lock to the side of her forehead. "Our next stop is Kirchheim, Madam," the conductor feels obliged to announce to her in person. After all, this lady is the holder of a ticket all the way from London. She stands at attention at the window for the rest of the train ride, a lady in a green tailored suit more befitting the overcast skies of her northern city than the lush southern German mountainous scenery she takes in with remembering eyes. Reminiscent of the coverlets on the headrests of the intercontinental Pullman car, her blouse collar is tucked over the lapels of her suit. She wears her clothes with leisurely elegance, buttoning her jacket over her slender waist. Only if one approaches her from the right can one detect the silvery cord of the hearing aid running like an antenna down her neck. She is accustomed to wearing gloves.

He stands on the other side of the turnstile, a light trench coat thrown over one arm, leaning with the other on a walking cane. Since his retirement from the bank he has gone back to wearing blue linen work shirts after the fashion of his father. He tells his in-laws, who disapprove, "old age lets you get away with things." His goatee isn't to everybody's liking either, but he feels it complements his salt-and-pepper hair.

The intensity of their greeting is pressed into their handshake. "You look marvelous, Grete." "So do you, Anton." "Your grip betrays the old horsewoman," he adds with some tenderness. They both stop talking after the initial signs of recognition, and gaze at one another. Their eyes are windows to their souls. His blue eyes suggest an iris with delicate and transparent petals growing in a moderate, moist climate. Lines like crow's feet wrinkle their corners and reveal that he likes to laugh. Her eyes are dark brown and begin to glow with the challenges of unexplored fields. They have the magic power of penetrating appearances without shifting their focus from the surfaces of things.

At the zebra stripes of the crosswalk where halting cars seem impatient with their gait, he takes her arm. The cafe under the linden tree is just around the corner from the station plaza. They find a shaded place in the courtyard. The foliage of the ancient tree spreads its umbrella over their table and she feels a refreshing coolness which reminds her of dipping her feet in the bucket her grandmother used to collect rain water. "Tea, Grete?" he asks. She nods. "Yes, of course, what else for a lady who has soaked up the English culture for more than a half century. I expected you to be as rotund as all of our surviving school friends," he teases her. "You know I would live on a diet of green apples if that ever happened," she retorts, slightly annoyed. How easy it is to restore familiarity by harking back to old vulnerabilities.

"How have you fared, world traveler?" he continues in a light vein. She touches her nose, groping for the appropriate reply. "I've had a blessed life," she finally answers. She has an envelope with photographs ready for him to view. One by one, from infancy to middle age, first her children, then her grandchildren are paraded before him. "Rena is the latest to arrive and is my favorite. From her very first step the world was hers to grasp, and she keeps on pursuing it with enthusiasm and success." "A chip off the old block, is that it?" he asks. "In a way, I guess. It does give me satisfaction to see one of my offspring follow in my footsteps." "And your late husband," he queries with a grin. "We are still bound by golden threads," she smiles, "that neither tarnish nor corrode." She reaches into the folds of her blouse for a gold locket which she wears close to her heart. "I'm really not interested in seeing his picture," he remarks. She lets the locket slide back to its accustomed place. "You know, I once read an article of yours," he continues, changing the subject. "Fred cut it out and sent it with some other clippings and a note which read, 'Father, is that not a lady you used to know in high school?' It was an article in a horticulture magazine, something about an airborne algae that attacks palm trees and the concrete walls of swimming pools," he chuckles. "Odd as it seems now, I filed it away somewhere, for old time's sake, I suppose." "Oh, dear," she admits, "I did take on odd jobs at times just to sustain my writing."

"But what about you, has life been good to you, Anton?" "More than that," he picks up the thread to unroll what has been woven into the fabric of his years. "I, too, got what I desired, a comfortable, secure life. Born in Kirchheim and grew up here. The surrounding mountains kept my travels to close range, and my professional aspirations remained modest. I married, had two sons, was respected and able to live out my idiosyncrasies, within limits, you understand."

A wind builds up, affecting their sheltered mood. "Let's start up to my place," he suggests, "it's quite a steep walk up the slope for folks our age. We'll need to take our time." "Did you marry Erika," Grete asks as they wander away from the protection of the linden tree. "Yes, I did. I married her for love." Grete swallows the gall of an old jealousy and hastily adds, "I always thought you two would make a good couple." Just then they begin the climb up the cobblestone sidewalk toward Anton's house which is perched between two hills like a bird's nest in the fork of a tree. Grete pauses to admire it.

Once inside, Anton shows Grete to the room that has always been what he calls his "home office." There, at a bay window, they linger to contemplate the broad vista of the town below a grassy incline, arms around each other's waists. After awhile they return to the living room where Grete makes herself comfortable on the overstuffed sofa facing the fireplace. Anton kneels and puts some dry kindling on the flickering fire. Grete suppresses an onslaught of images and faces him. "How does one do it after all these years?" her expression determined and lucid. "Does one pick up where one left off, as if half a century hadn't intervened?" Anton remains silent for a long moment, not wanting to be rushed. It is not that he fears failure, but he bargains for time to fully take in her presence.

What he really wants is caress her calves which he remembers as round and firm. Glancing up at her from close range he sees tiny bumps and swelling interlaced with creases and wrinkles, the hallmarks of the flow of her time. It is burdensome to raise himself from the crouching position. "Old age, Grete dear, wouldn't be so bad but for all its inconveniences." Movement has been painful since his hip operation last fall. She tries to be helpful, reaching for his arm. Zigzagging down a ski slope, coming to a halt, swishing a circle around her, he used to smile, confident, invincible. Neither of them really believed then that there would come a day when their bodies would disobey them. "Why, Grete, I would like to know, have you never come home to visit before now?" "I'm not certain," she says, thinking aloud. "I once took a holiday in Vermont, in the northeastern United States. It was late in the winter months, the sun of the new season already shining but the ground still buried in snow. The farmers had started sapping their maple trees. I suppose I felt no need to return here before. But the time of my harvesting is coming now."

Who is to say what is more beautiful, the sprouting sapling turning its fresh buds toward the sun or the knobby, gnarled tree, bearing fruit and providing rest.

When they had first made love in their teens, they had shaken like aspen leaves, limbs intertwined and nearly overcome by the newness of the encounter. Now, like leaves falling topsy-turvy, their edges wrinkled by the dryness of autumn, they sway back and forth firmly grounded in their individual identities, and more aware of each other than youthful love ever left room for. Nestled together, her back cupped by his chest and arms, the sap begins to flow, and fresh green shoots break through the bark along with the spicy aroma of wilting flowers.

Grete never liked to linger at bed's edge. Her children used to say that she vaulted into action at the first chirping of a bird in the morning. At this moment she feels like attending to her disheveled hair, freshening her make-up. Her tailored suit would fit her mood. She is ready for the bygone places. She already smells the musty halls of her high school where faces of teachers and students change from year to year but where the atmosphere of old will have stayed on in the cracks of the walls, behind blackboards and under the bicycle shelter. She has a foretaste of the firm, salty, crusty bagels she will buy at the bakery adjacent to the schoolyard. Munching, she will stroll to the house where she grew up, with its unkempt garden overgrown with weeds, and fruit trees needing pruning. Surely in the garden's thicket some wild berries will bring back the flavor of her youth. At the brick house on the corner between Friedrichstrasse and Mandering she envisions her friend, Karin, tugging at her bicycle in the shed. "Let's hurry to the stables, she'll shout. I want to ride Sultan today. Who will be your pick?" She will hear the town hall's clock strike the hours, and know where she is supposed to be, and how much time she has left. Anton, she realizes, is only one of the stops in all the harvesting she still has to do.

"Let's not get up, yet." It's Anton's soft, coaxing voice. He brings two flannel bathrobes, one green, the other crimson. She would like to resist his pleading and be on her way. Why doesn't she throw off this soothing languor? Perhaps for old time's sake, she suppresses her assertiveness and does not allow her desire to speed off to recapture the past on her own to take over. She sinks back into the chair next to the fireplace. The kindling is burned to ashes. But the big logs still smolder with a deep glow through and through. A warmth envelopes her body and all her limbs slacken. The rising smoke befogs her and she leans back in comfort and repose. "Tea, Grete?" "Yes, please, Anton."

For long hours they sit and talk, swinging back and forth between yesterday and today, never touching on tomorrow except when during silences their stares fix on the fire that alternately lures, fascinates and warms them.

Full Steam Ahead

By the time I was seven I was comfortable riding the train alone from our residence in southern Germany to where my maternal grandmother lived two hours to the north. I spent several weeks with her each summer, nourished by her stories and our outings into the countryside.

At twelve my summer vacation brought me my first earnings at the farm of my godmother. My task was to weed her flower garden and to pull small hand wagons loaded with hot luncheons out to the field workers. I was busy all day and tired at night, and very proud of the extra money I brought home to our meager household. As soon as my return train rolled into our station and I saw my mother standing on the platform, I could hardly wait to get off and throw my arms around her.

My heart leaped with joy when my uncle in Sweden needed day care for my little niece. I was thirteen and this was the longest train ride I had taken thus far. The journey included a night on the ferry where I was overwhelmed by the smorgasbord of foods. My stomach was also overwhelmed. Its contents landed in the spray over the railing. We were used to simple meals at home.

I like children and the two months with little Astrid flew by. Each week I was given a couple of free days. My frugal uncle handed me a few krona and showed me on the city map of Stockholm how to use the trolley. Upon my return in the evenings I had to account in writing for every krona I had spent. On my outings into the city I wandered through the cobblestone streets, explored different municipal parks and joined tour groups on numerous occasions, including three visits to City Hall. I also ventured out to the Scheren, rocky outcrops on the outskirts of the city. There one day tears dripped onto the sunbaked flat surface of a stone. I stirred the tiny teary puddle with my index finger and wrote, "I want to be home." Back in Germany I never mentioned my homesickness because my parents regarded these trips away as "blessed luxuries." But I felt a crack in my foundation.

I was thrilled when, a year later family friends invited me to join them and their large brood of 8 in Switzerland. From there they took me along on an excursion to the Côte d'Azur. Their chalet in the midst of blooming meadows and overripe blueberry patches with cowbells echoing through the valley evoked magical images. And the golden sun and pearly sand along the blue Mediterranean were unforgettable sights. Still, I was lonely. The small children were my only company. I was fourteen. The adults kept to themselves. At night I clutched the encouraging letters from my grandmother and wept. I was never mistreated, just ignored. Lying on the beach with a towel over my face, I overheard two women from the household exclaiming, "Let her be. She is always so sullen." The crack in my foundation widened and led from loneliness to depression.

With the passage of time, I became a self-sufficient traveler. I knew how to navigate a city, change trains, buy my meals from vendors and converse in a foreign language. But not until I befriended lighthearted Margot at nineteen and we both attended a summer language program in Neuchatel did I learn what a joyful time away from home can feel like. Soon after we arrived, we met two artists who took us boating and dancing.

Margot and I enrolled at the University of Hamburg. On completion of our first semester we signed up for a sojourn to the Middle East with other students. To earn money for the trip I secured a part-time job helping with children and Margot worked a few hours in a fabric store. We sewed all of our clothes for the upcoming adventure from remnants she brought to our student apartment.

Although my parents encouraged visits abroad, this one frightened them. As our train chugged out of the Stuttgart station destined for Istanbul, they dabbed their eyes with the handkerchiefs they had brought for waving.

My parents' foreboding did not prove altogether wrong. I met my husband on that long journey into wonderous lands. A year later I married him and followed him to the United States. My interest in different cultures was complemented by his passion for exploring regions far and wide. Through long years of married life we have traversed the world. I am never lonely with him at my side.

But my husband's wanderlust diverges from mine. As a youngster he had taken excursions with his parents across the United States, but an exchange year in Germany was his first solo stay with another family. Because he grew up in a stable environment, he is comfortable taking calculated risks. He never feels a stranger in a strange land. He pushes boundaries with confidence and curiosity, never minding an unfamiliar custom or a welcoming foreign bed. He loves to extend stays. When my husband comes back from abroad he immediately plans another trip. I always take my home with me wherever we go and try to replicate familiar features in my new experiences. I search for posters and cheap throw rugs to bring a touch of my taste to a foreign setting. For me even a most wonderful stay abroad is always temporary. I get restless for our return.

All through my happy years in America I have not been able to entirely shed homesickness. I still miss my childhood traditions with their intimacies and feelings of belonging. I miss the summers with my grandmother, and especially her warmth. I miss my early sense of security because I know from personal experience how quickly it can be taken away. After each trip I sink into the fluffy worn featherbed from my youth and sigh with gratefulness and relief, "Home again, home again, home sweet home."

Rumbling over Steel

I love trains, the slow commuter, the 200 mile-an-hour express. I have traveled on all sorts. There was the steam engine chugging from Dubrovnik to Sarajevo on a narrow-gauge rail line with women lugging baskets full of chickens and farm produce. My face was soot-smeared from coal dust wafting through the open windows. I have relished meals in elegant dining cars and munched on snacks on hard wooden commuter benches. Years ago, on a trip from Stuttgart to Istanbul I bedded down in a net luggage rack strung like a hammock above the compartment seats. I took a sleeper from London to Glasgow and was awakened with morning tea. As a child I fled westward from the Russian army atop a coal freighter with my fxamily.

A whistle, a hooting, and the wheels begin to sing on the tracks that look like ladders stretched end to end along the ground. A herd of sheep on the left, an onion-shaped church steeple on the right. In Ukraine a station master in a red cap motions with his hand signal as we pass through his village. A lady encumbered by fur steps down from a first class car in Finland, and in Italy students jump onto the caboose of our departing train just in time. I shiver in icy air-conditioned compartments or sweat alongside coughing old radiators.

A train ride is a journey not a trip. There are travel companions. I meet strangers, hear foreign languages, we tell stories. I can retreat, read, or watch the countryside pass by like a moving picture. The rocking, clanking and rumbling over steel lulls me.

The train is a symbol of traveling through life in alternating conditions, cherishing solitude or the company of others, at high speed or slow, wide awake or dozing.

Darning Socks

During long afternoons when I was about seven years-old and the war in Germany had ended, I learned to darn socks. Sitting beside my beloved grandmother, I felt safe. From my perch I watched her nimble fingers thread woolen yarn across large holes and small. And I asked countless questions as we did our handiwork. Although I did not understand it at the time, darning would come to mean much more to me than repairing worn socks.

I had experienced chaos and heartache in early childhood. When I was very small I overheard my mother's desperate sobs upon learning that her husband had been mortally wounded in the war. I witnessed my grandmother's deep sorrow when both her sonsv—one 19, the other 21—died in battle. As my mother, my grandmother and I fled from the advancing Russian army in 1945 I witnessed bloodied and delirious soldiers on a transport train from the front crying "Mama, Mama." When our westward trek ended, I saw bombed-out buildings everywhere and the bloated carcasses of animals littering the streets. In the icy winter of 1946 I was quarantined in a provisional children's hospital with diphtheria. Amid rampant contagion I contracted one life-threatening disease after another and survived them all. But when my friend Eric died in the bed next to mine, I dove under my blanket and could only be coaxed out for meals. I suffered with night-sweats, and hallucinated about losing my mother.

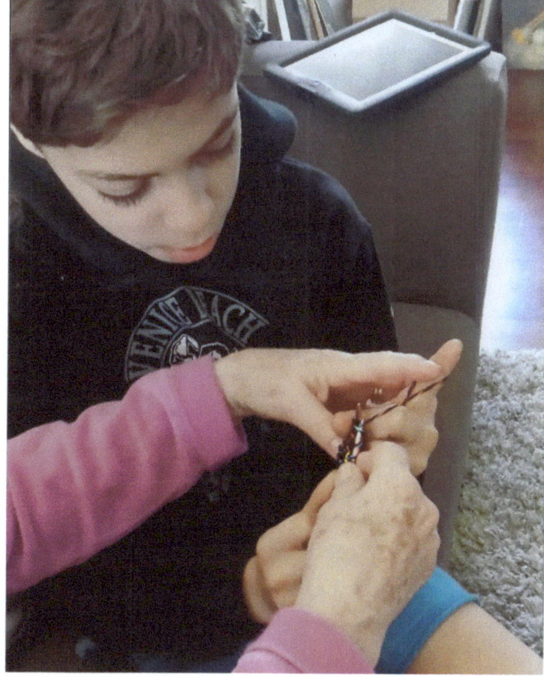

As the afternoon began to darken I laid my partially darned sock aside and asked my grandmother, "Are there any happy lives?" After a long pause she replied, "Our friends in Sweden have good lives. They have everyday concerns, of course, but tragedies are rare. When I visited them before the war, they were seldom gloomy. We laughed a lot and I felt lighthearted." I pressed her for more. "But why do *we* continue to live when there is so much sadness around us?" She put her darning down and drew me to her, tears filling her eyes. "We go on because we love each other so much. That's why." She held me for dear life and rocked me back and forth. Then she composed herself, took up her darning, and told me to do the same. Which I did.

Life's unpredictability still scares me. Childhood fears persist deep down. Nevertheless, looking back now, recalling my seven year-old self asking big questions about life's meaning, I realize that my grandmother's answer satisfied me for more than one reason. The words she said were simple and true to my experience of being loved by her and my mother in the midst of the upheavals of a war-torn time. But what clinched it for me, I now see, was her matter-of-fact return to *mending*—socks, lives—and her instruction to me to do likewise.

Live!

It is 1942. Miriam leans against an inside wall of the Jewish ghetto in Warsaw. Daily roundups and deportations have depleted the population and it is rumored that soon the ghetto will be burned down. All checkpoints are heavily guarded and anyone attempting to escape is shot on the spot. Hunger and exhaustion have wasted Miriam's body. Her precious three month-old daughter Rachel has sucked her breasts dry. Miriam presses her slumbering child to her heart one last time and wets her sleeping face with a flood of tears. The mild sedative for her daughter has cost Miriam the last keepsake from her grandparents, a gold pendant with a crest of tiny diamonds. She pins a note to the baby's shirt: Rachel, my love. Live! Then she tenderly wraps her infant firmly between two cushions, lashes them together with a scarf and heaves them with the last of her strength over the barbed wire atop the wall. Then Miriam sinks to her knees, sobbing uncontrollably. An SS man who has watched the spectacle from across the prison yard approaches and summarily executes her where she kneels. Outside the ghetto wall a passing stranger, happening upon the whimpering bundle, instinctively snatches it up and hurries home. As the ghetto goes up in flames days later, the Polish man and his wife keep Rachel safe and vow to raise her as their own.

A year later in a small coastal town on the Baltic Sea, Inge and Karl pack a rucksack for their only living son, Henrik, who has just turned 15. Their oldest son was killed at the beginning of the war in France and two other sons fell in the battle at Stalingrad. Inge, a busy mother and enthusiastic sports instructor, and Karl, a respected judge, are prominent members of their community. Though not fond of Hitler and his ilk, as patriotic German Nationalists they want to believe the government's promise to make Germany great again after the humiliating Versailles Treaty that marked the end of World War I. They willingly supported their sons' desire to serve their country. But now with the situation on the eastern front worsening and the regime announcing plans to conscript youngsters from high school, doubts and fear have crept in. Huddled together around roaring flames in the big brick fireplace in their villa, Inge and Karl's conversations grow heated and lengthy. Unable to sleep, Inge wanders the corridor between their upstairs bedrooms. Only the wind rattling the icicles on the eves of the roof picks up her lament. "I have lost three sons. I can't lose another."

A few nights later they resolve to send Henrik to visit relatives in Sweden for the Christmas break. Henrik has been raised in comfortable surroundings but his passion is for long hikes along the unspoiled dunes of the Baltic coast. He is not thrilled at the thought of spending the holidays away from his friends who are organizing a winter campout. Besides, he is ready to volunteer in the youth organization which will soon join the fight for the Fatherland. Inge and Karl reassure Henrik that Sweden in winter offers unique opportunities for forays into nature.

An attempt to bribe the captain of a fully booked boat to Stockholm to make room for an unaccompanied minor falls on deaf ears. But an invitation from a prominent Swedish cousin stating that the family was in need of a hardy young geology student to join them on an expedition to gather ice samples from frozen springs near Uppsala secures Henrik passage in steerage. The prospect of adventure excites Henrik and softens his reluctance to leave. And he is convinced that he will be back in time to start his final school semester. On the evening before his departure Henrik notices that his mother rumples his hair a bit longer than usual before bedtime and hands him her favorite collection of Schiller's dramas for the trip. It unnerves him momentarily when he glimpses his mother dabbing her eyes as she leaves the room, but he gives it no further thought. His father has bought him a fancy camera and encourages him to take as many pictures as he likes to show them when he returns. When Henrik boards the ship and stands at the railing vigorously waving a red-and-white checkered handkerchief, Inge clutches Karl's arm so forcefully that he winces.

Days later, Henrik feels betrayed when his Swedish aunt informs him that he has traveled to safety on a one-way ticket and that he will not return to his homeland until the war ends. She describes in great detail the increasingly dangerous situation in Germany. Retreating to his room, Henrik buries his head in a pillow and cries hot tears of fury. He harbors thoughts of running away but quickly realizes that he has no other place to go. He does not speak Swedish and has no money. He desperately misses his parents and feels like a kid again, imagining his mother's gentle fingers softly tousling his hair.

In the autumn of 1944 Inge and Karl decide to remain in their hometown even as a swarm of refugees treks through from farther east, telling of plunder and atrocities. When the Soviet army marches through their town, the family villa is sacked. As with other women in the town, Inge is repeatedly raped by rampaging soldiers. A lifelong swimmer, she makes her way to a nearby lake to wash away the traces of violation. Like a water turtle she plunges deep beneath the surface of the water. When she comes up for air a sniper's bullet strikes her forehead.

Now alone and bereft, Karl sets out from what remains of the villa on a cold February night in 1945, warmly dressed in fur but without luggage. He walks to the train station and joins the throng of waiting travelers, but no trains rumble through. As the temperature drops well below freezing, a mother carrying a child begs him for his coat. Karl hands it to her. When a crippled man hobbles up and points at his boots, Karl takes them off. Finally, with nothing on except his shirt and trousers, he slumps against a barren tree and sinks to the frozen ground. When a servant from the old days happens upon him and tries to drag him to safety, he realizes that Karl has died of the cold. In his hand he clutches a note: To my beloved son, Henrik. Live!

Permanence in Change

A huge oak tree stretches its leafy crown and branches, heavily laden with foliage, through a gaping window frame of castle Bielwiese. The tree looks like a giant firmly rooted in the ground, spreading its arms toward the sky.

Our family of six has arrived at the ruins of our former estate in Poland which was in the family from 1727 until 1932 when the land was in German hands. It has taken us much longer than the predicted two hours from Wroclaw (formerly Breslau) to the village of Wielowies. Our rented van has bumped over rutted country roads past golden wheat fields studded with poppies and blue cornflowers swaying in the summer breeze. Suddenly I hear my mother humming her favorite song, "Geh aus mein Herz und suche Freud in dieser schönen Sommerszeit." And when we pass by tiny ponds I remember her telling of swimming here as a child with her two brothers and other neighborhood kids among algae, water lilies and croaking frogs, always without a stitch on and giddy with joy.

We stand and gaze at the ruins of the castle, a massive heap of red brick and crumbling mortar. The entire front façade is still standing three stories high with the original molded crowned seals of ancestral Baron von Lüttwitz intact and a stork nest firmly planted atop the gable. Otherwise, jungle-like vegetation abounds in the rubble and makes climbing into the interior over walls and through high piles of stones difficult. My American family mistakes the nettles sprouting in huge clusters everywhere for poison ivy and retreats at first. Only when I assure them that nettles sting but cause no permanent discomfort does Zachary slip his shorts down slightly to protect his bare legs and follow my lead. The others explore the perimeter. Zachary and I continue to struggle over rugged obstacles, determined to venture into our family's past.

"Nothing is built to last forever," my son-in-law Tommy comments when he first spots the ruins. And my husband Ron sighs, "Everything vanishes in the end." But Zachary and I marvel at the abundance of nature that has endured here for centuries, always being reborn. As we forge through the thicket not entered by other people for many years we spread our T-shirts out like aprons and gather red bricks to take home as gifts for relatives. "Can you believe," Zachary says," that these bricks have survived?" As we swipe spider webs from our faces and trample down brush to make our way forward we suddenly halt at a huge black hole in the ground. It is still recognizable as the furnace in the cellar that heated the fireplaces for the large rooms in the upper stories. My maternal grandmother recalled waking up under thick feather bedding and hearing the servants stoking the coals downstairs on cold winter mornings.

We arrive at a window in a turret and survey what lies before us. The air is still, holding its breath before exhaling with stories which now resurface in the July calm. How much sadness and drama has played out in these serene surroundings. And how much happiness.

Adjacent to the main building we spot the ivy-covered guesthouse, now broken down, walls supported by large poles, with the roof caved in and swallows darting from under the eaves. In this guest house a Russian born piano teacher instructed our forebear, Clara. They fell in love. In 1832, having been married for twelve years to Rochus Baron von Lüttwitz and borne six children, Clara followed her teacher to America. It was said that her last child died of a broken heart after her mother left. There is a marker at the village church bearing the name of Clara's daughter. According to family legend, following Clara's departure, her husband had the interior walls of the mansion draped in black and forbade the utterance of his wife's name.

Still, this bucolic setting was the site of a great deal of gladness. In our mind's eye we see an aunt riding side-saddle and smiling. She was written up in the local newspaper as the first woman to go fox hunting with an all-male retinue. Of her carefree childhood my mother recalled, "We had so much freedom to roam and explore." When one of her brothers was killed at Stalingrad in the Second World War a letter was found in his tattered uniform pocket with the words, "Only the memory of our idyllic childhood in Bielwiese makes it possible for me to endure this hellhole."

The last owner of Bielwiese, Nicholaus Baron von Lüttwitz was adored by his family and servants alike. He was known for his kindness and generosity. Lavish events took place on his estate and in his manor. Wedding parties were celebrated under lanterns dangling from trees in the park. Wakes were held in the large entrance hall, and no birthday went by without surprises and sumptuous meals. At Christmas a tall fir tree was cut in the nearby forest and brought in, smelling of snow and green sap. It was decorated with white candles that lit up Christmas Eve festivities. My mother remembered how all the servants were given their presents first before any family member could approach their gifts. Easter was a holiday designed for the children. Adults and youngsters alike dressed in their finest clothes. Following obligatory church attendance, the park echoed with jubilant squeals and laughter. Children of all ages ran from nest to nest that they had made themselves with moss and grass the day before. Soon their baskets brimmed with painted eggs and freshly baked treats.

The highlight of the harvest festival was the arrival of a team of horses pulling a wagon carrying the last load of wheat into the courtyard. A crown woven by the field hands from grain stalks and held together with colorful ribbons hung from the rafters in the clean-swept barn. Before everyone was invited to an evening of dancing and fun, the Baron blessed the richness of the annual harvest. Then a band began to play and the entire community sat down at long tables stacked with food. Schnapps was poured in bountiful quantities. The Baron was lenient when his workers stumbled from their dwellings the following morning long after the rooster had crowed its wakeup call.

Opapa, as he was affectionately known by his offspring, was a man full of the joy of life. But he could not manage his money. He was deeply in debt by the time of his death in 1929. As his estate fell into disrepair, his beloved wife Isa became addicted to pain medication following a complicated childbirth. She was admitted to the hospital at the nearby Lubiáz monastery for treatment and died soon thereafter.

After Bielwiese was confiscated by the state, the mansion stood vacant for many years. It served as a hostel for local workers between World War I and World War II until the Russian army gutted it in 1945, leaving only the façade and front walls intact. The devastated interior gave free reign to plants, rain and wind as well as deer, rabbits and foxes. A farsighted aunt had transported much of the artwork and furniture to western Germany soon after Nicholaus died.

We sit down on some logs for a picnic, feeling that Bielwiese had become like an old friend to us in the short time since we arrived. As our fantasy wanders between recent stories and more remote ones, we experience a sense of déjà vu. We snap another round of pictures, knowing that these ruins have been designated for demolition by the government. Only their isolated location has spared them until now. A local priest had written to us prior to our trip, "Maybe the spirits of your ancestors have guarded the ruins so that you can see them before they disappear." The nettles' sting, the summer heat, the crumbling bricks, the imposing facade and the stories we recalled are all burned into our memories to be taken back across the ocean.

We are not yet finished with our journey into the past. Another family shrine awaits a visit. We drive from Poland into the Czech Republic to Svaty Jan Pad Skalan (Saint John Under the Cross) near Prague. The village is quite small, gently nestled in a sun-dappled valley near rugged rocks under a gigantic cliff where a cross stands like a weathervane. Before our family owned the castle which leans into these cliffs, legend has it that Saint Ivan lived in a cave beneath the manor house and performed miracles in the surrounding communities. Soon after our arrival we drink from the Fountain of Life that still bubbles fresh spring water from an ancient stone reservoir.

Once again it is a grandfather who connects us to this remote spot. He was a jeweler in Prague and quite wealthy, but a passion for gambling was his downfall. One night in desperation after losing large sums of money he shot and killed himself. As was the custom regarding suicides, he was not permitted to be buried in the church. Instead he was laid to rest adjacent to the family chapel. Only the chapel's stucco walls and lovely interior have been renovated. A weatherworn monument bearing the image of a guardian angel hovers above the grave, bearing barely visible the family name Berger. At the time of his death, that grandfather was survived by his wife and several daughters, one of whom was my great-grandmother Marie Berger. When she married in 1871 her dowry included an ornate hand-carved Baroque-style armoire with the artist's initials chiseled into the sideboards, a big rounded trunk for linen and a delicate hand-painted fan from one of her sisters who was a lady-in-waiting at the Prague court. These beautiful heirlooms now have an honored place in our American home.

To atone for the suicide, the family willed the castle and the estate to the Catholic Church which eventually turned it into a cloister. Subsequently, under the Communist regime, it served as a military academy, and is now a state music school. All the rooms are lovingly restored. The ceiling in the ample music room has been stripped of old plaster and paint, revealing beautiful original paintings of biblical scenes. A piano stands in the middle of the arch-domed room. Alexander gingerly approaches the instrument, lifts the lid and gently sits down on a swivel stool. Softly at first and then full-force, he starts to play. I am covered in goosebumps as the melody floats into the invisible realms above us, blending with the chorus of our ancestors.

Claudia has knelt against the statue with the guarding angel. She closes her eyes as the sun licks her face and a murmuring breeze plays with her hair. "I would want to be buried in this peaceful place," she whispers. "I feel at home here." We share her feelings and lower ourselves down next to her into the lush grass.

We have encountered enduring nature, seen impressive monumental ruins and artful handicrafts that defy time, and our souls have been touched by music echoing through ancient halls. We have shared many stories of family members. Before we departed on this journey we had leafed through old photo albums with faded, yellowed pictures and learned much about our ancestors. But it is as if these stories were phantoms when we first encountered them. The photos could have been of strangers. Now the places where the stories were lived have made the inhabitants spring to life in an unexpected and powerful way. They step from the shadows of oblivion and we see them walk around, talk, laugh and cry, and we feel as though we are among them. "It's not just in telling about historical places but also in visiting them," my husband muses, "that the past comes to life. Though there is always loss and sometimes tragedy as things fade away, one also sees love and joy. Everything changes, but embedded in that change is permanence. To keep the connection we have forged we must now add our own stories to those of bygone generations."

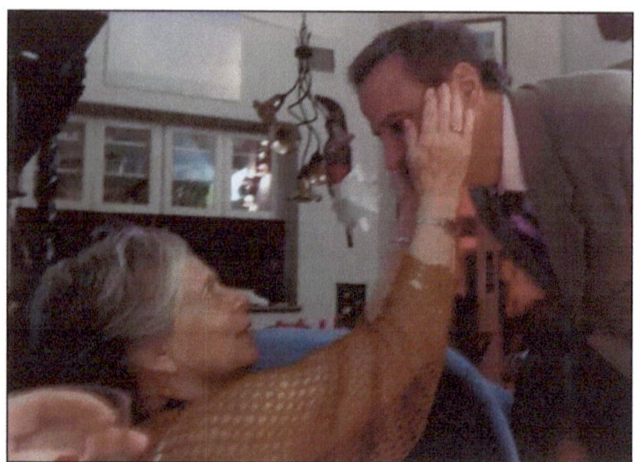

Acknowledgements

The Fall, *A Walk Through My Garden*, Edited by Whitney Scott, Outrider Press, 2007 (First Place winner).

Hope Diamond, and Letting Go, *Biostories Magazine*, April 2014.

Letting Go was reprinted in *Burningword Literary Journal*, No 71, July 2014.

Bedrock, *Firstwriter Magazine*, UK, Issue 28, Winter 2015/16.

Fear Not, *Lillypress*, Volume 10, Issue 2, Winter 2016.

In Search of My Father, *Nazar Look* ,Issue45, Winter 2015.

Birth as an Art, *New Look*, Vol. 5, No2, 1977.

A Fluke of Circumstance, *Writer's Haven*, Vol.1, No.1, May 2010.

Landings, *The Birthstory Project*, April 2016.

Your Two- or Three Year Old, *Living With Preschoolers*, Vol.11, No 4, July, August, September 1984.

An Emergency Room Experience, *Floridian*, February 27, 1977.

The Devil Runs Fast, *Southern Pacific Review*, January 2013.

Goodbye Balmy Gulf! Hello Ice-Glazed Snow, *The Writer Within*, August 2006.

For the Love of a Horse, *Sassafras Magazine*, Issue 5, October 2013.

Do Animals Grieve? *Death Studies*, Vol. 13, No.1, 1989.

Vanished, *Ascent Aspirations*, October 2013.

Horses Are a Valuable Part of Police Work, *Galveston Daily News*, October 9th, 1990.

Rumbling Over Steel, *Brilliant Flash Fiction*, September 30th, 2014.

Three Coins in a Fountain, *Danaliteray.org*, August 2006.

Take Two—They're Small, *Writings about Food*, edited by Whitney Scott, Outrider Press 2002

The Wife and the Piano Teacher, *34th Parallel Magazine*, Issue 22, 2013.

The Freedom to Be the Woman of One's Own Choosing, *St. Andrew's Review*, Issue No.25, 1983.

Here I Stand, *34th Parallel Magazine*, Issue 37, June 2016.

Nothing But Snake Oil? *Explore: The Journal of Science and Healing*, Vol.3, Issue 6, 2007.

Lightning Over Kaufman, *Houston Chronicle Texas Magazine*, January 4th, 2004.

The Hand That Feeds Us, *Short Story Us*, December 14th, 2008.

A Calf Skin Notebook with Rose-Colored Lines, *The Storyteller, A Writer's Magazine,* Fossil Creek Publications, November/December 2006.

Substitutes Are Not Supposed to Smile, *Capstone Journal of Education*, Vol.3, No. 1, Summer/Fall 1982.

The Device, *Vacations: The Good, the Bad and the Ugly,* edited by Whitney Scott, Outsider Press, 2006.

The Old Should Be Explorers, *PitWit.com.* July 25th, 2006, Republished in *Looking Back,* Anthology of Short Stories, Attitude and Culture Journal of Crimean Tatars in Romania.

In Defense of Wrinkles, *Galveston Daily News*, December 1st, 1987.

Turn Down the Lights Gently, *Family Gatherings,* Edited by Whitney Scott, Outrider Press 2003.

Stalingrad, a Lifetime Later, *History Magazine*, Canada, October/ November 2011.

He's My Brother, *Offbeat/Quirky, Journal of Experimental Fiction,* Vol.73, March 2017.

A Child Loses a Pet, *Death Education,* Vol.13, No.4, Winter 1980.

Teachable Moments Occasioned by "Small Deaths," *Children and Death,* Edited by Hannelore Wass and Charles A. Corr, 1984.

Death Rehearsal, *The Other Herald,* Winter Issue 2016

Gypsy Spirit, *Falling In Love Again, Love The Second Time Around*, Edited by Whitney Scott, Outrider Press, 2005. The Adoption, *NETSAGS,* Iceland, January 2011.

Forever Love, *Home Life,* Vol.44, No.11, August 1990.

For Old Time's Sake, *Wind, A Literary Journal,* Vol.14, No.50, 1984.

Darning Socks, *Foliate Oak Literary Journal,* October 1st, 2016.

The Dark Room, *Longshot Island Magazine,* May 2017.

Live!, *34th Parallel Magazine,* Issue 47, October 2017.

Learning from Snails, *Folded Word,* November 2017.

A Secret Hiding Place, and Liebe Grosse Mietze Katze, *Foliate Oak Literary Journal,* December 2017.

Permanence in Change, *34th Parallel Magazine,* Issue 49, December 2017.

The Quotidian, a poem, *The Pangolin Review,* June 8th, 2018.

Cradling the Heart, a poem, *Green Silk Journal,* Fall 2018.

Dem Herrgott Sei Skifahrer (Ridicule), *Heart & Humanity Magazine,* December, 2018.

Crying is a Gift, and Ode to Water, 2 poems, *Poethead/WordPress,* April 2019.

The House of Childhood, a poem, *Plainsongs,* Hastings College Press, July 2019.

Full Steam Ahead, *ArielChart,* June 2019.

About the Author

A writer from youth and an M.A. graduate in comparative literature from the University of Rochester, German-born Ute Carson published her first prose piece in 1977. *Colt Tailing*, a 2004 novel, was a finalist for the Peter Taylor Book Award. Carson's story "The Fall" won Outrider Press's Grand Prize and appeared in its short story and poetry anthology *A Walk through My Garden*, 2007. Her second novel *In Transit* was published in 2008. Her poems have appeared in numerous journals and magazines in the US and abroad. Carson's poetry was featured on the televised *Spoken Word Showcase* 2009, 2010, 2011, Channel Austin. A poetry collection *Just a Few Feathers* was published in 2011. The poem "A Tangled Nest of Moments" placed second in the Eleventh International Poetry Competition 2012. Her chapbook *Folding Washing* was published in 2013 and her collection of poems *My Gift to Life* was nominated for the 2015 Pushcart Award Prize. *Save the Last Kiss*, a novella, was published in 2016. Her poetry collection *Reflections* was out in 2018. She received the *Ovidiu-Bektore Literary Award 2018* from the Anticus Mulicultural Association in Constanta, Romania. In 2018 she was nominated a second time for the Pushcart Award Prize by the Plain View Press. Her website is www.utecarson.com.

Ute Carson resides in Austin, Texas with her husband. They have three daughters, six grandchildren, a horse and a clowder of cats.

www.ingramcontent.com/pod-product-compliance
Lightning Source LLC
Chambersburg PA
CBHW041125100726
47911CB00002B/46